THE BEST
MYSTERIES
OF ALL TIME

Most novels—even outstanding ones—fade from popular memory after a while. But John Buchan's *The Thirty-Nine Steps* (1915) has remained well-known to mystery fans for decades, both by virtue of the book itself and due to the fame of the 1935 Alfred Hitchcock film that was based on the story. Buchan was one of Hitchcock's favorite writers, and with good reason. Buchan's ability to create and build suspense through characters, plot development, and his unforgettable descriptions of the Scottish countryside made him a Hitchcockian natural.

Buchan wrote *The Thirty-Nine Steps* when he was convalescing from illness and was unable to join the army due to age and poor health. It was a resounding success immediately upon publication. In fact, it was so popular that Buchan quickly set about writing a sequel, *Greenmantle* (1916). Both books remain classics today, nearly a century after they were written.

The
Thirty-Nine
Steps

Greenmantle

Other books by
JOHN BUCHAN

Mr. Standfast
The Three Hostages
The Courts of the Morning
The Island of Sheep
The Power-House
John Macnab
The Dancing Floor
Sick Heart River
The Half-Hearted
A Lodge in the Wilderness
Prester John
Salute to Adventurers
The Path of the King
Huntingtower
Midwinter
Castle Gay
The Blanket of the Dark
The Gap in the Curtain
A Prince of the Captivity
The Free Fishers
A Lost Lady of Old Years
The House of the Four Winds
The Long Traverse
Mountain Meadow
John Burnet of Barns: A Romance

JOHN BUCHAN

The Thirty-Nine Steps

Greenmantle

THE BEST
MYSTERIES
OF ALL TIME

ImPress • Pleasantville, New York

THE BEST MYSTERIES OF ALL TIME

The Thirty-Nine Steps and *Greenmantle*

This Reader's Digest edition contains the complete text of John Buchan's *The Thirty-Nine Steps*, first published in 1915, and *Greenmantle*, first published in 1916.

ImPress is an imprint of The Reader's Digest Association, Inc., Bedford Road, Pleasantville, New York 10570.

ISSN 1544-4007

PRINTED IN THE UNITED STATES OF AMERICA

The Thirty-Nine Steps

The Thirty-Nine Steps

CHAPTER 1

The Man Who Died

I RETURNED from the city about three o'clock on that May afternoon pretty well disgusted with life. I had been three months in
the Old Country, and was fed up with it. If anyone had told me a
year ago that I would have been feeling like that I should have
laughed at him; but there was the fact. The weather made me
liverish, the talk of the ordinary Englishman made me sick, I
couldn't get enough exercise, and the amusements of London
seemed as flat as soda-water that has been standing in the sun.
"Richard Hannay," I kept telling myself, "you have got into the
wrong ditch, my friend, and you had better climb out."

It made me bite my lips to think of the plans I had been building up those last years in Bulawayo. I had got my pile—not one
of the big ones, but good enough for me; and I had figured out
all kinds of ways of enjoying myself. My father had brought me
out from Scotland at the age of six, and I had never been home
since; so England was a sort of Arabian Nights to me, and I
counted on stopping there for the rest of my days.

But from the first I was disappointed with it. In about a week I
was tired of seeing sights, and in less than a month I had had
enough of restaurants and theatres and race meetings. I had no
real pal to go about with, which probably explains things. Plenty
of people invited me to their houses, but they didn't seem much

interested in me. They would fling me a question or two about South Africa, and then get onto their own affairs. A lot of Imperialist ladies asked me to tea to meet schoolmasters from New Zealand and editors from Vancouver, and that was the dismallest business of all. Here was I, thirty-seven years old, sound in wind and limb, with enough money to have a good time, yawning my head off all day. I had just about settled to clear out and get back to the veld, for I was the best bored man in the United Kingdom.

That afternoon I had been worrying my brokers about investments to give my mind something to work on, and on my way home I turned into my club—rather a pot-house, which took in Colonial members. I had a long drink, and read the evening papers. They were full of the row in the Near East, and there was an article about Karolides, the Greek Premier. I rather fancied the chap. From all accounts he seemed the one big man in the show; and he played a straight game too, which was more than could be said for most of them. I gathered that they hated him pretty blackly in Berlin and Vienna, but that we were going to stick by him, and one paper said that he was the only barrier between Europe and Armageddon. I remember wondering if I could get a job in those parts. It struck me that Albania was the sort of place that might keep a man from yawning.

About six o'clock I went home, dressed, dined at the Café Royal, and turned into a music-hall. It was a silly show, all capering women and monkey-faced men, and I did not stay long. The night was fine and clear as I walked back to the flat I had hired near Portland Place. The crowd surged past me on the pavements, busy, and chattering, and I envied the people for having something to do. These shopgirls and clerks and dandies and policemen had some interest in life that kept them going. I gave half a crown to a beggar because I saw him yawn; he was a fellow sufferer. At Oxford Circus I looked up into the spring sky and I made a vow. I would give the Old Country another day to fit me into something; if nothing happened, I would take the next boat for the Cape.

My flat was the first floor in a new block behind Langham Place. There was a common staircase, with a porter and a lift-man at the entrance, but there was no restaurant or anything of that sort, and each flat was quite shut off from the others. I hate servants on the premises, so I had a fellow to look after me who came in by the day. He arrived before eight o'clock every morning and used to depart at seven, for I never dined at home.

I was just fitting my key into the door when I noticed a man at my elbow. I had not seen him approach, and the sudden appearance made me start. He was a slim man, with a short brown beard and small, gimlety blue eyes. I recognized him as the occupant of a flat on the top floor, with whom I had passed the time of day on the stairs.

"Can I speak to you?" he said. "May I come in for a minute?" He was steadying his voice with an effort, and his hand was pawing my arm.

I got my door open and motioned him in. No sooner was he over the threshold than he made a dash for my back room, where I used to smoke and write my letters. Then he bolted back.

"Is the door locked?" he asked feverishly, and he fastened the chain with his own hand.

"I'm very sorry," he said humbly. "It's a mighty liberty, but you looked the kind of man who would understand. I've had you in my mind all this week when things got troublesome. Say, will you do me a good turn?"

"I'll listen to you," I said. "That's all I'll promise." I was getting worried by the antics of this nervous little chap.

There was a tray of drinks on a table beside him, from which he filled himself a stiff whisky and soda. He drank it off in three gulps, and cracked the glass as he set it down.

"Pardon," he said, "I'm a bit rattled to-night. You see, I happen at this moment to be dead."

I sat down in an arm-chair and lit my pipe.

"What does it feel like?" I asked. I was pretty certain that I had to deal with a madman.

A smile flickered over his drawn face. "I'm not mad—yet. Say, sir, I've been watching you, and I reckon you're a cool customer. I reckon, too, you're an honest man, and not afraid of playing a bold hand. I'm going to confide in you. I need help worse than any man ever needed it, and I want to know if I can count you in."

"Get on with your yarn," I said, "and I'll tell you."

He seemed to brace himself for a great effort, and then started on the queerest rigmarole. I didn't get hold of it at first, and I had to stop and ask him questions. But here is the gist of it:

He was an American, from Kentucky, and after college, being pretty well off, he had started out to see the world. He wrote a bit, and acted as war correspondent for a Chicago paper, and spent a year or two in South-Eastern Europe. I gathered that he was a fine linguist, and had got to know pretty well the society in those parts. He spoke familiarly of many names that I remembered to have seen in the newspapers.

He had played about with politics, he told me, at first for the interest of them, and then because he couldn't help himself. I read him as a sharp, restless fellow, who always wanted to get down to the roots of things. He got a little further down than he wanted.

I am giving you what he told me as well as I could make it out. Away behind all the Governments and the armies there was a big subterranean movement going on, engineered by very dangerous people. He had come on it by accident; it fascinated him; he went further, and then he got caught. I gathered that most of the people in it were the sort of educated anarchists that make revolutions, but that beside them there were financiers who were playing for money. A clever man can make big profits on a falling market, and it suited the book of both classes to set Europe by the ears.

He told me some queer things that explained a lot that had puzzled me—things that happened in the Balkan War, how one state suddenly came out on top, why alliances were made and broken, why certain men disappeared, and where the sinews of war came from. The aim of the whole conspiracy was to get Russia and Germany at loggerheads.

When I asked Why, he said that the anarchist lot thought it

would give them their chance. Everything would be in the melting pot, and they looked to see a new world emerge. The capitalists would rake in the shekels, and make fortunes by buying up wreckage. Capital, he said, had no conscience and no fatherland. Besides, the Jew was behind it, and the Jew hated Russia worse than hell.

"Do you wonder?" he cried. "For three hundred years they have been persecuted, and this is the return match for the *pogroms*. The Jew is everywhere, but you have to go far down the backstairs to find him. Take any big Teutonic business concern. If you have dealings with it the first man you meet is Prince *von und zu* Something, an elegant young man who talks Eton-and-Harrow English. But he cuts no ice. If your business is big, you get behind him and find a prognathous Westphalian with a retreating brow and the manners of a hog. He is the German business man that gives your English papers the shakes. But if you're on the biggest kind of job and are bound to get to the real boss, ten to one you are brought up against a little white-faced Jew in a bath-chair with an eye like a rattlesnake. Yes, sir, he is the man who is ruling the world just now, and he has his knife in the Empire of the Tsar, because his aunt was outraged and his father flogged in some one-horse location on the Volga."

I could not help saying that his Jew-anarchists seemed to have got left behind a little.

"Yes and no," he said. "They won up to a point, but they struck a bigger thing than money, a thing that couldn't be bought, the old elemental fighting instincts of man. If you're going to be killed, you invent some kind of flag and country to fight for, and if you survive you get to love the thing. Those foolish devils of soldiers have found something they care for, and that has upset the pretty plan laid in Berlin and Vienna. But my friends haven't played their last card by a long sight. They've gotten the ace up their sleeves, and unless I can keep alive for a month they are going to play it and win."

"But I thought you were dead," I put in.

"*Mors janua vitae*," he smiled. (I recognized the quotation: it

was about all the Latin I knew.) "I'm coming to that, but I've got
to put you wise about a lot of things first. If you read your newspaper, I guess you know the name of Constantine Karolides?"

I sat up at that, for I had been reading about him that very
afternoon.

"He is the man that has wrecked all their games. He is the one
big brain in the whole show, and he happens also to be an honest
man. Therefore he has been marked down these twelve months
past. I found that out—not that it was difficult, for any fool could
guess as much. But I found out the way they were going to get
him, and that knowledge was deadly. That's why I have had to
decease."

He had another drink, and I mixed it for him myself, for I was
getting interested in the beggar.

"They can't get him in his own land, for he has a bodyguard of
Epirotes that would skin their grandmothers. But on the 15th
day of June he is coming to this city. The British Foreign Office
has taken to having International tea-parties, and the biggest of
them is due on that date. Now Karolides is reckoned the principal guest, and if my friends have their way he will never return
to his admiring countrymen."

"That's simple enough, anyhow," I said. "You can warn him
and keep him at home."

"And play their game?" he asked sharply. "If he does not come
they win, for he's the only man that can straighten out the tangle. And if his Government are warned he won't come, for he
does not know how big the stakes will be on June the 15th."

"What about the British Government?" I said. "They're not
going to let their guests be murdered. Tip them the wink, and
they'll take extra precautions."

"No good. They might stuff your city with plain-clothes detectives and double the police and Constantine would still be a
doomed man. My friends are not playing this game for candy.
They want a big occasion for the taking off, with the eyes of all
Europe on it. He'll be murdered by an Austrian, and there'll be
plenty of evidence to show the connivance of the big folk in

Vienna and Berlin. It will all be an infernal lie, of course, but the case will look black enough to the world. I'm not talking hot air, my friend. I happen to know every detail of the hellish contrivance, and I can tell you it will be the most finished piece of blackguardism since the Borgias. But it's not going to come off if there's a certain man who knows the wheels of the business alive right here in London on the 15th day of June. And that man is going to be your servant, Franklin P. Scudder."

I was getting to like the little chap. His jaw had shut like a rattrap, and there was the fire of battle in his gimlety eyes. If he was spinning me a yarn he could act up to it.

"Where did you find out this story?" I asked.

"I got the first hint in an inn on the Achensee in Tyrol. That set me inquiring, and I collected my other clues in a fur shop in the Galician quarter of Buda, in a Strangers' Club in Vienna, and in a little bookshop off the Racknitzstrasse in Leipsig. I completed my evidence ten days ago in Paris. I can't tell you the details now, for it's something of a history. When I was quite sure in my own mind I judged it my business to disappear, and I reached this city by a mighty queer circuit. I left Paris a dandified young French-American and I sailed from Hamburg a Jew diamond merchant. In Norway I was an English student of Ibsen collecting material for lectures, but when I left Bergen I was a cinema-man with special ski films. And I came here from Leith with a lot of pulpwood propositions in my pocket to put before the London newspapers. Till yesterday I thought I had muddied my trail some, and was feeling pretty happy. Then . . ."

The recollection seemed to upset him, and he gulped down some more whisky.

"Then I saw a man standing in the street outside this block. I used to stay close in my room all day, and only slip out after dark for an hour or two. I watched him for a bit from my window, and I thought I recognized him . . . He came in and spoke to the porter . . . When I came back from my walk last night I found a card in my letterbox. It bore the name of the man I want least to meet on God's earth."

I think that the look in my companion's eyes, the sheer naked scare on his face, completed my conviction of his honesty. My own voice sharpened a bit as I asked him what he did next.

"I realized that I was bottled as sure as a pickled herring, and that there was only one way out. I had to die. If my pursuers knew I was dead they would go to sleep again."

"How did you manage it?"

"I told the man that valets me that I was feeling pretty bad, and I got myself up to look like death. That wasn't difficult, for I'm no slouch at disguises. Then I got a corpse—you can always get a body in London if you know where to go for it. I fetched it back in a trunk on the top of a four-wheeler, and I had to be assisted upstairs to my room. You see I had to pile up some evidence for the inquest. I went to bed and got my man to mix me a sleeping draught, and then told him to clear out. He wanted to fetch a doctor, but I swore some and said I couldn't abide leeches. When I was left alone I started in to fake up that corpse. He was my size, and I judged had perished from too much alcohol, so I put some spirits handy about the place. The jaw was the weak point in the likeness, so I blew it away with a revolver. I dare say there will be somebody to-morrow to swear to having heard a shot, but there are no neighbours on my floor, and I guessed I could risk it. So I left the body in bed dressed up in my pyjamas, with a revolver lying on the bedclothes and a considerable mess around. Then I got into a suit of clothes I had kept waiting for emergencies. I didn't dare to shave for fear of leaving tracks, and besides, it wasn't any kind of use my trying to get into the streets. I had had you in my mind all day, and there seemed nothing to do but to make an appeal to you. I watched from my window till I saw you come home, and then slipped down the stair to meet you . . . There, sir, I guess you know about as much as me of this business."

He sat blinking like an owl, fluttering with nerves and yet desperately determined. By this time I was pretty well convinced that he was going straight with me. It was the wildest sort of narrative, but I had heard in my time many steep tales which had turned out to be true, and I had made a practice of judging the man rather than the story. If he had wanted to get a location in my flat, and then cut my throat, he would have pitched a milder yarn.

"Hand me your key," I said, "and I'll take a look at the corpse. Excuse my caution, but I'm bound to verify a bit if I can."

He shook his head mournfully. "I reckoned you'd ask for that, but I haven't got it. It's on my chain on the dressing-table. I had to leave it behind for I couldn't leave any clues to breed suspicions. The gentry who are after me are pretty bright-eyed citizens. You'll have to take me on trust for the night, and to-morrow you'll get proof of the corpse business right enough."

I thought for an instant or two. "Right. I'll trust you for the night. I'll lock you into this room and keep the key. Just one word, Mr. Scudder. I believe you're straight, but if so be you are not I should warn you that I'm a handy man with a gun."

"Sure," he said, jumping up with some briskness. "I haven't the privilege of your name, sir, but let me tell you that you're a white man. I'll thank you to lend me a razor."

I took him into my bedroom and turned him loose. In half an hour's time a figure came out that I scarcely recognized. Only his gimlety, hungry eyes were the same. He was shaved clean, his hair was parted in the middle, and he had cut his eyebrows. Further, he carried himself as if he had been drilled, and was the very model, even to the brown complexion, of some British officer who had had a long spell in India. He had a monocle, too, which he stuck in his eye, and every trace of the American had gone out of his speech.

"My hat! Mr. Scudder—" I stammered.

"Not Mr. Scudder," he corrected; "Captain Theophilus Digby, of the 40th Gurkhas, presently home on leave. I'll thank you to remember that, sir."

I made him up a bed in my smoking-room and sought my own couch, more cheerful than I had been for the past month. Things did happen occasionally, even in this God-forgotten metropolis.

I woke next morning to hear my man, Paddock, making the deuce of a row at the smoking-room door. Paddock was a fellow I had done a good turn to out on the Selakwi, and I had inspanned him as my servant as soon as I got to England. He had about as much gift of the gab as a hippopotamus, and was not a great hand at valeting, but I knew I could count on his loyalty.

"Stop that row, Paddock," I said. "There's a friend of mine, Captain—Captain" (I couldn't remember the name) "dossing down in there. Get breakfast for two and then come and speak to me."

I told Paddock a fine story about how my friend was a great swell, with his nerves pretty bad from overwork, who wanted absolute rest and stillness. Nobody had got to know he was here, or he would be besieged by communications from the India Office and the Prime Minister and his cure would be ruined. I am bound to say Scudder played up splendidly when he came to breakfast. He fixed Paddock with his eyeglass, just like a British officer, asked him about the Boer War, and slung out at me a lot of stuff about imaginary pals. Paddock couldn't learn to call me "sir," but he "sirred" Scudder as if his life depended on it.

I left him with the newspaper and a box of cigars, and went down to the City till luncheon. When I got back the liftman had an important face.

"Nawsty business 'ere this morning, sir. Gent in No. 15 has been and shot 'isself. They've just took 'im to the mortuary. The police are up there now."

I ascended to No. 15, and found a couple of bobbies and an inspector busy making an examination. I asked a few idiotic questions, and they soon kicked me out. Then I found the man that had valeted Scudder, and pumped him, but I could see he suspected nothing. He was a whining fellow with a churchyard face, and half a crown went far to console him.

I attended the inquest next day. A partner of some publishing firm gave evidence that the deceased had brought him woodpulp propositions, and had been, he believed, an agent of an American business. The jury found it a case of suicide while of unsound

mind, and the few effects were handed over to the American
Consul to deal with. I gave Scudder a full account of the affair,
and it interested him greatly. He said he wished he could have attended the inquest, for he reckoned it would be about as spicy as
to read one's own obituary notice.

The first two days he stayed with me in that back room he was
very peaceful. He read and smoked a bit, and made a heap of jottings in a notebook, and every night we had a game of chess, at
which he beat me hollow. I think he was nursing his nerves back
to health, for he had had a pretty trying time. But on the third
day I could see he was beginning to get restless. He fixed up a list
of the days till June 15th, and ticked each off with a red pencil,
making remarks in shorthand against them. I would find him
sunk in a brown study, with his sharp eyes abstracted, and after
those spells of meditation he was apt to be very despondent.

Then I could see that he began to get edgy again. He listened
for little noises, and was always asking me if Paddock could be
trusted. Once or twice he got very peevish, and apologized for it.
I didn't blame him. I made every allowance, for he had taken on
a fairly stiff job.

It was not the safety of his own skin that troubled him, but the
success of the scheme he had planned. That little man was clean
grit all through, without a soft spot in him. One night he was
very solemn.

"Say, Hannay," he said, "I judge I should let you a bit deeper
into this business. I should hate to go out without leaving somebody else to put up a fight." And he began to tell me in detail
what I had only heard from him vaguely.

I did not give him very close attention. The fact is, I was more
interested in his own adventures than in his high politics. I reckoned that Karolides and his affairs were not my business, leaving
all that to him. So a lot that he said slipped clean out of my
memory. I remember that he was very clear that the danger to
Karolides would not begin till he had got to London, and would
come from the very highest quarters, where there would be no
thought of suspicion. He mentioned the name of a woman—Julia

Czechenyi—as having something to do with the danger. She would be the decoy, I gathered, to get Karolides out of the care of his guards. He talked, too, about a Black Stone and a man that lisped in his speech, and he described very particularly somebody that he never referred to without a shudder—an old man with a young voice who could hood his eyes like a hawk.

He spoke a good deal about death, too. He was mortally anxious about winning through with his job, but he didn't care a rush for his life.

"I reckon it's like going to sleep when you are pretty well tired out, and waking to find a summer day with the scent of hay coming in at the window. I used to thank God for such mornings way back in the Blue-Grass country, and I guess I'll thank Him when I wake up on the other side of Jordan."

Next day he was much more cheerful, and read the life of Stonewall Jackson much of the time. I went out to dinner with a mining engineer I had got to see on business, and came back about half past ten in time for our game of chess before turning in.

I had a cigar in my mouth, I remember, as I pushed open the smoking-room door. The lights were not lit, which struck me as odd. I wondered if Scudder had turned in already.

I snapped the switch, but there was nobody there. Then I saw something in the far corner which made me drop my cigar and fall into a cold sweat.

My guest was lying sprawled on his back. There was a long knife through his heart which skewered him to the floor.

CHAPTER 2

The Milkman Sets Out on His Travels

I sat down in an arm-chair and felt very sick. That lasted for maybe five minutes, and was succeeded by a fit of the horrors. The poor staring white face on the floor was more than I could bear, and I managed to get a tablecloth and cover it. Then I staggered to a cupboard, found the brandy and swallowed several mouthfuls. I had seen men die violently before; indeed I had killed a few myself in the Matabele War; but this cold-blooded indoor business was different. Still I managed to pull myself together. I looked at my watch, and saw that it was half past ten.

An idea seized me, and I went over the flat with a small-tooth comb. There was nobody there, nor any trace of anybody, but I shuttered and bolted all the windows and put the chain on the door.

By this time my wits were coming back to me, and I could think again. It took me about an hour to figure the thing out, and I did not hurry, for, unless the murderer came back, I had till about six o'clock in the morning for my cogitations.

I was in the soup—that was pretty clear. Any shadow of a doubt I might have had about the truth of Scudder's tale was now gone. The proof of it was lying under the tablecloth. The men who knew that he knew what he knew had found him, and had taken the best way to make certain of his silence. Yes; but he had been in my rooms four days, and his enemies must have reckoned that he had confided in me. So I would be the next to go. It might be that very night, or next day, or the day after, but my number was up all right.

Then suddenly I thought of another probability. Supposing I went out now and called in the police, or went to bed and let Paddock find the body and call them in the morning. What kind of a story was I to tell about Scudder? I had lied to Paddock about him, and the whole thing looked desperately fishy. If I made a clean breast of it and told the police everything he had told me, they would simply laugh at me. The odds were a thousand to one that I would be charged with the murder, and the circumstantial evidence was strong enough to hang me. Few people knew me in England; I had no real pal who could come forward and swear to my character. Perhaps that was what those secret enemies were playing for. They were clever enough for anything, and an English prison was as good a way of getting rid of me till after June 15th as a knife in my chest.

Besides, if I told the whole story, and by any miracle was believed, I would be playing their game. Karolides would stay at home, which was what they wanted. Somehow or other the sight of Scudder's dead face had made me a passionate believer in his scheme. He was gone, but he had taken me into his confidence, and I was pretty well bound to carry on his work.

You may think this ridiculous for a man in danger of his life, but that was the way I looked at it. I am an ordinary sort of fellow, not braver than other people, but I hate to see a good man downed, and that long knife would not be the end of Scudder if I could play the game in his place.

It took me an hour or two to think this out, and by that time I had come to a decision. I must vanish somehow, and keep vanished till the end of the second week in June. Then I must somehow find a way to get in touch with the Government people and tell them what Scudder had told me. I wished to Heaven he had told me more, and that I had listened more carefully to the little he had told me. I knew nothing but the barest facts. There was a big risk that, even if I weathered the other dangers, I would not be believed in the end. I must take my chance of that, and hope that something might happen which would confirm my tale in the eyes of the Government.

My first job was to keep going for the next three weeks. It was now the 24th day of May, and that meant twenty days of hiding before I could venture to approach the powers that be. I reckoned that two sets of people would be looking for me—Scudder's enemies to put me out of existence, and the police, who would want me for Scudder's murder. It was going to be a giddy hunt, and it was queer how the prospect comforted me. I had been slack so long that almost any chance of activity was welcome. When I had to sit alone with that corpse and wait on Fortune I was no better than a crushed worm, but if my neck's safety was to hang on my own wits I was prepared to be cheerful about it.

My next thought was whether Scudder had any papers about him to give me a better clue to the business. I drew back the tablecloth and searched his pockets, for I had no longer any shrinking from the body. The face was wonderfully calm for a man who had been struck down in a moment. There was nothing in the breast pocket, and only a few loose coins and a cigar holder in the waistcoat. The trousers held a little penknife and some silver, and the side pocket of his jacket contained an old crocodile-skin cigar case. There was no sign of the little black book in which I had seen him making notes. That had no doubt been taken by his murderer.

But as I looked up from my task I saw that some drawers had been pulled out in the writing-table. Scudder would never have left them in that state, for he was the tidiest of mortals. Someone must have been searching for something—perhaps for the pocket-book.

I went round the flat and found that everything had been ransacked—the inside of books, drawers, cupboards, boxes, even the pockets of the clothes in my wardrobe, and the sideboard in the dining-room. There was no trace of the book. Most likely the enemy had found it, but they had not found it on Scudder's body.

Then I got out an atlas and looked at a big map of the British Isles. My notion was to get off to some wild district, where my veldcraft would be of some use to me, for I would be like a trapped rat in a city. I considered that Scotland would be best, for my people were Scotch and I could pass anywhere as an ordinary Scotsman. I had half an idea at first to be a German tourist, for my father had had German partners, and I had been brought up to speak the tongue pretty fluently, not to mention having put in three years prospecting for copper in German Damaraland. But I calculated that it would be less conspicuous to be a Scot, and less in a line with what the police might know of my past. I fixed on Galloway as the best place to go to. It was the nearest wild part of Scotland, so far as I could figure it out, and from the look of the map was not over thick with population.

A search in Bradshaw informed me that a train left St. Pancras at seven-ten, which would land me at any Galloway station in the late afternoon. That was well enough, but a more important matter was how I was to make my way to St. Pancras, for I was pretty certain that Scudder's friends would be watching outside. This puzzled me for a bit; then I had an inspiration, on which I went to bed and slept for two troubled hours.

I got up at four and opened my bedroom shutters. The faint light of a fine summer morning was flooding the skies, and the sparrows had begun to chatter. I had a great revulsion of feeling, and felt a God-forgotten fool. My inclination was to let things slide, and trust to the British police taking a reasonable view of my case. But as I reviewed the situation I could find no arguments to bring against my decision of the previous night, so with a wry mouth I resolved to go on with my plan. I was not feeling in any particular funk; only disinclined to go looking for trouble, if you understand me.

I hunted out a well-used tweed suit, a pair of strong nailed boots, and a flannel shirt with a collar. Into my pockets I stuffed a spare shirt, a cloth cap, some handkerchiefs, and a toothbrush.

I had drawn a good sum in gold from the bank two days before, in case Scudder should want money, and I took fifty pounds of it in sovereigns in a belt which I had brought back from Rhodesia. That was about all I wanted. Then I had a bath, and cut my moustache, which was long and drooping, into a short stubby fringe.

Now came the next step. Paddock used to arrive punctually at seven-thirty and let himself in with a latch-key. But about twenty minutes to seven, as I knew from bitter experience, the milkman turned up with a great clatter of cans, and deposited my share outside my door. I had seen that milkman sometimes when I had gone out for an early ride. He was a young man about my own height, with an ill-nourished moustache, and he wore a white overall. On him I staked all my chances.

I went into the darkened smoking-room where the rays of morning light were beginning to creep through the shutters. There I breakfasted off a whisky and soda and some biscuits from the cupboard. By this time it was getting on for six o'clock. I put a pipe in my pocket and filled my pouch from the tobacco jar on the table by the fireplace.

As I poked into the tobacco my fingers touched something hard, and I drew out Scudder's little black pocket-book . . .

That seemed to me a good omen. I lifted the cloth from the body and was amazed at the peace and dignity of the dead face. "Goodbye, old chap," I said; "I am going to do my best for you. Wish me well, wherever you are."

Then I hung about in the hall waiting for the milkman. That was the worst part of the business, for I was fairly choking to get out of doors. Six-thirty passed, then six-forty, but still he did not come. The fool had chosen this day of all days to be late.

At one minute after the quarter to seven I heard the rattle of the cans outside. I opened the front door, and there was my man, singling out my cans from a bunch he carried and whistling through his teeth. He jumped a bit at the sight of me.

"Come in here a moment," I said. "I want a word with you." And I led him into the dining-room.

"I reckon you're a bit of a sportsman," I said, "and I want you to do me a service. Lend me your cap and overall for ten minutes, and here's a sovereign for you."

His eyes opened at the sight of the gold, and he grinned broadly. "Wot's the gyme?" he asked.

"A bet," I said. "I haven't time to explain, but to win it I've got to be a milkman for the next ten minutes. All you've got to do is to stay here till I come back. You'll be a bit late, but nobody will complain, and you'll have that quid for yourself."

"Right-o!" he said cheerily. "I ain't the man to spoil a bit of sport. 'Ere's the rig, guv'nor."

I stuck on his flat blue hat and his white overall, picked up the cans, banged my door, and went whistling downstairs. The porter at the foot told me to shut my jaw, which sounded as if my make-up was adequate.

At first I thought there was nobody in the street. Then I caught sight of a policeman a hundred yards down, and a loafer shuffling past on the other side. Some impulse made me raise my eyes to the house opposite, and there at a first-floor window was a face. As the loafer passed he looked up, and I fancied a signal was exchanged.

I crossed the street, whistling gaily and imitating the jaunty swing of the milkman. Then I took the first side street, and went up a left-hand turning which led past a bit of vacant ground. There was no one in the little street, so I dropped the milk-cans inside the hoarding and sent the hat and overall after them. I had only just put on my cloth cap when a postman came round the corner. I gave him good morning and he answered me unsuspiciously. At that moment the clock of a neighbouring church struck the hour of seven.

There was not a second to spare. As soon as I got to Euston Road I took to my heels and ran. The clock at Euston Station showed five minutes past the hour. At St. Pancras I had no time to take a ticket, let alone that I had not settled upon my destination. A porter told me the platform, and as I entered it I saw the train already in motion. Two station officials blocked the way, but I dodged them and clambered into the last carriage.

Three minutes later, as we were roaring through the northern tunnels, an irate guard interviewed me. He wrote out for me a ticket to Newton Stewart, a name which had suddenly come back to my memory, and he conducted me from the first-class compartment where I had ensconced myself to a third-class smoker, occupied by a sailor and a stout woman with a child. He went off grumbling, and as I mopped my brow I observed to my companions in my broadest Scots that it was a sore job catching trains. I had already entered upon my part.

"The impidence o' that gyaird!" said the lady bitterly. "He needit a Scotch tongue to pit him in his place. He was complainin' o' this wean no haein' a ticket and her no fower till August twalmonth, and he was objectin' to this gentleman spittin'."

The sailor morosely agreed, and I started my new life in an atmosphere of protest against authority. I reminded myself that a week ago I had been finding the world dull.

CHAPTER 3

The Adventure of the Literary Innkeeper

I HAD a solemn time travelling north that day. It was fine May weather, with the hawthorn flowering on every hedge, and I asked myself why, when I was still a free man, I had stayed on in London and not got the good of this heavenly country. I didn't dare face the restaurant car, but I got a luncheon basket at Leeds and shared it with the fat woman. Also I got the morning's papers, with news about starters for the Derby and the beginning of the cricket season, and some paragraphs about how Balkan affairs were settling down and a British squadron was going to Kiel.

When I had done with them I got out Scudder's little black pocket-book and studied it. It was pretty well filled with jottings, chiefly figures, though now and then a name was printed in. For example, I found the words "Hofgaard," "Luneville," and "Avocado" pretty often, and especially the word "Pavia."

Now I was certain that Scudder never did anything without a reason, and I was pretty sure that there was a cypher in all this. That is a subject which has always interested me, and I did a bit at it myself once as intelligence-officer in Delagoa Bay during the Boer War. I have a head for things like chess and puzzles, and I used to reckon myself pretty good at finding out cyphers. This one looked like the numerical kind where sets of figures correspond to the letters of the alphabet, but any fairly shrewd man can find the clue to that sort after an hour or two's work, and I didn't think Scudder would have been content with anything so easy. So I fastened on the printed words, for you can make a pretty good numerical cypher if you have a key word which gives you the sequence of the letters.

I tried for hours, but none of the words answered. Then I fell asleep and woke at Dumfries just in time to bundle out and get into the slow Galloway train. There was a man on the platform whose looks I didn't like, but he never glanced at me, and when I caught sight of myself in the mirror of an automatic machine I didn't wonder. With my brown face, my old tweeds, and my slouch, I was the very model of one of the hill farmers who were crowding into the third-class carriages.

I travelled with half a dozen in an atmosphere of shag and clay pipes. They had come from the weekly market, and their mouths were full of prices. I heard accounts of how the lambing had gone up the Cairn and the Deuch and a dozen other mysterious waters. Above half the men had lunched heavily and were highly flavoured with whisky, but they took no notice of me. We rumbled slowly into a land of little wooded glens and then to a great wide moorland place, gleaming with lochs, with high hills showing northwards.

About five o'clock the carriage had emptied, and I was left alone as I had hoped. I got out at the next station, a little place whose name I scarcely noted, set right in the heart of a bog. It reminded me of one of those forgotten little stations in the Karroo. An old station-master was digging in his garden, and with his spade over his shoulder sauntered to the train, took charge of a parcel, and went back to his potatoes. A child of ten received my ticket, and I emerged on a white road that straggled over the brown moor.

It was a gorgeous spring evening, with every hill showing as clear as a cut amethyst. The air had the queer, rooty smell of bogs, but it was as fresh as mid-ocean, and it had the strangest effect on my spirits. I actually felt light-hearted. I might have been a boy out for a spring holiday tramp, instead of a man of thirty-seven very much wanted by the police. I felt just as I used to feel when I was starting for a big trek on a frosty morning on the high veld. If you believe me, I swung along that road whistling. There was no plan of campaign in my head, only just to go on and on in this blessed, honest-smelling hill country, for every mile put me in better humour with myself.

In a roadside planting I cut a walking-stick of hazel, and presently struck off the highway up a by-path which followed the glen of a brawling stream. I reckoned that I was still far ahead of any pursuit, and for that night might please myself. It was some hours since I had tasted food, and I was getting very hungry when I came to a herd's cottage set in a nook beside a waterfall. A brown-faced woman was standing by the door, and greeted me with the kindly shyness of moorland places. When I asked for a night's lodging she said I was welcome to the "bed in the loft," and very soon she set before me a hearty meal of ham and eggs, scones, and thick sweet milk.

At the darkening her man came in from the hills, a lean giant, who in one step covered as much ground as three paces of ordinary mortals. They asked no questions, for they had the perfect breeding of all dwellers in the wilds, but I could see they set me down as a kind of dealer, and I took some trouble to confirm their view. I spoke a lot about cattle, of which my host knew little, and I picked up from him a good deal about the local Galloway markets, which I tucked away in my memory for future use. At ten I was nodding in my chair, and the "bed in the loft" received a weary man who never opened his eyes till five o'clock set the little homestead a-going once more.

They refused any payment, and by six I had breakfasted and was striding southwards again. My notion was to return to the railway line a station or two farther on than the place where I had alighted yesterday and to double back. I reckoned that that was the safest way, for the police would naturally assume that I was always making farther from London in the direction of some western port. I thought I had still a good bit of a start, for, as I reasoned, it would take some hours to fix the blame on me, and several more to identify the fellow who got on board the train at St. Pancras.

It was the same jolly, clear spring weather, and I simply could not contrive to feel careworn. Indeed I was in better spirits than I had been for months. Over a long ridge of moorland I took my road, skirting the side of a high hill which the herd had called Cairnsmore of Fleet. Nesting curlews and plovers were crying everywhere, and the links of green pasture by the streams were dotted with young lambs. All the slackness of the past months was slipping from my bones, and I stepped out like a four-year-old. By and by I came to a swell of moorland which dipped to the vale of a little river, and a mile away in the heather I saw the smoke of a train.

The station, when I reached it, proved to be ideal for my purpose. The moor surged up around it and left room only for the single line, the slender siding, a waiting-room, an office, the station-master's cottage, and a tiny yard of gooseberries and sweet-william. There seemed no road to it from anywhere, and to increase the desolation the waves of a tarn lapped on their grey granite beach half a mile away. I waited in the deep heather till I saw the smoke of an east-going train on the horizon. Then I approached the tiny booking-office and took a ticket for Dumfries.

The only occupants of the carriage were an old shepherd and his dog—a wall-eyed brute that I mistrusted. The man was asleep, and on the cushions beside him was that morning's *Scotsman*. Eagerly I seized on it, for I fancied it would tell me something.

There were two columns about the Portland Place Murder, as it was called. My man Paddock had given the alarm and had the milkman arrested. Poor devil, it looked as if the latter had earned his sovereign hardly; but for me he had been cheap at the price, for he seemed to have occupied the police the better part of the day. In the latest news I found a further instalment of the story. The milkman had been released, I read, and the true criminal, about whose identity the police were reticent, was believed to have got away from London by one of the northern lines. There was a short note about me as the owner of the flat. I guessed the police had stuck that in, as a clumsy contrivance to persuade me that I was unsuspected.

There was nothing else in the paper, nothing about foreign politics or Karolides, or the things that had interested Scudder. I laid it down, and found that we were approaching the station at which I had got out yesterday. The potato-digging station-master had been gingered up into some activity, for the west-going train was waiting to let us pass, and from it had descended three men who were asking him questions. I supposed that they were the local police, who had been stirred up by Scotland Yard, and had traced me as far as this one-horse siding. Sitting well back in the shadow I watched them carefully. One of them had a book, and took down notes. The old potato-digger seemed to have turned peevish, but the child who had collected my ticket was talking volubly. All the party looked out across the moor where the white road departed. I hoped they were going to take up my tracks there.

As we moved away from the station my companion woke up. He fixed me with a wandering glance, kicked his dog viciously, and inquired where he was. Clearly he was very drunk.

"That's what comes o' bein' a teetotaller," he observed in bitter regret.

I expressed my surprise that in him I should have met a blue-ribbon stalwart.

"Ay, but I'm a strong teetotaller," he said pugnaciously. "I took the pledge last Martinmas, and I havena touched a drop o' whisky sinsyne. No even at Hogmanay, though I was sair temptit."

He swung his heels up on the seat, and burrowed a frowsy head into the cushions.

"And that's a' I get," he moaned. "A heid hetter than hell fire, and twae een lookin' different ways for the Sabbath."

"What did it?" I asked.

"A drink they ca' brandy. Bein' a teetotaller I keepit off the whisky, but I was nip-nippin' a' day at this brandy, and I doubt

I'll no be weel for a fortnicht." His voice died away into a stutter, and sleep once more laid its heavy hand on him.

My plan had been to get out at some station down the line, but the train suddenly gave me a better chance, for it came to a standstill at the end of a culvert which spanned a brawling porter-coloured river. I looked out and saw that every carriage window was closed and no human figure appeared in the landscape. So I opened the door, and dropped quickly into the tangle of hazels which edged the line.

It would have been all right but for that infernal dog. Under the impression that I was decamping with its master's belongings, it started to bark, and all but got me by the trousers. This woke up the herd, who stood bawling at the carriage door in the belief that I had committed suicide. I crawled through the thicket, reached the edge of the stream, and in cover of the bushes put a hundred yards or so behind me. Then from my shelter I peered back, and saw the guard and several passengers gathered round the open carriage door and staring in my direction. I could not have made a more public departure if I had left with a bugler and a brass band.

Happily the drunken herd provided a diversion. He and his dog, which was attached by a rope to his waist, suddenly cascaded out of the carriage, landed on their heads on the track, and rolled some way down the bank towards the water. In the rescue which followed the dog bit somebody, for I could hear the sound of hard swearing. Presently they had forgotten me, and when after a quarter of a mile's crawl I ventured to look back, the train had started again and was vanishing in the cutting.

I was in a wide semicircle of moorland, with the brown river as radius, and the high hills forming the northern circumference. There was not a sign or sound of a human being, only the splashing water and the interminable crying of curlews. Yet, oddly enough, for the first time I felt the terror of the hunted on me. It was not the police that I thought of, but the other folk, who knew that I knew Scudder's secret and dared not let me live. I was certain that they would pursue me with a keenness and vigilance unknown to the British law, and that once their grip closed on me I should find no mercy.

I looked back, but there was nothing in the landscape. The sun glinted on the metals of the line and the wet stones in the stream, and you could not have found a more peaceful sight in the world. Nevertheless I started to run. Crouching low in the runnels of the bog, I ran till the sweat blinded my eyes. The mood did not leave me till I had reached the rim of mountain and flung myself panting on a ridge high above the young waters of the brown river.

From my vantage-ground I could scan the whole moor right away to the railway line and to the south of it where green fields took the place of heather. I have eyes like a hawk, but I could see nothing moving in the whole countryside. Then I looked east beyond the ridge and saw a new kind of landscape—shallow green valleys with plentiful fir plantations and the faint lines of dust which spoke of highroads. Last of all I looked into the blue May sky and there I saw that which set my pulses racing . . .

Low down in the south a monoplane was climbing into the heavens. I was as certain as if I had been told that that aeroplane was looking for me, and that it did not belong to the police. For an hour or two I watched it from a pit of heather. It flew low along the hill-tops, and then in narrow circles over the valley up which I had come. Then it seemed to change its mind, rose to a great height, and flew away back to the south.

I did not like this espionage from the air, and I began to think less well of the countryside I had chosen for a refuge. These heather hills were no sort of cover if my enemies were in the sky, and I must find a different kind of sanctuary. I looked with more satisfaction to the green country beyond the ridge, for there I should find woods and stone houses.

About six in the evening I came out of the moorland to a white ribbon of road which wound up the narrow vale of a lowland stream. As I followed it, fields gave place to bent, the glen became a plateau, and presently I had reached a kind of pass where a solitary house smoked in the twilight. The road swung over a bridge, and leaning on the parapet was a young man.

He was smoking a long clay pipe and studying the water with spectacled eyes. In his left hand was a small book with a finger marking the place. Slowly he repeated:

"As when a Gryphon through the wilderness
With wingèd step, o'er hill and moory dale
Pursues the Arimaspian."

He jumped round as my step rung on the keystone, and I saw a pleasant sunburnt boyish face.

"Good evening to you," he said gravely. "It's a fine night for the road."

The smell of peat smoke and of some savoury roast floated to me from the house.

"Is that place an inn?" I asked.

"At your service," he said politely. "I am the landlord, sir, and I hope you will stay the night, for to tell you the truth I have had no company for a week."

I pulled myself up on the parapet of the bridge and filled my pipe. I began to detect an ally.

"You're young to be an innkeeper," I said.

"My father died a year ago and left me the business. I live there with my grandmother. It's a slow job for a young man, and it wasn't my choice of profession."

"Which was?"

He actually blushed. "I want to write books," he said.

"And what better chance could you ask?" I cried. "Man, I've often thought that an innkeeper would make the best story-teller in the world."

"Not now," he said eagerly. "Maybe in the old days when you had pilgrims and ballad-makers and highwaymen and mail coaches on the road. But not now. Nothing comes here but motor-cars full of fat women, who stop for lunch, and a fisherman or two in the spring, and the shooting tenants in August. There is not much material to be got out of that. I want to see life, to travel the world, and write things like Kipling and Conrad. But the most I've done yet is to get some verses printed in *Chambers's Journal*."

I looked at the inn standing golden in the sunset against the brown hills.

"I've knocked a bit about the world, and I wouldn't despise such a hermitage. D'you think that adventure is found only in the tropics or among the gentry in red shirts? Maybe you're rubbing shoulders with it at this moment."

"That's what Kipling says," he said, his eyes brightening, and he quoted some verse about "Romance bringing up the nine-fifteen."

"Here's a true tale for you then," I cried, "and a month from now you can make a novel out of it."

Sitting on the bridge in the soft May gloaming I pitched him a lovely yarn. It was true in essentials, too, though I altered the minor details. I made out that I was a mining magnate from Kimberley, who had had a lot of trouble with I.D.B. and had shown up a gang. They had pursued me across the ocean, and had killed my best friend, and were now on my tracks.

I told the story well, though I say it who shouldn't. I pictured a flight across the Kalahari to German Africa, the crackling, parching days, the wonderful blue-velvet nights. I described an attack on my life on the voyage home, and I made a really horrid affair of the Portland Place murder. "You're looking for adventure," I cried; "well, you've found it here. The devils are after me, and the police are after them. It's a race that I mean to win."

"By God!" he whispered, drawing his breath in sharply. "It is all pure Rider Haggard and Conan Doyle."

"You believe me," I said gratefully.

"Of course I do," and he held out his hand. "I believe everything out of the common. The only thing to distrust is the normal."

He was very young, but he was the man for my money.

"I think they're off my track for the moment, but I must lie close for a couple of days. Can you take me in?"

He caught my elbow in his eagerness and drew me towards the house. "You can lie as snug here as if you were in a moss-hole. I'll see that nobody blabs, either. And you'll give me some more material about your adventures?"

As I entered the inn porch I heard from far off the beat of an engine. There silhouetted against the dusky west was my friend, the monoplane.

HE GAVE me a room at the back of the house, with a fine out-look over the plateau, and he made me free of his own study, which was stacked with cheap editions of his favourite authors. I never saw the grandmother, so I guess she was bedridden. An old woman called Margit brought me my meals, and the innkeeper was around me at all hours. I wanted some time to myself, so I invented a job for him. He had a motor-bicycle and I sent him off next morning for the daily paper, which usually arrived with the post in the later afternoon. I told him to keep his eyes skinned, and make note of any strange figures he saw, keeping a special sharp look-out for motors and aeroplanes. Then I sat down in real earnest to Scudder's notebook.

He came back at midday with the *Scotsman*. There was nothing in it, except some further evidence of Paddock and the milkman, and a repetition of yesterday's statement that the murderer had gone north. But there was a long article, reprinted from *The Times*, about Karolides and the state of affairs in the Balkans, though there was no mention of any visit to England. I got rid of the innkeeper for the afternoon, for I was getting very warm in my search for the cypher.

As I told you, it was a numerical cypher, and by an elaborate system of experiments I had pretty well discovered what were the nulls and stops. The trouble was the key word, and when I thought of the odd million words he might have used I felt pretty hopeless. But about three o'clock I had a sudden inspiration.

The name Julia Czechenyi flashed across my memory. Scudder had said it was the key to the Karolides business, and it occurred to me to try it on his cypher.

It worked. The five letters of "Julia" gave me the position of the vowels. A was J, the tenth letter of the alphabet, and so represented by X in the cypher. E was U = XXI, and so on. "Czechenyi" gave me the numerals for the principal consonants. I scribbled that scheme on a bit of paper and sat down to read Scudder's pages.

In half an hour I was reading with a whitish face and fingers that drummed on the table.

I glanced out of the window and saw a big touring-car coming up the glen towards the inn. It drew up at the door, and there was the sound of people alighting. There seemed to be two of them, men in Aquascutums and tweed caps.

Ten minutes later the innkeeper slipped into the room, his eyes bright with excitement.

"There's two chaps below looking for you," he whispered. "They're in the dining-room having whiskies and sodas. They asked about you and said they had hoped to meet you here. Oh! and they described you jolly well, down to your boots and shirt. I told them you had been here last night and had gone off on a motor-bicycle this morning, and one of the chaps swore like a navvy."

I made him tell me what they looked like. One was a dark-eyed thin fellow with bushy eyebrows, the other was always smiling and lisped in his talk. Neither was any kind of foreigner; on this my young friend was positive.

I took a bit of paper and wrote these words in German as if they were part of a letter:

> *Black Stone. Scudder had got on to this, but he could not act for a fortnight. I doubt if I can do any good now, especially as Karolides is uncertain about his plans. But if Mr. T. advises I will do the best I . . .*

I manufactured it rather neatly, so that it looked like a loose page of a private letter.

"Take this down and say it was found in my bedroom, and ask them to return it to me if they overtake me."

Three minutes later I heard the car begin to move, and peeping from behind the curtain caught sight of the two figures. One was slim, the other was sleek; that was the most I could make of my reconnaissance.

The innkeeper appeared in great excitement. "Your paper woke them up," he said gleefully. "The dark fellow went as white as death and cursed like blazes, and the fat one whistled and looked ugly. They paid for their drinks with half a sovereign and wouldn't wait for change."

"Now I'll tell you what I want you to do," I said. "Get on your bicycle and go off to Newton Stewart to the Chief Constable. Describe the two men, and say you suspect them of having had something to do with the London murder. You can invent reasons. The two will come back, never fear. Not to-night, for they'll follow me forty miles along the road, but first thing to-morrow morning. Tell the police to be here bright and early."

He set off like a docile child, while I worked at Scudder's notes. When he came back we dined together, and in common decency I had to let him pump me. I gave him a lot of stuff about lion hunts and the Matabele War, thinking all the while what tame businesses these were compared to this I was now engaged in. When he went to bed I sat up and finished Scudder. I smoked in a chair till daylight, for I could not sleep.

About eight next morning I witnessed the arrival of two constables and a sergeant. They put their car in a coachhouse under the innkeeper's instructions, and entered the house. Twenty minutes later I saw from my window a second car come across the plateau from the opposite direction. It did not come up to the inn, but stopped two hundred yards off in the shelter of a patch of wood. I noticed that its occupants carefully reversed it before leaving it. A minute or two later I heard their steps on the gravel outside the window.

My plan had been to lie hid in my bedroom, and see what happened. I had a notion that, if I could bring the police and my other more dangerous pursuers together, something might work out of it to my advantage. But now I had a better idea. I scribbled a line of thanks to my host, opened the window, and dropped quietly into a gooseberry bush. Unobserved I crossed the dyke, crawled down the side of a tributary burn, and won the highroad on the far side of the patch of trees. There stood the car, very spick and span in the morning sunlight, but with the dust on her which told of a long journey. I started her, jumped into the chauffeur's seat, and stole gently out on to the plateau.

Almost at once the road dipped so that I lost sight of the inn, but the wind seemed to bring me the sound of angry voices.

CHAPTER 4

The Adventure of the Radical Candidate

You may picture me driving that 40 hp car for all she was worth over the crisp moor roads on that shining May morning; glancing back at first over my shoulder, and looking anxiously to the next turning; then driving with a vague eye, just wide enough awake to keep on the highway. For I was thinking desperately of what I had found in Scudder's pocket-book.

The little man had told me a pack of lies. All his yarns about the Balkans and the Jew-anarchists and the Foreign Office Conference were eyewash, and so was Karolides. And yet not quite, as you shall hear. I had staked everything on my belief in his story, and had been let down; here was his book telling me a different tale, and instead of being once-bit-twice-shy, I believed it absolutely.

Why, I don't know. It rang desperately true, and the first yarn, if you understand me, had been in a queer way true also in spirit. The fifteenth day of June was going to be a day of destiny, a bigger destiny than the killing of a Dago. It was so big that I didn't blame Scudder for keeping me out of the game and wanting to play a lone hand. That, I was pretty clear, was his intention. He had told me something which sounded big enough, but the real thing was so immortally big that he, the man who had found it out, wanted it all for himself. I didn't blame him. It was risks after all that he was chiefly greedy about.

The whole story was in the notes—with gaps, you understand, which he would have filled up from his memory. He stuck down his authorities, too, and had an odd trick of giving them all a numerical value and then striking a balance, which stood for the reliability of each stage in the yarn. The four names he had printed were authorities, and there was a man, Ducrosne, who got five out of a possible five; and another fellow, Ammersfoort, who got three. The bare bones of the tale were all that was in the book—these, and one queer phrase which occurred half a dozen times inside brackets. ("Thirty-nine steps") was the phrase; and at its last time of use it ran—("Thirty-nine steps, I counted them—high tide 10:17 p.m."). I could make nothing of that.

The first thing I learned was that it was no question of preventing a war. That was coming, as sure as Christmas: had been arranged, said Scudder, ever since February 1912. Karolides was going to be the occasion. He was booked all right, and was to hand in his checks on June 14th, two weeks and four days from that May morning. I gathered from Scudder's notes that nothing on earth could prevent that. His talk of Epirote guards that would skin their own grandmothers was all billy-o.

The second thing was that this war was going to come as a mighty surprise to Britain. Karolides' death would set the Balkans by the ears, and then Vienna would chip in with an ultimatum. Russia wouldn't like that, and there would be high words. But Berlin would play the peacemaker, and pour oil on the waters, till suddenly she would find a good cause for a quarrel, pick it up, and in five hours let fly at us. That was the idea, and a pretty good one too. Honey and fair speeches, and then a stroke in the dark. While we were talking about the goodwill and good intentions of Germany our coast would be silently ringed with mines, and submarines would be waiting for every battleship.

But all this depended upon the third thing, which was due to happen on June 15th. I would never have grasped this if I hadn't once happened to meet a French staff-officer, coming back from

West Africa, who had told me a lot of things. One was that, in spite of all the nonsense talked in Parliament, there was a real working alliance between France and Britain, and that the two General Staffs met every now and then, and made plans for joint action in case of war. Well, in June a very great swell was coming over from Paris, and he was going to get nothing less than a statement of the disposition of the British Home Fleet on mobilization. At least I gathered it was something like that; anyhow, it was something uncommonly important.

But on the 15th day of June there were to be others in London—others, at whom I could only guess. Scudder was content to call them collectively the "Black Stone." They represented not our Allies, but our deadly foes; and the information, destined for France, was to be diverted to their pockets. And it was to be used, remember—used a week or two later, with great guns and swift torpedoes, suddenly in the darkness of a summer night.

This was the story I had been deciphering in a back room of a country inn, overlooking a cabbage garden. This was the story that hummed in my brain as I swung in the big touring-car from glen to glen.

My first impulse had been to write a letter to the Prime Minister, but a little reflection convinced me that that would be useless. Who would believe my tale? I must show a sign, some token in proof, and Heaven knew what that could be. Above all, I must keep going myself, ready to act when things got riper, and that was going to be no light job with the police of the British Isles in full cry after me and the watchers of the Black Stone running silently and swiftly on my trail.

I had no very clear purpose in my journey, but I steered east by the sun, for I remembered from the map that if I went north I would come into a region of coal-pits and industrial towns. Presently I was down from the moorlands and traversing the broad haugh of a river. For miles I ran alongside a park wall, and in a break of the trees I saw a great castle. I swung through little old thatched villages, and over peaceful lowland streams, and past gardens blazing with hawthorn and yellow laburnum. The land was so deep in peace that I could scarcely believe that somewhere behind me were those who sought my life; ay, and that in a month's time, unless I had the almightiest of luck, these round country faces would be pinched and staring, and men would be lying dead in English fields.

About midday I entered a long straggling village, and had a mind to stop and eat. Halfway down was the Post Office, and on the steps of it stood the post-mistress and a policeman hard at work conning a telegram. When they saw me they wakened up, and the policeman advanced with raised hand, and cried on me to stop.

I nearly was fool enough to obey. Then it flashed upon me that the wire had to do with me; that my friends at the inn had come to an understanding, and were united in desiring to see more of me, and that it had been easy enough for them to wire the description of me and the car to thirty villages through which I might pass. I released the brakes just in time. As it was, the policeman made a claw at the hood, and only dropped off when he got my left in his eye.

I saw that main roads were no place for me, and turned into the by-ways. It wasn't an easy job without a map, for there was the risk of getting on to a farm road and ending in a duck-pond or a stable-yard, and I couldn't afford that kind of delay. I began to see what an ass I had been to steal the car. The big green brute would be the safest kind of clue to me over the breadth of Scotland. If I left it and took to my feet, it would be discovered in an hour or two and I would get no start in the race.

The immediate thing to do was to get to the loneliest roads. These I soon found when I struck up a tributary of the big river, and got into a glen with steep hills all about me, and a corkscrew road at the end which climbed over a pass. Here I met nobody, but it was taking me too far north, so I slewed east along a bad track and finally struck a big double-line railway. Away below me I saw another broadish valley, and it occurred to me that if I crossed it I might find some remote inn to pass the night. The evening was now drawing in, and I was furiously hungry, for I had eaten nothing since breakfast except a couple of buns I had bought from a baker's cart.

Just then I heard a noise in the sky, and lo and behold there was that infernal aeroplane, flying low, about a dozen miles to the south and rapidly coming towards me.

I had the sense to remember that on a bare moor I was at the aeroplane's mercy, and that my only chance was to get to the leafy cover of the valley. Down the hill I went like blue lightning, screwing my head round, whenever I dared, to watch that damned flying machine. Soon I was on a road between hedges, and dipping to the deep-cut glen of a stream. Then came a bit of thick wood where I slackened speed.

Suddenly on my left I heard the hoot of another car, and realized to my horror that I was almost upon a couple of gateposts through which a private road debouched on the highway. My horn gave an agonized roar, but it was too late. I clapped on my brakes, but my impetus was too great, and there before me a car was sliding athwart my course. In a second there would have been the deuce of a wreck. I did the only thing possible, and ran slap into the hedge on the right, trusting to find something soft beyond.

But there I was mistaken. My car slithered through the hedge like butter, and then gave a sickening plunge forward. I saw what was coming, leaped on the seat and would have jumped out. But a branch of hawthorn got me in the chest, lifted me up and held me, while a ton or two of expensive metal slipped below me, bucked and pitched, and then dropped with an almighty smash fifty feet to the bed of the stream.

SLOWLY that thorn let me go. I subsided first on the hedge, and then very gently on a bower of nettles. As I scrambled to my feet a hand took me by the arm, and a sympathetic and badly scared voice asked me if I were hurt.

I found myself looking at a tall young man in goggles and a leather ulster, who kept on blessing his soul and whinnying apologies. For myself, once I got my wind back, I was rather glad than otherwise. This was one way of getting rid of the car.

"My blame, sir," I answered him. "It's lucky that I did not add homicide to my follies. That's the end of my Scotch motor tour, but it might have been the end of my life."

He plucked out a watch and studied it. "You're the right sort of fellow," he said. "I can spare a quarter of an hour, and my house is two minutes off. I'll see you clothed and fed and snug in bed. Where's your kit, by the way? Is it in the burn along with the car?"

"It's in my pocket," I said, brandishing a toothbrush. "I'm a Colonial and travel light."

"A Colonial," he cried. "By Gad, you're the very man I've been praying for. Are you by any blessed chance a Free Trader?"

"I am," said I, without the foggiest notion of what he meant.

He patted my shoulder and hurried me into his car. Three minutes later we drew up before a comfortable-looking shooting-box set among pine-trees, and he ushered me indoors. He took me first to a bedroom and flung half a dozen of his suits before me, for my own had been pretty well reduced to rags. I selected a loose blue serge, which differed most conspicuously from my former garments, and borrowed a linen collar. Then he haled me to the dining-room, where the remnants of a meal stood on the table, and announced that I had just five minutes to feed. "You can take a snack in your pocket, and we'll have supper when we get back. I've got to be at the Masonic Hall at eight o'clock or my agent will comb my hair."

I had a cup of coffee and some cold ham, while he yarned away on the hearthrug.

"You find me in the deuce of a mess, Mr.—; by the by, you haven't told me your name. Twisdon? Any relation of old Tommy Twisdon of the Sixtieth? No? Well, you see I'm Liberal Candidate for this part of the world, and I had a meeting on to-night at Brattleburn—that's my chief town, and an infernal Tory strong-hold. I had got the Colonial ex-Premier fellow, Crumpleton, coming to speak for me to-night, and had the thing tremendously billed and the whole place ground-baited. This afternoon

I had a wire from the ruffian saying he had got influenza at Blackpool, and here am I left to do the whole thing myself. I had meant to speak for ten minutes and must now go on for forty, and, though I've been racking my brains for three hours to think of something, I simply cannot last the course. Now you've got to be a good chap and help me. You're a Free Trader and can tell our people what a wash-out Protection is in the Colonies. All you fellows have the gift of the gab—I wish to Heaven I had it. I'll be for evermore in your debt."

I had very few notions about Free Trade one way or the other, but I saw no other chance to get what I wanted. My young gentleman was far too absorbed in his own difficulties to think how odd it was to ask a stranger who had just missed death by an ace and had lost a thousand-guinea car to address a meeting for him on the spur of the moment. But my necessities did not allow me to contemplate oddnesses or to pick and choose my supports.

"All right," I said. "I'm not much good as a speaker, but I'll tell them a bit about Australia."

At my words the cares of the ages slipped from his shoulders, and he was rapturous in his thanks. He lent me a big driving coat—and never troubled to ask why I had started on a motor tour without possessing an ulster—and, as we slipped down the dusty roads, poured into my ears the simple facts of his history. He was an orphan, and his uncle had brought him up—I've forgotten the uncle's name, but he was in the Cabinet, and you can read his speeches in the papers. He had gone round the world after leaving Cambridge, and then, being short of a job, his uncle had advised politics. I gathered that he had no preference in parties. "Good chaps in both," he said cheerfully, "and plenty of blighters, too. I'm Liberal, because my family have always been Whigs." But if he was lukewarm politically he had strong views on other things. He found out I knew a bit about horses, and jawed away about the Derby entries; and he was full of plans for improving his shooting. Altogether, a very clean, decent, callow young man.

As we passed through a little town two policemen signalled us to stop, and flashed their lanterns on us.

"Beg pardon, Sir Harry," said one. "We've got instructions to look out for a car, and the description's no unlike yours."

"Right-o," said my host, while I thanked Providence for the devious ways I had been brought to safety. After that he spoke no more, for his mind began to labour heavily with his coming speech. His lips kept muttering, his eye wandered, and I began to prepare myself for a second catastrophe. I tried to think of something to say myself, but my mind was dry as a stone. The next thing I knew we had drawn up outside a door in a street, and were being welcomed by some noisy gentlemen with rosettes.

The hall had about five hundred in it, women mostly, a lot of bald heads, and a dozen or two young men. The chairman, a weaselly minister with a reddish nose, lamented Crumpleton's absence, soliloquized on his influenza, and gave me a certificate as a "trusted leader of Australian thought." There were two policemen at the door, and I hoped they took note of that testimonial. Then Sir Harry started.

I never heard anything like it. He didn't begin to know how to talk. He had about a bushel of notes from which he read, and when he let go of them he fell into one prolonged stutter. Every now and then he remembered a phrase he had learned by heart, straightened his back, and gave it off like Henry Irving, and the next moment he was bent double and crooning over his papers. It was the most appalling rot, too. He talked about the "German menace," and said it was all a Tory invention to cheat the poor of their rights and keep back the great flood of social reform, but that "organized labour" realized this and laughed the Tories to scorn. He was all for reducing our Navy as a proof of our good faith, and then sending Germany an ultimatum telling her to do the same or we would knock her into a cocked hat. He said that, but for the Tories, Germany and Britain would be fellow workers in peace and reform. I thought of the little black book in my pocket! A giddy lot Scudder's friends cared for peace and reform.

Yet in a queer way I liked the speech. You could see the niceness of the chap shining out behind the muck with which he had been spoon-fed. Also it took a load off my mind. I mightn't be much of an orator, but I was a thousand per cent better than Sir Harry.

I didn't get on so badly when it came to my turn. I simply told them all I could remember about Australia, praying there should be no Australian there—all about its labour party and emigration and universal service. I doubt if I remembered to mention Free Trade, but I said there were no Tories in Australia, only Labour and Liberals. That fetched a cheer, and I woke them up a bit when I started in to tell them the kind of glorious business I thought could be made out of the Empire if we really put our backs into it.

Altogether I fancy I was rather a success. The minister didn't like me, though, and when he proposed a vote of thanks, spoke of Sir Harry's speech as "statesmanlike" and mine as having "the eloquence of an emigration agent."

When we were in the car again my host was in wild spirits at having got his job over. "A ripping speech, Twisdon," he said. "Now, you're coming home with me. I'm all alone, and if you'll stop a day or two I'll show you some very decent fishing."

We had a hot supper—and I wanted it pretty badly—and then drank grog in a big cheery smoking-room with a crackling wood fire. I thought the time had come for me to put my cards on the table. I saw by this man's eye that he was the kind you can trust.

"Listen, Sir Harry," I said. "I've something pretty important to say to you. You're a good fellow, and I'm going to be frank. Where on earth did you get that poisonous rubbish you talked to-night?"

His face fell. "Was it as bad as that?" he asked ruefully. "It did sound rather thin. I got most of it out of the *Progressive Magazine* and pamphlets that agent chap of mine keeps sending me. But you surely don't think Germany would ever go to war with us?"

"Ask that question in six weeks and it won't need an answer," I said. "If you'll give me your attention for half an hour I am going to tell you a story."

I can see yet that bright room with the deers' heads and the old prints on the walls, Sir Harry standing restlessly on the stone curb of the hearth, and myself lying back in an arm-chair, speaking. I seemed to be another person, standing aside and listening to my own voice, and judging carefully the reliability of my tale. It was the first time I had ever told anyone the exact truth, as far as I understood it, and it did me no end of good, for it straightened out the thing in my own mind. I blinked no detail. He heard all about Scudder, and the milkman, and the notebook, and my doings in Galloway. Presently he got very excited and walked up and down the hearthrug.

"So you see," I concluded, "you have got here in your house the man that is wanted for the Portland Place murder. Your duty is to send your car for the police and give me up. I don't think I'll get very far. There'll be an accident, and I'll have a knife in my ribs an hour or so after arrest. Nevertheless it's your duty, as a law-abiding citizen. Perhaps in a month's time you'll be sorry, but you have no cause to think of that."

He was looking at me with bright steady eyes. "What was your job in Rhodesia, Mr. Hannay?" he asked.

"Mining engineer," I said. "I've made my pile cleanly, and I've had a good time in the making of it."

"Not a profession that weakens the nerves, is it?"

I laughed. "Oh, as to that, my nerves are good enough." I took down a hunting-knife from a stand on the wall, and did the old Mashona trick of tossing it and catching it in my lips. That wants a pretty steady heart.

He watched me with a smile. "I don't want proof. I may be an ass on the platform, but I can size up a man. You're no murderer and you're no fool, and I believe you are speaking the truth. I'm going to back you up. Now, what can I do?"

"First, I want you to write a letter to your uncle. I've got to get in touch with the Government people some time before the 15th of June."

He pulled his moustache. "That won't help you. This is Foreign Office business, and my uncle would have nothing to do with it. Besides, you'd never convince him. No, I'll go one better. I'll write to the Permanent Secretary at the Foreign Office. He's my godfather, and one of the best going. What do you want?"

He sat down at a table and wrote to my dictation. The gist of it was that if a man called Twisdon (I thought I had better stick to that name) turned up before June 15th he was to treat him kindly. He said Twisdon would prove his *bona fides* by passing the word "Black Stone" and whistling "Annie Laurie."

"Good," said Sir Harry. "That's the proper style. By the way, you'll find my godfather—his name's Sir Walter Bullivant—down at his country cottage for Whitsuntide. It's close to Artinswell on the Kennet. That's done. Now, what's the next thing?"

"You're about my height. Lend me the oldest tweed suit you've got. Anything will do, so long as the colour is the opposite of the clothes I destroyed this afternoon. Then show me a map of the neighbourhood and explain to me the lie of the land. Lastly, if the police come seeking me, just show them the car in the glen. If the other lot turn up, tell them I caught the south express after your meeting."

He did, or promised to do, all these things. I shaved off the remnants of my moustache, and got inside an ancient suit of what I believe is called heather mixture. The map gave me some notion of my whereabouts, and told me the two things I wanted to know—where the main railway to the south could be joined and what were the wildest districts near at hand.

At two o'clock he wakened me from my slumbers in the smoking-room arm-chair, and led me blinking into the dark starry night. An old bicycle was found in a tool-shed and handed over to me.

"First turn to the right up by the long fir-wood," he enjoined. "By daybreak you'll be well into the hills. Then I should pitch the machine into a bog and take to the moors on foot. You can put in a week among the shepherds, and be as safe as if you were in New Guinea."

I pedalled diligently up steep roads of hill gravel till the skies grew pale with morning. As the mists cleared before the sun, I found myself in a wide green world with glens falling on every side and a far-away blue horizon. Here, at any rate, I could get early news of my enemies.

CHAPTER 5

The Adventure of the Spectacled Roadman

I SAT down on the very crest of the pass and took stock of my position.

Behind me was the road climbing through a long cleft in the hills, which was the upper glen of some notable river. In front was a flat space of maybe a mile, all pitted with bog-holes and rough with tussocks, and then beyond it the road fell steeply down another glen to a plain whose blue dimness melted into the distance. To left and right were round-shouldered green hills as smooth as pancakes, but to the south—that is, the left hand— there was a glimpse of high heathery mountains, which I remembered from the map as the big knot of hill which I had chosen for my sanctuary. I was on the central boss of a huge upland country, and could see everything moving for miles. In the meadows below the road half a mile back a cottage smoked, but it was the only sign of human life. Otherwise there was only the calling of plovers and the tinkling of little streams.

It was now about seven o'clock, and as I waited I heard once again that ominous beat in the air. Then I realized that my vantage-ground might be in reality a trap. There was no cover for a tomtit in those bald green places.

I sat quite still and hopeless while the beat grew louder. Then I saw an aeroplane coming up from the east. It was flying high, but as I looked it dropped several hundred feet and began to circle round the knot of hill in narrowing circles, just as a hawk wheels before it pounces. Now it was flying very low, and now the observer on board caught sight of me. I could see one of the two occupants examining me through glasses.

Suddenly it began to rise in swift whorls, and the next I knew it was speeding eastward again till it became a speck in the blue morning.

That made me do some savage thinking. My enemies had located me, and the next thing would be a cordon round me. I didn't know what force they could command, but I was certain it would be sufficient. The aeroplane had seen my bicycle, and would conclude that I would try to escape by the road. In that case there might be a chance on the moors to the right or left. I wheeled the machine a hundred yards from the highway, and plunged it into a moss-hole, where it sank among pond-weed and water-buttercups. Then I climbed to a knoll which gave me a view of the two valleys. Nothing was stirring on the long white ribbon that threaded them.

I have said there was not cover in the whole place to hide a rat. As the day advanced it was flooded with soft fresh light till it had the fragrant sunniness of the South African veld. At other times I would have liked the place, but now it seemed to suffocate me. The free moorlands were prison walls, and the keen hill air was the breath of a dungeon.

I tossed a coin—heads right, tails left—and it fell heads, so I turned to the north. In a little I came to the brow of the ridge which was the containing wall of the pass. I saw the highroad for maybe ten miles, and far down it something that was moving, and that I took to be a motor-car. Beyond the ridge I looked on a rolling green moor, which fell away into wooded glens.

Now my life on the veld has given me the eyes of a kite, and I can see things for which most men need a telescope . . . Away down the slope, a couple of miles away, several men were advancing like a row of beaters at a shoot . . .

I dropped out of sight behind the skyline. That way was shut to me, and I must try the bigger hills to the south beyond the highway. The car I had noticed was getting nearer, but it was still a long way off with some very steep gradients before it. I ran hard, crouching low except in the hollows, and as I ran I kept scanning the brow of the hill before me. Was it imagination, or did I see figures—one, two, perhaps more—moving in a glen beyond the stream?

If you are hemmed in on all sides in a patch of land there is only one chance of escape. You must stay in the patch, and let your enemies search it and not find you. That was good sense, but how on earth was I to escape notice in that tablecloth of a place? I would have buried myself to the neck in mud or lain below water or climbed the tallest tree. But there was not a stick of wood, the bog-holes were little puddles, the stream was a slender trickle. There was nothing but short heather, and bare hill bent, and the white highway.

Then in a tiny bight of road, beside a heap of stones, I found the roadman.

He had just arrived, and was wearily flinging down his hammer. He looked at me with a fishy eye and yawned.

"Confoond the day I ever left the herdin'!" he said, as if to the world at large. "There I was my ain maister. Now I'm a slave to the Government, tethered to the roadside, wi' sair een, and a back like a suckle."

He took up the hammer, struck a stone, dropped the implement with an oath, and put both hands to his ears. "Mercy on me! My heid's burstin'!" he cried.

He was a wild figure, about my own size but much bent, with a week's beard on his chin, and a pair of big horn spectacles.

"I canna dae't," he cried again. "The Surveyor maun just report me. I'm for my bed."

I asked him what was the trouble, though indeed that was clear enough.

"The trouble is that I'm no sober. Last nicht my dochter Merran was waddit, and they danced till fower in the byre. Me and some ither chiels sat down to the drinkin', and here I am. Peety that I ever lookit on the wine when it was red!"

I agreed with him about bed.

"It's easy speakin'," he moaned. "But I got a post-caird yestreen sayin' that the new Road Surveyor would be round the day. He'll come and he'll no find me, or else he'll find me fou, and either way I'm a done man. I'll awa' back to my bed and say I'm no weel, but I doot that'll no help me, for they ken my kind o' no-weel-ness."

Then I had an inspiration. "Does the new Surveyor know you?" I asked.

"No him. He's just been a week at the job. He rins about in a wee motor-cawr, and wad speir the inside oot o' a whelk."

"Where's your house?" I asked, and was directed by a wavering finger to the cottage by the stream.

"Well, back to your bed," I said, "and sleep in peace. I'll take on your job for a bit and see the Surveyor."

He stared at me blankly; then, as the notion dawned on his fuddled brain, his face broke into the vacant drunkard's smile.

"You're the billy," he cried. "It'll be easy eneuch managed. I've finished that bing o' stanes, so you needna chap ony mair this forenoon. Just take the barry, and wheel eneuch metal frae yon quarry doon the road to make anither bing the morn. My name's Alexander Turnbull, and I've been seeven year at the trade, and twenty afore that herdin', on Leithen Water. My freens ca' me Ecky, and whiles Specky, for I wear glasses, being weak i' the sicht. Just you speak the Surveyor fair, and ca' him Sir, and he'll be fell pleased. I'll be back or midday."

I borrowed his spectacles and filthy old hat; stripped off coat, waistcoat, and collar, and gave him them to carry home; borrowed, too, the foul stump of a clay pipe as an extra property. He indicated my simple tasks, and without more ado set off at an amble bedwards. Bed may have been his chief object, but I think there was also something left in the foot of a bottle. I prayed that he might be safe under cover before my friends arrived on the scene.

Then I set to work to dress for the part. I opened the collar of my shirt—it was a vulgar blue-and-white check such as plough-men wear—and revealed a neck as brown as any tinker's. I rolled up my sleeves, and there was a forearm which might have been a blacksmith's, sunburnt and rough with old scars. I got my boots and trouser-legs all white from the dust of the road, and hitched up my trousers, tying them with string below the knee. Then I set to work on my face. With a handful of dust I made a water-mark round my neck, the place where Mr. Turnbull's Sunday ab-lutions might be expected to stop. I rubbed a good deal of dirt also into the sunburn of my cheeks. A roadman's eyes would no doubt be a little inflamed, so I contrived to get some dust in both of mine, and by dint of vigorous rubbing produced a bleary effect.

The sandwiches Sir Harry had given me had gone off with my coat, but the roadman's lunch, tied up in a red handkerchief, was at my disposal. I ate with great relish several of the thick slabs of scone and cheese and drank a little of the cold tea. In the hand-kerchief was a local paper tied with string and addressed to Mr. Turnbull—obviously meant to solace his midday leisure. I did up the bundle again, and put the paper conspicuously beside it.

My boots did not satisfy me, but by dint of kicking among the stones I reduced them to the granite-like surface which marks a roadman's footgear. Then I bit and scraped my fingernails till the edges were all cracked and uneven. The men I was matched against would miss no detail. I broke one of the bootlaces and retied it in a clumsy knot, and loosed the other so that my thick grey socks bulged over the uppers. Still no sign of anything on the road. The motor I had observed half an hour ago must have gone home.

My toilet complete, I took up the barrow and began my jour-neys to and from the quarry a hundred yards off.

I remember an old scout in Rhodesia, who had done many queer things in his day, once telling me that the secret of playing a part was to think yourself into it. You could never keep it up, he said, unless you could manage to convince yourself that you were *it*. So I shut off all other thoughts and switched them on to the road-mending. I thought of the little white cottage as my home, I recalled the years I had spent herding on Leithen Water, I made my mind dwell lovingly on sleep in a box-bed and a bottle of cheap whisky. Still nothing appeared on that long white road.

Now and then a sheep wandered off the heather to stare at me. A heron flopped down to a pool in the stream and started to fish, taking no more notice of me than if I had been a milestone. On I went, trundling my loads of stone, with the heavy step of the professional. Soon I grew warm, and the dust on my face changed into solid and abiding grit. I was already counting the hours till evening should put a limit to Mr. Turnbull's monotonous toil.

Suddenly a crisp voice from the road, and looking up I saw a little Ford two-seater, and a round-faced young man in a bowler hat.

"Are you Alexander Turnbull?" he asked. "I am the new County Road Surveyor. You live at Blackhopefoot, and have charge of the section from Laidlaw-byres to the Riggs? Good! A fair bit of road, Turnbull, and not badly engineered. A little soft about a mile off, and the edges want cleaning. See you look after that. Good morning. You'll know me the next time you see me."

Clearly my get-up was good enough for the dreaded Surveyor. I went on with my work, and as the morning grew towards noon I was cheered by a little traffic. A baker's van breasted the hill, and sold me a bag of ginger biscuits which I stowed in my trouser pockets against emergencies. Then a herd passed with sheep, and disturbed me somewhat by asking loudly, "What had become o' Specky?"

"In bed wi' the colic," I replied, and the herd passed on . . .

Just about midday a big car stole down the hill, glided past and drew up a hundred yards beyond. Its three occupants descended as if to stretch their legs, and sauntered towards me.

Two of the men I had seen before from the window of the Galloway inn—one lean, sharp, and dark, the other comfortable and smiling. The third had the look of a countryman—a vet, perhaps, or a small farmer. He was dressed in ill-cut knickerbockers, and the eye in his head was as bright and wary as a hen's.

" 'Morning," said the last. "That's a fine easy job o' yours."

I had not looked up on their approach, and now, when accosted, I slowly and painfully straightened my back, after the manner of roadmen; spat vigorously, after the manner of the low Scot; and regarded them steadily before replying. I confronted three pairs of eyes that missed nothing.

"There's waur jobs and there's better," I said sententiously. "I wad rather hae yours, sittin' a' day on your hinderlands on thae cushions. It's you and your muckle cawrs that wreck my roads! If we a' had oor richts, ye sud be made to mend what ye break."

The bright-eyed man was looking at the newspaper lying beside Turnbull's bundle.

"I see you get your papers in good time," he said.

I glanced at it casually. "Ay, in gude time. Seein' that that paper cam' out last Setterday I'm just sax days late."

He picked it up, glanced at the superscription, and laid it down again. One of the others had been looking at my boots, and a word in German called the speaker's attention to them.

"You've a fine taste in boots," he said. "These were never made by a country shoemaker."

"They were not," I said readily. "They were made in London. I got them frae the gentleman that was here last year for the shootin'. What was his name now?" And I scratched a forgetful head.

Again the sleek one spoke in German. "Let us get on," he said. "This fellow is all right."

They asked one last question.

"Did you see anyone pass early this morning? He might be on a bicycle or he might be on foot."

I very nearly fell into the trap and told a story of a bicyclist hurrying past in the grey dawn. But I had the sense to see my danger. I pretended to consider very deeply.

"I wasna up very early," I said. "Ye see, my dochter was merrit last nicht, and we keepit it up late. I opened the house door about seeven and there was naebody on the road then. Since I cam' up here there has just been the baker and the Ruchill herd, besides you gentlemen."

One of them gave me a cigar, which I smelt gingerly and stuck in Turnbull's bundle. They got into their car and were out of sight in three minutes.

My heart leaped with an enormous relief, but I went on wheeling my stones. It was as well, for ten minutes later the car returned, one of the occupants waving a hand to me. Those gentry left nothing to chance.

I finished Turnbull's bread and cheese, and pretty soon I had finished the stones. The next step was what puzzled me. I could not keep up this roadmaking business for long. A merciful Providence had kept Mr. Turnbull indoors, but if he appeared on the scene there would be trouble. I had a notion that the cordon was still tight round the glen, and that if I walked in any direction I should meet with questioners. But get out I must. No man's nerve could stand more than a day of being spied on.

I stayed at my post till about five o'clock. By that time I had resolved to go down to Turnbull's cottage at nightfall and take my chance of getting over the hills in the darkness. But suddenly a new car came up the road, and slowed down a yard or two from me. A fresh wind had risen, and the occupant wanted to light a cigarette.

It was a touring-car, with the tonneau full of an assortment of baggage. One man sat in it, and by an amazing chance I knew him. His name was Marmaduke Jopley, and he was an offence to creation. He was a sort of blood stockbroker, who did his business by toadying eldest sons and rich young peers and foolish old ladies. "Marmie" was a familiar figure, I understood, at balls and polo weeks and country houses. He was an adroit scandalmonger, and would crawl a mile on his belly to anything that had a title or a million. I had a business introduction to his firm when I came to London, and he was good enough to ask me to dinner at his club. There he showed off at a great rate, and pattered about his duchesses till the snobbery of the creature turned me sick. I asked a man afterwards why nobody kicked him, and was told that Englishmen reverenced the weaker sex.

Anyhow there he was now, nattily dressed, in a fine new car, obviously on his way to visit some of his smart friends. A sudden daftness took me, and in a second I had jumped into the tonneau and had him by the shoulder.

"Hullo, Jopley," I sang out. "Well met, my lad!" He got a horrid fright. His chin dropped as he stared at me. "Who the devil are you?" he gasped.

"My name's Hannay," I said. "From Rhodesia, you remember."

"Good God, the murderer!" he choked.

"Just so. And there'll be a second murder, my dear, if you don't do as I tell you. Give me that coat of yours. That cap, too."

He did as bid, for he was blind with terror. Over my dirty trousers and vulgar shirt I put on his smart driving coat, which buttoned high at the top and thereby hid the deficiencies of my collar. I stuck the cap on my head, and added his gloves to my get-up. The dusty roadman in a minute was transformed into one of the neatest motorists in Scotland. On Mr. Jopley's head I clapped Turnbull's unspeakable hat, and told him to keep it there.

Then with some difficulty I turned the car. My plan was to go back the road he had come, for the watchers, having seen it before, would probably let it pass unremarked, and Marmie's figure was in no way like mine.

"Now, my child," I said, "sit quite still and be a good boy. I mean you no harm. I'm only borrowing your car for an hour or two. But if you play me any tricks, and above all if you open your mouth, as sure as there's a God above me I'll wring your neck. *Savez?*"

I enjoyed that evening's ride. We ran eight miles down the valley, through a village or two, and I could not help noticing several strange-looking folk lounging by the roadside. These were the watchers who would have had much to say to me if I had come in other garb or company. As it was, they looked incuriously on. One touched his cap in salute, and I responded graciously.

As the dark fell I turned up a side-glen which, as I remembered from the map, led into an unfrequented corner of the hills. Soon the villages were left behind, then the farms, and then even the wayside cottages. Presently we came to a lonely moor where the night was blackening the sunset gleam in the bog pools. Here we stopped, and I obligingly reversed the car and restored to Mr. Jopley his belongings.

"A thousand thanks," I said. "There's more use in you than I thought. Now be off and find the police."

As I sat on the hillside, watching the tail-lights dwindle, I reflected on the various kinds of crime I had now sampled. Contrary to general belief, I was not a murderer, but I had become an unholy liar, a shameless impostor, and a highwayman with a marked taste for expensive motor-cars.

CHAPTER 6

The Adventure of the Bald Archaeologist

I SPENT the night on a shelf of the hillside, in the lee of a boulder where the heather grew long and soft. It was a cold business, for I had neither coat nor waistcoat. These were in Mr. Turnbull's keeping, as was Scudder's little book, my watch and—worst of all—my pipe and tobacco pouch. Only my money accompanied me in my belt, and about half a pound of ginger biscuits in my trousers pocket.

I supped off half those biscuits, and by worming myself deep into the heather got some kind of warmth. My spirits had risen, and I was beginning to enjoy this crazy game of hide-and-seek. So far I had been miraculously lucky. The milkman, the literary innkeeper, Sir Harry, the roadman, and the idiotic Marmie, were all pieces of undeserved good fortune. Somehow the first success gave me a feeling that I was going to pull the thing through.

My chief trouble was that I was desperately hungry. When a Jew shoots himself in the City and there is an inquest, the newspapers usually report that the deceased was "well-nourished." I remember thinking that they would not call me well-nourished if I broke my neck in a bog-hole. I lay and tortured myself—for the ginger biscuits merely emphasized the aching void—with the memory of all the good food I had thought so little of in London. There were Paddock's crisp sausages and fragrant shavings of bacon, and shapely poached eggs—how often I had turned up my nose at them! There were the cutlets they did at the club, and a particular ham that stood on the cold table, for which my soul lusted. My thoughts hovered over all varieties of mortal edible, and finally settled on a porter-house steak and a quart of bitter with a welsh rabbit to follow. In longing hopelessly for these dainties I fell asleep.

I woke very cold and stiff about an hour after dawn. It took me a little while to remember where I was, for I had been very weary and had slept heavily. I saw first the pale blue sky through a net of heather, then a big shoulder of hill, and then my own boots placed neatly in a blaeberry bush. I raised myself on my arms and looked down into the valley, and that one look set me lacing up my boots in mad haste.

For there were men below, not more than a quarter of a mile off, spaced out on the hillside like a fan, and beating the heather. Marmie had not been slow in looking for his revenge.

I crawled out of my shelf into the cover of a boulder, and from it gained a shallow trench which slanted up the mountain face. This led me presently into the narrow gully of a burn, by way of which I scrambled to the top of the ridge. From there I looked back, and saw that I was still undiscovered. My pursuers were patiently quartering the hillside and moving upwards.

Keeping behind the skyline I ran for maybe half a mile, till I judged I was above the uppermost end of the glen. Then I showed myself, and was instantly noted by one of the flankers, who passed the word to the others. I heard cries coming up from below, and saw that the line of search had changed its direction. I pretended to retreat over the skyline, but instead went back the way I had come, and in twenty minutes was behind the ridge overlooking my sleeping place. From that viewpoint I had the satisfaction of seeing the pursuit streaming up the hill at the top of the glen on a hopelessly false scent.

I had before me a choice of routes, and I chose a ridge which made an angle with the one I was on, and so would soon put a deep glen between me and my enemies. The exercise had warmed my blood, and I was beginning to enjoy myself amazingly. As I went I breakfasted on the dusty remnants of the ginger biscuits.

I knew very little about the country, and I hadn't a notion what I was going to do. I trusted to the strength of my legs, but I was well aware that those behind me would be familiar with the lie of the land, and that my ignorance would be a heavy handicap. I saw in front of me a sea of hills, rising very high towards the south, but northwards breaking down into broad ridges which separated wide and shallow dales. The ridge I had chosen seemed to sink after a mile or two to a moor which lay like a pocket in the uplands. That seemed as good a direction to take as any other.

My stratagem had given me a fair start—call it twenty minutes—and I had the width of a glen behind me before I saw the first heads of the pursuers. The police had evidently called in local talent to their aid, and the men I could see had the appearance of herds or gamekeepers. They hallooed at the sight of me, and I waved my hand. Two dived into the glen and began to climb my ridge, while the others kept their own side of the hill. I felt as if I were taking part in a schoolboy game of hare and hounds.

But very soon it began to seem less of a game. Those fellows behind were hefty men on their native heath. Looking back I saw that only three were following direct, and I guessed that the others had fetched a circuit to cut me off. My lack of local knowledge might very well be my undoing, and I resolved to get out of this tangle of glens to the pocket of moor I had seen from the tops. I must so increase my distance as to get clear away from them, and I believed I could do this if I could find the right ground for it. If there had been cover I would have tried a bit of stalking, but on these bare slopes you could see a fly a mile off. My hope must be in the length of my legs and the soundness of my wind, but I needed easier ground for that, for I was not bred a mountaineer. How I longed for a good Afrikander pony!

I put on a great spurt and got off my ridge and down into the moor before any figures appeared on the skyline behind me. I crossed a burn, and came out on a highroad which made a pass between two glens. All in front of me was a big field of heather sloping up to a crest which was crowned with an odd feather of trees. In the dyke by the roadside was a gate, from which a grass-grown track led over the first wave of the moor.

I jumped the dyke and followed it, and after a few hundred yards—as soon as it was out of sight of the highway—the grass stopped and it became a very respectable road, which was evidently kept with some care. Clearly it ran to a house, and I began to think of doing the same. Hitherto my luck had held, and it might be that my best chance would be found in this remote dwelling. Anyhow there were trees there, and that meant cover.

I did not follow the road, but the burnside which flanked it on the right, where the bracken grew deep and the high banks made a tolerable screen. It was well I did so, for no sooner had I gained the hollow than, looking back, I saw the pursuit topping the ridge from which I had descended.

After that I did not look back; I had no time. I ran up the burn-side, crawling over the open places, and for a large part wading in the shallow stream. I found a deserted cottage with a row of phantom peat-stacks and an overgrown garden. Then I was among young hay, and very soon had come to the edge of a plan-tation of wind-blown firs. From there I saw the chimneys of the house smoking a few hundred yards to my left. I forsook the burnside, crossed another dyke, and almost before I knew I was on a rough lawn. A glance back told me that I was well out of sight of the pursuit, which had not yet passed the first lift of the moor.

The lawn was a very rough place, cut with a scythe instead of a mower, and planted with beds of scrubby rhododendrons. A brace of black-game, which are not usually garden birds, rose at my approach. The house before me was the ordinary moorland farm, with a more pretentious whitewashed wing added. At-tached to this wing was a glass veranda, and through the glass I saw the face of an elderly gentleman meekly watching me.

I stalked over the border of coarse hill gravel and entered the open veranda door. Within was a pleasant room, glass on one side, and on the other a mass of books. More books showed in an inner room. On the floor, instead of tables, stood cases such as you see in a museum, filled with coins and queer stone implements.

There was a knee-hole desk in the middle, and seated at it, with some papers and open volumes before him, was the benevolent old gentleman. His face was round and shiny, like Mr. Pickwick's, big glasses were stuck on the end of his nose, and the top of his head was as bright and bare as a glass bottle. He never moved when I entered, but raised his placid eyebrows and waited on me to speak.

It was not an easy job, with about five minutes to spare, to tell a stranger who I was and what I wanted and to win his aid. I did not attempt it. There was something about the eye of the man before me, something so keen and knowledgeable, that I could not find a word. I simply stared at him and stuttered.

"You seem in a hurry, my friend," he said slowly.

I nodded towards the window. It gave a prospect across the moor through a gap in the plantation, and revealed certain figures half a mile off struggling through the heather.

"Ah, I see," he said, and took up a pair of field-glasses through which he patiently scrutinised the figures.

"A fugitive from justice, eh? Well, we'll go into the matter at our leisure. Meantime I object to my privacy being broken in upon by the clumsy rural policeman. Go into my study, and you will see two doors facing you. Take the one on the left and close it behind you. You will be perfectly safe."

And this extraordinary man took up his pen again.

I did as I was bid, and found myself in a little dark chamber which smelt of chemicals, and was lit only by a tiny window high up in the wall. The door had swung behind me with a click like the door of a safe. Once again I had found an unexpected sanctuary.

All the same I was not comfortable. There was something about the old gentleman which puzzled and rather terrified me.

He had been too easy and ready, almost as if he had expected me. And his eyes had been horribly intelligent.

No sound came to me in that dark place. For all I knew the police might be searching the house, and if they did they would want to know what was behind this door. I tried to possess my soul in patience, and to forget how hungry I was.

Then I took a more cheerful view. The old gentleman could scarcely refuse me a meal, and I fell to reconstructing my breakfast. Bacon and eggs would content me, but I wanted the better part of a flitch of bacon and half a hundred eggs. And then, while my mouth was watering in anticipation, there was a click and the door stood open.

I emerged into the sunlight to find the master of the house sitting in a deep arm-chair in the room he called his study, and regarding me with curious eyes.

"Have they gone?" I asked.

"They have gone. I convinced them that you had crossed the hill. I do not choose that the police should come between me and one whom I am delighted to honour. This is a lucky morning for you, Mr. Richard Hannay."

As he spoke his eyelids seemed to tremble and to fall a little over his keen grey eyes. In a flash the phrase of Scudder's came back to me, when he had described the man he most dreaded in the world. He had said that he "could hood his eyes like a hawk." Then I saw that I had walked straight into the enemy's headquarters.

My first impulse was to throttle the old ruffian and make for the open air. He seemed to anticipate my intention, for he smiled gently, and nodded to the door behind me. I turned, and saw two menservants who had me covered with pistols.

He knew my name, but he had never seen me before. And as the reflection darted across my mind I saw a slender chance.

"I don't know what you mean," I said roughly. "And who are you calling Richard Hannay? My name's Ainslie."

"So?" he said, still smiling. "But of course you have others. We won't quarrel about a name."

I was pulling myself together now, and I reflected that my

garb, lacking coat and waistcoat and collar, would at any rate not betray me. I put on my surliest face and shrugged my shoulders.

"I suppose you're going to give me up after all, and I call it a damned dirty trick. My God, I wish I had never seen that cursed motor-car! Here's the money and be damned to you," and I flung four sovereigns on the table.

He opened his eyes a little. "Oh no, I shall not give you up. My friends and I will have a little private settlement with you, that is all. You know a little too much, Mr. Hannay. You are a clever actor, but not quite clever enough."

He spoke with assurance, but I could see the dawning of a doubt in his mind.

"Oh, for God's sake stop jawing," I cried. "Everything's against me. I haven't had a bit of luck since I came on shore at Leith. What's the harm in a poor devil with an empty stomach picking up some money he finds in a bust-up motor-car? That's all I done, and for that I've been chivvied for two days by those blasted bobbies over those blasted hills. I tell you I'm fair sick of it. You can do what you like, old boy! Ned Ainslie's got no fight left in him."

I could see that the doubt was gaining.

"Will you oblige me with the story of your recent doings?" he asked.

"I can't, guv'nor," I said in a real beggar's whine. "I've not had a bite to eat for two days. Give me a mouthful of food, and then you'll hear God's truth."

I must have showed my hunger in my face, for he signalled to one of the men in the doorway. A bit of cold pie was brought and a glass of beer, and I wolfed them down like a pig—or rather, like Ned Ainslie, for I was keeping up my character. In the middle of my meal he spoke suddenly to me in German, but I turned on him a face as blank as a stone wall.

Then I told him my story—how I had come off an Archangel ship at Leith a week ago, and was making my way overland to my brother at Wigtown. I had run short of cash—I hinted vaguely at a spree—and I was pretty well on my uppers when I had come on a hole in a hedge, and, looking through, had seen a big motor-car lying in the burn. I had poked about to see what had happened, and had found three sovereigns lying on the seat and one on the floor. There was nobody there or any sign of an owner, so I had pocketed the cash. But somehow the law had got after me. When I had tried to change a sovereign in a baker's shop, the woman had cried on the police, and a little later, when I was washing my face in a burn, I had been nearly gripped, and had only got away by leaving my coat and waistcoat behind me.

"They can have the money back," I cried, "for a fat lot of good it's done me. Those perishers are all down on a poor man. Now, if it had been you, guv'nor, that had found the quids, nobody would have troubled you."

"You're a good liar, Hannay," he said.

I flew into a rage. "Stop fooling, damn you! I tell you my name is Ainslie, and I never heard of anyone called Hannay in my born days. I'd sooner have the police than you with your Hannays and your monkey-faced pistol tricks . . . No, guv'nor, I beg pardon, I don't mean that. I'm much obliged to you for the grub, and I'll thank you to let me go now the coast's clear."

It was obvious that he was badly puzzled. You see he had never seen me, and my appearance must have altered considerably from my photographs, if he had got one of them. I was pretty smart and well dressed in London, and now I was a regular tramp.

"I do not propose to let you go. If you are what you say you are, you will soon have a chance of clearing yourself. If you are what I believe you are, I do not think you will see the light much longer."

He rang a bell, and a third servant appeared from the veranda.

"I want the Lanchester in five minutes," he said. "There will be three to luncheon."

Then he looked steadily at me, and that was the hardest ordeal of all.

There was something weird and devilish in those eyes, cold, malignant, unearthly, and most hellishly clever. They fascinated me like the bright eyes of a snake. I had a strong impulse to throw myself on his mercy and offer to join his side, and if you consider the way I felt about the whole thing you will see that that impulse must have been purely physical, the weakness of a brain mesmerized and mastered by a stronger spirit. But I managed to stick it out and even to grin.

"You'll know me next time, guv'nor," I said.

"Karl," he spoke in German to one of the men in the doorway, "you will put this fellow in the storeroom till I return, and you will be answerable to me for his keeping."

I was marched out of the room with a pistol at each ear.

THE storeroom was a damp chamber in what had been the old farmhouse. There was no carpet on the uneven floor, and nothing to sit down on but a school form. It was black as pitch, for the windows were heavily shuttered. I made out by groping that the walls were lined with boxes and barrels and sacks of some heavy stuff. The whole place smelt of mould and disuse. My jailers turned the key in the door, and I could hear them shifting their feet as they stood on guard outside.

I sat down in that chilly darkness in a very miserable frame of mind. The old boy had gone off in a motor to collect the two ruffians who had interviewed me yesterday. Now, they had seen me as the roadman, and they would remember me, for I was in the same rig. What was a roadman doing twenty miles from his beat, pursued by the police? A question or two would put them on the track. Probably they had seen Mr. Turnbull, probably Marmie too; most likely they could link me up with Sir Harry, and then the whole thing would be crystal clear. What chance had I in this moorland house with three desperadoes and their armed servants?

I began to think wistfully of the police, now plodding over the hills after my wraith. They at any rate were fellow-countrymen and honest men, and their tender mercies would be kinder than these ghoulish aliens. But they wouldn't have listened to me. That old devil with the eyelids had not taken long to get rid of them. I thought he probably had some kind of graft with the constabulary. Most likely he had letters from Cabinet Ministers saying he was to be given every facility for plotting against Britain. That's the sort of owlish way we run our politics in the Old Country.

The three would be back for lunch, so I hadn't more than a couple of hours to wait. It was simply waiting on destruction, for I could see no way out of this mess. I wished that I had Scudder's courage, for I am free to confess I didn't feel any great fortitude. The only thing that kept me going was that I was pretty furious. It made me boil with rage to think of those three spies getting the pull on me like this. I hoped that at any rate I might be able to twist one of their necks before they downed me.

The more I thought of it the angrier I grew, and I had to get up and move about the room. I tried the shutters, but they were the kind that locked with a key, and I couldn't move them. From the outside came the faint clucking of hens in the warm sun. Then I groped among the sacks and boxes. I couldn't open the latter, and the sacks seemed to be full of things like dog-biscuits that smelt of cinnamon. But, as I circumnavigated the room, I found a handle in the wall which seemed worth investigating.

It was the door of a wall cupboard—what they call a "press" in Scotland—and it was locked. I shook it, and it seemed rather flimsy. For want of something better to do I put out my strength on that door, getting some purchase on the handle by looping my braces round it. Presently the thing gave with a crash which I thought would bring in my warders to inquire. I waited for a bit, and then started to explore the cupboard shelves.

There was a multitude of queer things there. I found an odd vesta or two in my trouser pockets and struck a light. It went out in a second, but it showed me one thing. There was a little stock of electric torches on one shelf. I picked up one, and found it was in working order.

With the torch to help me I investigated further. There were bottles and cases of queer-smelling stuffs, chemicals no doubt for experiments, and there were coils of fine copper wire and hanks and hanks of a thin oiled silk. There was a box of detonators, and a lot of cord for fuses. Then away at the back of a shelf I found a stout brown cardboard box, and inside it a wooden case. I managed to wrench it open, and within lay half a dozen little grey bricks, each a couple of inches square.

I took up one, and found that it crumbled easily in my hand. Then I smelt it and put my tongue to it. After that I sat down to think. I hadn't been a mining engineer for nothing, and I knew lentonite when I saw it.

With one of these bricks I could blow the house to smithereens. I had used the stuff in Rhodesia and knew its power. But the trouble was that my knowledge wasn't exact. I had forgotten the proper charge and the right way of preparing it, and I wasn't sure about the timing. I had only a vague notion, too, as to its power, for though I had used it I had not handled it with my own fingers.

But it was a chance, the only possible chance. It was a mighty risk, but against it was an absolute black certainty. If I used it the odds were, as I reckoned, about five to one in favour of my blowing myself into the tree-tops; but if I didn't I should very likely be occupying a six-foot hole in the garden by the evening. That was the way I had to look at it. The prospect was pretty dark either way, but anyhow there was a chance, both for myself and for my country.

The remembrance of little Scudder decided me. It was about the beastliest moment of my life, for I'm no good at these cold-blooded resolutions. Still I managed to rake up the pluck to set my teeth and choke back the horrid doubts that flooded in on me. I simply shut off my mind and pretended I was doing an experiment as simple as Guy Fawkes' fireworks.

I got a detonator, and fixed it to a couple of feet of fuse. Then I took a quarter of a lentonite brick, and buried it near the door below one of the sacks in a crack of the floor, fixing the detonator in it. For all I knew half those boxes might be dynamite. If the cupboard held such deadly explosives, why not the boxes? In that case there would be a glorious skyward journey for me and the German servants and about an acre of the surrounding country. There was also the risk that the detonation might set off the other bricks in the cupboard, for I had forgotten most that I knew about lentonite. But it didn't do to begin thinking about the possibilities. The odds were horrible, but I had to take them.

I ensconced myself just below the sill of the window, and lit the fuse. Then I waited for a moment or two. There was dead silence—only a shuffle of heavy boots in the passage, and the peaceful cluck of the hens from the warm out-of-doors. I commended my soul to my Maker, and wondered where I would be in five seconds.

A great wave of heat seemed to surge upwards from the floor, and hang for a blistering instant in the air. Then the wall opposite me flashed into a golden yellow and dissolved with a rending thunder that hammered my brain into a pulp. Something dropped on me, catching the point of my left shoulder.

And then I think I became unconscious.

My stupor can scarcely have lasted beyond a few seconds. I felt myself being choked by thick yellow fumes, and struggled out of the debris to my feet. Somewhere behind me I felt fresh air. The jambs of the window had fallen, and through the ragged rent the smoke was pouring out to the summer noon. I stepped over the broken lintel, and found myself standing in a yard in a dense and acrid fog. I felt very sick and ill, but I could move my limbs, and I staggered blindly forward away from the house.

A small mill-lade ran in a wooden aqueduct at the other side of the yard, and into this I fell. The cool water revived me, and I had just enough wits left to think of escape. I squirmed up the lade among the slippery green slime till I reached the mill-wheel. Then I wriggled through the axle hole into the old mill and tumbled on to a bed of chaff. A nail caught the seat of my trousers, and I left a wisp of heather-mixture behind me.

The mill had been long out of use. The ladders were rotten with age, and in the loft the rats had gnawed great holes in the floor. Nausea shook me, and a wheel in my head kept turning, while my left shoulder and arm seemed to be stricken with the palsy. I looked out of the window and saw a fog still hanging over the house and smoke escaping from an upper window. Please God I had set the place on fire, for I could hear confused cries coming from the other side.

But I had no time to linger, since this mill was obviously a bad hiding-place. Anybody looking for me would naturally follow the lade, and I made certain the search would begin as soon as they found that my body was not in the storeroom. From another window I saw that on the far side of the mill stood an old stone dovecot. If I could get there without leaving tracks I might find a hiding-place, for I argued that my enemies, if they thought I could move, would conclude I had made for open country, and would go seeking me on the moor.

I crawled down the broken ladder, scattering chaff behind me to cover my footsteps. I did the same on the mill floor, and on the threshold where the door hung on broken hinges. Peeping out, I saw that between me and the dovecot was a piece of bare cobbled ground, where no footmarks would show. Also it was mercifully hid by the mill buildings from any view from the house. I slipped across the space, got to the back of the dovecot and prospected a way of ascent.

That was one of the hardest jobs I ever took on. My shoulder and arm ached like hell, and I was so sick and giddy that I was always on the verge of falling. But I managed it somehow. By the use of out-jutting stones and gaps in the masonry and a tough ivy root I got to the top in the end. There was a little parapet behind which I found space to lie down. Then I proceeded to go off into an old-fashioned swoon.

I woke with a burning head and the sun glaring in my face. For a long time I lay motionless, for those horrible fumes seemed to have loosened my joints and dulled my brain. Sounds came to me from the house—men speaking throatily and the throbbing of a stationary car. There was a little gap in the parapet to which I wriggled, and from which I had some sort of prospect of the yard. I saw figures come out—a servant with his head bound up, and then a younger man in knickerbockers. They were looking for something, and moved towards the mill. Then one of them caught sight of the wisp of cloth on the nail, and cried out to the other. They both went back to the house, and brought two more to look at it. I saw the rotund figure of my late captor, and I thought I made out the man with the lisp. I noticed that all had pistols.

For half an hour they ransacked the mill. I could hear them kicking over the barrels and pulling up the rotten planking. Then they came outside, and stood just below the dovecot, arguing fiercely. The servant with the bandage was being soundly rated. I heard them fiddling with the door of the dovecot, and for one horrid moment I fancied they were coming up. Then they thought better of it, and went back to the house.

All that long blistering afternoon I lay baking on the roof-top. Thirst was my chief torment. My tongue was like a stick, and to make it worse I could hear the cool drip of water from the mill-lade. I watched the course of the little stream as it came in from the moor, and my fancy followed it to the top of the glen, where it must issue from an icy fountain fringed with cool ferns and mosses. I would have given a thousand pounds to plunge my face into that.

I had a fine prospect of the whole ring of moorland. I saw the car speed away with two occupants, and a man on a hill pony riding east. I judged they were looking for me, and I wished them joy of their quest.

But I saw something else more interesting. The house stood almost on the summit of a swell of moorland which crowned a sort of plateau, and there was no higher point nearer than the big hills six miles off. The actual summit, as I have mentioned, was a biggish clump of trees—firs mostly, with a few ashes and beeches. On the dovecot I was almost on a level with the tree-tops, and could see what lay beyond. The wood was not solid, but only a ring, and inside was an oval of green turf, for all the world like a big cricket field.

I didn't take long to guess what it was. It was an aerodrome, and a secret one. The place had been most cunningly chosen. For suppose anyone were watching an aeroplane descending here, he would think it had gone over the hill beyond the trees. As the place was on the top of a rise in the midst of a big amphitheatre, any observer from any direction would conclude it had passed out of view behind the hill. Only a man very close at hand would realize that the aeroplane had not gone over but had descended in the midst of the wood. An observer with a telescope on one of the higher hills might have discovered the truth, but only herds went there, and herds do not carry spy-glasses. When I looked from the dovecot I could see far away a blue line which I knew was the sea, and I grew furious to think that our enemies had this secret conning-tower to rake our waterways.

Then I reflected that if that aeroplane came back the chances were ten to one that I would be discovered. So through the afternoon I lay and prayed for the coming of darkness, and glad I was when the sun went down over the big western hills and the twilight haze crept over the moor. The aeroplane was late. The gloaming was far advanced when I heard the beat of wings and saw it vol-planing downward to its home in the wood. Lights twinkled for a bit and there was much coming and going from the house. Then the dark fell and silence.

Thank God it was black night. The moon was well on its last quarter and would not rise till late. My thirst was too great to allow me to tarry, so about nine o'clock, so far as I could judge, I started to descend. It wasn't easy, and halfway down I heard the back door of the house open, and saw the gleam of a lantern against the mill wall. For some agonizing minutes I hung by the ivy and prayed that whoever it was would not come round by the dovecot. Then the light disappeared, and I dropped as softly as I could on to the hard soil of the yard.

I crawled on my belly in the lee of a stone dyke till I reached the fringe of trees which surrounded the house. If I had known how to do it I would have tried to put that aeroplane out of action, but I realized that any attempt would probably be futile. I was pretty certain that there would be some kind of defence round the house, so I went through the wood on hands and knees, feeling carefully every inch before me. It was as well, for presently I came on a wire about two feet from the ground. If I had tripped over that, it would doubtless have rung some bell in the house and I would have been captured.

A hundred yards farther on I found another wire cunningly placed on the edge of a small stream. Beyond that lay the moor, and in five minutes I was deep in bracken and heather. Soon I was round the shoulder of the rise, in the little glen from which the mill-lade flowed. Ten minutes later my face was in the spring, and I was soaking down pints of the blessed water.

But I did not stop till I had put half a dozen miles between me and that accursed dwelling.

The Dry-Fly Fisherman

I sat down on a hill-top and took stock of my position. I wasn't feeling very happy, for my natural thankfulness at my escape was clouded by my severe bodily discomfort. Those lentonite fumes had fairly poisoned me, and the baking hours on the dovecot hadn't helped matters. I had a crushing headache, and felt as sick as a cat. Also my shoulder was in a bad way. At first I thought it was only a bruise, but it seemed to be swelling, and I had no use of my left arm.

My plan was to seek Mr. Turnbull's cottage, recover my garments, and especially Scudder's notebook, and then make for the main line and get back to the south. It seemed to me that the sooner I got in touch with the Foreign Office man, Sir Walter Bullivant, the better. I didn't see how I could get more proof than I had got already. He must just take or leave my story, and anyway, with him I would be in better hands than those devilish Germans. I had begun to feel quite kindly towards the British police.

It was a wonderful starry night, and I had not much difficulty about the road. Sir Harry's map had given me the lie of the land, and all I had to do was to steer a point or two west of south-west to come to the stream where I had met the roadman. In all these travels I never knew the names of the places, but I believe this stream was no less than the upper waters of the River Tweed. I calculated I must be about eighteen miles distant, and that meant I could not get there before morning. So I must lie up a day somewhere, for I was too outrageous a figure to be seen in the sunlight. I had neither coat, waistcoat, collar, nor hat, my trousers were badly torn, and my face and hands were black with the explosion. I dare say I had other beauties, for my eyes felt as if they were furiously bloodshot. Altogether I was no spectacle for God-fearing citizens to see on a highroad.

Very soon after daybreak I made an attempt to clean myself in a hill burn, and then approached a herd's cottage, for I was feeling the need of food. He was away from home, and his wife was alone, with no neighbour for five miles. She was a decent old body, and a plucky one, for though she got a fright when she saw me, she had an axe handy, and would have used it on any evildoer. I told her that I had had a fall—I didn't say how—and she saw by my looks that I was pretty sick. Like a true Samaritan she asked no questions, but gave me a bowl of milk with a dash of whisky in it, and let me sit for a little by her kitchen fire. She would have bathed my shoulder, but it ached so badly that I would not let her touch it.

I don't know what she took me for—a repentant burglar, perhaps; for when I wanted to pay her for the milk and tendered a sovereign, which was the smallest coin I had, she shook her head and said something about "giving it to them that had a right to it." At this I protested so strongly that I think she believed me honest, for she took the money and gave me a warm new plaid for it, and an old hat of her man's. She showed me how to wrap the plaid round my shoulders, and when I left that cottage I was the living image of the kind of Scotsman you see in the illustrations to Burns's poems. But at any rate I was more or less clad.

It was as well, for the weather changed before midday to a thick drizzle of rain. I found shelter below an overhanging rock in the crook of a burn, where a drift of dead brackens made a tolerable bed. There I managed to sleep till nightfall, waking very cramped and wretched, with my shoulder gnawing like a toothache. I ate the oatcake and cheese the old wife had given me and set out again just before the darkening.

I pass over the miseries of that night among the wet hills. There were no stars to steer by, and I had to do the best I could from my memory of the map. Twice I lost my way, and I had some nasty falls into peat-bogs. I had only about ten miles to go as the crow flies, but my mistakes made it nearer twenty. The last bit was completed with set teeth and a very light and dizzy head. But I managed it, and in the early dawn I was knocking at Mr. Turnbull's door. The mist lay close and thick, and from the cottage I could not see the highroad.

Mr. Turnbull himself opened to me—sober and something more than sober. He was primly dressed in an ancient but well-tended suit of black; he had been shaved not later than the night before; he wore a linen collar; and in his left hand he carried a pocket Bible. At first he did not recognize me.

"Whae are ye that comes stravaigin' here on the Sabbath mornin'?" he asked.

I had lost all count of the days. So the Sabbath was the reason for this strange decorum.

My head was swimming so wildly that I could not frame a coherent answer. But he recognized me, and he saw that I was ill.

"Hae ye got my specs?" he asked.

I fetched them out of my trouser pocket and gave him them.

"Ye'll hae come for your jacket and westcoat," he said. "Come in-bye. Losh, man, ye're terrible dune i' the legs. Haud up till I get ye to a chair."

I perceived I was in for a bout of malaria. I had a good deal of fever in my bones, and the wet night had brought it out, while my shoulder and the effects of the fumes combined to make me feel pretty bad. Before I knew, Mr. Turnbull was helping me off with my clothes, and putting me to bed in one of the two cupboards that lined the kitchen walls.

He was a true friend in need, that old roadman. His wife was dead years ago, and since his daughter's marriage he lived alone.

For the better part of ten days he did all the rough nursing I needed. I simply wanted to be left in peace while the fever took its course, and when my skin was cool again I found that the bout had more or less cured my shoulder. But it was a baddish go, and though I was out of bed in five days, it took me some time to get my legs again.

He went out each morning, leaving me milk for the day, and locking the door behind him; and came in in the evening to sit silent in the chimney corner. Not a soul came near the place. When I was getting better, he never bothered me with a question. Several times he fetched me a two days' old *Scotsman*, and I noticed that the interest in the Portland Place murder seemed to have died down. There was no mention of it, and I could find very little about anything except a thing called the General Assembly—some ecclesiastical spree, I gathered.

One day he produced my belt from a lockfast drawer. "There's a terrible heap o' siller in't," he said. "Ye'd better coont it to see it's a' there."

He never even sought my name. I asked him if anybody had been around making inquiries subsequent to my spell at the roadmaking.

"Ay, there was a man in a motor-cawr. He speired whae had ta'en my place that day, and I let on I thocht him daft. But he keepit on at me, and syne I said he maun be thinkin' o' my gude-brither frae the Cleuch that whiles lent me a haun'. He was a wersh-lookin' sowl, and I couldna understand the half o' his English tongue."

I was getting restless those last days, and as soon as I felt myself fit I decided to be off. That was not till the twelfth day of June, and as luck would have it a drover went past that morning taking some cattle to Moffat. He was a man named Hislop, a friend of Turnbull's, and he came in to his breakfast with us and offered to take me with him.

I made Turnbull accept five pounds for my lodging, and a hard job I had of it. There never was a more independent being. He grew positively rude when I pressed him, and shy and red, and took the money at last without a thank-you. When I told him how much I owed him, he grunted something about "ae guid turn deservin' anither." You would have thought from our leave-taking that we had parted in disgust.

Hislop was a cheery soul, who chattered all the way over the pass and down the sunny vale of Annan. I talked of Galloway markets and sheep prices, and he made up his mind I was a "pack-shepherd" from those parts—whatever that may be. My plaid and my old hat, as I have said, gave me a fine theatrical Scots look. But driving cattle is a mortally slow job, and we took the better part of the day to cover a dozen miles.

If I had not had such an anxious heart I would have enjoyed that time. It was shining blue weather, with a constantly changing prospect of brown hills and far green meadows, and a continual sound of larks and curlews and falling streams. But I had no mind for the summer, and little for Hislop's conversation, for as the fateful fifteenth of June drew near I was overweighted with the hopeless difficulties of my enterprise.

I got some dinner in a humble Moffat public-house, and walked the two miles to the junction on the main line. The night express for the south was not due till near midnight, and to fill up the time I went up on the hillside and fell asleep, for the walk had tired me. I all but slept too long, and had to run to the station and catch the train with two minutes to spare. The feel of the hard third-class cushions and the smell of stale tobacco cheered me up wonderfully. At any rate, I felt now that I was getting to grips with my job.

I was decanted at Crewe in the small hours and had to wait till six to get a train for Birmingham. In the afternoon I got to Reading, and changed into a local train which journeyed into the deeps of Berkshire. Presently I was in a land of lush water-meadows and slow reedy streams. About eight o'clock in the evening, a weary and travel-stained being—a cross between a farm-labourer and a vet—with a checked black-and-white plaid over his arm (for I did not dare to wear it south of the Border), descended at the little station of Artinswell. There were several people on the platform, and I thought I had better wait to ask my way till I was clear of the place.

The road led through a wood of great beeches and then into a shallow valley, with the green backs of downs peeping over the distant trees. After Scotland the air smelt heavy and flat, but infinitely sweet, for the limes and chestnuts and lilac bushes were domes of blossom. Presently I came to a bridge, below which a clear slow stream flowed between snowy beds of water-buttercups. A little above it was a mill; and the lasher made a pleasant cool sound in the scented dusk. Somehow the place soothed me and put me at my ease. I fell to whistling as I looked into the green depths, and the tune which came to my lips was "Annie Laurie."

A fisherman came up from the waterside, and as he neared me he too began to whistle. The tune was infectious, for he followed my suit. He was a huge man in untidy old flannels and a wide-brimmed hat, with a canvas bag slung on his shoulder. He nodded to me, and I thought I had never seen a shrewder or better-tempered face. He leaned his delicate ten-foot split-cane rod against the bridge, and looked with me at the water.

"Clear, isn't it?" he said pleasantly. "I back our Kennet any day against the Test. Look at that big fellow. Four pounds if he's an ounce. But the evening rise is over and you can't tempt 'em."

"I don't see him," said I.

"Look! There! A yard from the reeds just above that stickle."

"I've got him now. You might swear he was a black stone."

"So," he said, and whistled another bar of "Annie Laurie."

"Twisdon's the name, isn't it?" he said over his shoulder, his eyes still fixed on the stream.

"No," I said. "I mean to say, Yes." I had forgotten all about my *alias*.

"It's a wise conspirator that knows his own name," he observed, grinning broadly at a moor-hen that emerged from the bridge's shadow.

I stood up and looked at him, at the square, cleft jaw and broad, lined brow and the firm folds of cheek, and began to think that here at last was an ally worth having. His whimsical blue eyes seemed to go very deep.

Suddenly he frowned. "I call it disgraceful," he said, raising his voice. "Disgraceful that an able-bodied man like you should dare to beg. You can get a meal from my kitchen, but you'll get no money from me."

A dog-cart was passing, driven by a young man who raised his whip to salute the fisherman. When he had gone, he picked up his rod.

"That's my house," he said, pointing to a white gate a hundred yards on. "Wait five minutes and then go round to the back door." And with that he left me.

I did as I was bidden. I found a pretty cottage with a lawn running down to the stream, and a perfect jungle of guelder-rose and lilac flanking the path. The back door stood open, and a grave butler was awaiting me.

"Come this way, sir," he said, and he led me along a passage and up a back staircase to a pleasant bedroom looking towards the river. There I found a complete outfit laid out for me—dress clothes with all the fixings, a brown flannel suit, shirts, collars, ties, shaving things and hair-brushes, even a pair of patent shoes. "Sir Walter thought as how Mr. Reggie's things would fit you, sir," said the butler. "He keeps some clothes 'ere, for he comes regular on the weekends. There's a bathroom next door, and I've prepared a 'ot bath. Dinner in 'alf an hour, sir. You'll 'ear the gong."

The grave being withdrew, and I sat down in a chintz-covered easy chair and gaped. It was like a pantomime, to come suddenly out of beggardom into this orderly comfort. Obviously Sir Walter believed in me, though why he did I could not guess. I looked at myself in the mirror and saw a wild, haggard brown fellow, with a fortnight's ragged beard, and dust in ears and eyes, collarless, vulgarly shirted, with shapeless old tweed clothes and boots that had not been cleaned for the better part of a month. I made a fine tramp and a fair drover; and here I was ushered by a prim butler into this temple of gracious ease. And the best of it was that they did not even know my name.

I resolved not to puzzle my head but to take the gifts the gods had provided. I shaved and bathed luxuriously and got into the dress clothes, and clean crackling shirt, which fitted me not so badly. When I had finished the looking-glass showed a not un-personable young man.

Sir Walter awaited me in a dusky dining-room where a little round table was lit with silver candles. The sight of him—so re-spectable and established and secure, the embodiment of law and government and all the conventions—took me aback and made me feel an interloper. He couldn't know the truth about me, or he wouldn't treat me like this. I simply could not accept his hos-pitality on false pretences.

"I'm more obliged to you than I can say, but I'm bound to make things clear," I said. "I'm an innocent man, but I'm wanted by the police. I've got to tell you this, and I won't be surprised if you kick me out."

He smiled. "That's all right. Don't let that interfere with your appetite. We can talk about these things after dinner."

I never ate a meal with greater relish, for I had had nothing all day but railway sandwiches. Sir Walter did me proud, for we drank a good champagne and had some uncommon fine port af-terwards. It made me almost hysterical to be sitting there, waited on by a footman and a sleek butler, and remember that I had been living for three weeks like a brigand, with every man's hand against me. I told Sir Walter about tiger-fish in the Zam-besi that bite off your fingers if you give them a chance, and we discussed sport up and down the globe, for he had hunted a bit in his day.

We went to his study for coffee, a jolly room full of books and trophies and untidiness and comfort. I made up my mind that if ever I got rid of this business and had a house of my own, I would create just such a room. Then when the coffee-cups were cleared away, and we had got our cigars alight, my host swung his long legs over the side of his chair and bade me get started with my yarn.

"I've obeyed Harry's instructions," he said, "and the bribe he offered me was that you would tell me something to wake me up. I'm ready, Mr. Hannay."

I noticed with a start that he called me by my proper name.

I began at the very beginning. I told of my boredom in London, and the night I had come back to find Scudder gibbering on my doorstep. I told him all Scudder had told me about Karolides and the Foreign Office conference, and that made him purse his lips and grin.

Then I got to the murder, and he grew solemn again. He heard all about the milkman and my time in Galloway, and my deciphering Scudder's notes at the inn.

"You've got them here?" he asked sharply, and drew a long breath when I whipped the little book from my pocket.

I said nothing of the contents. Then I described my meeting with Sir Harry, and the speeches at the hall. At that he laughed uproariously.

"Harry talked dashed nonsense, did he? I quite believe it. He's as good a chap as ever breathed, but his idiot of an uncle has stuffed his head with maggots. Go on, Mr. Hannay."

My day as roadman excited him a bit. He made me describe the two fellows in the car very closely and seemed to be raking back in his memory. He grew merry again when he heard of the fate of that ass Jopley.

But the old man in the moorland house solemnized him. Again I had to describe every detail of his appearance.

"Bland and bald-headed and hooded his eyes like a bird . . . He sounds a sinister wild-fowl! And you dynamited his hermitage, after he had saved you from the police. Spirited piece of work, that!"

Presently I reached the end of my wanderings. He got up slowly, and looked down at me from the hearthrug.

"You may dismiss the police from your mind," he said. "You're in no danger from the law of this land."

"Great Scot!" I cried. "Have they got the murderer?"

"No. But for the last fortnight they have dropped you from the list of possibles."

"Why?" I asked in amazement.

"Principally because I received a letter from Scudder. I knew something of the man, and he did several jobs for me. He was half crank, half genius, but he was wholly honest. The trouble about him was his partiality for playing a lone hand. That made him pretty well useless in any Secret Service—a pity, for he had uncommon gifts. I think he was the bravest man in the world, for he was always shivering with fright, and yet nothing would choke him off. I had a letter from him on the 31st of May."

"But he had been dead a week by then."

"The letter was written and posted on the 23rd. He evidently did not anticipate an immediate decease. His communications usually took a week to reach me, for they were sent under cover to Spain and then to Newcastle. He had a mania, you know, for concealing his tracks."

"What did he say?" I stammered.

"Nothing. Merely that he was in danger, but had found shelter with a good friend, and that I would hear from him before the 15th of June. He gave me no address, but said he was living near Portland Place. I think his object was to clear you if anything happened. When I got it I went to Scotland Yard, went over the details of the inquest, and concluded that you were the friend. We made inquiries about you, Mr. Hannay, and found you were respectable. I thought I knew the motives for your disappearance— not only the police, the other one too—and when I got Harry's scrawl I guessed at the rest. I have been expecting you any time this past week."

You can imagine what a load this took off my mind. I felt a free man once more, for I was now up against my country's enemies only, and not my country's law.

"Now let us have the little notebook," said Sir Walter.

It took us a good hour to work through it. I explained the cypher, and he was jolly quick at picking it up. He emended my reading of it on several points, but I had been fairly correct, on the whole. His face was very grave before he had finished, and he sat silent for a while.

"I don't know what to make of it," he said at last. "He is right about one thing—what is going to happen the day after to-morrow. How the devil can it have got known? That is ugly enough in itself. But all this about war and the Black Stone—it reads like some wild melodrama. If only I had more confidence in Scudder's judgment. The trouble about him was that he was too romantic. He had the artistic temperament, and wanted a story to be better than God meant it to be. He had a lot of odd biases, too. Jews, for example, made him see red. Jews and the high finance.

"The Black Stone," he repeated. "*Der Schwarzestein.* It's like a penny novelette. And all this stuff about Karolides. That is the weak part of the tale, for I happen to know that the virtuous Karolides is likely to outlast us both. There is no state in Europe that wants him gone. Besides, he has just been playing up to Berlin and Vienna and giving my Chief some uneasy moments. No! Scudder has gone off the track there. Frankly, Hannay, I don't believe that part of his story. There's some nasty business afoot, and he found out too much and lost his life over it. But I am ready to take my oath that it is ordinary spy work. A certain great European Power makes a hobby of her spy system, and her methods are not too particular. Since she pays by piecework her blackguards are not likely to stick at a murder or two. They want our naval dispositions for their collection at the Marineamt; but they will be pigeonholed—nothing more."

Just then the butler entered the room.

"There's a trunk call from London, Sir Walter. It's Mr. 'Eath, and he wants to speak to you personally."

My host went off to the telephone.

He returned in five minutes with a whitish face. "I apologize to the shade of Scudder," he said. "Karolides was shot dead this evening at a few minutes after seven."

The Coming of the Black Stone

I CAME down to breakfast next morning, after eight hours of blessed dreamless sleep, to find Sir Walter decoding a telegram in the midst of muffins and marmalade. His fresh rosiness of yesterday seemed a thought tarnished.

"I had a busy hour on the telephone after you went to bed," he said. "I got my Chief to speak to the First Lord and the Secretary for War, and they are bringing Royer over a day sooner. This wire clinches it. He will be in London at five. Odd that the code word for a *Sous-chef d'Etat Major-General* should be 'Porker.' "

He directed me to the hot dishes and went on.

"Not that I think it will do much good. If your friends were clever enough to find out the first arrangement they are clever enough to discover the change. I would give my head to know where the leak is. We believed there were only five men in England who knew about Royer's visit, and you may be certain there were fewer in France, for they manage these things better there."

While I ate he continued to talk, making me to my surprise a present of his full confidence.

"Can the dispositions not be changed?" I asked.

"They could," he said. "But we want to avoid that if possible. They are the result of immense thought, and no alteration would be as good. Besides, on one or two points change is simply impossible. Still, something could be done, I suppose, if it were absolutely necessary. But you see the difficulty, Hannay. Our enemies are not going to be such fools as to pick Royer's pocket or any childish game like that. They know that would mean a row and put us on our guard. Their aim is to get the details without any one of us knowing, so that Royer will go back to Paris in the belief that the whole business is still deadly secret. If they can't do that they fail, for, once we suspect, they know that the whole thing must be altered."

"Then we must stick by the Frenchman's side till he is home again," I said. "If they thought they could get the information in Paris they would try there. It means that they have some deep scheme on foot in London which they reckon is going to win out."

"Royer dines with my Chief, and then comes to my house where four people will see him—Whittaker from the Admiralty, myself, Sir Arthur Drew, and General Winstanley. The First Lord is ill, and has gone to Sheringham. At my house he will get a certain document from Whittaker, and after that he will be motored to Portsmouth where a destroyer will take him to Havre. His journey is too important for the ordinary boat-train. He will never be left unattended for a moment till he is safe on French soil. The same with Whittaker till he meets Royer. That is the best we can do, and it's hard to see how there can be any miscarriage. But I don't mind admitting that I'm horribly nervous. This murder of Karolides will play the deuce in the chancelleries of Europe."

After breakfast he asked me if I could drive a car.

"Well, you'll be my chauffeur to-day and wear Hudson's rig. You're about his size. You have a hand in this business and we are taking no risks. There are desperate men against us, who will not respect the country retreat of an overworked official."

When I first came to London I had bought a car and amused

myself with running about the south of England, so I knew something of the geography. I took Sir Walter to town by the Bath Road and made good going. It was a soft breathless June morning, with a promise of sultriness later, but it was delicious enough swinging through the little towns with their freshly watered streets, and past the summer gardens of the Thames valley. I landed Sir Walter at his house in Queen Anne's Gate punctually by half past eleven. The butler was coming up by train with the luggage.

The first thing he did was to take me round to Scotland Yard. There we saw a prim gentleman, with a clean-shaven, lawyer's face.

"I've brought you the Portland Place murderer," was Sir Walter's introduction.

The reply was a wry smile. "It would have been a welcome present, Bullivant. This, I presume, is Mr. Richard Hannay, who for some days greatly interested my department."

"Mr. Hannay will interest it again. He has much to tell you, but not to-day. For certain grave reasons his tale must wait for twenty-four hours. Then, I can promise you, you will be entertained and possibly edified. I want you to assure Mr. Hannay that he will suffer no further inconvenience."

This assurance was promptly given. "You can take up your life where you left off," I was told. "Your flat, which probably you no longer wish to occupy, is waiting for you, and your man is still there. As you were never publicly accused, we considered that there was no need of a public exculpation. But on that, of course, you must please yourself."

"We may want your assistance later on, MacGillivray," Sir Walter said as we left.

Then he turned me loose.

"Come and see me to-morrow, Hannay. I needn't tell you to keep deadly quiet. If I were you I would go to bed, for you must have considerable arrears of sleep to overtake. You had better lie low, for if one of your Black Stone friends saw you there might be trouble."

I FELT CURIOUSLY AT A LOOSE end. At first it was very pleasant to be a free man, able to go where I wanted without fearing anything. I had only been a month under the ban of the law, and it was quite enough for me. I went to the Savoy and ordered very carefully a very good luncheon, and then smoked the best cigar the house could provide. But I was still feeling nervous. When I saw anybody look at me in the lounge, I grew shy, and wondered if they were thinking about the murder.

After that I took a taxi and drove miles away up into North London. I walked back through fields and lines of villas and terraces and then slums and mean streets, and it took me pretty nearly two hours. All the while my restlessness was growing worse. I felt that great things, tremendous things, were happening or about to happen, and I, who was the cog-wheel of the whole business, was out of it. Royer would be landing at Dover, Sir Walter would be making plans with the few people in England who were in the secret, and somewhere in the darkness the Black Stone would be working. I felt the sense of danger and impending calamity, and I had the curious feeling, too, that I alone could avert it, alone could grapple with it. But I was out of the game now. How could it be otherwise? It was not likely that Cabinet Ministers and Admiralty Lords and Generals would admit me to their councils.

I actually began to wish that I could run up against one of my three enemies. That would lead to developments. I felt that I wanted enormously to have a vulgar scrap with those gentry, where I could hit out and flatten something. I was rapidly getting into a very bad temper.

I didn't feel like going back to my flat. That had to be faced some time, but as I still had sufficient money I thought I would put it off till next morning, and go to an hotel for the night.

My irritation lasted through dinner, which I had at a restaurant in Jermyn Street. I was no longer hungry, and let several courses pass untasted. I drank the best part of a bottle of Burgundy, but it did nothing to cheer me. An abominable restlessness had taken possession of me. Here was I, a very ordinary fellow, with no particular brains, and yet I was convinced that somehow I was needed to help this business through—that without me it would all go to blazes. I told myself it was sheer silly conceit, that four or five of the cleverest people living, with all the might of the British Empire at their back, had the job in hand. Yet I couldn't be convinced. It seemed as if a voice kept speaking in my ear, telling me to be up and doing, or I would never sleep again.

The upshot was that about half past nine I made up my mind to go to Queen Anne's Gate. Very likely I would not be admitted, but it would ease my conscience to try.

I walked down Jermyn Street, and at the corner of Duke Street passed a group of young men. They were in evening dress, had been dining somewhere, and were going on to a music-hall. One of them was Mr. Marmaduke Jopley.

He saw me and stopped short.

"By God, the murderer!" he cried. "Here, you fellows, hold him! That's Hannay, the man who did the Portland Place murder!" He gripped me by the arm, and the others crowded round.

I wasn't looking for any trouble, but my ill-temper made me play the fool. A policeman came up, and I should have told him the truth, and, if he didn't believe it, demanded to be taken to Scotland Yard, or for that matter to the nearest police station. But a delay at that moment seemed to me unendurable, and the sight of Marmie's imbecile face was more than I could bear. I let out with my left, and had the satisfaction of seeing him measure his length in the gutter.

Then began an unholy row. They were all on me at once, and the policeman took me in the rear. I got in one or two good blows, for I think, with fair play, I could have licked the lot of them, but the policeman pinned me behind, and one of them got his fingers on my throat.

Through a black cloud of rage I heard the officer of the law asking what was the matter, and Marmie, between his broken teeth, declaring that I was Hannay the murderer.

"Oh, damn it all," I cried, "make the fellow shut up. I advise you to leave me alone, constable. Scotland Yard knows all about me, and you'll get a proper wigging if you interfere with me."

"You've got to come along of me, young man," said the policeman. "I saw you strike that gentleman crool 'ard. You began it too, for he wasn't doing nothing. I seen you. Best go quietly or I'll have to fix you up."

Exasperation and an overwhelming sense that at no cost must I delay gave me the strength of a bull elephant. I fairly wrenched the constable off his feet, floored the man who was gripping my collar, and set off at my best pace down Duke Street. I heard a whistle being blown, and the rush of men behind me.

I have a very fair turn of speed, and that night I had wings. In a jiffy I was in Pall Mall and had turned down towards St. James's Park. I dodged the policeman at the Palace gates, dived through a press of carriages at the entrance to the Mall, and was making for the bridge before my pursuers had crossed the roadway. In the open ways of the Park I put on a spurt. Happily there were few people about and no one tried to stop me. I was staking all on getting to Queen Anne's Gate.

When I entered that quiet thoroughfare it seemed deserted. Sir Walter's house was in the narrow part, and outside it three or four motor-cars were drawn up. I slackened speed some yards off and walked briskly up to the door. If the butler refused me admission, or if he even delayed to open the door, I was done.

He didn't delay. I had scarcely rung before the door opened.

"I must see Sir Walter," I panted. "My business is desperately important."

That butler was a great man. Without moving a muscle he held the door open, and then shut it behind me. "Sir Walter is engaged, sir, and I have orders to admit no one. Perhaps you will wait."

The house was of the old-fashioned kind, with a wide hall and rooms on both sides of it. At the far end was an alcove with a telephone and a couple of chairs, and there the butler offered me a seat.

"See here," I whispered. "There's trouble about and I'm in it. But Sir Walter knows, and I'm working for him. If anyone comes and asks if I am here, tell him a lie."

He nodded, and presently there was a noise of voices in the street, and a furious ringing at the bell. I never admired a man more than that butler. He opened the door, and with a face like a graven image waited to be questioned. Then he gave them it. He told them whose house it was, and what his orders were, and simply froze them off the doorstep. I could see it all from my alcove, and it was better than any play.

I HADN'T waited long till there came another ring at the bell. The butler made no bones about admitting this new visitor.

While he was taking off his coat I saw who it was. You couldn't open a newspaper or a magazine without seeing that face—the grey beard cut like a spade, the firm fighting mouth, the blunt square nose, and the keen blue eyes. I recognized the First Sea Lord, the man, they say, that made the new British Navy.

He passed my alcove and was ushered into a room at the back of the hall. As the door opened I could hear the sound of low voices. It shut, and I was left alone again. For twenty minutes I sat there, wondering what I was to do next. I was still perfectly convinced that I was wanted, but when or how I had no notion. I kept looking at my watch, and as the time crept on to half past ten I began to think that the conference must soon end. In a quarter of an hour Royer should be speeding along the road to Portsmouth . . .

Then I heard a bell ring, and the butler appeared. The door of the back room opened, and the First Sea Lord came out. He walked past me, and in passing he glanced in my direction, and for a second we looked each other in the face.

Only for a second, but it was enough to make my heart jump. I had never seen the great man before, and he had never seen me. But in that fraction of time something sprang into his eyes, and that something was recognition. You can't mistake it. It is a flicker, a spark of light, a minute shade of difference which means one thing and one thing only. It came involuntarily, for in a moment it died, and he passed on. In a maze of wild fancies I heard the street door close behind him.

I picked up the telephone book and looked up the number of his house. We were connected at once, and I heard a servant's voice.

"Is his Lordship at home?" I asked.

"His Lordship returned half an hour ago," said the voice, "and has gone to bed. He is not very well to-night. Will you leave a message, sir?"

I rang off and almost tumbled into a chair. My part in this business was not yet ended. It had been a close shave, but I had been in time.

Not a moment could be lost, so I marched boldly to the door of that back room and entered without knocking.

Five surprised faces looked up from a round table. There was Sir Walter, and Drew the War Minister, whom I knew from his photographs. There was a slim elderly man, who was probably Whittaker, the Admiralty official, and there was General Winstanley, conspicuous from the long scar on his forehead. Lastly there was a short stout man with an iron-grey moustache and bushy eyebrows, who had been arrested in the middle of a sentence.

Sir Walter's face showed surprise and annoyance.

"This is Mr. Hannay, of whom I have spoken to you," he said apologetically to the company. "I'm afraid, Hannay, this visit is ill-timed."

I was getting back my coolness. "That remains to be seen, sir," I said; "but I think it may be in the nick of time. For God's sake, gentlemen, tell me who went out a minute ago?"

"Lord Alloa," Sir Walter said, reddening with anger.

"It was not," I cried; "it was his living image, but it was not Lord Alloa. It was someone who recognized me, someone I have seen in the last month. He had scarcely left the doorstep when I rang up Lord Alloa's house and was told he had come in half an hour before and had gone to bed."

"Who—who—" someone stammered.

"The Black Stone," I cried, and I sat down in the chair so recently vacated and looked round at five badly scared gentlemen.

The Thirty-Nine Steps

"Nonsense!" said the official from the Admiralty.

Sir Walter got up and left the room while we looked blankly at the table. He came back in ten minutes with a long face. "I have spoken to Alloa," he said. "Had him out of bed—very grumpy. He went straight home after Mulross's dinner."

"But it's madness," broke in General Winstanley. "Do you mean to tell me that that man came here and sat beside me for the best part of half an hour and that I didn't detect the imposture? Alloa must be out of his mind."

"Don't you see the cleverness of it?" I said. "You were too interested in other things to have any eyes. You took Lord Alloa for granted. If it had been anybody else you might have looked more closely, but it was natural for him to be here, and that put you all to sleep."

Then the Frenchman spoke, very slowly, and in good English.

"The young man is right! His psychology is good. Our enemies have not been foolish!"

He bent his wise brows on the assembly.

"I will tell you a tale," he said. "It happened many years ago in Senegal. I was quartered in a remote station, and to pass the time used to go fishing for big barbel in the river. A little Arab mare used to carry my luncheon basket—one of the salted dun breed you got at Timbuktu in the old days. Well, one morning I had good sport, and the mare was unaccountably restless. I could hear her whinnying and squealing and stamping her feet, and I kept soothing her with my voice while my mind was intent on fish. I could see her all the time, as I thought, out of a corner of my eye, tethered to a tree twenty yards away. After a couple of hours I began to think of food. I collected my fish in a tarpaulin bag, and moved down the stream towards the mare, trolling my line. When I got up to her I flung the tarpaulin on her back . . ."

He paused and looked round.

"It was the smell that gave me warning. I turned my head and found myself looking at a lion three feet off . . . An old man-eater, that was the terror of the village . . . What was left of the mare, a mass of blood and bones and hide, was behind him."

"What happened?" I asked. I was enough of a hunter to know a true yarn when I heard it.

"I stuffed my fishing-rod into his jaws, and I had a pistol. Also my servants came presently with rifles. But he left his mark on me." He held up a hand which lacked three fingers.

"Consider," he said. "The mare had been dead more than an hour, and the brute had been patiently watching me ever since. I never saw the kill, for I was accustomed to the mare's fretting, and I never marked her absence, for my consciousness of her was only of something tawny, and the lion filled that part. If I could blunder thus, gentlemen, in a land where men's senses are keen, why should we busy preoccupied urban folk not err also?"

Sir Walter nodded. No one was ready to gainsay him.

"But I don't see," went on Winstanley. "Their object was to get these dispositions without our knowing it. Now it only required one of us to mention to Alloa our meeting to-night for the whole fraud to be exposed."

Sir Walter laughed dryly. "The selection of Alloa shows their acumen. Which of us was likely to speak to him about to-night? Or was he likely to open the subject?"

I remembered the First Sea Lord's reputation for taciturnity and shortness of temper.

"The one thing that puzzles me," said the General, "is what good his visit here would do that spy fellow? He could not carry away several pages of figures and strange names in his head."

"That is not difficult," the Frenchman replied. "A good spy is trained to have a photographic memory. Like your own Macaulay. You noticed he said nothing, but went through these papers again and again. I think we may assume that he has every detail stamped on his mind. When I was younger I could do the same trick."

"Well, I suppose there is nothing for it but to change the plans," said Sir Walter ruefully.

Whittaker was looking very glum. "Did you tell Lord Alloa what has happened?" he asked. "No? Well, I can't speak with absolute assurance, but I'm nearly certain we can't make any serious change unless we alter the geography of England."

"Another thing must be said." It was Royer who spoke. "I talked freely when that man was here. I told something of the military plans of my Government. I was permitted to say so much. But that information would be worth many millions to our enemies. No, my friends, I see no other way. The man who came here and his confederates must be taken, and taken at once."

"Good God," I cried, "and we have not a rag of a clue."

"Besides," said Whittaker, "there is the post. By this time the news will be on its way."

"No," said the Frenchman. "You do not understand the habits of the spy. He receives personally his reward, and he delivers personally his intelligence. We in France know something of the breed. There is still a chance, *mes amis*. These men must cross the sea, and there are ships to be searched and ports to be watched. Believe me, the need is desperate for both France and Britain."

Royer's grave good sense seemed to pull us together. He was the man of action among fumblers. But I saw no hope in any face, and I felt none. Where among the fifty millions of these islands and within a dozen hours were we to lay hands on the three cleverest rogues in Europe?

THEN SUDDENLY I had an inspiration.

"Where is Scudder's book?" I cried to Sir Walter. "Quick, man, I remember something in it."

He unlocked the door of a bureau and gave it to me.

I found the place. "*Thirty-nine steps*," I read, and again, "*Thirty-nine steps—I counted them—High tide, 10:17 p.m.*"

The Admiralty man was looking at me as if he thought I had gone mad.

"Don't you see it's a clue," I shouted. "Scudder knew where these fellows laired—he knew where they were going to leave the country, though he kept the name to himself. To-morrow was the day, and it was some place where high tide was at ten-seventeen."

"They may have gone to-night," someone said.

"Not they. They have their own snug secret way, and they won't be hurried. I know Germans, and they are mad about working to a plan. Where the devil can I get a book of Tide Tables?"

Whittaker brightened up. "It's a chance," he said. "Let's go over to the Admiralty."

We got into two of the waiting motor-cars—all but Sir Walter, who went off to Scotland Yard—to "mobilize MacGillivray," so he said.

We marched through empty corridors and big bare chambers where the charwomen were busy, till we reached a little room lined with books and maps. A resident clerk was unearthed, who presently fetched from the library the Admiralty Tide Tables. I sat at the desk and the others stood round, for somehow or other I had got charge of this expedition.

It was no good. There were hundreds of entries, and so far as I could see ten-seventeen might cover fifty places. We had to find some way of narrowing the possibilities.

I took my head in my hands and thought. There must be some way of reading this riddle. What did Scudder mean by steps? I thought of dock steps, but if he had meant that I didn't think he would have mentioned the number. It must be some place where there were several staircases, and one marked out from the others by having thirty-nine steps.

Then I had a sudden thought, and hunted up all the steamer sailings. There was no boat which left for the Continent at 10:17 p.m.

Why was high tide important? If it was a harbour it must be some little place where the tide mattered, or else it was a heavy-draught boat. But there was no regular steamer sailing at that hour, and somehow I didn't think they would travel by a big boat from a regular harbour. So it must be some little harbour where the tide was important, or perhaps no harbour at all.

But if it was a little port I couldn't see what the steps signified. There were no sets of staircases on any harbour that I had ever seen. It must be some place which a particular staircase identified, and where the tide was full at ten-seventeen. On the whole it seemed to me that the place must be a bit of open coast. But the staircases kept puzzling me.

Then I went back to wider considerations. Whereabouts would a man be likely to leave for Germany, a man in a hurry, who wanted a speedy and a secret passage? Not from any of the big harbours. And not from the Channel or the West Coast or Scotland, for, remember, he was starting from London. I measured the distance on the map, and tried to put myself in the enemy's shoes. I should try for Ostend or Antwerp or Rotterdam, and I should sail from somewhere on the East Coast between Cromer and Dover.

All this was very loose guessing, and I don't pretend it was ingenious or scientific. I wasn't any kind of Sherlock Holmes. But I have always fancied I had a kind of instinct about questions like this. I don't know if I can explain myself, but I used to use my brains as far as they went, and after they came to a blank wall I guessed, and I usually found my guesses pretty right.

So I set out all my conclusions on a bit of Admiralty paper. They ran like this:

FAIRLY CERTAIN

(1) Place where there are several sets of stairs; one that matters distinguished by having thirty-nine steps.

(2) Full tide at 10:17 p.m. Leaving shore only possible at full tide.

(3) Steps not dock steps, and so place probably not harbour.

(4) No regular night steamer at 10:17. Means of transport must be tramp (unlikely), yacht, or fishing-boat.

There my reasoning stopped. I made another list, which I headed "Guessed," but I was just as sure of the one as the other.

GUESSED

(1) Place not harbour but open coast.

(2) Boat small—trawler, yacht, or launch.

(3) Place somewhere on East Coast between Cromer and Dover.

It struck me as odd that I should be sitting at that desk with a Cabinet Minister, a Field-Marshal, two high Government officials, and a French General watching me, while from the scribble of a dead man I was trying to drag a secret which meant life or death for us.

Sir Walter had joined us, and presently MacGillivray arrived. He had sent out instructions to watch the ports and railway stations for the three men whom I had described to Sir Walter. Not that he or anybody else thought that that would do much good.

"Here's the most I can make of it," I said. "We have got to find a place where there are several staircases down to the beach, one of which has thirty-nine steps. I think it's a piece of open coast with biggish cliffs, somewhere between the Wash and the Channel. Also it's a place where full tide is at ten-seventeen to-morrow night."

Then an idea struck me. "Is there no Inspector of Coastguards or some fellow like that who knows the East Coast?"

Whittaker said there was, and that he lived in Clapham. He went off in a car to fetch him, and the rest of us sat about the little room and talked of anything that came into our heads. I lit a pipe and went over the whole thing again till my brain grew weary.

About one in the morning the coastguard man arrived. He was a fine old fellow, with the look of a naval officer, and was desperately respectful to the company. I left the War Minister to cross-examine him, for I felt he would think it cheek in me to talk.

"We want you to tell us the places you know on the East Coast where there are cliffs, and where several sets of steps run down to the beach."

He thought for a bit. "What kind of steps do you mean, sir? There are plenty of places with roads cut down through the cliffs, and most roads have a step or two in them. Or do you mean regular staircases—all steps, so to speak?"

Sir Arthur looked towards me. "We mean regular staircases," I said.

He reflected a minute or two. "I don't know that I can think of any. Wait a second. There's a place in Norfolk—Brattlesham—beside a golf course, where there are a couple of staircases to let the gentlemen get a lost ball."

"That's not it," I said.

"Then there are plenty of Marine Parades, if that's what you mean. Every seaside resort has them."

I shook my head.

"It's got to be more retired than that," I said.

"Well, gentlemen, I can't think of anywhere else. Of course, there's the Ruff—"

"What's that?" I asked.

"The big chalk headland in Kent, close to Bradgate. It's got a lot of villas on the top, and some of the houses have staircases down to a private beach. It's a very high-toned sort of place, and the residents there like to keep by themselves."

I tore open the Tide Tables and found Bradgate. High tide there was at 10:27 p.m. on the 15th of June.

"We're on the scent at last," I cried excitedly. "How can I find out what is the tide at the Ruff?"

"I can tell you that, sir," said the coastguard man. "I once was lent a house there in this very month, and I used to go out at night to the deep-sea fishing. The tide's ten minutes before Bradgate."

I closed the book and looked round at the company.

"If one of those staircases has thirty-nine steps we have solved the mystery, gentlemen," I said. "I want the loan of your car, Sir Walter, and a map of the roads. If Mr. MacGillivray will spare me ten minutes, I think we can prepare something for to-morrow."

It was ridiculous of me to take charge of the business like this, but they didn't seem to mind, and after all I had been in the show from the start. Besides, I was used to rough jobs, and these eminent gentlemen were too clever not to see it. It was General Royer who gave me my commission. "I for one," he said, "am content to leave the matter in Mr. Hannay's hands."

By half past three I was tearing past the moonlit hedgerows of Kent, with MacGillivray's best man on the seat beside me.

Various Parties Converging on the Sea

A PINK and blue June morning found me at Bradgate looking from the Griffin Hotel over a smooth sea to the lightship on the Cock sands which seemed the size of a bell-buoy. A couple of miles farther south and much nearer the shore a small destroyer was anchored. Scaife, MacGillivray's man, who had been in the Navy, knew the boat, and told me her name and her commander's, so I sent off a wire to Sir Walter.

After breakfast Scaife got from a house-agent a key for the gates of the staircases on the Ruff. I walked with him along the sands, and sat down in a nook of the cliffs while he investigated the half dozen of them. I didn't want to be seen, but the place at this hour was quite deserted, and all the time I was on that beach I saw nothing but the seagulls.

It took him more than an hour to do the job, and when I saw him coming towards me, conning a bit of paper, I can tell you my heart was in my mouth. Everything depended, you see, on my guess proving right.

He read aloud the number of steps in the different stairs. "Thirty-four, thirty-five, thirty-nine, forty-two, forty-seven," and "twenty-one" where the cliffs grew lower. I almost got up and shouted.

We hurried back to the town and sent a wire to MacGillivray.

I wanted half a dozen men, and I directed them to divide themselves among different specified hotels. Then Scaife set out to
prospect the house at the head of the thirty-nine steps.

He came back with news that both puzzled and reassured me.
The house was called Trafalgar Lodge, and belonged to an old
gentleman called Appleton—a retired stockbroker, the house-
agent said. Mr. Appleton was there a good deal in the summer-
time, and was in residence now—had been for the better part of
a week. Scaife could pick up very little information about him,
except that he was a decent old fellow, who paid his bills regularly, and was always good for a fiver for a local charity. Then
Scaife seems to have penetrated to the back door of the house,
pretending he was an agent for sewing-machines. Only three
servants were kept, a cook, a parlourmaid, and a housemaid,
and they were just the sort that you would find in a respectable
middle-class household. The cook was not the gossiping kind,
and had pretty soon shut the door in his face, but Scaife said he
was positive she knew nothing. Next door there was a new
house building which would give good cover for observation,
and the villa on the other side was to let, and its garden was
rough and shrubby.

I borrowed Scaife's telescope, and before lunch went for a walk
along the Ruff. I kept well behind the rows of villas, and found a
good observation point on the edge of the golf course. There I
had a view of the line of turf along the cliff-top, with seats placed
at intervals, and the little square plots, railed in and planted with
bushes, whence the staircases descended to the beach. I saw Trafalgar Lodge very plainly, a red-brick villa with a veranda, a tennis lawn behind, and in front the ordinary seaside flower-garden
full of marguerites and scraggy geraniums. There was a flagstaff
from which an enormous Union Jack hung limply in the still air.

Presently I observed someone leave the house and saunter
along the cliff. When I got my glasses on him I saw it was an old
man, wearing white flannel trousers, a blue serge jacket, and a
straw hat. He carried field-glasses and a newspaper, and sat down
on one of the iron seats and began to read. Sometimes he would

lay down the paper and turn his glasses on the sea. He looked for a long time at the destroyer. I watched him for half an hour, till he got up and went back to the house for his luncheon, when I returned to the hotel for mine.

I wasn't feeling very confident. This decent commonplace dwelling was not what I had expected. The man might be the bald archaeologist of the horrible moorland farm, or he might not. He was exactly the kind of satisfied old bird you will find in every suburb and every holiday place. If you wanted a type of the perfectly harmless person you would probably pitch on that.

But after lunch, as I sat in the hotel porch, I perked up, for I saw the thing I hoped for and had dreaded to miss. A yacht came up from the south and dropped anchor pretty well opposite the Ruff. She seemed about a hundred and fifty tons, and I saw she belonged to the Squadron from the white ensign. So Scaife and I went down to the harbour and hired a boatman for an afternoon's fishing.

I spent a warm and peaceful afternoon. We caught between us about twenty pounds of cod and lythe, and out in that dancing blue sea I took a cheerier view of things. Above the white cliffs of the Ruff I saw the green and red of the villas, and especially the great flagstaff of Trafalgar Lodge. About four o'clock, when we had fished enough, I made the boatman row us round the yacht, which lay like a delicate white bird, ready at a moment to flee. Scaife said she must be a fast boat from her build, and that she was pretty heavily engined.

Her name was the *Ariadne*, as I discovered from the cap of one of the men who was polishing brasswork. I spoke to him, and got an answer in the soft dialect of Essex. Another hand that came along passed me the time of day in an unmistakable English tongue. Our boatman had an argument with one of them about the weather, and for a few minutes we lay on our oars close to the starboard bow.

Then the men suddenly disregarded us and bent their heads to their work as an officer came along the deck. He was a pleasant, clean-looking young fellow, and he put a question to us about our fishing in very good English. But there could be no doubt about him. His close-cropped head and the cut of his collar and tie never came out of England.

That did something to reassure me, but as we rowed back to Bradgate my obstinate doubts would not be dismissed. The thing that worried me was the reflection that my enemies knew that I had got my knowledge from Scudder, and it was Scudder who had given me the clue to this place. If they knew that Scudder had this clue, would they not be certain to change their plans? Too much depended on their success for them to take any risks. The whole question was how much they understood about Scudder's knowledge. I had talked confidently last night about Germans always sticking to a scheme, but if they had any suspicions that I was on their track they would be fools not to cover it. I wondered if the man last night had seen that I recognized him. Somehow I did not think he had, and to that I clung. But the whole business had never seemed so difficult as that afternoon when by all calculations I should have been rejoicing in assured success.

In the hotel I met the commander of the destroyer, to whom Scaife introduced me, and with whom I had a few words. Then I thought I would put in an hour or two watching Trafalgar Lodge.

I found a place farther up the hill, in the garden of an empty house. From that I had a full view of the court, on which two figures were having a game of tennis. One was the old man, whom I had already seen; the other was a younger fellow, wearing some club colours in the scarf round his middle. They played with tremendous zest, like two city gents who wanted hard exercise to open their pores. You couldn't conceive a more innocent spectacle. They shouted and laughed and stopped for drinks, when a maid brought out two tankards on a salver. I rubbed my eyes and asked myself if I was not the most immortal fool on earth. Mystery and darkness had hung about the men who hunted me over the Scotch moor in aeroplane and motor-car, and notably about that infernal antiquarian. It was easy enough to connect those folk with the knife that pinned Scudder to the floor, and with fell designs on the world's peace. But here were two guileless citizens taking their innocuous exercise, and soon about to go indoors to a humdrum dinner, where they would talk of market prices and the last cricket scores and the gossip of their native Surbiton. I had been making a net to catch vultures and falcons, and lo and behold! two plump thrushes had blundered into it.

Presently a third figure arrived, a young man on a bicycle, with a bag of golf clubs slung on his back. He strolled round to the tennis lawn and was welcomed riotously by the players. Evidently they were chaffing him, and their chaff sounded horribly English. Then the plump man, mopping his brow with a silk handkerchief, announced that he must have a tub. I heard his very words—"I've got into a proper lather," he said. "This will bring down my weight and my handicap, Bob. I'll take you on to-morrow and give you a stroke a hole." You couldn't find anything much more English than that.

They all went into the house, and left me feeling a precious idiot. I had been barking up the wrong tree this time. These men might be acting; but if they were, where was their audience? They didn't know I was sitting thirty yards off in a rhododendron. It was simply impossible to believe that these three hearty fellows were anything but what they seemed—three ordinary, game-playing, suburban Englishmen, wearisome, if you like, but sordidly innocent.

AND yet there were three of them; and one was old, and one was plump, and one was lean and dark; and their house chimed in with Scudder's notes; and half a mile off was lying a steam yacht with at least one German officer. I thought of Karolides lying dead, and all Europe trembling on the edge of earthquake, and the men I had left behind me in London who were waiting anxiously for the events of the next hours. There was no doubt that hell was afoot somewhere. The Black Stone had won, and if it survived this June night would bank its winnings.

There seemed only one thing to do—go forward as if I had no

doubts, and if I was going to make a fool of myself to do it handsomely. Never in my life have I faced a job with greater disinclination. I would rather in my then mind have walked into a den of anarchists, each with his Browning handy, or faced a charging lion with a popgun, than enter that happy home of three cheerful Englishmen and tell them that their game was up. How they would laugh at me!

But suddenly I remembered a thing I once heard in Rhodesia from old Peter Pienaar. I have quoted Peter already in this narrative. He was the best scout I ever knew, and before he had turned respectable he had been pretty often on the windy side of the law, when he had been wanted badly by the authorities. Peter once discussed with me the question of disguises, and he had a theory which struck me at the time. He said, barring absolute certainties like fingerprints, mere physical traits were very little use for identification if the fugitive really knew his business. He laughed at things like dyed hair and false beards and such childish follies. The only thing that mattered was what Peter called "atmosphere."

If a man could get into perfectly different surroundings from those in which he had been first observed, and—this is the important part—really play up to these surroundings and behave as if he had never been out of them, he would puzzle the cleverest detectives on earth. And he used to tell a story of how he once borrowed a black coat and went to church and shared the same hymn-book with the man that was looking for him. If that man had seen him in decent company before he would have recognized him; but he had only seen him snuffing the lights in a public-house with a revolver.

The recollection of Peter's talk gave me the first real comfort I had had that day. Peter had been a wise old bird, and these fellows I was after were about the pick of the aviary. What if they were playing Peter's game? A fool tries to look different: a clever man looks the same and *is* different.

Again, there was that other maxim of Peter's which had helped me when I had been a roadman. "If you are playing a part, you

will never keep it up unless you convince yourself that you are
it." That would explain the game of tennis. Those chaps didn't
need to act, they just turned a handle and passed into another
life, which came as naturally to them as the first. It sounds a
platitude, but Peter used to say that it was the big secret of all the
famous criminals.

It was now getting on for eight o'clock, and I went back and
saw Scaife to give him his instructions. I arranged with him how
to place his men, and then I went for a walk, for I didn't feel up
to any dinner. I went round the deserted golf course, and then to
a point on the cliffs farther north beyond the line of the villas.

On the little trim newly made roads I met people in flannels
coming back from tennis and the beach, and a coastguard from
the wireless station, and donkeys and pierrots padding home-
wards. Out at sea in the blue dusk I saw lights appear on the
Ariadne and on the destroyer away to the south, and beyond the
Cock sands the bigger lights of steamers making for the Thames.
The whole scene was so peaceful and ordinary that I got more
dashed in spirits every second. It took all my resolution to stroll
towards Trafalgar Lodge about half past nine.

On the way I got a piece of solid comfort from the sight of a
greyhound that was swinging along at a nursemaid's heels. He
reminded me of a dog I used to have in Rhodesia, and of the time
when I took him hunting with me in the Pali hills. We were after
rhebok, the dun kind, and I recollected how we had followed one
beast, and both he and I had clean lost it. A greyhound works by
sight, and my eyes are good enough, but that buck simply leaked
out of the landscape. Afterwards I found out how it managed it.
Against the grey rock of the kopje it showed no more than a crow
against a thunder-cloud. It didn't need to run away; all it had to
do was to stand still and melt into the background.

Suddenly as these memories chased across my brain I thought
of my present case and applied the moral. The Black Stone didn't
need to bolt. They were quietly absorbed into the landscape. I
was on the right track, and I jammed that down in my mind and
vowed never to forget it. The last word was with Peter Pienaar.

Scaife's men would be posted now, but there was no sign of a soul. The house stood as open as a market-place for anybody to observe. A three-foot railing separated it from the cliff road; the windows on the ground floor were all open, and shaded lights and the low sound of voices revealed where the occupants were finishing dinner. Everything was as public and above-board as a charity bazaar. Feeling the greatest fool on earth, I opened the gate and rang the bell.

A MAN of my sort, who has travelled about the world in rough places, gets on perfectly well with two classes, what you may call the upper and the lower. He understands them and they understand him. I was at home with herds and tramps and roadmen, and I was sufficiently at my ease with people like Sir Walter and the men I had met the night before. I can't explain why, but it is a fact. But what fellows like me don't understand is the great comfortable, satisfied middle-class world, the folk that live in villas and suburbs. He doesn't know how they look at things, he doesn't understand their conventions, and he is as shy of them as of a black mamba. When a trim parlourmaid opened the door, I could hardly find my voice.

I asked for Mr. Appleton, and was ushered in. My plan had been to walk straight into the dining-room, and by a sudden appearance wake in the men that start of recognition which would confirm my theory. But when I found myself in that neat hall the place mastered me. There were the golf clubs and tennis rackets, the straw hats and caps, the rows of gloves, the sheaf of walking-sticks, which you will find in ten thousand British homes. A stack of neatly folded coats and waterproofs covered the top of an old oak chest; there was a grandfather clock ticking; and some polished brass warming-pans on the walls, and a barometer, and a print of Chiltern winning the St. Leger. The place was as orthodox as an Anglican church. When the maid asked me for my name I gave it automatically, and was shown into the smoking-room, on the right side of the hall.

That room was even worse. I hadn't time to examine it, but I could see some framed group photographs above the mantel-piece, and I could have sworn they were English public school or college. I had only one glance, for I managed to pull myself together and go after the maid. But I was too late. She had already entered the dining-room and given my name to her master, and I had missed the chance of seeing how the three took it.

When I walked into the room the old man at the head of the table had risen and turned round to meet me. He was in evening dress—a short coat and black tie—as was the other, whom I called in my own mind the plump one. The third, the dark fellow, wore a blue serge suit and a soft white collar, and the colours of some club or school.

The old man's manner was perfect. "Mr. Hannay?" he said hesitatingly. "Did you wish to see me? One moment, you fellows, and I'll rejoin you. We had better go to the smoking-room."

Though I hadn't an ounce of confidence in me, I forced myself to play the game. I pulled up a chair and sat down on it.

"I think we have met before," I said, "and I guess you know my business."

The light in the room was dim, but so far as I could see their faces, they played the part of mystification very well.

"Maybe, maybe," said the old man. "I haven't a very good memory, but I'm afraid you must tell me your errand, sir, for I really don't know it."

"Well, then," I said, and all the time I seemed to myself to be talking pure foolishness—"I have come to tell you that the game's up. I have here a warrant for the arrest of you three gentlemen."

"Arrest," said the old man, and he looked really shocked. "Arrest! Good God, what for?"

"For the murder of Franklin Scudder in London on the 23rd day of last month."

"I never heard the name before," said the old man in a dazed voice.

One of the others spoke up. "That was the Portland Place murder. I read about it. Good Heavens, you must be mad, sir! Where do you come from?"

"Scotland Yard," I said.

After that for a minute there was utter silence. The old man was staring at his plate and fumbling with a nut, the very model of innocent bewilderment.

Then the plump one spoke up. He stammered a little, like a man picking his words.

"Don't get flustered, uncle," he said. "It is all a ridiculous mistake; but these things happen sometimes, and we can easily set it right. It won't be hard to prove our innocence. I can show that I was out of the country on the 23rd of May, and Bob was in a nursing home. You were in London, but you can explain what you were doing."

"Right, Percy! Of course that's easy enough. The 23rd! That was the day after Agatha's wedding. Let me see. What was I doing? I came up in the morning from Woking, and lunched at the club with Charlie Symons. Then—oh yes, I dined with the Fishmongers. I remember, for the punch didn't agree with me, and I was seedy next morning. Hang it all, there's the cigar-box I brought back from the dinner." He pointed to an object on the table, and laughed nervously.

"I think, sir," said the young man, addressing me respectfully, "you will see you are mistaken. We want to assist the law like all Englishmen, and we don't want Scotland Yard to be making fools of themselves. That's so, uncle?"

"Certainly, Bob." The old fellow seemed to be recovering his voice. "Certainly, we'll do anything in our power to assist the authorities. But—but this is a bit too much. I can't get over it."

"How Nellie will chuckle," said the plump man. "She always said that you would die of boredom because nothing ever happened to you. And now you've got it thick and strong," and he began to laugh very pleasantly.

"By Jove, yes. Just think of it! What a story to tell at the club. Really, Mr. Hannay, I suppose I should be angry, to show my innocence, but it's too funny! I almost forgive you the fright you gave me! You looked so glum, I thought I might have been walking in my sleep and killing people."

It couldn't be acting, it was too confoundedly genuine. My heart went into my boots, and my first impulse was to apologize and clear out. But I told myself I must see it through, even though I was to be the laughing-stock of Britain. The light from the dinner-table candlesticks was not very good, and to cover my confusion I got up, walked to the door and switched on the electric light. The sudden glare made them blink, and I stood scanning the three faces.

Well, I made nothing of it. One was old and bald, one was stout, one was dark and thin. There was nothing in their appearance to prevent them being the three who had hunted me in Scotland, but there was nothing to identify them. I simply can't explain why I who, as a roadman, had looked into two pairs of eyes, and as Ned Ainslie into another pair, why I, who have a good memory and reasonable powers of observation, could find no satisfaction. They seemed exactly what they professed to be, and I could not have sworn to one of them.

There in that pleasant dining-room, with etchings on the walls, and a picture of an old lady in a bib above the mantelpiece, I could see nothing to connect them with the moorland desperadoes. There was a silver cigarette-box beside me, and I saw that it had been won by Percival Appleton, Esq., of the St. Bede's Club, in a golf tournament. I had to keep firm hold of Peter Pienaar to prevent myself bolting out of that house.

"Well," said the old man politely, "are you reassured by your scrutiny, sir?"

I couldn't find a word.

"I hope you'll find it consistent with your duty to drop this ridiculous business. I make no complaint, but you'll see how annoying it must be to respectable people."

I shook my head.

"Oh Lord," said the young man. "This is a bit too thick!"

"Do you propose to march us off to the police station?" asked the plump one. "That might be the best way out of it, but I suppose you won't be content with the local branch. I have the right to ask to see your warrant, but I don't wish to cast any aspersions upon you. You are only doing your duty. But you'll admit it's horribly awkward. What do you propose to do?"

There was nothing to do except to call in my men and have them arrested, or to confess my blunder and clear out. I felt mesmerized by the whole place, by the air of obvious innocence—not innocence merely, but frank honest bewilderment and concern in the three faces.

"Oh, Peter Pienaar," I groaned inwardly, and for a moment I was very near damning myself for a fool and asking their pardon.

"Meantime I vote we have a game of bridge," said the plump one. "It will give Mr. Hannay time to think over things, and you know we have been wanting a fourth player. Do you play, sir?"

I accepted as if it had been an ordinary invitation at the club. The whole business had mesmerized me. We went into the smoking-room where a card-table was set out, and I was offered things to smoke and drink. I took my place at the table in a kind of dream. The window was open and the moon was flooding the cliffs and sea with a great tide of yellow light. There was moonshine, too, in my head. The three had recovered their composure, and were talking easily—just the kind of slangy talk you will hear in any golf club-house. I must have cut a rum figure, sitting there knitting my brows with my eyes wandering.

My partner was the young dark one. I play a fair hand at bridge, but I must have been rank bad that night. They saw that they had got me puzzled, and that put them more than ever at their ease. I kept looking at their faces, but they conveyed nothing to me. It was not that they looked different; they *were* different. I clung desperately to the words of Peter Pienaar.

THEN something awoke me.

The old man laid down his hand to light a cigar. He didn't pick it up at once, but sat back for a moment in his chair, with his fingers tapping on his knees.

It was the movement I remembered when I had stood before him in the moorland farm, with the pistols of his servants behind me.

A little thing, lasting only a second, and the odds were a thousand to one that I might have had my eyes on my cards at the time and missed it. But I didn't, and, in a flash, the air seemed to clear. Some shadow lifted from my brain, and I was looking at the three men with full and absolute recognition.

The clock on the mantelpiece struck ten o'clock.

The three faces seemed to change before my eyes and reveal their secrets. The young one was the murderer. Now I saw cruelty and ruthlessness, where before I had only seen good humour. His knife, I made certain, had skewered Scudder to the floor. His kind had put the bullet in Karolides.

The plump man's features seemed to dislimn, and form again, as I looked at them. He hadn't a face, only a hundred masks that he could assume when he pleased. That chap must have been a superb actor. Perhaps he had been Lord Alloa of the night before; perhaps not, it didn't matter. I wondered if he was the fellow who had first tracked Scudder, and left his card on him. Scudder had said he lisped, and I could imagine how the adoption of a lisp might add terror.

But the old man was the pick of the lot. He was sheer brain, icy, cool, calculating, as ruthless as a steam hammer. Now that my eyes were opened I wondered where I had seen the benevolence. His jaw was like chilled steel, and his eyes had the inhuman luminosity of a bird's. I went on playing, and every second a greater hate welled up in my heart. It almost choked me, and I couldn't answer when my partner spoke. Only a little longer could I endure their company.

"Whew! Bob! Look at the time," said the old man. "You'd better think about catching your train. Bob's got to go to town tonight," he added, turning to me. The voice rang now as false as hell.

I looked at the clock, and it was nearly half past ten.

"I am afraid he must put off his journey," I said.

"Oh, damn," said the young man, "I thought you had dropped that rot. I've simply got to go. You can have my address, and I'll give any security you like."

"No," I said, "you must stay."

At that I think they must have realized that the game was desperate. Their only chance had been to convince me that I was playing the fool, and that had failed. But the old man spoke again.

"I'll go bail for my nephew. That ought to content you, Mr. Hannay." Was it fancy, or did I detect some halt in the smoothness of that voice?

There must have been, for as I glanced at him, his eyelids fell in that hawk-like hood which fear had stamped on my memory.

I blew my whistle.

In an instant the lights were out. A pair of strong arms gripped me round the waist, covering the pockets in which a man might be expected to carry a pistol.

"*Schnell, Franz,*" cried a voice, "*das Boot, das Boot!*" As it spoke, I saw two of my fellows emerge on the moonlit lawn.

The young dark man leaped for the window, was through it, and over the low fence before a hand could touch him. I grappled the old chap, and the room seemed to fill with figures. I saw the plump one collared, but my eyes were all for the out-of-doors, where Franz sped on over the road towards the railed entrance to the beach stairs. One man followed him, but he had no chance. The gates of the stairs locked behind the fugitive, and I stood staring, with my hands on the old boy's throat, for such a time as a man might take to descend those steps to the sea.

Suddenly my prisoner broke from me and flung himself on the wall. There was a click as if a lever had been pulled. Then came a low rumbling, far far below the ground, and through the window I saw a cloud of chalky dust pouring out of the shaft of the stairway.

Someone switched on the light.

The old man was looking at me with blazing eyes.

"He is safe," he cried. "You cannot follow in time . . . He is gone. He has triumphed . . . *Der Schwarzestein ist in der Siegeskrone.*"

There was more in those eyes than any common triumph. They had been hooded like a bird of prey, and now they flamed with a hawk's pride. A white fanatic heat burned in them, and I realized for the first time the terrible thing I had been up against. This man was more than a spy; in his foul way he had been a patriot.

As the handcuffs clinked on his wrists I said my last word to him.

"I hope Franz will bear his triumph well. I ought to tell you that the *Ariadne* for the last hour has been in our hands."

SEVEN weeks later, as all the world knows, we went to war. I joined the New Army the first week, and owing to my Matabele experience got a captain's commission straight off. But I had done my best service, I think, before I put on khaki.

Greenmantle

Greenmantle

CHAPTER 1

A Mission Is Proposed

I HAD just finished breakfast and was filling my pipe when I got Bullivant's telegram. It was at Furling, the big country house in Hampshire where I had come to convalesce after Loos, and Sandy, who was in the same case, was hunting for the marmalade. I flung him the flimsy with the blue strip pasted down on it, and he whistled.

"Hullo, Dick, you've got the battalion. Or maybe it's a staff billet. You'll be a blighted brass-hat, coming it heavy over the hard-working regimental officer. And to think of the language you've wasted on brass-hats in your time!"

I sat and thought for a bit, for that name "Bullivant" carried me back eighteen months to the hot summer before the war. I had not seen the man since, though I had read about him in the papers. For more than a year I had been a busy battalion officer, with no other thought than to hammer a lot of raw stuff into good soldiers. I had succeeded pretty well, and there was no prouder man on earth than Richard Hannay when he took his Lennox Highlanders over the parapets on that glorious and bloody 25th day of September. Loos was no picnic, and we had had some ugly bits of scrapping before that, but the worst bit of the campaign I had seen was a tea-party to the show I had been in with Bullivant before the war started.

The sight of his name on a telegram form seemed to change all my outlook on life. I had been hoping for the command of the battalion, and looking forward to being in at the finish with Brother Boche. But this message jerked my thoughts on to a new road. There might be other things in the war than straight-forward fighting. Why on earth should the Foreign Office want to see an obscure major of the New Army, and want to see him in double-quick time?

"I'm going up to town by the ten train," I announced; "I'll be back in time for dinner."

"Try my tailor," said Sandy. "He's got a very nice taste in red tabs. You can use my name."

An idea struck me. "You're pretty well all right now. If I wire for you, will you pack your own kit and mine and join me?"

"Right-o! I'll accept a job on your staff if they give you a corps. If so be as you come down to-night, be a good chap and bring a barrel of oysters from Sweeting's."

I travelled up to London in a regular November drizzle, which cleared up about Wimbledon to watery sunshine. I never could stand London during the war. It seemed to have lost its bearings and broken out into all manner of badges and uniforms which did not fit in with my notion of it. One felt the war more in its streets than in the field, or rather one felt the confusion of war without feeling the purpose. I dare say it was all right; but since August 1914 I never spent a day in town without coming home depressed to my boots.

I took a taxi and drove straight to the Foreign Office. Sir Walter did not keep me waiting long. But when his secretary took me to his room I would not have recognized the man I had known eighteen months before.

His big frame seemed to have dropped flesh and there was a stoop in the square shoulders. His face had lost its rosiness and was red in patches, like that of a man who gets too little fresh air. His hair was much greyer and very thin about the temples, and there were lines of overwork below the eyes. But the eyes were the same as before, keen and kindly and shrewd, and there was no change in the firm set of the jaw.

"We must on no account be disturbed for the next hour," he told his secretary. When the young man had gone he went across to both doors and turned the keys in them.

"Well, Major Hannay," he said, flinging himself into a chair beside the fire. "How do you like soldiering?"

"Right enough," I said, "though this isn't just the kind of war I would have picked myself. It's a comfortless, bloody business. But we've got the measure of the old Boche now, and it's dogged as does it. I count on getting back to the front in a week or two."

"Will you get the battalion?" he asked. He seemed to have followed my doings pretty closely.

"I believe I've a good chance. I'm not in this show for honour and glory, though. I want to do the best I can, but I wish to Heaven it was over. All I think of is coming out of it with a whole skin."

He laughed. "You do yourself an injustice. What about the forward observation post at the Lone Tree? You forgot about the whole skin then."

I felt myself getting red. "That was all rot," I said, "and I can't think who told you about it. I hated the job, but I had to do it to prevent my subalterns going to glory. They were a lot of fire-eating young lunatics. If I had sent one of them he'd have gone on his knees to Providence and asked for trouble."

Sir Walter was still grinning.

"I'm not questioning your caution. You have the rudiments of it, or our friends of the Black Stone would have gathered you in at our last merry meeting. I would question it as little as your courage. What exercises my mind is whether it is best employed in the trenches."

"Is the War Office dissatisfied with me?" I asked sharply.

"They are profoundly satisfied. They propose to give you command of your battalion. Presently, if you escape a stray bullet, you will no doubt be a Brigadier. It is a wonderful war for youth and brains. But, I take it you are in this business to serve your country, Hannay?"

"I reckon I am," I said. "I am certainly not in it for my health."

He looked at my leg, where the doctors had dug out the shrapnel fragments, and smiled quizzically.

"Pretty fit again?" he asked.

"Tough as a sjambok. I thrive on the racket and eat and sleep like a schoolboy."

He got up and stood with his back to the fire, his eyes staring abstractedly out of the window at the wintry park.

"It is a great game, and you are the man for it, no doubt. But there are others who can play it, for soldiering to-day asks for the average rather than the exception in human nature. It is like a big machine where the parts are standardized. You are fighting, not because you are short of a job, but because you want to help England. How if you could help her better than by commanding a battalion—or brigade—or, if it comes to that, a division? How if there is a thing which you alone can do? Not some *embusqué* business in an office, but a thing compared to which your fight at Loos was a Sunday-school picnic. You are not afraid of danger? Well, in this job you would not be fighting with an army around you, but alone. You are fond of tackling difficulties? Well, I can give you a task which will try all your powers. Have you anything to say?"

My heart was beginning to thump uncomfortably. Sir Walter was not the man to pitch a case too high.

"I am a soldier," I said, "and under orders."

"True; but what I am about to propose does not come by any conceivable stretch within the scope of a soldier's duties. I shall perfectly understand if you decline. You will be acting as I should act myself—as any sane man would. I would not press you for worlds. If you wish it, I will not even make the proposal, but let you go here and now, and wish you good luck with your battalion. I do not wish to perplex a good soldier with impossible decisions."

This piqued me and put me on my mettle.

"I am not going to run away before the guns fire. Let me hear what you propose."

Sir Walter crossed to a cabinet, unlocked it with a key from his chain, and took a piece of paper from a drawer. It looked like an ordinary half-sheet of note-paper.

"I take it," he said, "that your travels have not extended to the East."

"No," I said, "barring a shooting trip in East Africa."

"Have you by any chance been following the present campaign there?"

"I've read the newspapers pretty regularly since I went to hospital. I've got some pals in the Mesopotamia show, and of course I'm keen to know what is going to happen at Gallipoli and Salonika. I gather that Egypt is pretty safe."

"If you will give me your attention for ten minutes I will supplement your newspaper reading."

Sir Walter lay back in an arm-chair and spoke to the ceiling. It was the best story, the clearest and the fullest, I had ever got of any bit of the war. He told me just how and why and when Turkey had left the rails. I heard about her grievances over our seizure of her ironclads, of the mischief the coming of the *Goeben* had wrought, of Enver and his precious Committee and the way they had got a cinch on the old Turk. When he had spoken for a bit, he began to question me.

"You are an intelligent fellow, and you will ask how a Polish adventurer, meaning Enver, and a collection of Jews and gipsies should have got control of a proud race. The ordinary man will tell you that it was German organization backed up with German money and German arms. You will inquire again how, since Turkey is primarily a religious power, Islam has played so small a part in it all. The Sheikh-ul-Islam is neglected, and though the Kaiser proclaims a Holy War and calls himself Hadji Mohammed Guilliamo, and says the Hohenzollerns are descended from the Prophet, that seems to have fallen pretty flat. The ordinary man again will answer that Islam in Turkey is becoming a back number, and that Krupp guns are the new gods. Yet—I don't know. I do not quite believe in Islam becoming a back number.

"Look at it in another way," he went on. "If it were Enver and

Germany alone dragging Turkey into a European war for purposes that no Turk cared a rush about, we might expect to find the regular army obedient, and Constantinople. But in the provinces, where Islam is strong, there would be trouble. Many of us counted on that. But we have been disappointed. The Syrian army is as fanatical as the hordes of the Mahdi. The Senussi have taken a hand in the game. The Persian Moslems are threatening trouble. There is a dry wind blowing through the East, and the parched grasses wait the spark. And the wind is blowing towards the Indian border. Whence comes that wind, think you?"

Sir Walter had lowered his voice and was speaking very slow and distinct. I could hear the rain dripping from the eaves of the window, and far off the hoot of taxis in Whitehall.

"Have you an explanation, Hannay?" he asked again.

"It looks as if Islam had a bigger hand in the thing than we thought," I said. "I fancy religion is the only thing to knit up such a scattered empire."

"You are right," he said. "You must be right. We have laughed at the Holy War, the Jehad that old Von der Goltz prophesied. But I believe that stupid old man with the big spectacles was right. There is a Jehad preparing. The question is, How?"

"I'm hanged if I know," I said; "but I'll bet it won't be done by a pack of stout German officers in *Pickelhaubes*. I fancy you can't manufacture Holy Wars out of Krupp guns alone and a few staff-officers and a battle cruiser with her boilers burst."

"Agreed. They are not fools, however much we try to persuade ourselves of the contrary. But supposing they had got some tremendous sacred sanction—some holy thing, some book or gospel or some new prophet from the desert, something which would cast over the whole ugly mechanism of German war the glamour of the old torrential raids which crumpled the Byzantine Empire and shook the walls of Vienna? Islam is a fighting creed, and the mullah still stands in the pulpit with the Koran in one hand and a drawn sword in the other. Supposing there is some Ark of the Covenant which will madden the remotest Moslem peasant with dreams of Paradise? What then, my friend?"

"Then there will be hell let loose in those parts pretty soon."

"Hell which may spread. Beyond Persia, remember, lies India."

"You keep to suppositions. How much do you know?" I asked.

"Very little, except the fact. But the fact is beyond dispute. I have reports from agents everywhere—pedlars in South Russia, Afghan horse-dealers, Turcoman merchants, pilgrims on the road to Mecca, sheikhs in North Africa, sailors on the Black Sea coasters, sheep-skinned Mongols, Hindu fakirs, Greek traders in the Gulf, as well as respectable Consuls who use cyphers. They tell the same story. The East is waiting for a revelation. It has been promised one. Some star—man, prophecy, or trinket—is coming out of the West. The Germans know, and that is the card with which they are going to astonish the world."

"And the mission you spoke of for me is to go and find out?"

He nodded gravely. "That is the crazy and impossible mission."

"Tell me one thing, Sir Walter," I said. "I know it is the fashion in this country if a man has a special knowledge to set him to some job exactly the opposite. I know all about Damaraland, but instead of being put on Botha's staff, as I applied to be, I was kept in Hampshire mud till the campaign in German South West Africa was over. I know a man who could pass as an Arab, but do you think they would send him to the East? They left him in my battalion—a lucky thing for me, for he saved my live at Loos. I know the fashion, but isn't this just carrying it a bit too far? There must be thousands of men who have spent years in the East and talk any language. They're the fellows for this job. I never saw a Turk in my life except a chap who did wrestling turns in a show at Kimberley. You've picked about the most useless man on earth."

"You've been a mining engineer, Hannay," Sir Walter said. "If you wanted a man to prospect for gold in Barotseland you would of course like to get one who knew the country and the people and the language. But the first thing you would require in him would be that he had a nose for finding gold and knew his business. That is the position now. I believe that you have a nose for finding out what our enemies try to hide. I know that you are brave and cool and resourceful. That is why I tell you the story. Besides . . ."

He unrolled a big map of Europe on the wall.

"I can't tell you where you'll get on the track of the secret, but I can put a limit to the quest. You won't find it east of the Bosporus—not yet. It is still in Europe. It may be in Constantinople, or in Thrace. It may be farther west. But it is moving eastwards. If you are in time you may cut into its march to Constantinople. That much I can tell you. The secret is known in Germany, too, to those whom it concerns. It is in Europe that the seeker must search—at present."

"Tell me more," I said. "You can give me no details and no instructions. Obviously you can give me no help if I come to grief."

He nodded. "You would be beyond the pale."

"You give me a free hand."

"Absolutely. You can have what money you like, and you can get what help you like. You can follow any plan you fancy, and go anywhere you think fruitful. We can give no directions."

"One last question. You say it is important. Tell me just how important."

"It is life and death," he said solemnly. "I can put it no higher and no lower. Once we know what is the menace we can meet it. As long as we are in the dark it works unchecked and we may be too late. The war must be won or lost in Europe. Yes; but if the East blazes up, our effort will be distracted from Europe and the great *coup* may fail. The stakes are no less than victory and defeat, Hannay."

I got out of my chair and walked to the window. It was a difficult moment in my life. I was happy in my soldiering; above all, happy in the company of my brother officers. I was asked to go off into the enemy's lands on a quest for which I believed I was manifestly unfitted—a business of lonely days and nights, of nerve-racking strain, of deadly peril shrouding me like a garment.

Looking out on the bleak weather I shivered. It was too grim a business, too inhuman for flesh and blood. But Sir Walter had called it a matter of life and death, and I had told him that I was out to serve my country. He could not give me orders, but was I not under orders—higher orders than my Brigadier's? I thought myself incompetent, but cleverer men than me thought me competent, or at least competent enough for a sporting chance. I knew in my soul that if I declined I should never be quite at peace in the world again. And yet Sir Walter had called the scheme madness, and said that he himself would never have accepted.

How does one make a great decision? I swear that when I turned round to speak I meant to refuse. But my answer was Yes, and I had crossed the Rubicon. My voice sounded cracked and far away.

Sir Walter shook hands with me and his eyes blinked a little.

"I may be sending you to your death, Hannay—Good God, what a damned task-mistress duty is!—If so, I shall be haunted with regrets, but *you* will never repent. Have no fear of that. You have chosen the roughest road, but it goes straight to the hill-tops."

He handed me the half-sheet of note-paper. On it were written three words—"*Kasredin,*" "*cancer,*" and "*v. I.*"

"That is the only clue we possess," he said. "I cannot construe it, but I can tell you the story. We have had our agents working in Persia and Mesopotamia for years—mostly young officers of the Indian Army. They carry their lives in their hands, and now and then one disappears, and the sewers of Bagdad might tell a tale. But they find out many things, and they count the game worth the candle. They have told us of the star rising in the West, but they could give us no details. All but one—the best of them. He had been working between Mosul and the Persian frontier as a muleteer, and had been south into the Bakhtiari hills. He found out something, but his enemies knew that he knew and he was pursued. Three months ago, just before Kut, he staggered into Delamain's camp with ten bullet holes in him and a knife slash on his forehead. He mumbled his name, but beyond that and the fact that there was a Something coming from the West he told them nothing. He died in ten minutes. They found this paper on him, and since he cried out the word 'Kasredin' in his last moments, it must have had something to do with his quest. It is for you to find out if it has any meaning."

I folded it up and placed it in my pocket-book.

"What a great fellow! What was his name?" I asked.

Sir Walter did not answer at once. He was looking out of the window. "His name," he said at last, "was Harry Bullivant. He was my son. God rest his brave soul!"

CHAPTER 2

The Gathering of the Missionaries

I WROTE out a wire to Sandy, asking him to come up by the two-fifteen train and meet me at my flat.

"I have chosen my colleague," I said.

"Billy Arbuthnot's boy? His father was at Harrow with me. I know the fellow—Harry used to bring him down to fish—tallish, with a lean, high-boned face and a pair of brown eyes like a pretty girl's. I know his record, too. There's a good deal about him in this office. He rode through Yemen, which no white man ever did before. The Arabs let him pass, for they thought him stark mad and argued that the hand of Allah was heavy enough on him without their efforts. He's blood-brother to every kind of Albanian bandit. Also he used to take a hand in Turkish politics, and got a huge reputation. Some Englishman was once complaining to old Mahmoud Shevkat about the scarcity of statesmen in Western Europe, and Mahmoud broke in with, 'Have you not the Honourable Arbuthnot?' You say he's in your battalion. I was wondering what had become of him, for we tried to get hold of him here, but he had left no address. Ludovick Arbuthnot—yes, that's the man. Buried deep in the commissioned ranks of the New Army? Well, we'll get him out pretty quick!"

"I knew he had knocked about the East, but I didn't know he

was that kind of swell. Sandy's not the chap to buck about himself."

"He wouldn't," said Sir Walter. "He had always a more than Oriental reticence. I've got another colleague for you, if you like him."

He looked at his watch. "You can get to the Savoy Grill Room in five minutes by taxi-cab. Go in from the Strand, turn to your left, and you will see in the alcove on the right-hand side a table with one large American gentleman sitting at it. They know him there, so he will have the table to himself. I want you to go and sit down beside him. Say you come from me. His name is Mr. John Scantlebury Blenkiron, now a citizen of Boston, Mass., but born and raised in Indiana. Put this envelope in your pocket, but don't read its contents till you have talked to him. I want you to form your own opinion about Mr. Blenkiron."

I went out of the Foreign Office in as muddled a frame of mind as any diplomatist who ever left its portals. I was most desperately depressed. To begin with, I was in a complete funk. I had always thought I was about as brave as the average man, but there's courage and courage, and mine was certainly not the impassive kind. Stick me down in a trench and I could stand being shot at as well as most people, and my blood could get hot if it were given the chance. But I think I had too much imagination. I couldn't shake off the beastly forecasts that kept crowding my mind.

In about a fortnight, I calculated, I would be dead. Shot as a spy—a rotten sort of ending! At the moment I was quite safe, looking for a taxi in the middle of Whitehall, but the sweat broke on my forehead. I felt as I had felt in my adventure before the war. But this was far worse, for it was more cold-blooded and premeditated, and I didn't seem to have even a sporting chance. I watched the figures in khaki passing on the pavement, and thought what a nice safe prospect they had compared to mine. Yes, even if next week they were in the Hohenzollern, or the Hairpin trench at the Quarries, or that ugly angle at Hooge. I wondered why I had not been happier that morning before I got that infernal wire. Suddenly all the trivialities of English life seemed to me inexpressibly dear and terribly far away. I was very angry with Bullivant, till I remembered how fair he had been. My fate was my own choosing.

When I was hunting the Black Stone the interest of the problem had helped to keep me going. But now I could see no problem. My mind had nothing to work on but three words of gibberish on a sheet of paper and a mystery of which Sir Walter had been convinced, but to which he couldn't give a name. It was like the story I had read of St. Teresa setting off at the age of ten with her small brother to convert the Moors. I sat huddled in the taxi with my chin on my breast, wishing that I had lost a leg at Loos and been comfortably tucked away for the rest of the war.

Sure enough I found my man in the Grill Room. There he was, feeding solemnly, with a napkin tucked under his chin. He was a big fellow with a fat, sallow, clean-shaven face. I disregarded the hovering waiter and pulled up a chair beside the American at the little table. He turned on me a pair of full sleepy eyes, like a ruminating ox.

"Mr. Blenkiron?" I asked.

"You have my name, sir," he said. "Mr. John Scantlebury Blenkiron. I would wish you a good morning if I saw anything good in this darned British weather."

"I come from Sir Walter Bullivant," I said, speaking low.

"So?" said he. "Sir Walter is a very good friend of mine. Pleased to meet you, Mr.—or I guess it's Colonel—"

"Hannay," I said; "Major Hannay." I was wondering what this sleepy Yankee could do to help me.

"Allow me to offer you luncheon, Major. Here, waiter, bring the *carte*. I regret that I cannot join you in sampling the efforts of the management of this hotel. I suffer, sir, from dyspepsia—duodenal dyspepsia. It gets me two hours after a meal and gives me hell just below the breast-bone. So I am obliged to adopt a diet. My nourishment is fish, sir, and boiled milk and a little dry toast. It's a melancholy descent from the days when I could do justice to a lunch at Sherry's and sup off oyster-crabs and devilled bones." He sighed from the depths of his capacious frame.

I ordered an omelette and a chop, and took another look at him. The large eyes seemed to be gazing steadily at me without seeing me. They were as vacant as an abstracted child's; but I had an uncomfortable feeling that they saw more than mine.

"You have been fighting, Major? The Battle of Loos? Well, I guess that must have been some battle. We in America respect the fighting of the British soldier, but we don't quite catch on to the de-vices of the British Generals. We opine that there is more bellicosity than science among your highbrows. That is so? My father fought at Chattanooga, but these eyes have seen nothing gorier than a Presidential election. Say, is there any way I could be let into a scene of real bloodshed?"

His serious tone made me laugh. "There are plenty of your country-men in the present show," I said. "The French Foreign Legion is full of young Americans, and so is our Army Service Corps. Half the chauffeurs you strike in France seem to come from the States."

He sighed. "I did think of some belligerent stunt a year back. But I reflected that the good God had not given John S. Blenkiron the kind of martial figure that would do credit to the tented field. Also I recollected that we Americans were nootrals—benevolent nootrals—and that it did not become me to be butting into the struggles of the effete monarchies of Europe. So I stopped at home. It was a big renunciation, Major, for I was lying sick during the Philippines business, and I have never seen the lawless passions of men let loose on a battlefield. And, as a stoodent of humanity, I hankered for the experience."

"What have you been doing?" I asked. The calm gentleman had begun to interest me.

"Waal," he said, "I just waited. The Lord has blessed me with money to burn, so I didn't need to go scrambling like a wild cat for war contracts. But I reckoned I would get let into the game somehow, and I was. Being a nootral, I was in an advantageous position to take a hand. I had a pretty hectic time for a while, and then I reckoned I would leave God's country and see what was doing in Europe. I have counted myself out of the bloodshed business, but, as your poet sings, peace has its victories not less renowned than war, and I reckon that means that a nootral can have a share in a scrap as well as a belligerent."

"That's the best kind of neutrality I've ever heard of," I said.

"It's the right kind," he replied solemnly. "Say, Major, what are your lot fighting for? For your own skins and your Empire and the peace of Europe. Waal, those ideals don't concern us one cent. We're not Europeans, and there aren't any German trenches on Long Island yet. You've made the ring in Europe, and if we came butting in it wouldn't be the rules of the game. You wouldn't welcome us, and I guess you'd be right. We're that delicate-minded we can't interfere and that was what my friend, President Wilson, meant when he opined that America was too proud to fight. So we're nootrals. But likewise we're benevolent nootrals. As I follow events, there's a skunk been let loose in the world, and the odour of it is going to make life none too sweet till it is cleared away. It wasn't us that stirred up that skunk, but we've got to take a hand in disinfecting the planet. See? We can't fight, but, by God! some of us are going to sweat blood to sweep the mess up. Officially we do nothing except give off Notes like a leaky boiler gives off steam. But as individooal citizens we're in it up to the neck. So, in the spirit of Jefferson Davis and Woodrow Wilson, I'm going to be the nootralist kind of nootral till Kaiser will be sorry he didn't declare war on America at the beginning."

I was completely recovering my temper. This fellow was a perfect jewel, and his spirit put purpose into me.

"I guess you British were the same kind of nootral when your Admiral warned off the German fleet from interfering with Dewey in Manila Bay in '98." Mr. Blenkiron drank up the last drop of his boiled milk, and lit a thin black cigar.

I leaned forward. "Have you talked to Sir Walter?" I asked.

"I have talked to him, and he has given me to understand that there's a deal ahead which you're going to boss. There are no flies on that big man, and if he says it's good business then you can count me in."

"You know that it's uncommonly dangerous?"

"I judged so. But it don't do to begin counting risks. I believe in an all-wise beneficent Providence, but you have got to trust Him and give Him a chance. What's life anyhow? For me, it's living on a strict diet and having frequent pains in my stomach. It isn't such an almighty lot to give up, provided you get a good price in the deal. Besides, how big is the risk? About one o'clock in the morning, when you can't sleep, it will be the size of Mount Everest, but if you run out to meet it, it will be a hillock you can jump over. The grizzly looks very fierce when you're taking your ticket for the Rockies and wondering if you'll come back, but he's just an ordinary bear when you've got the sight of your rifle on him. I won't think about risks till I'm up to my neck in them and don't see the road out."

I scribbled my address on a piece of paper and handed it to the stout philosopher. "Come to dinner to-night at eight," I said.

"I thank you, Major. A little fish, please, plain-boiled, and some hot milk. You will forgive me if I borrow your couch after the meal and spend the evening on my back. That is the advice of my noo doctor."

I got a taxi and drove to my club. On the way I opened the envelope Sir Walter had given me. It contained a number of jottings, the dossier of Mr. Blenkiron. He had done wonders for the Allies in the States. He had nosed out the Dumba plot, and had been instrumental in getting the portfolio of Dr. Albert. Von Papen's spies had tried to murder him, after he had defeated an attempt to blow up one of the big gun factories. Sir Walter had written at the end: "The best man we ever had. Better than Scudder. He would go through hell with a box of bismuth tablets and a pack of Patience cards."

I went into the little back smoking-room, borrowed an atlas from the library, poked up the fire, and sat down to think. Mr. Blenkiron had given me the fillip I needed. My mind was beginning to work now, and was running wide over the whole business. Not that I hoped to find anything by my cogitations. It wasn't thinking in an arm-chair that would solve the mystery.

But I was getting a sort of grip on a plan of operations. And to my relief I had stopped thinking about the risks. Blenkiron had shamed me out of that. If a sedentary dyspeptic could show that kind of nerve, I wasn't going to be behind him.

I went back to my flat about five o'clock. My man Paddock had gone to the wars long ago, so I had shifted to one of the new blocks in Park Lane where they provide food and service. I kept the place on to have a home to go to when I got leave. It's a miserable business holidaying in an hotel.

Sandy was devouring tea-cakes with the serious resolution of a convalescent.

"Well, Dick, what's the news? Is it a brass-hat or the boot?"

"Neither," I said. "But you and I are going to disappear from His Majesty's forces. Seconded for special service."

"Oh my sainted aunt!" said Sandy. "What is it? For Heaven's sake put me out of pain. Have we to tout deputations of suspicious neutrals over munition works or take the shivering journalist in a motor-car where he can imagine he sees a Boche?"

"The news will keep. But I can tell you this much. It's about as safe and easy as to go through the German lines with a walking-stick."

"Come, that's not so dusty," said Sandy, and began cheerfully on the muffins.

I must spare a moment to introduce Sandy to the reader, for he cannot be allowed to slip into this tale by a side-door. If you will consult the Peerage you will find that to Edward Cospatrick, fifteenth Baron Clanroyden, there was born in the year 1882, as his second son, Ludovick Gustavus Arbuthnot, commonly called the Honourable, etc. The said son was educated at Eton and New College, Oxford, was a captain in the Tweeddale Yeomanry, and served for some years as honorary attaché at various embassies. The Peerage will stop short at this point, but that is by no means the end of the story. For the rest you must consult very different authorities. Lean brown men from the ends of the earth may be seen on the London pavements now and then in creased clothes, walking with the light outland step, slinking into clubs as if they could not remember whether or not they belonged to them. From them you may get news of Sandy. Better still, you will hear of him at little forgotten fishing ports where the Albanian mountains dip to the Adriatic. If you struck a Mecca pilgrimage the odds are you would meet a dozen of Sandy's friends in it. In shepherds' huts in the Caucasus you will find bits of his cast-off clothing, for he has a knack of shedding garments as he goes. In the caravanserais of Bokhara and Samarkand he is known, and there are shikaris in the Pamirs who still speak of him around their fires. If you were going to visit Petrograd or Rome or Cairo it would be no use asking him for introductions; if he gave them, they would lead you into strange haunts. But if Fate compelled you to go to Llasa or Yarkand or Seistan he could map out your road for you and pass the word to potent friends. We call ourselves insular, but the truth is that we are the only race on earth that can produce men capable of getting inside the skin of remote peoples. Perhaps the Scots are better than the English, but we're all a thousand per cent better than anybody else. Sandy was the wandering Scot carried to the pitch of genius. In old days he would have led a crusade or discovered a new road to the Indies. To-day he merely roamed as the spirit moved him, till the war swept him up and dumped him down in my battalion.

I got out Sir Walter's half-sheet of note-paper. It was not the original—naturally he wanted to keep that—but it was a careful tracing. I took it that Harry Bullivant had not written down the words as a memo for his own use. People who follow his career have good memories. He must have written them in order that, if he perished and his body was found, his friends might get a clue. Wherefore, I argued, the words must be intelligible to somebody or other of our persuasion, and likewise they must be pretty well gibberish to any Turk or German that found them.

The first, "*Kasredin*," I could make nothing of.

I asked Sandy.

"You mean Nasr-ed-din," he said, still munching crumpets.

"What's that?" I asked sharply.

"He's the General believed to be commanding against us in Mesopotamia. I remember him years ago in Aleppo. He talked bad French and drank the sweetest of sweet champagne."

I looked closely at the paper. The "K" was unmistakable.

"Kasredin is nothing. It means in Arabic the House of Faith, and might cover anything from Hagia Sofia to a suburban villa. What's your next puzzle, Dick? Have you entered for a prize competition in a weekly paper?"

"*Cancer*," I read out.

"It is the Latin for a crab. Likewise it is the name of a painful disease. It is also a sign of the Zodiac."

"*v. I*," I read.

"There you have me. It sounds like the number of a motor-car. The police would find out for you. I call this a rather difficult competition. What's the prize?"

I passed him the paper. "Who wrote it? It looks as if he had been in a hurry."

"Harry Bullivant," I said.

Sandy's face grew solemn. "Old Harry. He was at my tutor's. The best fellow God ever made. I saw his name in the casualty list before Kut . . . Harry didn't do things without a purpose. What's the story of this paper?"

"Wait till after dinner," I said. "I'm going to change and have a bath. There's an American coming to dine, and he's part of the business."

Mr. Blenkiron arrived punctual to the minute in a fur coat like a Russian prince's. Now that I saw him on his feet I could judge him better. He had a fat face, but was not too plump in figure, and very muscular wrists showed below his shirt-cuffs. I fancied that, if the occasion called, he might be a good man with his hands.

Sandy and I ate a hearty meal, but the American picked at his boiled fish and sipped his milk a drop at a time. When the servant had cleared away, he was as good as his word and laid himself out on my sofa. I offered him a good cigar, but he preferred one of his own lean black abominations. Sandy stretched his length in an easy-chair and lit his pipe. "Now for your story, Dick," he said.

I began, as Sir Walter had begun with me, by telling them about the puzzle in the Near East. I pitched a pretty good yarn, for I had been thinking a lot about it, and the mystery of the business had caught my fancy. Sandy got very keen.

"It is possible enough. Indeed, I've been expecting it, though I'm hanged if I can imagine what card the Germans have got up their sleeve. It might be any one of twenty things. Thirty years ago there was a bogus prophecy that played the devil in Yemen. Or it might be a flag such as Ali Wad Helu had, or a jewel like Solomon's necklace in Abyssinia. You never know what will start off a Jehad! But I rather think it's a man."

"Where could he get his purchase?" I asked.

"It's hard to say. If it were merely wild tribesmen like the Bed-ouin he might have got a reputation as a saint and miracle-worker. Or he might be a fellow that preached a pure religion, like the chap that founded the Senussi. But I'm inclined to think he must be something extra special if he can put a spell on the whole Moslem world. The Turk and the Persian wouldn't follow the ordinary new theology game. He must be of the Blood. Your Mahdis and Mullahs and Imams were nobodies, but they had only a local prestige. To capture all Islam—and I gather that is what we fear—the man must be of the Koreish, the tribe of the Prophet himself."

"But how could any impostor prove that? For I suppose he's an impostor."

"He would have to combine a lot of claims. His descent must be pretty good to begin with, and there are families, remember, that claim the Koreish blood. Then he'd have to be rather a won-der on his own account—saintly, eloquent, and that sort of thing. And I expect he'd have to show a sign, though what that could be I haven't a notion."

"You know the East about as well as any living man. Do you think that kind of thing is possible?" I asked.

"Perfectly," said Sandy, with a grave face.

"Well, there's the ground cleared to begin with. Then there's the evidence of pretty well every secret agent we possess. That all seems to prove the fact. But we have no details and no clues except that bit of paper." I told them the story of it.

Sandy studied it with wrinkled brows. "It beats me. But it may be the key for all that. A clue may be dumb in London and shout aloud at Bagdad."

"That's just the point I was coming to. Sir Walter says this thing is about as important for our cause as big guns. He can't give me orders, but he offers the job of going out to find what the mischief is. Once he knows that, he says he can checkmate it. But it's got to be found out soon, for the mine may be sprung at any moment. I've taken on the job. Will you help?"

Sandy was studying the ceiling.

"I should add that it's about as safe as playing chuck-farthing at the Loos Cross-roads, the day you and I went in. And if we fail nobody can help us."

"Oh, of course, of course," said Sandy in an abstracted voice.

Mr. Blenkiron, having finished his after-dinner recumbency, had sat up and pulled a small table towards him. From his pocket he had taken a pack of Patience cards and had begun to play the game called the Double Napoleon. He seemed to be oblivious of the conversation.

Suddenly I had the feeling that the whole affair was stark lunacy. Here were we three simpletons sitting in a London flat and projecting a mission into the enemy's citadel without an idea what we were to do or how we were to do it. And one of the three was looking at the ceiling, and whistling softly through his teeth, and another was playing Patience. The farce of the thing struck me so keenly that I laughed.

Sandy looked at me sharply. "You feel like that? Same with me. It's idiocy, but all war is idiotic, and the most whole-hearted idiot is apt to win. We're to go on this mad trail wherever we think we can hit it. Well, I'm with you. But I don't mind admitting that I'm in a blue funk. I had got myself adjusted to this trench business and was quite happy. And now you have hoicked me out, and my feet are cold."

"I don't believe you know what fear is," I said.

"There you're wrong, Dick," he said earnestly. "Every man who isn't a maniac knows fear. I have done some daft things, but I never started on them without wishing they were over. Once I'm in the show I get easier, and by the time I'm coming out I'm sorry to leave it. But at the start my feet are icy."

"Then I take it you're coming?"

"Rather," he said. "You didn't imagine I would go back on you?"

"And you, sir?" I addressed Blenkiron.

His game of Patience seemed to be coming out. He was completing eight little heaps of cards with a contented grunt. As I spoke, he raised his sleepy eyes and nodded.

"Why, yes," he said. "You gentlemen mustn't think that I haven't been following your most engrossing conversation. I guess I haven't missed a syllable. I find that a game of Patience stimulates the digestion after meals and conduces to quiet reflection. John S. Blenkiron is with you all the time."

He shuffled the cards and dealt for a new game.

I don't think I ever expected a refusal, but this ready assent cheered me wonderfully. I couldn't have faced the thing alone.

"Well, that's settled. Now for ways and means. We three have got to put ourselves in the way of finding out Germany's secret, and we have to go where it is known. Somehow or other we have to reach Constantinople, and to beat the biggest area of country we must go by different roads. Sandy, my lad, you've got to get into Turkey. You're the only one of us that knows that engaging people. You can't get in by Europe very easily, so you must try Asia. What about the coast of Asia Minor?"

"It could be done," he said. "You'd better leave that entirely to me. I'll find out the best way. I suppose the Foreign Office will help me to get to the jumping-off place?"

"Remember," I said, "it's no good getting too far east. The secret, so far as concerns us, is still west of Constantinople."

"I see that. I'll blow in on the Bosporus by a short tack."

"For you, Mr. Blenkiron, I would suggest a straight journey. You're an American, and can travel through Germany direct. But I wonder how far your activities in New York will allow you to pass as a neutral?"

"I have considered that, sir," he said. "I have given some thought to the pecooliar psychology of the great German nation. As I read them they're as cunning as cats, and if you play the feline game they will outwit you every time. Yes, sir, they are no slouches at sleuth-work. If I were to buy a pair of false whiskers and dye my hair and dress like a Baptist parson and go into Germany on the peace racket, I guess they'd be on my trail like a knife, and I should be shot as a spy inside of a week or doing solitary in the Moabit prison. But they lack the larger vision. They can be bluffed, sir. With your approval I shall visit the Fatherland as John S. Blenkiron, once a thorn in the side of their brightest boys on the other side. But it will be a different John S. I reckon he will have experienced a change of heart. He will have come to appreciate the great, pure, noble soul of Germany, and he will be sorrowing for his past like a converted gun-man at a camp meeting. He will be a victim of the meanness and perfidy of the British Government. I am going to have a first-class row with your Foreign Office about my passport, and I am going to speak harsh words about them up and down this metropolis. I am going to be shadowed by your sleuths at my port of embarkation, and I guess I shall run up hard against the British Legations in Scandinavia. By that time our Teutonic friends will have begun to wonder what has happened to John S., and to think that maybe they have been mistaken in that child. So, when I get to Germany they will be waiting for me with an open mind. Then I judge my conduct will surprise and encourage them. I will confide to them valuable secret information about British preparations, and I will show up the British lion as the meanest kind of cur. You may trust me to make a good impression. After that I'll move eastwards, to see the demolition of the British Empire in those parts. By the way, where is the rendezvous?"

"This is the 17th day of November. If we can't find out what we want in two months we may chuck the job. On the 17th of January we should forgather in Constantinople. You fix the meeting-place."

"I've already thought of that," he said, and going to the writing-table he drew a little plan on a sheet of paper. "That lane runs down from the Kurdish Bazaar in Galata to the ferry of Ratchik. Halfway down on the left-hand side is a café kept by a Greek called Kuprasso. Behind the café is a garden, surrounded by high walls which were parts of the old Byzantine Theatre. At the end of the garden is a shanty called the Garden-House of Suliman the Red. It has been in its time a dancing-hall and a gambling hell and God knows what else. It's not a place for respectable people, but the ends of the earth converge there and no questions are asked. That's the best spot I can think of for a meeting-place."

The kettle was simmering by the fire, the night was raw, and it seemed the hour for whisky-punch. I made a brew for Sandy and myself and boiled some milk for Blenkiron.

"What about language?" I asked. "You're all right, Sandy?"

"I know German fairly well; and I can pass anywhere as a Turk. The first will do for eavesdropping and the second for ordinary business."

"And you?" I asked Blenkiron.

"I was left out at Pentecost," he said. "I regret to confess I have no gift of tongues. But the part I have chosen for myself don't require the polyglot. Never forget I'm plain John S. Blenkiron, a citizen of the great American Republic."

"You haven't told us your own line, Dick," Sandy said.

"I am going to the Bosporus through Germany, and, not being a neutral, it won't be a very cushioned journey."

Sandy looked grave.

"That sounds pretty desperate. Is your German good enough?"

"Pretty fair; quite good enough to pass as a native. But officially I shall not understand one word. I shall be a Boer from Western Cape Colony: one of Maritz's old lot who after a bit of trouble has got through Angola and reached Europe. I shall talk Dutch and nothing else. And, my hat! I shall be pretty bitter about the British. There's a powerful lot of good swear-words in the *taal*. I shall know all about Africa, and be panting to get another whack at the *verdommt rooinek*. With luck they may send me to the Uganda show or to Egypt, and I shall take care to go by Constantinople. If I'm to deal with the Mohammedan natives they're bound to show me what hand they hold. At least, that's the way I look at it."

We filled our glasses—two of punch and one of milk—and drank to our next merry meeting. Then Sandy began to laugh, and I joined in. The sense of hopeless folly again descended on me. The best plans we could make were like a few buckets of water to ease the drought of the Sahara or the old lady who would have stopped the Atlantic with a broom. I thought with sympathy of little St. Teresa.

CHAPTER 3

Peter Pienaar

OUR various departures were unassuming, all but the American's. Sandy spent a busy fortnight in his subterranean fashion, now in the British Museum, now running about the country to see old exploring companions, now at the War Office, now at the Foreign Office, but mostly in my flat, sunk in an arm-chair and meditating. He left finally on December 1 as a King's Messenger for Cairo. Once there I knew the King's Messenger would disappear, and some queer Oriental ruffian take his place. It would have been impertinence in me to inquire into his plans. He was the real professional, and I was only a dabbler.

Blenkiron was a different matter. Sir Walter told me to look out for squalls, and the twinkle in his eye gave me a notion of what was coming. The first thing the sportsman did was to write a letter to the papers signed with his name. There had been a debate in the House of Commons on foreign policy, and the speech of some idiot there gave him his cue. He declared that he had been heart and soul with the British at the start, but that he was reluctantly compelled to change his views. He said our blockade of Germany had broken all the laws of God and humanity, and he reckoned that Britain was now the worst exponent of Prussianism going. That letter made a fine racket, and the paper that printed it had a row with the Censor.

But that was only the beginning of Mr. Blenkiron's campaign. He got mixed up with some mountebanks called the League of Democrats against Aggression, gentlemen who thought that Germany was all right if we could only keep from hurting her feelings. He addressed a meeting under their auspices, which was broken up by the crowd, but not before John S. had got off his chest a lot of amazing stuff. I wasn't there, but a man who was told me that he never heard such clotted nonsense. He said that Germany was right in wanting the freedom of the seas, and that America would back her up, and that the British Navy was a bigger menace to the peace of the world than the Kaiser's army. He admitted that he had once thought differently, but he was an honest man and not afraid to face facts. The oration closed suddenly, when he got a brussels-sprout in the eye, at which my friend said he swore in a very unpacifist style.

After that he wrote other letters to the Press, saying that there was no more liberty of speech in England, and a lot of scallywags backed him up. Some Americans wanted to tar and feather him, and he got kicked out of the Savoy. There was an agitation to get him deported, and questions were asked in Parliament, and the Under-Secretary for Foreign Affairs said his department had the matter in hand. I was beginning to think that Blenkiron was carrying his tomfoolery too far, so I went to see Sir Walter, but he told me to keep my mind easy.

"Our friend's motto is 'Thorough,' " he said, "and he knows very well what he is about. We have officially requested him to leave, and he sails from Newcastle on Monday. He will be shadowed wherever he goes, and we hope to provoke more outbreaks. He is a very capable fellow."

The last I saw of him was on the Saturday afternoon when I met him in St. James's Street and offered to shake hands. He told me that my uniform was a pollution, and made a speech to a small crowd about it. They hissed him and he had to get into a taxi. As he departed there was just the suspicion of a wink in his left eye. On Monday I read that he had gone off, and the papers observed that our shores were well quit of him.

I sailed on December 3 from Liverpool in a boat bound for the Argentine that was due to put in at Lisbon. I had of course to get a Foreign Office passport to leave England, but after that my connexion with the Government ceased. All the details of my journey were carefully thought out. Lisbon would be a good jumping-off place, for it was the rendezvous of scallywags from most parts of Africa. My kit was an old Gladstone bag, and my clothes were the relics of my South African wardrobe. I let my beard grow for some days before I sailed, and, since it grows fast, I went on board with the kind of hairy chin you will see on the young Boer. My name was now Brandt, Cornelis Brandt—at least so my passport said, and passports never lie.

There were just two other passengers on that beastly boat, and they never appeared till we were out of the Bay. I was pretty bad myself, but managed to move about all the time, for the frowst in my cabin would have sickened a hippo. The old tub took two days and a night to waddle from Ushant to Finisterre. Then the weather changed and we came out of snow-squalls into something very like summer. The hills of Portugal were all blue and yellow like the Kalahari, and before we made the Tagus I was beginning to forget I had ever left Rhodesia. There was a Dutchman among the sailors with whom I used to patter the *taal*, and but for "Good morning" and "Good evening" in broken English to the captain, that was about all the talking I did on the cruise.

We dropped anchor off the quays of Lisbon on a shiny blue morning, pretty near warm enough to wear flannels. I had now got to be very wary. I did not leave the ship with the shore-going boat, but made a leisurely breakfast. Then I strolled on deck, and there, just casting anchor in the middle of the stream, was another ship with the blue and white funnel I knew so well. I calculated that a month before she had been smelling the mangrove swamps of Angola. Nothing could better answer my purpose. I proposed to board her, pretending I was looking for a friend, and come on shore from her, so that anyone in Lisbon who chose to be curious would think I had landed straight from Portuguese Africa.

I hailed one of the adjacent ruffians, and got into his row-boat, with my kit. We reached the vessel—they called her the *Henry the Navigator*—just as the first shore-boat was leaving. The crowd in it were all Portuguese, which suited my book.

But when I went up the ladder the first man I met was old Peter Pienaar.

Here was a piece of sheer monumental luck. Peter had opened his eyes and his mouth, and had got as far as *"Allemachtig,"* when I shut him up.

"Brandt," I said, "Cornelis Brandt. That's my name now, and don't you forget it. Who is the captain here? Is it still old Sloggett?"

"Ja," said Peter, pulling himself together. "He was speaking about you yesterday."

This was better and better. I sent Peter below to get hold of Sloggett, and presently I had a few words with that gentleman in his cabin with the door shut.

"You've got to enter my name in the ship's books. I came aboard at Mossamedes. And my name's Cornelis Brandt."

At first Sloggett was for objecting. He said it was a felony. I told him that I dared say it was, but he had got to do it, for reasons which I couldn't give, but which were highly creditable to all parties. In the end he agreed, and I saw it done. I had a pull on old Sloggett, for I had known him ever since he owned a dissolute tug-boat at Delagoa Bay.

Then Peter and I went ashore and swaggered into Lisbon as if we owned De Beers. We put up at the big hotel opposite the railway station, and looked and behaved like a pair of low-bred South Africans home for a spree. It was a fine bright day, so I hired a motor-car and said I would drive it myself. We asked the name of some beauty-spot to visit, and were told Cintra and shown the road to it. I wanted a quiet place to talk, for I had a good deal to say to Peter Pienaar.

I christened that car the Lusitanian Terror, and it was a marvel that we did not smash ourselves up. There was something immortally wrong with its steering gear. Half a dozen times we slewed across the road, inviting destruction. But we got there in the end, and had luncheon in an hotel opposite the Moorish palace. There we left the car and wandered up the slopes of a hill, where, sitting among scrub very like the veld, I told Peter the situation of affairs.

But first a word must be said about Peter. He was the man that taught me all I ever knew of veldcraft, and a good deal about human nature besides. He was out of the Old Colony—Burgersdorp, I think—but he had come to the Transvaal when the Lydenburg goldfields started. He was prospector, transport-rider, and hunter in turns, but principally hunter. In those early days he was none too good a citizen. He was in Swaziland with Bob Macnab, and you know what that means. Then he took to working off bogus gold propositions on Kimberley and Johannesburg magnates, and what he didn't know about salting a mine wasn't knowledge. After that he was in the Kalahari, where he and Scotty Smith were familiar names. An era of comparative respectability dawned for him with the Matabele War, when he did uncommon good scouting and transport work. Cecil Rhodes wanted to establish him on a stock farm down Salisbury way, but Peter was an independent devil and would call no man master. He took to big-game hunting, which was what God intended him for, for he could track a tsessebe in thick bush, and was far the finest shot I have seen in my life. He took parties to the Pungwe flats, and Barotseland, and up to Tanganyika. Then he made a speciality of the Ngami region, where I once hunted with him, and he was with me when I went prospecting in Damaraland.

When the Boer War started, Peter, like many of the very great hunters, took the British side and did most of our intelligence work in the North Transvaal. Beyers would have hanged him if he could have caught him, and there was no love lost between Peter and his own people for many a day. When it was all over and things had calmed down a bit, he settled in Bulawayo and used to go with me when I went on trek. At the time when I left Africa two years before, I had lost sight of him for months, and heard that he was somewhere on the Congo poaching elephants.

He had always a great idea of making things hum so loud in Angola that the Union Government would have to step in and annex it. After Rhodes Peter had the biggest notions south of the Line.

He was a man of about five foot ten, very thin and active, and as strong as a buffalo. He had pale blue eyes, a face as gentle as a girl's, and a soft sleepy voice. From his present appearance it looked as if he had been living hard lately. His clothes were of the cut you might expect to get at Lobito Bay, he was as lean as a rake, deeply browned with the sun, and there was a lot of grey in his beard. He was fifty-six years old, and used to be taken for forty. Now he looked about his age.

I first asked him what he had been up to since the war began. He spat, in the Kaffir way he had, and said he had been having hell's time.

"I got hung up on the Kafue," he said. "When I heard from old Letsitela that the white men were fighting I had a bright idea that I might get into German South West from the north. You see I knew that Botha couldn't long keep out of the war. Well, I got into German territory all right, and then a *skellum* of an officer came along, and commandeered all my mules, and wanted to commandeer me with them for his fool army. He was a very ugly man with a yellow face." Peter filled a deep pipe from a kudu-skin pouch.

"Were you commandeered?" I asked.

"No. I shot him—not so as to kill, but to wound badly. It was all right, for he fired first on me. Got me too in the left shoulder. But that was the beginning of bad trouble. I trekked east pretty fast, and got over the border among the Ovamba. I have made many journeys, but that was the worst. Four days I went without water, and six without food. Then by bad luck I fell in with 'Nkitla—you remember, the half-caste chief. He said I owed him money for cattle which I bought when I came there with Carowab. It was a lie, but he held to it, and would give me no transport. So I crossed the Kalahari on my feet. Ugh, it was as slow as a vrouw coming from *nachtmaal*. It took weeks and weeks, and when I came to Lechwe's kraal, I heard that the fighting was over and that Botha had conquered the Germans. That, too, was a lie, but it deceived me, and I went north into Rhodesia, where I learned the truth. But by then I judged the war had gone too far for me to make any profit out of it, so I went into Angola to look for German refugees. By that time I was hating Germans worse than hell."

"But what did you propose to do with them?" I asked.

"I had a notion they would make trouble with the Government in those parts. I don't specially love the Portugoose, but I'm for him against the Germans every day. Well, there was trouble, and I had a merry time for a month or two. But by and by it petered out, and I thought I had better clear for Europe, for South Africa was settling down just as the big show was getting really interesting. So here I am, Cornelis, my old friend. If I shave my beard will they let me join the Flying Corps?"

I looked at Peter sitting there smoking, as imperturbable as if he had been growing mealies in Natal all his life and had run home for a month's holiday with his people in Peckham.

"You're coming with me, my lad," I said. "We're going into Germany."

Peter showed no surprise. "Keep in mind that I don't like the Germans," was all he said. "I'm a quiet Christian man, but I've the devil of a temper."

Then I told him the story of our mission.

"You and I have got to be Maritz's men. We went into Angola, and now we're trekking for the Fatherland to get a bit of our own back from the infernal English. Neither of us knows any German—publicly. We'd better plan out the fighting we were in—Kakamas will do for one, and Schuit Drift. You were a Ngamiland hunter before the war. They won't have your dossier, so you can tell any lie you like. I'd better be an educated Afrikander, one of Beyer's bright lads, and a pal of old Hertzog. We can let our imagination loose about that part, but we must stick to the same yarn about the fighting."

"*Ja*, Cornelis," said Peter. (He had called me Cornelis ever since I had told him my new name. He was a wonderful chap for catching on to any game.) "But after we get into Germany, what then? There can't be much difficulty about the beginning. But once we're among the beer-swillers I don't quite see our line. We're to find out about something that's going on in Turkey? When I was a boy the predikant used to preach about Turkey. I wish I was better educated and remembered whereabouts in the map it was."

"You leave that to me," I said; "I'll explain it all to you before we get there. We haven't got much of a spoor, but we'll cast about, and with luck will pick it up. I've seen you do it often enough when we hunted kudu on the Kafue."

Peter nodded. "Do we sit still in a German town?" he asked anxiously. "I shouldn't like that, Cornelis."

"We move gently eastward to Constantinople," I said.

Peter grinned. "We should cover a lot of new country. You can reckon on me, friend Cornelis. I've always had a hankering to see Europe."

He rose to his feet and stretched his long arms.

"We'd better begin at once. God, I wonder what's happened to old Solly Maritz, with his bottle face? Yon was a fine battle at the drift when I was sitting up to my neck in the Orange praying that Brits' lads would take my head for a stone."

Peter was as thorough a mountebank, when he got started, as Blenkiron himself. All the way back to Lisbon he yarned about Maritz and his adventures in German South West till I half believed they were true. He made a very good story of our doings, and by his constant harping on it I pretty soon got it into my memory. That was always Peter's way. He said if you were going to play a part, you must think yourself into it, convince yourself that you were *it*, till you really were it and didn't act but behaved naturally. The two men who had started that morning from the hotel door had been bogus enough, but the two men that returned were genuine desperadoes itching to get a shot at England.

We spent the evening piling up evidence in our favour. Some

kind of republic had been started in Portugal, and ordinarily the cafés would have been full of politicians, but the war had quieted all these local squabbles, and the talk was of nothing but what was doing in France and Russia. The place we went to was a big, well-lighted show on a main street, and there were a lot of sharp-eyed fellows wandering about that I guessed were spies and police agents. I knew that Britain was the one country that doesn't bother about this kind of game, and that it would be safe enough to let ourselves go.

I talked Portuguese fairly well, and Peter spoke it like a Lourenço Marques bar-keeper, with a lot of Shangaan words to fill up. He started on curaçao, which I reckoned was a new drink to him, and presently his tongue ran freely. Several neighbours pricked up their ears, and soon we had a small crowd round our table.

We talked to each other of Maritz and our doings. It didn't seem to be a popular subject in that café. One big blue-black fellow said that Maritz was a dirty swine who would soon be hanged. Peter quickly caught his knife-wrist with one hand and his throat with the other, and demanded an apology. He got it. The Lisbon *boulevardiers* have not lost any lions.

After that there was a bit of a squash in our corner. Those near to us were very quiet and polite, but the outer fringe made remarks. When Peter said that if Portugal, which he admitted he loved, was going to stick to England she was backing the wrong horse, there was a murmur of disapproval. One decent-looking fellow, who had the air of a ship's captain, flushed all over his honest face, and stood up looking straight at Peter. I saw that we had struck an Englishman, and mentioned it to Peter in Dutch.

Peter played his part perfectly. He suddenly shut up, and, with furtive looks around him, began to jabber to me in a low voice. He was the very picture of the old stage conspirator.

The old fellow stood staring at us. "I don't very well understand this damned lingo," he said; "but if so be you dirty Dutchmen are sayin' anything against England, I'll ask you to repeat it. And if so be as you repeats it I'll take either of you on and knock the face off him."

He was a chap after my own heart, but I had to keep the game up. I said in Dutch to Peter that we mustn't get brawling in a public-house. "Remember the big thing," I said darkly. Peter nodded, and the old fellow, after staring at us for a bit, spat scornfully, and walked out.

"The time is coming when the Englander will sing small," I observed to the crowd. We stood drinks to one or two, and then swaggered into the street. At the door a hand touched my arm, and, looking down, I saw a little scrap of a man in a fur coat.

"Will the gentleman walk a step with me and drink a glass of beer?" he said in very stiff Dutch.

"Who the devil are you?" I asked.

"*Gott strafe England!*" was his answer, and, turning back the lapel of his coat, he showed some kind of ribbon in his buttonhole.

"Amen," said Peter. "Lead on, friend. We don't mind if we do."

He led us to a back street and then up two pairs of stairs to a very snug little flat. The place was filled with fine red lacquer, and I guessed that art-dealing was his nominal business. Portugal, since the republic broke up the convents and sold up the big royalist grandees, was full of bargains in the lacquer and curio line.

He filled us two long tankards of very good Munich beer.

"*Prosit*," he said, raising his glass. "You are from South Africa. What make you in Europe?"

We both looked sullen and secretive.

"That's our own business," I answered. "You don't expect to buy our confidence with a glass of beer."

"So?" he said. "Then I will put it differently. From your speech in the café I judge you do not love the English."

Peter said something about stamping on their grandmothers, a Kaffir phrase which sounded gruesome in Dutch.

The man laughed. "That is all I want to know. You are on the German side?"

"That remains to be seen," I said. "If they treat me fair I'll fight for them, or for anybody else that makes war on England.

England has stolen my country and corrupted my people and made me an exile. We Afrikanders do not forget. We may be slow but we win in the end. We two are men worth a great price. Germany fights England in East Africa. We know the natives as no Englishmen can ever know them. They are too soft and easy and the Kaffirs laugh at them. But we can handle the blacks so that they will fight like devils for fear of us. What is the reward, little man, for our services? I will tell you. There will be no reward. We ask none. We fight for hate of England."

Peter grunted a deep approval.

"That is good talk," said our entertainer, and his close-set eyes flashed. "There is room in Germany for such men as you. Where are you going now, I beg to know?"

"To Holland," I said. "Then maybe we will go to Germany. We are tired with travel and may rest a bit. This war will last long and our chance will come."

"But you may miss your market," he said significantly. "A ship sails to-morrow for Rotterdam. If you take my advice, you will go with her."

This was what I wanted, for if we stayed in Lisbon some real soldier of Maritz might drop in any day and blow the gaff.

"I recommend you to sail in the *Machado*," he repeated. "There is work for you in Germany—oh yes, much work; but if you delay the chance may pass. I will arrange your journey. It is my business to help the allies of my fatherland."

He wrote down our names and an epitome of our doings contributed by Peter, who required two mugs of beer to help him through. He was a Bavarian, it seemed, and we drank to the health of Prince Rupprecht, the same blighter I was trying to do in at Loos. That was an irony which Peter unfortunately could not appreciate. If he could he would have enjoyed it.

The little chap saw us back to our hotel, and was with us the next morning after breakfast, bringing the steamer tickets. We got on board about two in the afternoon, but on my advice he did not see us off. I told him that, being British subjects and rebels at that, we did not want to run any risks on board, assuming a

British cruiser caught us up and searched us. But Peter took twenty pounds off him for travelling expenses, it being his rule never to miss an opportunity of spoiling the Egyptians.

As we were dropping down the Tagus we passed the old *Henry the Navigator.*

"I met Sloggett in the street this morning," said Peter, "and he told me a little German man had been off in a boat at daybreak looking up the passenger list. Yon was a right notion of yours, Cornelis. I am glad we are going among Germans. They are careful people whom it is a pleasure to meet."

CHAPTER 4

Adventures of Two Dutchmen on the Loose

THE Germans, as Peter said, are a careful people. A man met us on the quay at Rotterdam. I was a bit afraid that something might have turned up in Lisbon to discredit us, and that our little friend might have warned his pals by telegram. But apparently all was serene.

Peter and I had made our plans pretty carefully on the voyage. We had talked nothing but Dutch, and had kept up between ourselves the rôle of Maritz's men, which Peter said was the only way to play a part well. Upon my soul, before we got to Holland I was not very clear in my own mind what my past had been. Indeed the danger was that the other side of my mind, which should be busy with the great problem, would get atrophied, and that I should soon be mentally on a par with the ordinary backveld desperado. We had agreed that it would be best to get into Germany at once, and when the agent on the quay told us of a train at midday we decided to take it.

I had another fit of cold feet before we got over the frontier. At the station there was a King's Messenger whom I had seen in France, and a war correspondent who had been trotting round our part of the front before Loos. I heard a woman speaking pretty clean-cut English, which amid the hoarse Dutch jabber sounded like a lark among crows. There were copies of the

English papers for sale, and English cheap editions. I felt pretty bad about the whole business, and wondered if I should ever see these homely sights again.

But the mood passed when the train started. It was a clear blowing day, and as we crawled through the flat pastures of Holland my time was taken up answering Peter's questions. He had never been in Europe before, and formed a high opinion of the farming. He said he reckoned that such land would carry four sheep a morgen. We were thick in talk when we reached the frontier station and jolted over a canal bridge into Germany.

I had expected a big barricade with barbed wire and entrenchments. But there was nothing to see on the German side but half a dozen sentries in the field-grey I had hunted at Loos. An under-officer, with the black-and-gold button of the Landsturm, hoicked us out of the train, and we were all shepherded in a big bare waiting-room where a large stove burned. They took us two at a time into an inner room for examination. I had explained to Peter all about this formality, but I was glad we went in together, for they made us strip to the skin, and I had to curse him pretty seriously to make him keep quiet. The men who did the job were fairly civil, but they were mighty thorough. They took down a list of all we had in our pockets and bags, and all the details from the passports the Rotterdam agent had given us.

We were dressing when a man in a lieutenant's uniform came in with a paper in his hand. He was a fresh-faced lad of about twenty, with short-sighted spectacled eyes.

"Herr Brandt," he called out.

I nodded.

"And this is Herr Pienaar?" he asked in Dutch.

He saluted. "Gentlemen, I apologize. I am late because of the slowness of the Herr Commandant's motor-car. Had I been in time you would not have been required to go through this ceremony. We have been advised of your coming, and I am instructed to attend you on your journey. The train for Berlin leaves in half an hour. Pray do me the honour to join me in a bock."

With a feeling of distinction we stalked out of the ordinary

ruck of passengers and followed the lieutenant to the station restaurant. He plunged at once into conversation, talking the Dutch
of Holland, which Peter, who had forgotten his schooldays, found
a bit hard to follow. He was unfit for active service, because of
his eyes and a weak heart, but he was a desperate fire-eater in
that stuffy restaurant. By his way of it Germany could gobble up
the French and the Russians whenever she cared, but she was
aiming at getting all the Middle East in her hands first, so that
she could come out conqueror with the practical control of half
the world.

"Your friends the English," he said grinning, "will come last.
When we have starved them and destroyed their commerce with
our under-sea boats we will show them what our navy can do.
For a year they have been wasting their time in brag and politics,
and we have been building great ships—oh, so many! My cousin
at Kiel—" and he looked over his shoulder.

But we never heard about that cousin at Kiel. A short sunburnt
man came in and our friend sprang up and saluted, clicking his
heels like a pair of tongs.

"These are the South African Dutch, Herr Captain," he said.

The new-comer looked us over with bright intelligent eyes,
and started questioning Peter in the *taal*. It was well that we had
taken some pains with our story, for this man had been years in
German South West, and knew every mile of the borders. Zorn
was his name, and both Peter and I thought we remembered
hearing him spoken of.

I am thankful to say that we both showed up pretty well. Peter
told his story to perfection, not pitching it too high, and asking
me now and then for a name or to verify some detail. Captain
Zorn looked satisfied.

"You seem the right kind of fellows," he said. "But remember"—
and he bent his brows on us—"we do not understand slimness in
this land. If you are honest you will be rewarded, but if you dare
to play a double game you will be shot like dogs. Your race has
produced over many traitors for my taste."

"I ask no reward," I said gruffly. "We are not Germans or

Germany's slaves. But so long as she fights against England we will fight for her."

"Bold words," he said; "but you must bow your stiff necks to discipline first. Discipline has been the weak point of you Boers, and you have suffered for it. You are no more a nation. In Germany we put discipline first and last, and therefore we will conquer the world. Off with you now. Your train starts in three minutes. We will see what von Stumm will make of you."

That fellow gave me the best "feel" of any German I had yet met. He was a white man and I could have worked with him. I liked his stiff chin and steady blue eyes.

My chief recollection of our journey to Berlin was its commonplaceness. The spectacled lieutenant fell asleep, and for the most part we had the carriage to ourselves. Now and again a soldier on leave would drop in, most of them tired men with heavy eyes. No wonder, poor devils, for they were coming back from the Yser or the Ypres salient. I would have liked to talk to them, but officially of course I knew no German, and the conversation I overheard did not signify much. It was mostly about regimental details, though one chap, who was in better spirits than the rest, observed that this was the last Christmas of misery, and that next year he would be holidaying at home with full pockets. The others assented, but without much conviction.

The winter day was short, and most of the journey was made in the dark. I could see from the window the lights of little villages, and now and then the blaze of ironworks and forges. We stopped at a town for dinner, where the platform was crowded with drafts waiting to go westward. We saw no signs of any scarcity of food, such as the English newspapers wrote about. We had an excellent dinner at the station restaurant, which, with a bottle of white wine, cost just three shillings apiece. The bread, to be sure, was poor, but I can put up with the absence of bread if I get a juicy fillet of beef and as good vegetables as you will see in the Savoy.

I was a little afraid of our giving ourselves away in our sleep, but I need have had no fear, for our escort slumbered like a hog

with his mouth wide open. As we roared through the darkness I
kept pinching myself to make myself feel that I was in the enemy's land on a wild mission. The rain came on, and we passed
through dripping towns, with the lights shining from the wet
streets. As we went eastward the lighting seemed to grow more
generous. After the murk of London it was queer to slip through
garish stations with a hundred arc lights glowing, and to see long
lines of lamps running to the horizon. Peter dropped off early,
but I kept awake till midnight, trying to focus thoughts that per-
sistently strayed. Then I, too, dozed, and did not awake till about
five in the morning, when we ran into a great busy terminus as
bright as midday. It was the easiest and most unsuspicious journey I ever made.

The lieutenant stretched himself and smoothed his rumpled
uniform. We carried our scanty luggage to a *droschke*, for there
seemed to be no porters. Our escort gave the address of some
hotel and we rumbled out into brightly lit empty streets.

"A mighty dorp," said Peter. "Of a truth the Germans are a
great people."

The lieutenant nodded good-humouredly.

"The greatest people on earth," he said, "as their enemies will
soon bear witness."

I would have given a lot for a bath, but I felt that it would be
outside my part, and Peter was not of the washing persuasion.
But we had a very good breakfast of coffee and eggs, and then
the lieutenant started on the telephone. He began by being dic-
tatorial, then he seemed to be switched on to higher authorities,
for he grew more polite, and at the end he fairly crawled. He
made some arrangements, for he informed us that in the afternoon we would see some fellow whose title he could not translate
into Dutch. I judged he was a great swell, for his voice became
reverential at the mention of him.

He took us for a walk that morning after Peter and I had attended to our toilets. We were an odd pair of scallywags to look
at, but as South African as a wait-a-bit bush. Both of us had ready-
made tweed suits, grey flannel shirts with flannel collars, and felt

hats with broader brims than they like in Europe. I had strong nailed brown boots, Peter a pair of those mustard-coloured abominations which the Portuguese affect and which made him hobble like a Chinese lady. He had a scarlet satin tie which you could hear a mile off. My beard had grown to quite a respectable length, and I trimmed it like General Smuts'. Peter's was the kind of loose flapping thing the *taakhaar* loves, which has scarcely ever been shaved, and is combed once in a blue moon. I must say we made a pretty solid pair. Any South African would have set us down as a Boer from the backveld who had bought a suit of clothes in the nearest store, and his cousin from some one-horse dorp who had been to school and thought himself the devil of a fellow. We fairly reeked of the sub-continent, as the papers call it.

It was a fine morning after the rain, and we wandered about in the streets for a couple of hours. They were busy enough, and the shops looked rich and bright with their Christmas goods, and one big store where I went to buy a pocket-knife was packed with customers. One didn't see very many young men, and most of the women wore mourning. Uniforms were everywhere, but their wearers generally looked like dug-outs or office fellows. We had a glimpse of the squat building which housed the General Staff and took off our hats to it. Then we stared at the Marineamt, and I wondered what plots were hatching there behind old Tirpitz's whiskers. The capital gave one an impression of ugly cleanness and a sort of dreary effectiveness. And yet I found it depressing—more depressing than London. I don't know how to put it, but the whole big concern seemed to have no soul in it, to be like a big factory instead of a city. You won't make a factory look like a house, though you decorate its front and plant rosebushes all round it. The place depressed and yet cheered me. It somehow made the German people seem smaller.

At three o'clock the lieutenant took us to a plain white building in a side street with sentries at the door. A young staff-officer met us and made us wait for five minutes in an ante-room. Then we were ushered into a big room with a polished floor on which Peter nearly sat down. There was a log fire burning, and seated at a table was a little man in spectacles with his hair brushed back from his brow like a popular violinist. He was the boss, for the lieutenant saluted him and announced our names. Then he disappeared, and the man at the table motioned us to sit down in two chairs before him.

"Herr Brandt and Herr Pienaar?" he asked, looking over his glasses.

But it was the other man that caught my eye. He stood with his back to the fire leaning his elbows on the mantelpiece. He was a perfect mountain of a fellow, six and a half feet if he was an inch, with shoulders on him like a shorthorn bull. He was in uniform, and the black-and-white ribbon of the Iron Cross showed at a buttonhole. His tunic was all wrinkled and strained as if it could scarcely contain his huge chest, and mighty hands were clasped over his stomach. That man must have had the length of reach of a gorilla. He had a great, lazy, smiling face, with a square cleft chin which stuck out beyond the rest. His brow retreated and the stubby back of his head ran forward to meet it, while his neck below bulged out over his collar. His head was exactly the shape of a pear with the sharp end topmost.

He stared at me with his small bright eyes and I stared back. I had struck something I had been looking for for a long time, and till that moment I wasn't sure that it existed. Here was the German of caricature, the real German, the fellow we were up against. He was as hideous as a hippopotamus, but effective. Every bristle on his odd head was effective.

The man at the table was speaking. I took him to be a civilian official of sorts, pretty high up from his surroundings, perhaps an Under-Secretary. His Dutch was slow and careful, but good—too good for Peter. He had a paper before him and was asking us questions from it. They did not amount to much, being pretty well a repetition of those Zorn had asked us at the frontier. I answered fluently, for I had all our lies by heart.

Then the man on the hearthrug broke in. "I'll talk to them, Excellency," he said in German. "You are too academic for these outland swine."

He began in the *taal*, with the thick guttural accent that you get in German South West. "You have heard of me," he said. "I am the Colonel von Stumm who fought the Hereros."

Peter pricked up his ears. "*Ja*, Baas, you cut off the chief Baviaan's head and sent it in pickle about the country. I have seen it."

The big man laughed. "You see I am not forgotten," he said to his friend, and then to us: "So I treat my enemies, and so will Germany treat hers. You, too, if you fail me by a fraction of an inch." And he laughed loud again.

There was something horrible in that boisterousness. Peter was watching him from below his eyelids, as I have seen him watch a lion about to charge.

He flung himself on a chair, put his elbows on the table, and thrust his face forward.

"You have come from a damned muddled show. If I had Maritz in my power I would have him flogged at a wagon's end. Fools and pig-dogs, they had the game in their hands and they flung it away. We could have raised a fire that would have burned the English into the sea, and for lack of fuel they let it die down. Then they try to fan it when the ashes are cold."

He rolled a paper pellet and flicked it into the air. "That is what I think of your idiot general," he said, "and of all you Dutch. As slow as a fat vrouw and as greedy as an aasvogel."

We looked very glum and sullen.

"A pair of dumb dogs," he cried. "A thousand Brandenburgers would have won in a fortnight. Seitz hadn't much to boast of, mostly clerks and farmers and half-castes, and no soldier worth the name to lead them, but it took Botha and Smuts and a dozen generals to hunt him down. But Maritz!" His scorn came like a gust of wind.

"Maritz did all the fighting there was," said Peter sulkily. "At any rate he wasn't afraid of the sight of khaki like you lot."

"Maybe he wasn't," said the giant in a cooing voice; "maybe he had his reasons for that. You Dutchmen have always a feather-bed to fall on. You can always turn traitor. Maritz now calls himself Robinson, and has a pension from his friend Botha."

"That," said Peter, "is a very damned lie."

"I asked for information," said Stumm with a sudden politeness. "But that is all past and done with. Maritz matters no more than your old Cronjes and Krugers. The show is over, and you are looking for safety. For a new master perhaps? But, man, what can you bring? What can you offer? You and your Dutch are lying in the dust with the yoke on your necks. The Pretoria lawyers have talked you round. You see that map," and he pointed to a big one on the wall. "South Africa is coloured green. Not red for the English, or yellow for the Germans. Some day it will be yellow, but for a little it will be green—the colour of neutrals, of nothings, of boys and young ladies and chicken-hearts."

I kept wondering what he was playing at.

Then he fixed his eyes on Peter. "What do you come here for? The game's up in your own country. What can you offer us Germans? If we gave you ten million marks and sent you back you could do nothing. Stir up a village row, perhaps, and shoot a policeman. South Africa is counted out in this war. Botha is a cleverish man and has beaten you calves'-heads of rebels. Can you deny it?"

Peter couldn't. He was terribly honest in some things, and these were for certain his opinions.

"No," he said, "that is true, Baas."

"Then what in God's name can you do?" shouted Stumm.

Peter mumbled some foolishness about nobbling Angola for Germany and starting a revolution among the natives. Stumm flung up his arms and cursed, and the Under-Secretary laughed.

It was high time for me to chip in. I was beginning to see the kind of fellow this Stumm was, and as he talked I thought of my mission, which had got overlaid by my Boer past. It looked as if he might be useful.

"Let me speak," I said. "My friend is a great hunter, but he fights better than he talks. He is no politician. You speak truth. South Africa is a closed door for the present, and the key to it is elsewhere. Here in Europe, and in the East, and in other parts of Africa. We have come to help you to find the key."

Stumm was listening. "Go on, my little Boer. It will be a new thing to hear a *taakhaar* on world-politics."

"You are fighting," I said, "in East Africa; and soon you may fight in Egypt. All the east coast north of the Zambesi will be your battleground. The English run about the world with little expeditions. I do not know where the places are, though I read of them in the papers. But I know my Africa. You want to beat them here in Europe and on the seas. Therefore, like wise generals, you try to divide them and have them scattered throughout the globe while you stick at home. That is your plan?"

"A second Falkenhayn," said Stumm, laughing.

"Well, England will not let East Africa go. She fears for Egypt and she fears, too, for India. If you press her there she will send armies and more armies till she is so weak in Europe that a child can crush her. That is England's way. She cares more for her Empire than for what may happen to her allies. So I say press and still press there, destroy the railway to the Lakes, burn her capital, pen up every Englishman in Mombasa island. At this moment it is worth for you a thousand Damaralands."

The man was really interested and the Under-Secretary, too, pricked up his ears.

"We can keep our territory," said the former; "but as for pressing, how the devil are we to press? The accursed English hold the sea. We cannot ship men or guns there. South are the Portuguese and west the Belgians. You cannot move a mass without a lever."

"The lever is there, ready for you," I said.

"Then for God's sake show it me," he cried.

I looked at the door to see that it was shut, as if what I had to say was very secret.

"You need men, and the men are waiting. They are black, but they are the stuff of warriors. All round your borders you have the remains of great fighting tribes, the Angoni, the Masai, the Manyumwezi, and above all the Somalis of the north, and the dwellers on the Upper Nile. The British recruit their black regiments there, and so do you. But to get recruits is not enough.

You must set whole nations moving, as the Zulu under Tchaka flowed over South Africa."

"It cannot be done," said the Under-Secretary.

"It can be done," I said quietly. "We two are here to do it."

This kind of talk was jolly difficult for me, chiefly because of Stumm's asides in German to the official. I had, above all things, to get the credit of knowing no German, and, if you understand a language well, it is not very easy when you are interrupted not to show that you know it, either by a direct answer, or by referring to the interruption in what you say next. I had to be always on my guard, and yet it was up to me to be very persuasive and convince these fellows that I would be useful. Somehow or other I had to get into their confidence.

"I have been for years up and down in Africa—Uganda and the Congo and the Upper Nile. I know the ways of the Kaffir as no Englishman does. We Afrikanders see into the black man's heart, and though he may hate us he does our will. You Germans are like the English; you are too big folk to understand plain men. 'Civilize,' you cry. 'Educate,' say the English. The black man obeys and puts away his gods, but he worships them all the time in his soul. We must get his gods on our side, and then he will move mountains. We must do as John Laputa did with Sheba's necklace."

"That's all in the air," said Stumm, but he did not laugh.

"It is sober common sense," I said. "But you must begin at the right end. First find the race that fears its priests. It is waiting for you—the Mussulmans of Somaliland and the Abyssinian border and the Blue and White Nile. They would be like dried grasses to catch fire if you used the flint and steel of their religion. Look what the English suffered from a crazy mullah who ruled only a dozen villages. Once get the flames going and they will lick up the pagans of the west and south. That is the way of Africa. How many thousands, think you, were in the Mahdi's army who never heard of the Prophet till they saw the black flags of the Emirs going into battle?"

Stumm was smiling. He turned his face to the official and

spoke with his hand over his mouth, but I caught his words. They were: "This is the man for Hilda." The other pursed his lips and looked a little scared.

Stumm rang a bell and the lieutenant came in and clicked his heels. He nodded towards Peter. "Take this man away with you. We have done with him. The other fellow will follow presently."

Peter went out with a puzzled face and Stumm turned to me.

"You are a dreamer, Brandt," he said. "But I do not reject you on that account. Dreams sometimes come true, when an army follows the visionary. But who is going to kindle the flame?"

"You," I said.

"What the devil do you mean?" he asked.

"That is your part. You are the cleverest people in the world. You have already half the Mussulman lands in your power. It is for you to show us how to kindle a Holy War, for clearly you have the secret of it. Never fear but we will carry out your order."

"We have no secret," he said shortly, and glanced at the official, who stared out of the window.

I dropped my jaw and looked the picture of disappointment. "I do not believe you," I said slowly. "You play a game with me. I have not come six thousand miles to be made a fool of."

"Discipline, by God," Stumm cried. "This is none of your ragged commandos." In two strides he was above me and had lifted me out of my seat. His great hands clutched my shoulders, and his thumbs gouged my armpits. I felt as if I were in the grip of a big ape. Then very slowly he shook me so that my teeth seemed loosened and my head swam. He let me go and I dropped limply back in the chair.

"Now, go! *Futsack!* And remember that I am your master. I, Ulric von Stumm, who owns you as a Kaffir owns his mongrel. Germany may have some use for you, my friend, when you fear me as you never feared your God."

As I walked dizzily away the big man was smiling in his horrible way, and that little official was blinking and smiling too. I had struck a dashed queer country, so queer that I had had no time to remember that for the first time in my life I had been bullied without hitting back. When I realized it I nearly choked with anger. But I thanked Heaven I had shown no temper, for I remembered my mission. Luck seemed to have brought me into useful company.

CHAPTER 5

Further Adventures of the Same

NEXT morning there was a touch of frost and a nip in the air which stirred my blood and put me in buoyant spirits. I forgot my precarious position and the long road I had still to travel. I came down to breakfast in great form, to find Peter's even temper badly ruffled. He had remembered Stumm in the night and disliked the memory; this he muttered to me as we rubbed shoulders at the dining-room door. Peter and I got no opportunity for private talk. The lieutenant was with us all the time, and at night we were locked in our rooms. Peter discovered this through trying to get out to find matches, for he had the bad habit of smoking in bed.

Our guide started on the telephone, and announced that we were to be taken to see a prisoners' camp. In the afternoon I was to go somewhere with Stumm, but the morning was for sightseeing. "You will see," he told us, "how merciful is a great people. You will also see some of the hated English in our power. That will delight you. They are the forerunners of all their nation."

We drove in a taxi through the suburbs and then over a stretch of flat market-garden-like country to a low rise of wooded hills. After an hour's ride we entered the gate of what looked like a big reformatory or hospital. I believe it had been a home for destitute children. There were sentries at the gate and massive concentric circles of barbed wire through which we passed under an arch that was let down like a portcullis at nightfall. The lieutenant showed his permit, and we ran the car into a brick-paved yard and marched through a lot more sentries to the office of the commandant.

He was away from home, and we were welcomed by his deputy, a pale young man with a head nearly bald. There were introductions in German which our guide translated into Dutch, and a lot of elegant speeches about how Germany was foremost in humanity as well as martial valour. Then they stood us sandwiches and beer, and we formed a procession for a tour of inspection. There were two doctors, both mild-looking men in spectacles, and a couple of warders—under-officers of the good old burly, bullying sort I knew well. That was the cement which kept the German army together. Her men were nothing to boast of on the average; no more were the officers, even in crack corps like the Guards and the Brandenburgers; but they seemed to have an inexhaustible supply of hard, competent N.C.O.s.

We marched round the wash-houses, the recreation-ground, the kitchens, the hospital—with nobody in it save one chap with the 'flu. It didn't seem to be badly done. This place was entirely for officers, and I expect it was a show place where American visitors were taken. If half the stories one heard were true there were some pretty ghastly prisons away in South and East Germany.

I didn't half like the business. To be a prisoner has always seemed to me about the worst thing that could happen to a man. The sight of German prisoners used to give me a bad feeling inside, whereas I looked at dead Boches with nothing but satisfaction. Besides, there was the off-chance that I might be recognized. So I kept very much in the shadow whenever we passed anybody in the corridors. The few we met passed us incuriously. They saluted the deputy-commandant, but scarcely wasted a glance on us. No doubt they thought we were inquisitive Germans come to gloat over them. They looked fairly fit, but a little puffy about the eyes, like men who get too little exercise. They seemed thin, too. I expect the food, for all the commandant's talk, was nothing to boast of. In one room people were writing letters. It was a big place with only a tiny stove to warm it, and the windows were shut so that the atmosphere was a cold frowst. In another room a fellow was lecturing on something to a dozen hearers and drawing figures on a blackboard. Some were in ordinary khaki, others in any old thing they could pick up, and most wore greatcoats. Your blood gets thin when you have nothing to do but hope against hope and think of your pals and the old days.

I was moving along, listening with half an ear to the lieutenant's prattle and the loud explanations of the deputy-commandant, when I pitchforked into what might have been the end of my business. We were going through a sort of convalescent room, where people were sitting who had been in hospital. It was a big place, a little warmer than the rest of the building, but still abominably fuggy. There were about half a dozen men in the room, reading and playing games. They looked at us with lack-lustre eyes for a moment, and then returned to their occupations. Being convalescents I suppose they were not expected to get up and salute.

All but one, who was playing Patience at a little table by which we passed. I was feeling very bad about the thing, for I hated to see these good fellows locked away in this infernal German hole when they might have been giving the Boche his deserts at the front. The commandant went first with Peter, who had developed a great interest in prisons. Then came our lieutenant with one of the doctors; then a couple of warders; and then the second doctor and myself. I was absent-minded at the moment and was last in the queue.

The Patience-player suddenly looked up and I saw his face. I'm hanged if it wasn't Dolly Riddell, who was our brigade machine-gun officer at Loos. I had heard that the Germans had got him when they blew up a mine at the Quarries.

I had to act pretty quick, for his mouth was agape, and I saw he was going to speak. The doctor was a yard ahead of me.

I stumbled and spilt his cards on the floor. Then I kneeled to pick them up and gripped his knee. His head bent to help me and I spoke low in his ear.

"I'm Hannay all right. For God's sake don't wink an eye. I'm here on a secret job."

The doctor had turned to see what was the matter. I got a few more words in. "Cheer up, old man. We're winning hands down."

Then I began to talk excited Dutch and finished the collection of the cards. Dolly was playing his part well, smiling as if he was amused by the antics of a monkey. The others were coming back, the deputy-commandant with an angry light in his dull eye. "Speaking to the prisoners is forbidden," he shouted.

I looked blankly at him till the lieutenant translated.

"What kind of fellow is he?" said Dolly in English to the doctor. "He spoils my game and then jabbers High-Dutch at me."

Officially I knew English, and that speech of Dolly's gave me my cue. I pretended to be very angry with the very damned Englishman, and went out of the room close by the deputy-commandant, grumbling like a sick jackal. After that I had to act a bit. The last place we visited was the close-confinement part where prisoners were kept as a punishment for some breach of the rules. They looked cheerless enough, but I pretended to gloat over the sight, and said so to the lieutenant, who passed it on to the others. I have rarely in my life felt such a cad.

On the way home the lieutenant discoursed a lot about prisoners and detention-camps, for at one time he had been on duty at Ruhleben. Peter, who had been in quod more than once in his life, was deeply interested and kept on questioning him. Among other things he told us was that they often put bogus prisoners among the rest, who acted as spies. If any plot to escape was hatched these fellows got into it and encouraged it. They never interfered till the attempt was actually made and then they had them on toast. There was nothing the Boche liked so much as an excuse for sending a poor devil to "solitary."

That afternoon Peter and I separated. He was left behind with the lieutenant and I was sent off to the station with my bag in the company of a Landsturm sergeant. Peter was very cross, and I didn't care for the look of things; but I brightened up when I heard I was going somewhere with Stumm. If he wanted to see me again he must think me of some use, and if he was going to use me he was bound to let me into his game. I liked Stumm about as much as a dog likes a scorpion, but I hankered for his society.

At the station platform, where the ornament of the Landsturm saved me all the trouble about tickets, I could not see my companion. I stood waiting, while a great crowd, mostly of soldiers, swayed past me and filled all the front carriages. An officer spoke to me gruffly and told me to stand aside behind a wooden rail. I obeyed, and suddenly found Stumm's eyes looking down at me.

"You know German?" he asked sharply.

"A dozen words," I said carelessly. "I've been to Windhuk and learned enough to ask for my dinner. Peter—my friend—speaks it a bit."

"So," said Stumm. "Well, get into the carriage. Not that one! There, thickhead!"

I did as I was bid, he followed, and the door was locked behind us. The precaution was needless, for the sight of Stumm's profile at the platform end would have kept out the most brazen. I wondered if I had woken up his suspicions. I must be on my guard to show no signs of intelligence if he suddenly tried me in German, and that wouldn't be easy, for I knew it as well as I knew Dutch.

We moved into the country, but the windows were blurred with frost, and I saw nothing of the landscape. Stumm was busy with papers and let me alone. I read on a notice that one was forbidden to smoke, so to show my ignorance of German I pulled out my pipe. Stumm raised his head, saw what I was doing, and gruffly bade me put it away, as if he were an old lady that disliked the smell of tobacco.

In half an hour I got very bored, for I had nothing to read and my pipe was *verboten*. People passed now and then in the corridors, but no one offered to enter. No doubt they saw the big figure in uniform and thought he was the deuce of a staff swell who wanted solitude. I thought of stretching my legs in the corridor, and was just getting up to do it when somebody slid the door back and a big figure blocked the light.

He was wearing a heavy ulster and a green felt hat. He saluted Stumm, who looked up angrily, and smiled pleasantly on us both.

"Say, gentlemen," he said, "have you room in here for a little one? I guess I'm about smoked out of my car by your brave soldiers. I've gotten a delicate stomach . . ."

Stumm had risen with a brow of wrath, and looked as if he were going to pitch the intruder off the train. Then he seemed to halt and collect himself, and the other's face broke into a friendly grin.

"Why, it's Colonel Stumm," he cried. (He pronounced it like the first syllable in "stomach.") "Very pleased to meet you again, Colonel. I had the honour of making your acquaintance at our Embassy. I reckon Ambassador Gerard didn't cotton to our conversation that night." And the new-comer plumped himself down in the corner opposite me.

I had been pretty certain I would run across Blenkiron somewhere in Germany, but I didn't think it would be so soon. There he sat staring at me with his full, unseeing eyes, rolling out platitudes to Stumm, who was nearly bursting in his effort to keep civil. I looked moody and suspicious, which I took to be the right line.

"Things are getting a bit dead at Salonika," said Mr. Blenkiron, by way of a conversational opening.

Stumm pointed to a notice which warned officers to refrain from discussing military operations with mixed company in a railway carriage.

"Sorry," said Blenkiron, "I can't read that tombstone language of yours. But I reckon that that notice to trespassers, whatever it signifies, don't apply to you and me. I take it this gentleman is in your party."

I sat and scowled, fixing the American with suspicious eyes.

"He is a Dutchman," said Stumm; "South African Dutch, and he is not happy, for he doesn't like to hear English spoken."

"We'll shake on that," said Blenkiron cordially. "But who said I spoke English? It's good American. Cheer up, friend, for it isn't the call that makes the big wapiti, as they say out west in my country. I hate John Bull worse than a poison rattle. The Colonel can tell you that."

I dare say he could, but at that moment we slowed down at a station and Stumm got up to leave. "Good day to you, Herr Blenkiron," he cried over his shoulder. "If you consider your comfort, don't talk English to strange travellers. They don't distinguish between the different brands."

I followed him in a hurry, but was recalled by Blenkiron's voice.

"Say, friend," he shouted, "you've left your grip," and he handed me my bag from the luggage rack. But he showed no sign of recognition, and the last I saw of him was sitting sunk in a corner with his head on his chest as if he were going to sleep. He was a man who kept up his parts well.

There was a motor-car waiting—one of the grey military kind—and we started at a terrific pace over bad forest roads. Stumm had put away his papers in a portfolio, and flung me a few sentences on the journey.

"I haven't made up my mind about you, Brandt," he announced. "You may be a fool or a knave or a good man. If you are a knave, we will shoot you."

"And if I am a fool?" I asked.

"Send you to the Yser or the Dvina. You will be respectable cannon-fodder."

"You cannot do that unless I consent," I said.

"Can't we?" he said, smiling wickedly. "Remember you are a citizen of nowhere. Technically, you are a rebel, and the British, if you go to them, will hang you, supposing they have any sense. You are in our power, my friend, to do precisely what we like with you." He was silent for a second, and then he said, meditatively:

"But I don't think you are a fool. You may be a scoundrel.

Some kinds of scoundrel are useful enough. Other kinds are strung up with a rope. Of that we shall know more soon."

"And if I am a good man?"

"You will be given a chance to serve Germany, the proudest privilege a mortal man can have." The strange man said this with a ringing sincerity in his voice that impressed me.

The car swung out from the trees into a park lined with saplings, and in the twilight I saw before me a biggish house like an overgrown Swiss chalet. There was a kind of archway with a sham portcullis, and a terrace with battlements which looked as if they were made of stucco. We drew up at a Gothic front door, where a thin middle-aged man in a shooting jacket was waiting.

As we moved into the lighted hall I got a good look at our host. He was very lean and brown, with the stoop in the shoulder that one gets from being constantly on horseback. He had untidy grizzled hair and a ragged beard, and a pair of pleasant, short-sighted brown eyes.

"Welcome, my Colonel," he said. "Is this the friend you spoke of?"

"This is the Dutchman," said Stumm. "His name is Brandt. Brandt, you see before you Herr Gaudian."

I knew the name, of course; there weren't many in my profession that didn't. He was one of the biggest railway engineers in the world, the man who had built the Bagdad and Syrian railways, and the new lines in German East. I suppose he was about the greatest living authority on tropical construction. He knew the East and he knew Africa; clearly I had been brought down for him to put me through my paces.

A blonde maidservant took me to my room, which had a bare polished floor, a stove, and windows that, unlike most of the German kind I had sampled, seemed made to open. When I had washed I descended to the hall, which was hung round with trophies of travel, like Dervish jibbahs and Masai shields and one or two good buffalo heads. Presently a bell was rung. Stumm appeared with his host, and we went in to supper.

I was jolly hungry and would have made a good meal if I hadn't constantly had to keep jogging my wits. The other two talked in German, and when a question was put to me Stumm translated. The first thing I had to do was to pretend I didn't know German and look listlessly round the room while they were talking. The second was to miss not a word, for there lay my chance. The third was to be ready to answer questions at any moment, and to show in the answering that I had not followed the previous conversation. Likewise, I must not prove myself a fool in these answers, for I had to convince them that I was useful. It took some doing, and I felt like a witness in a box under a stiff cross-examination, or a man trying to play three games of chess at once.

I heard Stumm telling Gaudian the gist of my plan. The engineer shook his head.

"Too late," he said. "It should have been done at the beginning. We neglected Africa. You know the reason why."

Stumm laughed. "The von Einem! Perhaps, but her charm works well enough."

Gaudian glanced towards me while I was busy with an orange salad. "I have much to tell you of that. But it can wait. Your friend is right in one thing. Uganda is a vital spot for the English, and a blow there will make their whole fabric shiver. But how can we strike? They have still the coast, and our supplies grow daily smaller."

"We can send no reinforcements, but have we used all the local resources? That is what I cannot satisfy myself about. Zimmerman says we have, but Tressler thinks differently, and now we have this fellow coming out of the void with a story which confirms my doubt. He seems to know his job. You try him."

Thereupon Gaudian set about questioning me, and his questions were very thorough. I knew just enough and no more to get through, but I think I came out with credit. You see I have a capacious memory, and in my time I had met scores of hunters and pioneers and listened to their yarns, so I could pretend to knowledge of a place even when I hadn't been there. Besides, I had once been on the point of undertaking a job up Tanganyika way, and I had got up that countryside pretty accurately.

"You say that with our help you can make trouble for the British on the three borders?" Gaudian asked at length.

"I can spread the fire if someone else will kindle it," I said.

"But there are thousands of tribes with no affinities."

"They are all African. You can bear me out. All African peoples are alike in one thing—they can go mad, and the madness of one infects the others. The English know this well enough."

"Where would you start the fire?" he asked.

"Where the fuel is dryest. Up in the North among the Mussulman peoples. But there you must help me. I know nothing about Islam, and I gather that you do."

"Why?" he asked.

"Because of what you have done already," I answered.

Stumm had translated all this time, and had given the sense of my words very fairly. But with my last answer he took liberties. What he gave was: "Because the Dutchman thinks that we have some big card in dealing with the Moslem world." Then, lowering his voice and raising his eyebrows, he said some word like "Uhnmantl."

The other looked with a quick glance of apprehension at me. "We had better continue our talk in private, Herr Colonel," he said. "If Herr Brandt will forgive us, we will leave him for a little to entertain himself." He pushed the cigar-box towards me and the two got up and left the room.

I pulled my chair up to the stove, and would have liked to drop off to sleep. The tension of the talk at supper had made me very tired. I was accepted by these men for exactly what I professed to be. Stumm might suspect me of being a rascal, but it was a Dutch rascal. But all the same I was skating on thin ice. I could not sink myself utterly in the part, for if I did I would get no good out of being there. I had to keep my wits going all the time, and join the appearance and manners of a backveld Boer with the mentality of a British intelligence-officer. Any moment the two parts might clash and I would be faced with the most alert and deadly suspicion.

There would be no mercy from Stumm. That large man was

beginning to fascinate me, even though I hated him. Gaudian was clearly a good fellow, a white man and a gentleman. I could have worked with him for he belonged to my own totem. But the other was an incarnation of all that makes Germany detested, and yet he wasn't altogether the ordinary German, and I couldn't help admiring him. I noticed he neither smoked nor drank. His grossness was apparently not in the way of fleshly appetites. Cruelty, from all I had heard of him in German South West, was his hobby; but there were other things in him, some of them good, and he had that kind of crazy patriotism which becomes a religion. I wondered why he had not some high command in the field, for he had had the name of a good soldier. But probably he was a big man in his own line, whatever it was, for the Under-Secretary fellow had talked small in his presence, and so great a man as Gaudian clearly respected him. There must be no lack of brains inside that funny pyramidal head.

As I sat beside the stove I was casting back to think if I had got the slightest clue to my real job. There seemed to be nothing so far. Stumm had talked of a von Einem woman who was interested in his department, perhaps the same woman as the Hilda he had mentioned the day before to the Under-Secretary. There was not much in that. She was probably some minister's or ambassador's wife who had a finger in high politics. If I could have caught the word Stumm had whispered to Gaudian which made him start and look askance at me! But I had only heard a gurgle of something like "Uhnmantl," which wasn't any German word that I knew.

The heat put me into a half-doze and I began dreamily to wonder what other people were doing. Where had Blenkiron been posting to in that train, and what was he up to at this moment? He had been hobnobbing with ambassadors and swells—I wondered if he had found out anything. What was Peter doing? I fervently hoped he was behaving himself, for I doubted if Peter had really tumbled to the delicacy of our job. Where was Sandy, too? As like as not bucketing in the hold of some Greek coaster in the Aegean. Then I thought of my battalion somewhere on the line between Hulluch and La Bassée, hammering at the Boche, while I was five hundred miles or so inside the Boche frontier.

It was a comic reflection, so comic that it woke me up. After trying in vain to find a way of stoking that stove, for it was a cold night, I got up and walked about the room. There were portraits of two decent old fellows, probably Gaudian's parents. There were enlarged photographs, too, of engineering works, and a good picture of Bismarck. And close to the stove there was a case of maps mounted on rollers.

I pulled out one at random. It was a geological map of Germany, and with some trouble I found out where I was. I was an enormous distance from my goal, and moreover I was clean off the road to the East. To go there I must first go to Bavaria and then into Austria. I noticed the Danube flowing eastwards and remembered that that was one way to Constantinople.

Then I tried another map. This one covered a big area, all Europe from the Rhine and as far east as Persia. I guessed that it was meant to show the Bagdad railway and the through routes from Germany to Mesopotamia. There were markings on it; and, as I looked closer, I saw that there were dates scribbled in blue pencil, as if to denote the stages of a journey. The dates began in Europe, and continued right on into Asia Minor and then south to Syria.

For a moment my heart jumped, for I thought I had fallen by accident on the clue I wanted. But I never got that map examined. I heard footsteps in the corridor, and very gently I let the map roll up and turned away. When the door opened I was bending over the stove trying to get a light for my pipe.

It was Gaudian, to bid me join him and Stumm in his study.

On our way there he put a kindly hand on my shoulder. I think he thought I was bullied by Stumm and wanted to tell me that he was my friend, and he had no other language than a pat on the back.

The soldier was in his old position with his elbows on the mantelpiece and his formidable great jaw stuck out.

"Listen to me," he said. "Herr Gaudian and I are inclined to make use of you. You may be a charlatan, in which case you will be in the devil of a mess and have yourself to thank for it. If you are a rogue you will have little scope for roguery. We will see to that. If you are a fool, you will yourself suffer for it. But if you are a good man, you will have a fair chance, and if you succeed we will not forget it. To-morrow I go home and you will come with me and get your orders."

I made shift to stand at attention and salute.

Gaudian spoke in a pleasant voice, as if he wanted to atone for Stumm's imperiousness. "We are men who love our Fatherland, Herr Brandt," he said. "You are not of that Fatherland, but at least you hate its enemies. Therefore we are allies, and trust each other like allies. Our victory is ordained by God, and we are none of us more than His instruments."

Stumm translated in a sentence, and his voice was quite solemn. He held up his right hand and so did Gaudian, like a man taking an oath or a parson blessing his congregation. Then I realized something of the might of Germany. She produced good and bad, cads and gentlemen, but she could put a bit of the fanatic into them all.

The Indiscretions of the Same

I was standing stark naked next morning in that icy bedroom, trying to bathe in about a quart of water, when Stumm entered. He strode up to me and stared me in the face. I was half a head shorter than him to begin with, and a man does not feel his stoutest when he has no clothes, so he had the pull on me every way.

"I have reason to believe that you are a liar," he growled.

I pulled the bed-cover round me, for I was shivering with cold, and the German idea of a towel is a pocket-handkerchief. I own I was in a pretty blue funk.

"A liar!" he repeated. "You and that swine Pienaar."

With my best effort at surliness I asked what we had done.

"You lied, because you said you knew no German. Apparently your friend knows enough to talk treason and blasphemy."

This gave me back some heart.

"I told you I knew a dozen words. But I told you Peter could talk it a bit. I told you that yesterday at the station." Fervently I blessed my luck for that casual remark.

He evidently remembered, for his tone became a trifle more civil.

"You are a precious pair. If one of you is a scoundrel, why not the other?"

"I take no responsibility for Peter," I said. I felt I was a cad in saying it, but that was the bargain we had made at the start. "I have known him for years as a great hunter and a brave man. I know he fought well against the English. But more I cannot tell you. You have to judge him for yourself. What has he done?"

I was told, for Stumm had got it that morning on the telephone. While telling it he was kind enough to allow me to put on my trousers.

It was just the sort of thing I might have foreseen. Peter, left alone, had become first bored and then reckless. He had persuaded the lieutenant to take him out to supper at a big Berlin restaurant. There, inspired by the lights and music—novel things for a backveld hunter—and no doubt bored stiff by his company, he had proceeded to get drunk. That had happened in my experience with Peter about once in every three years, and it always happened for the same reason. Peter, bored and solitary in a town, went on the spree. He had a head like a rock, but he got to the required condition by wild mixing. He was quite a gentleman in his cups, and not in the least violent, but he was apt to be very free with his tongue. And that was what occurred at the Franciscana.

He had begun by insulting the Emperor, it seemed. He drank his health, but said he reminded him of a wart-hog, and thereby scarified the lieutenant's soul. Then an officer—some tremendous swell—at an adjoining table had objected to his talking so loud, and Peter had replied insolently in respectable German. After that things became mixed. There was some kind of a fight, during which Peter calumniated the German army and all its female ancestry. How he wasn't shot or run through I can't imagine, except that the lieutenant loudly proclaimed that he was a crazy Boer. Anyhow the upshot was that Peter was marched off to gaol, and I was left in a pretty pickle.

"I don't believe a word of it," I said firmly. I had most of my clothes on now and felt more courageous. "It is all a plot to get him into disgrace and draft him off to the front."

Stumm did not storm as I expected, but smiled.

"That was always his destiny," he said, "ever since I saw him. He was no use to us except as a man with a rifle. Cannon-fodder, nothing else. Do you imagine, you fool, that this great Empire in the thick of a world-war is going to trouble its head to lay snares for an ignorant *taakhaar?*"

"I wash my hands of him," I said. "If what you say of his folly is true I have no part in it. But he was my companion and I wish him well. What do you propose to do with him?"

"We will keep him under our eye," he said, with a wicked twist of the mouth. "I have a notion that there is more at the back of this than appears. We will investigate the antecedents of Herr Pienaar. And you, too, my friend. On you also we have our eye."

I did the best thing I could have done, for what with anxiety and disgust I lost my temper.

"Look here, sir," I cried, "I've had about enough of this. I came to Germany abominating the English and burning to strike a blow for you. But you haven't given me much cause to love you. For the last two days I've had nothing from you but suspicion and insult. The only decent man I've met is Herr Gaudian. It's because I believe that there are many in Germany like him that I'm prepared to go on with this business and do the best I can. But, by God, I wouldn't raise my little finger for your sake."

He looked at me very steadily for a minute. "That sounds like honesty," he said at last in a civil voice. "You had better come down and get your coffee."

I was safe for the moment but in very low spirits. What on earth would happen to poor old Peter? I could do nothing even if I wanted, and, besides, my first duty was to my mission. I had made this very clear to him at Lisbon and he had agreed, but all the same it was a beastly reflection. Here was the ancient worthy left to the tender mercies of the people he most detested on earth. My only comfort was that they couldn't do very much with him. If they sent him to the front, which was the worst they could do, he would escape, for I would have backed him to get through any mortal lines. It wasn't much fun for me either. Only when I was to be deprived of it did I realize how much his company had meant to me. I was absolutely alone now, and I didn't like it. I seemed to have about as much chance of joining Blenkiron and Sandy as of flying to the moon.

After breakfast I was told to get ready. When I asked where I was going Stumm advised me to mind my own business, but I remembered that last night he had talked of taking me home with him and giving me my orders. I wondered where his home was.

Gaudian patted me on the back when we started and wrung my hand. He was a capital good fellow, and it made me feel sick to think that I was humbugging him. We got into the same big grey car, with Stumm's servant sitting beside the chauffeur. It was a morning of hard frost, the bare fields were white with rime, and the fir-trees powdered like a wedding-cake. We took a different road from the night before, and after a run of half a dozen miles came to a little town with a big railway station. It was a junction on some main line, and after five minutes' waiting we found our train.

Once again we were alone in the carriage. Stumm must have had some colossal graft, for the train was crowded.

I had another three hours of complete boredom. I dared not smoke, and could do nothing but stare out of the window. We soon got into hilly country, where a good deal of snow was lying. It was the 23rd day of December, and even in war time one had a sort of feel of Christmas. You could see girls carrying evergreens, and when we stopped at a station the soldiers on leave had all the air of holiday making. The middle of Germany was a cheerier place than Berlin or the western parts. I liked the look of the old peasants, and the women in their neat Sunday best, but I noticed, too, how pinched they were. Here in the country, where no neutral tourists came, there was not the same stage-management as in the capital.

Stumm made no attempt to talk to me on the journey. I could see his aim. Before this he had cross-examined me, but now he wanted to draw me into ordinary conversation. He had no notion how to do it. He was either peremptory and provocative, like a drill-sergeant, or so obviously diplomatic that any fool would have been put on his guard. That is the weakness of the German. He has no gift for laying himself alongside different types of men. He is such a hard-shell being that he cannot put out feelers to his kind. He may have plenty of brains, as Stumm had, but he has the poorest notion of psychology of any of God's creatures. In Germany only the Jew can get outside himself, and that is why, if you look into the matter, you will find that the Jew is at the back of most German enterprises.

After midday we stopped at a station for luncheon. We had a very good meal in the restaurant, and when we were finishing two officers entered. Stumm got up and saluted and went aside to talk to them. Then he came back and made me follow him to a waiting-room, where he told me to stay till he fetched me. I noticed that he called a porter and had the door locked when he went out.

It was a chilly place with no fire, and I kicked my heels there for twenty minutes. I was living by the hour now, and did not trouble to worry about this strange behaviour. There was a volume of time-tables on a shelf, and I turned the pages idly till I struck a big railway map. Then it occurred to me to find out where we were going. I had heard Stumm take my ticket for a place called Schwandorf, and after a lot of searching I found it. It was away south in Bavaria, and so far as I could make out less than fifty miles from the Danube. That cheered me enormously. If Stumm lived there he would most likely start me off on my travels by the railway which I saw running to Vienna and then on to the East. It looked as if I might get to Constantinople after all. But I feared it would be a useless achievement, for what could I do when I got there? I was being hustled out of Germany without picking up the slenderest clue.

The door opened and Stumm entered. He seemed to have got bigger in the interval and to carry his head higher. There was a proud light, too, in his eye.

"Brandt," he said, "you are about to receive the greatest privilege that ever fell to one of your race. His Imperial Majesty is passing through here, and has halted for a few minutes. He has done me the honour to receive me, and when he heard my story he expressed a wish to see you. You will follow me to his presence. Do not be afraid. The All-Highest is merciful and gracious. Answer his questions like a man."

I followed him with a quickened pulse. Here was a bit of luck I had never dreamed of. At the far side of the station a train had drawn up, a train consisting of three big coaches, chocolate-coloured and picked out with gold. On the platform beside it stood a small group of officers, tall men in long grey-blue cloaks. They seemed to be mostly elderly, and one or two of the faces I thought I remembered from photographs in the picture papers.

As we approached they drew apart, and left us face to face with one man. He was a little below middle height, and all muffled in a thick coat with a fur collar. He wore a silver helmet with an eagle atop of it, and kept his left hand resting on his sword. Below the helmet was a face the colour of grey paper, from which shone curious sombre restless eyes with dark pouches beneath them. There was no fear of my mistaking him. These were the features which, since Napoleon, have been best known to the world.

I stood as stiff as a ramrod and saluted. I was perfectly cool and most desperately interested. For such a moment I would have gone through fire and water.

"Majesty, this is the Dutchman I spoke of," I heard Stumm say.

"What language does he speak?" the Emperor asked.

"Dutch," was the reply; "but being a South African he also speaks good English."

A spasm of pain seemed to flit over the face before me. Then he addressed me in English.

"You have come from a land which will yet be our ally to offer your sword to our service? I accept the gift and hail it as a good omen. I would have given your race its freedom, but there were fools and traitors among you who misjudged me. But that freedom I shall yet give you in spite of yourselves. Are there many like you in your country?"

"There are thousands, sire," I said, lying cheerfully. "I am one of many who think that my race's life lies in your victory. And I think that that victory must be won not in Europe alone. In South Africa for the moment there is no chance, so we look to other parts of the continent. You will win in Europe. You have won in the East, and it now remains to strike the English where they cannot fend the blow. If we take Uganda, Egypt will fall. By your permission I go there to make trouble for your enemies."

A flicker of a smile passed over the worn face. It was the face of one who slept little and whose thoughts rode him like a nightmare.

"That is well," he said. "Some Englishman once said that he would call in the New World to redress the balance of the Old. We Germans will summon the whole earth to suppress the infamies of England. Serve us well, and you will not be forgotten."

Then he suddenly asked: "Did you fight in the last South African War?"

"Yes, sire," I said. "I was in the commando of that Smuts who has now been bought by England."

"What were your countrymen's losses?" he asked eagerly.

I did not know, but I hazarded a guess. "In the field some twenty thousand. But many more by sickness and in the accursed prison-camps of the English."

Again a spasm of pain crossed his face.

"Twenty thousand," he repeated huskily. "A mere handful. To-day we lose as many in a skirmish in the Polish marshes."

Then he broke out fiercely.

"I did not seek the war . . . It was forced on me . . . I laboured for peace . . . The blood of millions is on the heads of England and Russia, but England most of all. God will yet avenge it. He that takes the sword will perish by the sword. Mine was forced from the scabbard in self-defence, and I am guiltless. Do they know that among your people?"

"All the world knows it, sire," I said.

He gave his hand to Stumm and turned away. The last I saw of him was a figure moving like a sleep-walker, with no spring in his step, amid his tall suite. I felt that I was looking on at a far bigger tragedy than any I had seen in action. Here was one that had loosed Hell, and the furies of Hell had got hold of him. He was no common man, for in his presence I felt an attraction which was not merely the mastery of one used to command. That would not have impressed me, for I had never owned a master. But here was a human being who, unlike Stumm and his kind, had the power of laying himself alongside other men. That was the irony of it. Stumm would not have cared a tinker's curse for all the massacres in history. But this man, the chief of a nation of Stumms, paid the price in war for the gifts that had made him successful in peace. He had imagination and nerves, and the one was white hot and the others were quivering. I would not have been in his shoes for the throne of the Universe . . .

ALL afternoon we sped southward, mostly in a country of hills and wooded valleys. Stumm, for him, was very pleasant. His Imperial master must have been gracious to him, and he passed a bit of it on to me. But he was anxious to see that I had got the right impression.

"The All-Highest is merciful, as I told you," he said.

I agreed with him.

"Mercy is the prerogative of kings," he said sententiously, "but for us lesser folks it is a trimming we can well do without."

I nodded my approval.

"I am not merciful," he went on, as if I needed telling that. "If any man stands in my way I trample the life out of him. That is the German fashion. That is what has made us great. We do not make war with lavender gloves and fine phrases, but with hard steel and hard brains. We Germans will cure the green-sickness of the world. The nations rise against us. Pouf! They are soft flesh, and flesh cannot resist iron. The shining ploughshare will cut its way through acres of mud."

I hastened to add that these were also my opinions.

"What the hell do your opinions matter? You are a thick-headed boor of the veld . . . Not but what," he added, "there is metal in you slow Dutchmen once we Germans have had the forging of it!"

The winter evening closed in, and I saw that we had come out of the hills and were in flat country. Sometimes a big sweep of river showed, and, looking out at one station, I saw a funny church with a thing like an onion on top of its spire. It might almost have been a mosque, judging from the pictures I remembered of mosques. I wished to Heaven I had given geography more attention in my time.

Presently we stopped, and Stumm led the way out. The train must have been specially halted for him, for it was a one-horse little place whose name I could not make out. The station-master was waiting, bowing and saluting, and outside was a motor-car with big headlights. Next minute we were sliding through dark woods where the snow lay far deeper than in the north. There was a mild frost in the air, and the tyres slipped and skidded at the corners.

We hadn't far to go. We climbed a little hill and on the top of it stopped at the door of a big black castle. It looked enormous in the winter night, with not a light showing anywhere on its front. The door was opened by an old fellow who took a long time about it and got well cursed for his slowness. Inside the place was very noble and ancient. Stumm switched on the electric light, and there was a great hall with black tarnished portraits of men and women in old-fashioned clothes, and mighty horns of deer on the walls.

There seemed to be no superfluity of servants. The old fellow said that food was ready, and without more ado we went into the dining-room—another vast chamber with rough stone walls above the panelling—and found some cold meats on a table beside a big fire. The servant presently brought in a ham omelette, and on that and the cold stuff we dined. I remember there was nothing to drink but water. It puzzled me how Stumm kept his great body going on the very moderate amount of food he ate. He was the type you expect to swill beer by the bucket and put away a pie at a sitting.

When we had finished, he rang for the old man and told him that we should be in the study for the rest of the evening. "You can lock up and go to bed when you like," he said, "but see you have coffee ready at seven sharp in the morning."

Ever since I entered that house I had the uncomfortable feeling of being in a prison. Here was I alone in this great place with a fellow who could, and would, wring my neck if he wanted. Berlin and all the rest of it had seemed comparatively open country; I had felt that I could move freely and at the worst make a bolt for it. But here I was trapped, and I had to tell myself every minute that I was there as a friend and colleague. The fact is, I was afraid of Stumm, and I don't mind admitting it. He was a new thing in my experience and I didn't like it. If only he had drunk and guzzled a bit I should have been happier.

We went up a staircase to a room at the end of a long corridor. Stumm locked the door behind him and laid the key on the table. That room took my breath away, it was so unexpected. In place of the grim bareness of downstairs here was a place all luxury and colour and light. It was very large, but low in the ceiling, and the walls were full of little recesses with statues in them. A thick grey carpet of velvet pile covered the floor, and the chairs were low and soft and upholstered like a lady's boudoir. A pleasant fire burned on the hearth and there was a flavour of scent in the air, something like incense or burnt sandalwood. A French clock on the mantelpiece told me that it was ten minutes past eight. Everywhere on little tables and in cabinets was a profusion of knickknacks, and there was some beautiful embroidery framed on screens. At first sight you would have said it was a woman's drawing-room.

But it wasn't. I soon saw the difference. There had never been a woman's hand in that place. It was the room of a man who had a passion for frippery, who had a perverted taste for soft delicate things. It was the complement to his bluff brutality. I began to see the queer other side of my host, that evil side which gossip had spoken of as not unknown in the German army. The room seemed a horribly unwholesome place, and I was more than ever afraid of Stumm.

The hearthrug was a wonderful old Persian thing, all faint greens and pinks. As he stood on it he looked uncommonly like a bull in a china-shop. He seemed to bask in the comfort of it, and sniffed like a satisfied animal. Then he sat down at an escritoire, unlocked a drawer and took out some papers.

"We will now settle your business, friend Brandt," he said. "You will go to Egypt and there take your orders from one whose name and address are in this envelope. This card," and he lifted a square piece of grey pasteboard with a big stamp at the corner and some code words stencilled on it, "will be your passport. You will show it to the man you seek. Keep it jealously, and never use it save under orders or in the last necessity. It is your badge as an accredited agent of the German Crown."

I took the card and the envelope and put them in my pocket-book.

"Where do I go after Egypt?" I asked.

"That remains to be seen. Probably you will go up the Blue Nile. Riza, the man you will meet, will direct you. Egypt is a nest of our agents who work peacefully under the nose of the English Secret Service."

"I am willing," I said. "But how do I reach Egypt?"

"You will travel by Holland and London. Here is your route," and he took a paper from his pocket. "Your passports are ready and will be given you at the frontier."

This was a pretty kettle of fish. I was to be packed off to Cairo by sea, which would take weeks, and God knows how I would get from Egypt to Constantinople. I saw all my plans falling to pieces about my ears, and just when I thought they were shaping nicely.

Stumm must have interpreted the look on my face as fear.

"You have no cause to be afraid," he said. "We have passed the word to the English police to look out for a suspicious South African named Brandt, one of Maritz's rebels. It is not difficult to have that kind of a hint conveyed to the proper quarter. But the description will not be yours. Your name will be Van der Linden, a respectable Java merchant going home to his plantations after a visit to his native shores. You had better get your dossier by heart, but I guarantee you will be asked no questions. We manage these things well in Germany."

I kept my eyes on the fire, while I did some savage thinking. I knew they would not let me out of their sight till they saw me in Holland, and, once there, there would be no possibility of getting back. When I left this house I would have no chance of giving them the slip. And yet I was well on my way to the East, the Danube could not be fifty miles off, and that way ran the road to Constantinople. It was a fairly desperate position. If I tried to get away Stumm would prevent me, and the odds were that I would go to join Peter in some infernal prison-camp.

Those moments were some of the worst I ever spent. I was absolutely and utterly baffled, like a rat in a trap. There seemed nothing for it but to go back to London and tell Sir Walter the game was up. And that was about as bitter as death.

He saw my face and laughed.

"Does your heart fail you, my little Dutchman? You funk the English? I will tell you one thing for your comfort. There is nothing in the world to be feared except me. Fail, and you have cause to shiver. Play me false and you had far better never have been born."

His ugly sneering face was close above mine. Then he put out his hands and gripped my shoulders as he had done the first afternoon.

I forget if I mentioned that part of the damage I got at Loos was a shrapnel bullet low down at the back of my neck. The wound had healed well enough, but I had pains there on a cold day. His fingers found the place and it hurt like hell.

There is a very narrow line between despair and black rage. I had about given up the game, but the sudden ache of my shoulders gave me purpose again. He must have seen the rage in my eyes for his own became cruel.

"The weasel would like to bite," he cried. "But the poor weasel has found its master. Stand still, vermin. Smile, look pleasant, or I will make pulp of you. Do you dare to frown at me?"

I shut my teeth and said never a word. I was choking in my throat and could not have uttered a syllable if I had tried.

Then he let me go, grinning like an ape.

I stepped back a pace and gave him my left between the eyes.

For a second he did not realize what had happened, for I don't suppose anyone had dared to lift a hand to him since he was a child. He blinked at me mildly. Then his face grew as red as fire.

"God in Heaven," he said quietly. "I am going to kill you," and he flung himself on me like a mountain.

I was expecting him and dodged the attack. I was quite calm now, but pretty helpless. The man had a gorilla's reach and could give me at least a couple of stone. He wasn't soft either, but looked as hard as granite. I was only just from hospital and absurdly out of training. He would certainly kill me if he could, and I saw nothing to prevent him.

My only chance was to keep him from getting to grips, for he could have squeezed in my ribs in two seconds. I fancied I was lighter on my legs than him, and I had a good eye. Black Monty at Kimberley had taught me to fight a bit, but there is no art on earth which can prevent a big man in a narrow space from sooner or later cornering a lesser one. That was the danger.

Backwards and forwards we padded on the soft carpet. He had no notion of guarding himself, and I got in a good few blows. Then I saw a queer thing. Every time I hit him he blinked and seemed to pause. I guessed the reason for that. He had gone through life keeping the crown of the causeway, and nobody had ever stood up to him. He wasn't a coward by a long chalk, but he was a bully, and had never been struck in his life. He was getting struck now in real earnest, and he didn't like it. He had lost his bearings and was growing as mad as a hatter.

I kept half an eye on the clock. I was hopeful now, and was looking for the right kind of chance. The risk was that I might tire sooner than him and be at his mercy.

Then I learned a truth I have never forgotten. If you are fighting a man who means to kill you, he will be apt to down you unless you mean to kill him too. Stumm did not know any rules to this game, and I forgot to allow for that. Suddenly, when I was watching his eyes, he launched a mighty kick at my stomach. If he had got me, this yarn would have had an abrupt ending. But by the mercy of God I was moving sideways when he let out, and his heavy boot just grazed my left thigh.

It was the place where most of the shrapnel had lodged, and for a second I was sick with pain and stumbled. Then I was on my feet again but with a new feeling in my blood. I had to smash Stumm or never sleep in my bed again.

I got a wonderful power from this new cold rage of mine. I felt I couldn't tire, and I danced round and dotted his face till it was streaming with blood. His bulky padded chest was no good to me, so I couldn't try for the mark.

He began to snort now and his breath came heavily. "You infernal cad," I said in good round English, "I'm going to knock the stuffing out of you," but he didn't know what I was saying.

Then at last he gave me my chance. He half tripped over a little table and his face stuck forward. I got him on the point of the chin, and put every ounce of weight I possessed behind the blow. He crumpled up in a heap and rolled over, upsetting a lamp and knocking a big china jar in two. His head, I remember, lay under the escritoire from which he had taken my passport.

I picked up the key and unlocked the door. In one of the gilded mirrors I smoothed my hair and tidied up my clothes. My anger had completely gone and I had no particular ill-will left against Stumm. He was a man of remarkable qualities, which would have brought him to the highest distinction in the Stone Age. But for all that he and his kind were back numbers.

I stepped out of the room, locked the door behind me, and started out on the second stage of my travels.

Christmastide

Everything depended on whether the servant was in the hall. I had put Stumm to sleep for a bit, but I couldn't flatter myself he would long be quiet, and when he came to he would kick the locked door to matchwood. I must get out of the house without a minute's delay, and if the door was shut and the old man gone to bed I was done.

I met him at the foot of the stairs, carrying a candle.

"Your master wants me to send off an important telegram. Where is the nearest office? There's one in the village, isn't there?" I spoke in my best German, the first time I had used the tongue since I crossed the frontier.

"The village is five minutes off at the foot of the avenue," he said. "Will you be long, sir?"

"I'll be back in a quarter of an hour," I said. "Don't lock up till I get in."

I put on my ulster and walked out into a clear starry night. My bag I left lying on a settle in the hall. There was nothing in it to compromise me, but I wished I could have got a toothbrush and some tobacco out of it. So began one of the craziest escapades you can well imagine. I couldn't stop to think of the future yet, but must take one step at a time. I ran down the avenue, my feet crackling on the hard snow, planning hard my programme for the next hour.

I found the village—half a dozen houses with one biggish place that looked like an inn. The moon was rising, and as I approached I saw that it was some kind of store. A funny little two-seated car was purring before the door, and I guessed this was also the telegraph office.

I marched in and told my story to a stout woman with spectacles on her nose who was talking to a young man.

"It is too late," she shook her head. "The Herr Burgrave knows that well. There is no connexion from here after eight o'clock. If the matter is urgent you must go to Schwandorf."

"How far is that?" I asked, looking for some excuse to get decently out of the shop.

"Seven miles," she said, "but here is Franz and the post-wagon. Franz, you will be glad to give the gentleman a seat beside you."

The sheepish-looking youth muttered something which I took to be assent, and finished off a glass of beer. From his eyes and manner he looked as if he were half drunk.

I thanked the woman, and went out to the car, for I was in a fever to take advantage of this unexpected bit of luck. I could hear the post-mistress enjoining Franz not to keep the gentleman waiting, and presently he came out and flopped into the driver's seat. We started in a series of voluptuous curves, till his eyes got accustomed to the darkness.

At first we made good going along the straight, broad highway lined with woods on one side and on the other snowy fields melting into haze. Then he began to talk, and, as he talked, he slowed down. This by no means suited my book, and I seriously wondered whether I should pitch him out and take charge of the thing. He was obviously a weakling, left behind in the conscription, and I could have done it with one hand. But by a fortunate chance I left him alone.

"That is a fine hat of yours, mein Herr," he said. He took off his own blue peaked cap, the uniform, I suppose, of the driver of the post-wagon, and laid it on his knee. The night air ruffled a shock of tow-coloured hair.

Then he calmly took my hat and clapped it on his head.

"With this thing I should be a gentleman," he said.

I said nothing, but put on his cap and waited.

"That is a noble overcoat, mein Herr," he went on. "It goes well with the hat. It is the kind of garment I have always desired to own. In two days it will be the holy Christmas, when gifts are given. Would that the good God sent me such a coat as yours!"

"You can try it on to see how it looks," I said good-humouredly.

He stopped the car with a jerk, and pulled off his blue coat. The exchange was soon effected. He was about my height, and my ulster fitted not so badly. I put on his overcoat, which had a big collar that buttoned round the neck.

The idiot preened himself like a girl. Drink and vanity had primed him for any folly. He drove so carelessly for a bit that he nearly put us into a ditch. We passed several cottages and at the last he slowed down.

"A friend of mine lives here," he announced. "Gertrud would like to see me in the fine clothes which the most amiable Herr has given me. Wait for me, I will not be long." And he scrambled out of the car and lurched into the little garden.

I took his place and moved very slowly forward. I heard the door open and the sound of laughing and loud voices. Then it shut, and looking back I saw that my idiot had been absorbed into the dwelling of his Gertrud. I waited no longer, but sent the car forward at its best speed.

Five minutes later the infernal thing began to give trouble—a nut loose in the antiquated steering-gear. I unhooked a lamp, examined it, and put the mischief right, but I was a quarter of an hour doing it. The highway ran now in a thick forest and I noticed branches going off now and then to the right. I was just thinking of turning up one of them, for I had no anxiety to visit Schwandorf, when I heard behind me the sound of a great car driven furiously.

I drew in to the right side—thank goodness I remembered the

rule of the road—and proceeded decorously, wondering what was going to happen. I could hear the brakes being clamped on and the car slowing down. Suddenly a big grey bonnet slipped past me and as I turned my head I heard a familiar voice.

It was Stumm, looking like something that has been run over. He had his jaw in a sling, so that I wondered if I had broken it, and his eyes were beautifully bunged up. It was that that saved me, that and his raging temper. The collar of the postman's coat was round my chin, hiding my beard, and I had his cap pulled well down on my brow. I remembered what Blenkiron had said—that the only way to deal with the Germans was naked bluff. Mine was naked enough, for it was all that was left to me.

"Where is the man you brought from Andersbach?" he roared, as well as his jaw would allow him.

I pretended to be mortally scared, and spoke in the best imitation I could manage of the postman's high cracked voice.

"He got out a mile back, Herr Burgrave," I quavered. "He was a rude fellow who wanted to go to Schwandorf, and then changed his mind."

"Where, you fool? Say exactly where he got down or I will wring your neck."

"In the wood this side of Gertrud's cottage . . . on the left hand . . . I left him running among the trees." I put all the terror I knew into my pipe, and it wasn't all acting.

"He means the Henrichs' cottage, Herr Colonel," said the chauffeur. "This man is courting the daughter."

Stumm gave an order and the great car backed, and, as I looked round, I saw it turning. Then as it gathered speed it shot forward, and presently was lost in the shadows. I had got over the first hurdle.

But there was no time to be lost. Stumm would meet the postman and would be tearing after me any minute. I took the first turning, and bucketed along a narrow woodland road. The hard ground would show very few tracks, I thought, and I hoped the pursuit would think I had gone on to Schwandorf. But it wouldn't do to risk it, and I was determined very soon to get the car off the road, leave it, and take to the forest. I took out my watch and calculated I could give myself ten minutes.

I was very nearly caught. Presently I came on a bit of rough heath, with a slope away from the road and here and there a patch of black which I took to be a sandpit. Opposite one of these I slewed the car to the edge, got out, started it again and saw it pitch head-foremost into the darkness. There was a splash of water and then silence. Craning over I could see nothing but murk, and the marks at the lip where the wheels had passed. They would find my tracks in the daylight but scarcely at this time of night.

Then I ran across the road to the forest. I was only just in time, for the echoes of the splash had hardly died away when I heard the sound of another car. I lay flat in a hollow below a tangle of snow-laden brambles and looked between the pine-trees at the moonlit road. It was Stumm's car again and to my consternation it stopped just a little short of the sandpit.

I saw an electric torch flashed, and Stumm himself got out and examined the tracks on the highway. Thank God, they would be still there for him to find, but had he tried half a dozen yards on he would have seen them turn towards the sandpit. If that had happened he would have beaten the adjacent woods and most certainly found me. There was a third man in the car, with my hat and coat on him. That poor devil of a postman had paid dear for his vanity.

They took a long time before they started again, and I was jolly well relieved when they went scouring down the road. I ran deeper into the woods till I found a track which—as I judged from the sky which I saw in a clearing—took me nearly due west. That wasn't the direction I wanted, so I bore off at right angles, and presently struck another road which I crossed in a hurry. After that I got entangled in some confounded kind of enclosure and had to climb paling after paling of rough stakes plaited with osiers. Then came a rise in the ground and I was on a low hill of pines which seemed to last for miles. All the time I was going at a good pace, and before I stopped to rest I calculated I had put six miles between me and the sandpit.

My mind was getting a little more active now; for the first part of the journey I had simply staggered from impulse to impulse. These impulses had been uncommon lucky, but I couldn't go on like that for ever. *Ek sal 'n plan maak*, says the old Boer when he gets into trouble, and it was up to me now to make a plan.

As soon as I began to think I saw the desperate business I was in for. Here was I, with nothing except what I stood up in—including a coat and cap that weren't mine—alone in mid-winter in the heart of South Germany. There was a man behind me looking for my blood, and soon there would be a hue-and-cry for me up and down the land. I had heard that the German police were pretty efficient, and I couldn't see that I stood the slimmest chance. If they caught me they would shoot me beyond doubt. I asked myself on what charge, and answered, "For knocking about a German officer." They couldn't have me up for espionage, for as far as I knew they had no evidence. I was simply a Dutchman that had got riled and had run amok. But if they cut down a cobbler for laughing at a second lieutenant—which is what happened at Zabern—I calculated that hanging would be too good for a man that had broken a colonel's jaw.

To make things worse my job was not to escape—though that would have been hard enough—but to get to Constantinople, more than a thousand miles off, and I reckoned I couldn't get there as a tramp. I had to be sent there, and now I had flung away my chance. If I had been a Catholic I would have said a prayer to St. Teresa, for she would have understood my troubles.

My mother used to say that when you felt down on your luck it was a good cure to count your mercies. So I set about counting mine. The first was that I was well started on my journey, for I couldn't be above two score miles from the Danube. The second was that I had Stumm's pass. I didn't see how I could use it, but there it was. Lastly I had plenty of money—fifty-three English sovereigns and the equivalent of three pounds in German paper which I had changed at the hotel. Also I had squared accounts with old Stumm. That was the biggest mercy of all.

I thought I'd better get some sleep, so I found a dryish hole below an oak root and squeezed myself into it. The snow lay deep in these woods and I was sopping wet up to my knees. All the same I managed to sleep for some hours, and got up and shook myself just as the winter's dawn was breaking through the tree-tops. Breakfast was the next thing, and I must find some sort of dwelling.

Almost at once I struck a road, a big highway running north and south. I trotted along in the bitter morning to get my circulation started, and presently I began to feel a little better. In a little I saw a church-spire, which meant a village. Stumm wouldn't be likely to have got on my tracks yet, I calculated, but there was always the chance that he had warned all the villages round by telephone and that they might be on the look-out for me. But that risk had to be taken, for I must have food.

It was the day before Christmas, I remembered, and people would be holidaying. The village was quite a big place, but at this hour—just after eight o'clock—there was nobody in the street except a wandering dog. I chose the most unassuming shop I could find, where a little boy was taking down the shutters—one of those general stores where they sell everything. The boy fetched a very old woman, who hobbled in from the back, fitting on her spectacles.

"*Grüss Gott,*" she said in a friendly voice, and I took off my cap. I saw from my reflection in a saucepan that I looked moderately respectable in spite of my night in the woods.

I told her a story of how I was walking from Schwandorf to see my mother at an imaginary place called Judenfeld, banking on the ignorance of villagers about any place five miles from their homes. I said my luggage had gone astray, and I hadn't time to wait for it, since my leave was short. The old lady was sympathetic and unsuspecting. She sold me a pound of chocolate, a box of biscuits, the better part of a ham, two tins of sardines and a rucksack to carry them. I also bought some soap, a comb and a cheap razor, and a small Tourists' Guide, published by a Leipzig firm. As I was leaving I saw what seemed like garments hanging up in the back shop, and turned to have a look at them. They were the kind of thing that Germans wear on their summer walking tours—long shooting capes made of a green stuff they call *loden*. I bought one, and a green felt hat and an alpenstock to keep it company. Then wishing the old woman and her belongings a merry Christmas, I departed and took the shortest cut out of the village. There were one or two people about now, but they did not seem to notice me.

I went into the woods again and walked for two miles till I halted for breakfast. I was not feeling quite so fit now, and I did not make much of my provisions, beyond eating a biscuit and some chocolate. I felt very thirsty and longed for hot tea. In an icy pool I washed and with infinite agony shaved my beard. That razor was the worst of its species, and my eyes were running all the time with the pain of the operation. Then I took off the postman's coat and cap, and buried them below some bushes. I was now a clean-shaven German pedestrian with a green cape and hat, and an absurd walking-stick with an iron-shod end—the sort of person who roams in thousands over the Fatherland in summer, but is a rarish bird in mid-winter.

The Tourists' Guide was a fortunate purchase, for it contained a big map of Bavaria which gave me my bearings. I was certainly not forty miles from the Danube—more like thirty. The road through the village I had left would have taken me to it. I had only to walk due south and I would reach it before night. So far as I could make out there were long tongues of forest running down to the river, and I resolved to keep to the woodlands. At the worst I would meet a forester or two, and I had a good enough story for them. On the highroad there might be awkward questions.

When I started out again I felt very stiff and the cold seemed to be growing intense. This puzzled me, for I had not minded it much up to now, and, being warm-blooded by nature, it never used to worry me. A sharp winter night on the high-veld was a long sight chillier than anything I had struck so far in Europe. But now my teeth were chattering and the marrow seemed to be freezing in my bones.

The day had started bright and clear, but a wrack of grey clouds soon covered the sky, and a wind from the east began to whistle. As I stumbled along through the snowy undergrowth I kept longing for bright warm places. I thought of those long days on the veld when the earth was like a great yellow bowl, with white roads running to the horizon and a tiny white farm basking in the heart of it, with its blue dam and patches of bright green lucerne. I thought of those baking days on the east coast, when the sea was like mother-of-pearl and the sky one burning turquoise. But most of all I thought of warm scented noons on trek, when one dozed in the shadow of the wagon and sniffed the wood smoke from the fire where the boys were cooking dinner.

From these pleasant pictures I returned to the beastly present— the thick snowy woods, the lowering sky, wet clothes, a hunted present, and a dismal future. I felt miserably depressed, and I couldn't think of any mercies to count. It struck me that I might be falling sick.

About midday I awoke with a start to the belief that I was being pursued. I cannot explain how or why the feeling came, except that it is a kind of instinct that men get who have lived much in wild countries. My senses, which had been numbed, suddenly grew keen, and my brain began to work double quick.

I asked myself what I would do if I were Stumm, with hatred in my heart, a broken jaw to avenge, and pretty well limitless powers. He must have found the car in the sandpit and seen my tracks in the wood opposite. I didn't know how good he and his men might be at following a spoor, but I knew that any ordinary Kaffir could have nosed it out easily. But he didn't need to do that. This was a civilized country full of roads and railways. I must some time and somewhere come out of the woods. He could have all the roads watched, and the telephone would set everyone on my track within a radius of fifty miles. Besides, he would soon pick up my trail in the village I had visited that morning. From the map I learned that it was called Greif, and it was likely to live up to that name with me.

Presently I came to a rocky knoll which rose out of the forest.

Keeping well in shelter I climbed to the top and cautiously looked around me. Away to the east I saw the vale of a river with broad fields and church-spires. West and south the forest rolled unbroken in a wilderness of snowy tree-tops. There was no sign of life anywhere, not even a bird, but I knew very well that behind me in the woods were men moving swiftly on my track, and that it was pretty well impossible for me to get away.

There was nothing for it but to go on till I dropped or was taken. I shaped my course south with a shade of west in it, for the map showed me that in that direction I would soonest strike the Danube. What I was going to do when I got there I didn't trouble to think. I had fixed the river as my immediate goal and the future must take care of itself.

I was now certain that I had fever on me. It was still in my bones, as a legacy from Africa, and had come out once or twice when I was with the battalion in Hampshire. The bouts had been short for I had known of their coming and dosed myself. But now I had no quinine, and it looked as if I were in for a heavy go. It made me feel desperately wretched and stupid, and I all but blundered into capture.

For suddenly I came on a road and was going to cross it blindly, when a man rode slowly past on a bicycle. Luckily I was in the shade of a clump of hollies and he was not looking my way, though he was not three yards off. I crawled forward to reconnoitre. I saw about half a mile of road running straight through the forest and every two hundred yards was a bicyclist. They wore uniform and appeared to be acting as sentries.

This could only have one meaning. Stumm had picketed all the roads and cut me off in an angle of the woods. There was no chance of getting across unobserved. As I lay there with my heart sinking, I had the horrible feeling that the pursuit might be following me from behind, and that at any moment I would be enclosed between two fires.

For more than an hour I stayed there with my chin in the snow. I didn't see any way out, and I was feeling so ill that I didn't seem to care. Then my chance came suddenly out of the skies.

The wind rose, and a great gust of snow blew from the east. In five minutes it was so thick that I couldn't see across the road. At first I thought it a new addition to my troubles, and then very slowly I saw the opportunity. I slipped down the bank and made ready to cross.

I almost blundered into one of the bicyclists. He cried out and fell off his machine, but I didn't wait to investigate. A sudden access of strength came to me and I darted into the woods on the farther side. I knew I would be soon swallowed from sight in the drift, and I knew that the falling snow would hide my tracks. So I put my best foot forward.

I must have run miles before the hot fit passed, and I stopped from sheer bodily weakness. There was no sound except the crush of falling snow, the wind seemed to have gone, and the place was very solemn and quiet. But Heavens! how the snow fell! It was partly screened by the branches, but all the same it was piling itself up deep everywhere. My legs seemed made of lead, my head burned, and there were fiery pains over all my body. I stumbled on blindly, without a notion of any direction, determined only to keep going to the last. For I knew that if I once lay down I would never rise again.

When I was a boy I was fond of fairy tales, and most of the stories I remembered had been about great German forests and snow and charcoal burners and woodmen's huts. Once I had longed to see these things, and now I was fairly in the thick of them. There had been wolves, too, and I wondered idly if I should fall in with a pack. I felt myself getting light-headed. I fell repeatedly and laughed sillily every time. Once I dropped into a hole and lay for some time at the bottom giggling. If anyone had found me then he would have taken me for a madman.

The twilight of the forest grew dimmer, but I scarcely noticed it. Evening was falling, and soon it would be night, a night without morning for me.

My body was going on without the direction of my brain, for my mind was filled with craziness. I was like a drunk man who keeps running, for he knows that if he stops he will fall, and I had a sort of bet with myself not to lie down—not at any rate just yet. If I lay down I should feel the pain in my head worse. Once I had ridden for five days down country with fever on me and the flat bush trees had seemed to melt into one big mirage and dance quadrilles before my eyes. But then I had more or less kept my wits. Now I was fairly daft, and every minute growing dafter.

Then the trees seemed to stop and I was walking on flat ground. It was a clearing, and before me twinkled a little light. The change restored me to consciousness, and suddenly I felt with horrid intensity the fire in my head and bones and the weakness of my limbs. I longed to sleep, and I had a notion that a place to sleep was before me. I moved towards the light and presently saw through a screen of snow the outline of a cottage.

I had no fear, only an intolerable longing to lie down. Very slowly I made my way to the door and knocked. My weakness was so great that I could hardly lift my hand.

There were voices within, and a corner of the curtain was lifted from the window. Then the door opened and a woman stood before me, a woman with a thin, kindly face.

"*Grüss Gott*," she said, while children peeped from behind her skirts.

"*Grüss Gott*," I replied. I leaned against the door-post, and speech forsook me.

She saw my condition. "Come in, sir," she said. "You are sick and it is no weather for a sick man."

I stumbled after her and stood dripping in the centre of the little kitchen, while three wondering children stared at me. It was a poor place, scantily furnished, but a good log-fire burned on the hearth. The shock of warmth gave me one of those minutes of self-possession which come sometimes in the middle of a fever.

"I am sick, mother, and I have walked far in the storm and lost my way. I am from Africa, where the climate is hot, and your cold brings me fever. It will pass in a day or two if you can give me a bed."

"You are welcome," she said; "but first I will make you coffee."

I took off my dripping cloak, and crouched close to the hearth. She gave me coffee—poor washy stuff, but blessedly hot. Poverty was spelled large in everything I saw. I felt the tides of fever beginning to overflow my brain again, and I made a great attempt to set my affairs straight before I was overtaken. With difficulty I took out Stumm's pass from my pocket-book.

"That is my warrant," I said. "I am a member of the Imperial Secret Service and for the sake of my work I must move in the dark. If you will permit it, mother, I will sleep till I am better, but no one must know that I am here. If anyone comes, you must deny my presence."

She looked at the big seal as if it were a talisman.

"Yes, yes," she said, "you will have the bed in the garret and be left in peace till you are well. We have no neighbours near, and the storm will shut the roads. I will be silent, I and the little ones."

My head was beginning to swim, but I made one more effort.

"There is food in my rucksack—biscuits and ham and chocolate. Pray take it for your use. And here is some money to buy Christmas fare for the little ones." And I gave her some of the German notes.

After that my recollection becomes dim. She helped me up a ladder to the garret, undressed me, and gave me a thick coarse nightgown. I seem to remember that she kissed my hand, and that she was crying. "The good Lord has sent you," she said. "Now the little ones have their prayers answered and the Christkind will not pass by our door."

The Essen Barges

I LAY for four days like a log in that garret bed. The storm died down, the thaw set in, and the snow melted. The children played about the doors and told stories at night round the fire. Stumm's myrmidons no doubt beset every road and troubled the lives of innocent wayfarers. But no one came near the cottage, and the fever worked itself out while I lay in peace.

It was a bad bout, but on the fifth day it left me, and I lay, as weak as a kitten, staring at the rafters and the little skylight. It was a leaky, draughty old place, but the woman of the cottage had heaped deerskins and blankets on my bed and kept me warm. She came in now and then, and once she brought me a brew of some bitter herbs which greatly refreshed me. A little thin porridge was all the food I could eat, and some chocolate made from the slabs in my rucksack.

I lay and dozed through the day, hearing the faint chatter of children below, and getting stronger hourly. Malaria passes as quickly as it comes and leaves a man little the worse, though this was one of the sharpest turns I ever had. As I lay I thought, and my thoughts followed curious lines. One queer thing was that Stumm and his doings seemed to have been shot back into a lumber-room of my brain and the door locked. He didn't seem to be a creature of the living present, but a distant memory on which I could look calmly. I thought a good deal about my battalion and the comedy of my present position. You see I was getting better, for I called it comedy now, not tragedy.

But chiefly I thought of my mission. All that wild day in the snow it had seemed the merest farce. The three words Harry Bullivant had scribbled had danced through my head in a crazy fandango. They were present to me now, but coolly and sanely in all their meagreness.

I remember that I took each one separately and chewed on it for hours. *Kasredin*—there was nothing to be got out of that. *Cancer*—there were too many meanings, all blind. *v. I*—that was the worst gibberish of all.

Before this I had always taken the *I* as the letter of the alphabet. I had thought the *v.* must stand for *von*, and I had considered the German names beginning with I—Ingolstadt, Ingeburg, Ingenohl, and all the rest of them. I had made a list of about seventy at the British Museum before I left London.

Now I suddenly found myself taking the *I* as the numeral One. Idly, not thinking what I was doing, I put it into German.

Then I nearly fell out of the bed. *Von Einem*—the name I had heard at Gaudian's house, the name Stumm had spoken behind his hand, the name to which Hilda was probably the prefix. It was a tremendous discovery—the first real bit of light I had found. Harry Bullivant knew that some man or woman called von Einem was at the heart of the mystery. Stumm had spoken of the same personage with respect and in connexion with the work I proposed to do in raising the Moslem Africans. If I found von Einem I would be getting very warm. What was the word that Stumm had whispered to Gaudian and scared that worthy? It had sounded like Uhnmantl. If I could only get that clear, I would solve the riddle.

I think that discovery completed my cure. At any rate on the evening of the fifth day—it was Wednesday, the 29th of December—I was well enough to get up. When the dark had fallen and it was too late to fear a visitor, I came downstairs and, wrapped in my green cape, took a seat by the fire.

As we sat there in the firelight, with the three white-headed children staring at me with saucer eyes, and smiling when I looked their way, the woman talked. Her man had gone to the wars on the Eastern front, and the last she had heard from him he was in a Polish bog and longing for his dry native woodlands. The struggle meant little to her. It was an act of God, a thunderbolt out of the sky, which had taken a husband from her, and might soon make her a widow and her children fatherless. She knew nothing of its causes and purposes, and thought of the Russians as a gigantic nation of savages, heathens who had never been converted, and who would eat up German homes if the good Lord and the brave German soldiers did not stop them. I tried hard to find out if she had any notion of affairs in the West, but she hadn't beyond the fact that there was trouble with the French. I doubt if she knew of England's share in it. She was a decent soul, with no bitterness against anybody, not even the Russians if they would spare her man.

That night I realized the crazy folly of war. When I saw the splintered shell of Ypres and heard hideous tales of German doings, I used to want to see the whole land of the Boche given up to fire and sword. I thought we could never end the war properly without giving the Huns some of their own medicine. But that woodcutter's cottage cured me of such nightmares. I was for punishing the guilty but letting the innocent go free. It was our business to thank God and keep our hands clean from the ugly blunders to which Germany's madness had driven her. What good would it do Christian folk to burn poor little huts like this and leave children's bodies by the wayside? To be able to laugh and to be merciful are the only things that make man better than the beasts.

The place, as I have said, was desperately poor. The woman's face had the skin stretched tight over the bones and that transparency which means under-feeding; I fancied she did not have the liberal allowance that soldiers' wives get in England. The children looked better nourished, but it was by their mother's sacrifice. I did my best to cheer them up. I told them long yarns about Africa and lions and tigers, and I got some pieces of wood and whittled them into toys. I am fairly good with a knife, and I carved very presentable likenesses of a monkey, a springbok, and a rhinoceros. The children went to bed hugging the first toys, I expect, they ever possessed.

It was clear to me that I must leave as soon as possible. I had to get on with my business, and besides, it was not fair to the woman. Any moment I might be found here, and she would get into trouble for harbouring me. I asked her if she knew where the Danube was, and her answer surprised me. "You will reach it in an hour's walk," she said. "The track through the wood runs straight to the ferry."

Next morning after breakfast I took my departure. It was drizzling weather, and I was feeling very lean. Before going I presented my hostess and the children with two sovereigns apiece. "It is English gold," I said, "for I have to travel among our enemies and use our enemies' money. But the gold is good, and if you go to any town they will change it for you. But I advise you to put it in your stocking-foot and use it only if all else fails. You must keep your home going, for some day there will be peace and your man will come back from the wars."

I kissed the children, shook the woman's hand, and went off down the clearing. They had cried "*Auf Wiedersehen,*" but it wasn't likely I would ever see them again.

The snow had all gone, except in patches in the deep hollows. The ground was like a full sponge, and a cold rain drifted in my eyes. After half an hour's steady trudge the trees thinned, and presently I came out on a knuckle of open ground cloaked in dwarf junipers. And there before me lay the plain, and a mile off a broad brimming river.

I sat down and looked dismally at the prospect. The exhilaration of my discovery the day before had gone. I had stumbled on a worthless piece of knowledge, for I could not use it. Hilda von Einem, if such a person existed and possessed the great secret, was probably living in some big house in Berlin, and I was about as likely to get anything out of her as to be asked to dine with the Kaiser. Blenkiron might do something, but where on earth was Blenkiron? I dared say Sir Walter would value the information, but I could not get to Sir Walter. I was to go on to Constantinople, running away from the people who really pulled the ropes. But if I stayed I could do nothing, and I could not stay. I must go on and I didn't see how I could go on. Every course seemed shut to me, and I was in as pretty a tangle as any man ever stumbled into.

For I was morally certain that Stumm would not let the thing drop. I knew too much, and besides I had outraged his pride. He would beat the countryside till he got me, and he undoubtedly would get me if I waited much longer. But how was I to get over the border? My passport would be no good, for the number of that pass would long ere this have been wired to every police station in Germany, and to produce it would be to ask for trouble. Without it I could not cross the borders by any railway. My studies of the Tourists' Guide had suggested that once I was in Austria I might find things slacker and move about easier. I thought of having a try at the Tyrol and I also thought of Bohemia. But these places were a long way off, and there were several thousand chances each day that I would be caught on the road.

This was Thursday, the 30th of December, the second last day of the year. I was due in Constantinople on the 17th of January. Constantinople! I had thought myself a long way from it in Berlin, but now it seemed as distant as the moon.

But that big sullen river in front of me led to it. And as I looked my attention was caught by a curious sight. On the far eastern horizon, where the water slipped round a corner of hill, there was a long trail of smoke. The streamers thinned out, and seemed to come from some boat well round the corner, but I could see at least two boats in view. Therefore there must be a long train of barges, with a tug in tow.

I looked to the west and saw another such procession coming into sight. First went a big river steamer—it can't have been much less than 1,000 tons—and after came a string of barges. I counted no less than six besides the tug. They were heavily loaded and their draught must have been considerable, but there was plenty of depth in the flooded river.

A moment's reflection told me what I was looking at. Once Sandy, in one of the discussions you have in hospital, had told us just how the Germans munitioned their Balkan campaign. They were pretty certain of dishing Serbia at the first go, and it was up to them to get through guns and shells to the old Turk, who was running pretty short in his first supply. Sandy said that they wanted the railway, but they wanted still more the river, and they could make certain of that in a week. He told us how endless strings of barges, loaded up at the big factories of Westphalia, were moving through the canals from the Rhine or the Elbe to the Danube. Once the first reached Turkey, there would be regular delivery, you see—as quick as the Turks could handle the stuff. And they didn't return empty, Sandy said, but came back full of Turkish cotton and Bulgarian beef and Rumanian corn. I don't know where Sandy got the knowledge, but there was the proof of it before my eyes.

It was a wonderful sight, and I could have gnashed my teeth to see those loads of munitions going snugly off to the enemy. I calculated they would give our poor chaps hell in Gallipoli. And then, as I looked, an idea came into my head and with it an eighth part of a hope.

There was only one way for me to get out of Germany, and that was to leave in such good company that I would be asked no questions. That was plain enough. If I travelled to Turkey, for instance, in the Kaiser's suite, I would be as safe as the mail; but if I went on my own I was done. I had, so to speak, to get my passport *inside* Germany, to join some caravan which had free marching powers. And there was the kind of caravan before me—the Essen barges.

It sounded lunacy, for I guessed that munitions of war would be as jealously guarded as old Hindenburg's health. All the safer, I replied to myself, once I get there. If you are looking for a deserter you don't seek him at the favourite regimental public-house. If you're after a thief, among the places you'd be apt to leave unsearched would be Scotland Yard.

It was sound reasoning, but how was I to get on board? Probably the beastly things did not stop once in a hundred miles, and Stumm would get me long before I struck a halting-place. And even if I did get a chance like that, how was I to get permission to travel?

One step was clearly indicated—to get down to the river bank at once. So I set off at a sharp walk across squelchy fields, till I struck a road where the ditches had overflowed so as almost to meet in the middle. The place was so bad that I hoped travellers might be few. And as I trudged, my thoughts were busy with my prospects as a stowaway. If I bought food, I might get a chance to lie snug on one of the barges. They would not break bulk till they got to their journey's end.

Suddenly I noticed that the steamer, which was now abreast me, began to move towards the shore, and as I came over a low rise, I saw on my left a straggling village with a church, and a small landing-stage. The houses stood about a quarter of a mile from the stream, and between them was a straight, poplar-fringed road.

Soon there could be no doubt about it. The procession was coming to a standstill. The big tug nosed her way in and lay up alongside the pier, where in that season of flood there was enough depth of water. She signalled to the barges and they also started to drop anchors, which showed that there must be at least two men aboard each. Some of them dragged a bit and it was rather a cock-eyed train that lay in mid-stream. The tug got out a gangway, and from where I lay I saw half a dozen men leave it, carrying something on their shoulders.

It could be only one thing—a dead body. Someone of the crew must have died, and this halt was to bury him. I watched the procession move towards the village and I reckoned they would take some time there, though they might have wired ahead for a grave to be dug. Anyhow, they would be long enough to give me a chance.

For I had decided upon the brazen course. Blenkiron had said you couldn't cheat the Boche, but you could bluff him. I was going to put up the most monstrous bluff. If the whole country-side was hunting for Richard Hannay, Richard Hannay would walk through as a pal of the hunters. For I remembered the pass Stumm had given me. If that was worth a tinker's curse it should be good enough to impress a ship's captain.

Of course there were a thousand risks. They might have heard of me in the village and told the ship's party the story. For that reason I resolved not to go there but to meet the sailors when they were returning to the boat. Or the captain might have been warned and got the number of my pass, in which case Stumm would have his hands on me pretty soon. Or the captain might be an ignorant fellow who had never seen a Secret Service pass and did not know what it meant, and would refuse me transport by the letter of his instructions. In that case I might wait on another convoy.

I had shaved and made myself a fairly respectable figure before I left the cottage. It was my cue to wait for the men when they left the church, wait on that quarter-mile of straight highway. I judged the captain must be in the party. The village, I was glad to observe, seemed very empty. I have my own notions about the Bavarians as fighting men, but I am bound to say that, judging by my observations, very few of them stayed at home.

That funeral took hours. They must have had to dig the grave, for I waited near the road in a clump of cherry-trees, with my feet in two inches of mud and water, till I felt chilled to the bone. I prayed to God it would not bring back my fever, for I was only one day out of bed. I had very little tobacco left in my pouch, but I stood myself one pipe, and I ate one of the three cakes of chocolate I still carried.

At last, well after midday, I could see the ship's party returning. They marched two by two and I was thankful to see that they had no villagers with them. I walked to the road, turned up it, and met the vanguard, carrying my head as high as I knew how.

"Where's your captain?" I asked, and a man jerked his thumb over his shoulder. The others wore thick jerseys and knitted caps, but there was one man at the rear in uniform. He was a short, broad man with a weather-beaten face and an anxious eye.

"May I have a word with you, Herr Captain?" I said, with what I hoped was a judicious blend of authority and conciliation.

He nodded to his companion, who walked on.

"Yes?" he asked rather impatiently.

I proffered him my pass. Thank Heaven he had seen the kind of thing before, for his face at once took on that curious look which one person in authority always wears when he is confronted with another. He studied it closely and then raised his eyes.

"Well, sir?" he said. "I observe your credentials. What can I do for you?"

"I take it you are bound for Constantinople?" I asked.

"The boats go as far as Rustchuk," he replied. "There the stuff is transferred to the railway."

"And you reach Rustchuk when?"

"In ten days, bar accidents. Let us say twelve to be safe."

"I want to accompany you," I said. "In my profession, Herr Captain, it is necessary sometimes to make journeys by other than the common route. That is now my desire. I have the right to call upon some other branch of our country's service to help me. Hence my request."

Very plainly he did not like it.

"I must telegraph about it. My instructions are to let no one aboard, not even a man like you. I am sorry, sir, but I must get authority first before I can fall in with your desire. Besides, my boat is ill-found. You had better wait for the next batch and ask Dreyser to take you. I lost Walter to-day. He was ill when he came aboard—a disease of the heart—but he would not be persuaded. And last night he died."

"Was that him you have been burying?" I asked.

"Even so. He was a good man and my wife's cousin, and now I have no engineer. Only a fool of a boy from Hamburg. I have just come from wiring to my owners for a fresh man, but even if he comes by the quickest train he will scarcely overtake us before Vienna or even Buda."

I saw light at last.

"We will go together," I said, "and cancel that wire. For behold, Herr Captain, I am an engineer, and will gladly keep an eye on your boilers till we get to Rustchuk."

He looked at me doubtfully.

"I am speaking truth," I said. "Before the war I was an engineer in Damaraland. Mining was my branch, but I had a good general training, and I know enough to run a river-boat. Have no fear. I promise you I will earn my passage."

His face cleared, and he looked what he was, an honest, good-humoured North German seaman.

"Come then in God's name," he cried, "and we will make a bargain. I will let the telegraph sleep. I require authority from the Government to take a passenger, but I need none to engage a new engineer."

He sent one of the hands back to the village to cancel his wire. In ten minutes I found myself on board, and ten minutes later we were out in mid-stream and our tows were lumbering into line. Coffee was being made ready in the cabin, and while I waited for it I picked up the captain's binoculars and scanned the place I had left.

I saw some curious things. On the first road I had struck on leaving the cottage there were men on bicycles moving rapidly. They seemed to wear uniform. On the next parallel road, the one that ran through the village, I could see others. I noticed, too, that several figures appeared to be beating the intervening fields.

Stumm's cordon had got busy at last, and I thanked my stars that not one of the villagers had seen me. I had not got away much too soon, for in another half-hour he would have had me.

The Return of the Straggler

BEFORE I turned in that evening I had done some good hours' work in the engine-room. The boat was oil-fired, and in very fair order, so my duties did not look as if they would be heavy. There was nobody who could be properly called an engineer; only, besides the furnace-men, a couple of lads from Hamburg who had been a year ago apprentices in a ship-building yard. They were civil fellows, both of them consumptive, who did what I told them and said little. By bed-time, if you had seen me in my blue jumper, a pair of carpet slippers, and a flat cap—all the property of the deceased Walter—you would have sworn I had been bred to the firing of river-boats, whereas I had acquired most of my knowledge on one run down the Zambesi, when the proper engineer got drunk and fell overboard among the crocodiles.

The captain—they called him Schenk—was out of his bearings in the job. He was a Frisian and a first-class deep-water seaman, but, since he knew the Rhine delta, and because the German mercantile marine was laid on the ice till the end of war, they had turned him on to this show. He was bored by the business, and didn't understand it very well. The river charts puzzled him, and though it was pretty plain going for hundreds of miles, yet he was in a perpetual fidget about the pilotage. You could see that he would have been far more in his element smelling his way through the shoals of the Ems mouth, or beating against a north-easter in the shallow Baltic. He had six barges in tow, but the heavy flood of the Danube made it an easy job except when it came to going slow. There were two men on each barge, who came aboard every morning to draw rations. That was a funny business, for we never lay to if we could help it. There was a dinghy belonging to each barge, and the men used to row to the next and get a lift in that barge's dinghy, and so forth. Six men would appear in the dinghy of the barge nearest us and carry off supplies for the rest. The men were mostly Frisians, slow-spoken, sandy-haired lads, very like the breed you strike on the Essex coast.

It was the fact that Schenk was really a deep-water sailor, and so a novice to the job, that made me get on with him. He was a good fellow and quite willing to take a hint, so before I had been twenty-four hours on board he was telling me all his difficulties, and I was doing my best to cheer him. And difficulties came thick, because the next night was New Year's Eve.

I knew that that night was a season of gaiety in Scotland, but Scotland wasn't in it with the Fatherland. Even Schenk, though he was in charge of valuable stores and was voyaging against time, was quite clear that the men must have permission for some kind of beano. Just before darkness we came abreast a fair-sized town, whose name I never discovered, and decided to lie to for the night. The arrangement was that one man should be left on guard in each barge, and the other get four hours' leave ashore. Then he would return and relieve his friend, who should proceed to do the same thing. I foresaw that there would be some fun when the first batch returned, but I did not dare to protest. I was desperately anxious to get past the Austrian frontier, for I had a half-notion we might be searched there, but Schenk took this *Sylvesterabend* business so seriously that I would have risked a row if I had tried to argue.

The upshot was what I expected. We got the first batch aboard about midnight, blind to the world, and the others straggled in at all hours next morning. I stuck to the boat for obvious reasons, but next day it became too serious, and I had to go ashore with the captain to try and round up the stragglers. We got them all in but two, and I am inclined to think these two had never meant to come back. If I had a soft job like a river-boat I shouldn't be inclined to run away in the middle of Germany with the certainty that my best fate would be to be scooped up for the trenches, but your Frisian has no more imagination than a haddock. The absentees were both watchmen from the barges, and I fancy the monotony of the life had got on their nerves.

The captain was in a raging temper, for he was short-handed to begin with. He would have started a press-gang, but there was no superfluity of men in that township: nothing but boys and grandfathers. As I was helping to run the trip I was pretty annoyed also, and I sluiced down the drunkards with icy Danube water, using all the worst language I knew in Dutch and German. It was a raw morning, and as we raged through the riverside streets I remember I heard the dry crackle of wild geese going overhead, and wished I could get a shot at them. I told one fellow—he was the most troublesome—that he was a disgrace to a great Empire, and was only fit to fight with the filthy English.

"God in Heaven!" said the captain, "we can delay no longer. We must make shift the best we can. I can spare one man from the deck hands, and you must give up one from the engine-room."

That was arranged, and we were tearing back rather short in the wind when I espied a figure sitting on a bench beside the booking-office on the pier. It was a slim figure, in an old suit of khaki: some cast-off duds which had long lost the semblance of a uniform. It had a gentle face, and was smoking peacefully, looking out upon the river and the boats and us noisy fellows with meek philosophical eyes. If I had seen General French sitting there and looking like nothing on earth I couldn't have been more surprised.

The man stared at me without recognition. He was waiting for his cue.

I spoke rapidly in Sesutu, for I was afraid the captain might know Dutch.

"Where have you come from?" I asked.

"They shut me up in *tronk*," said Peter, "and I ran away. I am tired, Cornelis, and want to continue the journey by boat."

"Remember you have worked for me in Africa," I said. "You are just home from Damaraland. You are a German who has lived thirty years away from home. You can tend a furnace and have worked in mines."

Then I spoke to the captain.

"Here is a fellow who used to be in my employ, Captain Schenk. It's almighty luck we've struck him. He's old, and not very strong in the head, but I'll go bail he's a good worker. He says he'll come with us and I can use him in the engine-room."

"Stand up," said the captain.

Peter stood up, light and slim and wiry as a leopard. A sailor does not judge men by girth and weight.

"He'll do," said Schenk, and the next minute he was readjusting his crews and giving the strayed revellers the rough side of his tongue. As it chanced, I couldn't keep Peter with me, but had to send him to one of the barges, and I had time for no more than five words with him, when I told him to hold his tongue and live up to his reputation as a half-wit. That accursed *Sylvesterabend* had played havoc with the whole outfit, and the captain and I were weary men before we got things straight.

In one way it turned out well. That afternoon we passed the frontier and I never knew it till I saw a man in a strange uniform come aboard, who copied some figures on a schedule, and brought us a mail. With my dirty face and general air of absorption in duty, I must have been an unsuspicious figure. He took down the names of the men in the barges, and Peter's name was given as it appeared on the ship's roll—Anton Blum.

"You must feel it strange, Herr Brandt," said the captain, "to be scrutinized by a policeman, you who give orders, I doubt not, to many policemen."

I shrugged my shoulders. "It is my profession. It is my business to go unrecognized often by my own servants." I could see that I was becoming rather a figure in the captain's eyes. He liked the way I kept the men up to their work, for I hadn't been a nigger-driver for nothing.

Late on that Sunday night we passed through a great city which the captain told me was Vienna. It seemed to last for miles and miles, and to be as brightly lit as a circus. After that, we were in big plains and the air grew perishing cold. Peter had come aboard once for his rations, but usually he left it to his partner, for he was lying very low. But one morning—I think it was the 5th of January, when we had passed Buda and were moving through great sodden flats just sprinkled with snow—the captain took it into his head to get me to overhaul the barge loads. Armed with a mighty typewritten list, I made a tour of the barges, beginning with the hindmost. There was a fine old stock of deadly weapons—mostly machine-guns and some field-pieces, and enough shells to blow up the Gallipoli peninsula. All kinds of shell were there, from the big 14-inch crumps to rifle grenades and trench-mortars. It made me fairly sick to see all these good things preparing for our own fellows, and I wondered whether I would not be doing my best service if I engineered a big explosion. Happily I had the common sense to remember my job and my duty and to stick to it.

Peter was in the middle of the convoy, and I found him pretty unhappy, principally through not being allowed to smoke. His companion was an ox-eyed lad, whom I ordered to look-out while Peter and I went over the lists.

"Cornelis, my old friend," he said, "there are some pretty toys here. With a spanner and a couple of clear hours I could make these maxims about as deadly as bicycles. What do you say to a try?"

"I've considered that," I said, "but it won't do. We're on a bigger business than wrecking munition convoys. I want to know how you got here."

He smiled with that extraordinary Sunday-school docility of his.

"It was very simple, Cornelis. I was foolish in the café—but they have told you of that. You see I was angry and did not reflect. They had separated us, and I could see would treat me as dirt. Therefore, my bad temper came out, for, as I have told you, I do not like Germans."

Peter gazed lovingly at the little bleak farms which dotted the Hungarian plain.

"All night I lay in *tronk* with no food. In the morning they fed me, and took me hundreds of miles in a train to a place which I think is called Neuburg. It was a great prison, full of English officers . . . I asked myself many times on the journey what was the reason of this treatment, for I could see no sense in it. If they wanted to punish me for insulting them they had the chance to send me off to the trenches. No one could have objected. If they thought me useless they could have turned me back to Holland. I could not have stopped them. But they treated me as if I were a dangerous man, whereas all their conduct hitherto had shown that they thought me a fool. I could not understand it.

"But I had not been one night in that Neuburg place before I thought of the reason. They wanted to keep me under observation as a check upon you, Cornelis. I figured it out this way. They had given you some very important work which required them to let you into some big secret. So far, good. They evidently thought much of you, even yon Stumm man, though he was as rude as a buffalo. But they did not know you fully, and they wanted a check on you. That check they found in Peter Pienaar. Peter was a fool, and if there was anything to blab, sooner or later Peter would blab it. Then they would stretch out a long arm and nip you short, wherever you were. Therefore they must keep old Peter under their eye."

"That sounds likely enough," I said.

"It was God's truth," said Peter. "And when it was all clear to me I settled that I must escape. Partly because I am a free man and do not like to be in prison, but mostly because I was not sure of myself. Some day my temper would go again, and I might say foolish things for which Cornelis would suffer. So it was very certain that I must escape.

"Now, Cornelis, I noticed pretty soon that there were two

kinds among the prisoners. There were the real prisoners, mostly English and French, and there were humbugs. The humbugs were treated, apparently, like the others, but not really, as I soon perceived. There was one man who passed as an English officer, another as a French Canadian, and the others called themselves Russians. None of the honest men suspected them, but they were there as spies to hatch plots for escape and get the poor devils caught in the act, and to worm out confidences which might be of value. That is the German notion of good business. I am not a British soldier to think all men are gentlemen. I know that amongst men there are desperate *skellums*, so I soon picked up this game. It made me very angry, but it was a good thing for my plan. I made my resolution to escape the day I arrived at Neuburg, and on Christmas Day I had a plan made."

"Peter, you're an old marvel. Do you mean to say you were quite certain of getting away whenever you wanted?"

"Quite certain, Cornelis. You see, I have been wicked in my time and know something about the inside of prisons. You may build them like great castles, or they may be like a backveld *tronk*, only mud and corrugated iron, but there is always a key and a man who keeps it, and that man can be bested. I knew I could get away, but I did not think it would be so easy. That was due to the bogus prisoners, my friends, the spies.

"I made great pals with them. On Christmas night we were very jolly together. I think I spotted every one of them the first day. I bragged about my past and all I had done, and I told them I was going to escape. They backed me up and promised to help. Next morning I had a plan. In the afternoon, just after dinner, I had to go to the commandant's room. They treated me a little differently from the others, for I was not a prisoner of war, and I went there to be asked questions and to be cursed as a stupid Dutchman. There was no strict guard kept there, for the place was on the second floor, and distant by many yards from any staircase. In the corridor outside the commandant's room there was a window which had no bars, and four feet from the window the limb of a great tree. A man might reach that limb, and if he were active as a monkey might descend to the ground. Beyond that I knew nothing, but I am a good climber, Cornelis.

"I told the others of my plan. They said it was good, but no one offered to come with me. They were very noble; they declared that the scheme was mine and I should have the fruit of it, for if more than one tried, detection was certain. I agreed and thanked them—thanked them with tears in my eyes. Then one of them very secretly produced a map. We planned out my road, for I was going straight to Holland. It was a long road, and I had no money, for they had taken all my sovereigns when I was arrested, but they promised to get a subscription up among themselves to start me. Again I wept tears of gratitude. This was on Sunday, the day after Christmas. I settled to make the attempt on the Wednesday afternoon.

"Now, Cornelis, when the lieutenant took us to see the British prisoners, you remember, he told us many things about the ways of prisons. He told us how they loved to catch a man in the act of escape, so that they could use him harshly with a clear conscience. I thought of that, and calculated that now my friends would have told everything to the commandant, and that they would be waiting to bottle me on the Wednesday. Till then I reckoned I would be slackly guarded, for they would look on me as safe in the net . . .

"So I went out of the window the next day. It was the Monday afternoon . . ."

"That was a bold stroke," I said admiringly.

"The plan was bold, but it was not skilful," said Peter modestly. "I had no money beyond seven marks, and I had but one stick of chocolate. I had no overcoat, and it was snowing hard. Further, I could not get down the tree, which had a trunk as smooth and branchless as a blue gum. For a little I thought I should be compelled to give in, and I was not happy.

"But I had leisure, for I did not think I would be missed before nightfall, and given time a man can do most things. By and by I found a branch which led beyond the outer wall of the yard and hung above the river. This I followed, and then dropped from it into the stream. It was a drop of some yards, and the water was very swift, so that I nearly drowned. I would rather swim the Limpopo, Cornelis, among all the crocodiles than that icy river. Yet I managed to reach the shore and get my breath lying in the bushes . . .

"After that it was plain going, though I was very cold. I knew that I would be sought on the northern roads, as I had told my friends, for no one would dream of an ignorant Dutchman going south away from his kinsfolk. But I had learned enough from the map to know that our road lay south-east, and I had marked this big river."

"Did you hope to pick me up?" I asked.

"No, Cornelis. I thought you would be travelling in first-class carriages while I should be plodding on foot. But I was set on getting to the place you spoke of (how do you call it? Constant Nople?), where our big business lay. I thought I might be in time for that."

"You're an old Trojan, Peter," I said; "but go on. How did you get to that landing-stage where I found you?"

"It was a hard journey," he said meditatively. "It was not easy to get beyond the barbed-wire entanglements which surrounded Neuburg—yes, even across the river. But in time I reached the woods and was safe, for I did not think any German could equal me in wild country. The best of them, even their foresters, are but babes in veldcraft compared with such as me . . . My troubles came only from hunger and cold. Then I met a Peruvian smouse,* and sold him my clothes and bought from him these. I did not want to part with my own, which were better, but he gave me ten marks on the deal. After that I went into a village and ate heavily."

"Were you pursued?" I asked.

"I do not think so. They had gone north, as I expected, and were looking for me at the railway stations which my friends had marked for me. I walked happily and put a bold face on it. If I saw a man or woman look at me suspiciously I went up to them at

---

* Peter meant a Polish-Jew pedlar.

once and talked. I told a sad tale, and all believed it. I was a poor Dutchman travelling home on foot to see a dying mother, and I had been told that by the Danube I should find the main railway to take me to Holland. There were kind people who gave me food, and one woman gave me half a mark, and wished me God speed . . . Then on the last day of the year I came to the river and found many drunkards."

"Was that when you resolved to get on one of the river-boats?"

"*Ja*, Cornelis. As soon as I heard of the boats I saw where my chance lay. But you might have knocked me over with a straw when I saw you come on shore. That was good fortune, my friend . . . I have been thinking much about the Germans, and I will tell you the truth. It is only boldness that can baffle them. They are a most diligent people. They will think of all likely difficulties, but not of all possible ones. They have not much imagination. They are like steam engines which must keep to prepared tracks. There they will hunt any man down, but let him trek for open country and they will be at a loss. Therefore boldness, my friend; for ever boldness. Remember as a nation they wear spectacles, which means that they are always peering."

Peter broke off to gloat over the wedges of geese and the strings of wild swans that were always winging across those plains. His tale had bucked me up wonderfully. Our luck had held beyond all belief, and I had a kind of hope in the business now which had been wanting before. That afternoon, too, I got another fillip.

I came on deck for a breath of air and found it pretty cold after the heat of the engine-room. So I called to one of the deck hands to fetch me up my cloak from the cabin—the same I had bought that first morning in the Greif village.

"*Der grüne mantel?*" the man shouted up, and I cried, "Yes." But the words seemed to echo in my ears, and long after he had given me the garment I stood staring abstractedly over the bulwarks.

His tone had awakened a chord of memory, or, to be accurate, they had given emphasis to what before had been only blurred and vague. For he had spoken the words which Stumm had uttered behind his hand to Gaudian. I had heard something like "*Uhnmantl*," and could make nothing of it. Now I was as certain of those words as of my own existence. They had been "*Grüne mantel.*" *Grüne mantel*, whatever it might be, was the name which Stumm had not meant me to hear, which was some talisman for the task I had proposed, and which was connected in some way with the mysterious von Einem.

This discovery put me in high fettle. I told myself that, considering the difficulties, I had managed to find out a wonderful amount in a very few days. It only shows what a man can do with the slenderest evidence if he keeps chewing and chewing on it . . .

Two mornings later we lay alongside the quays at Belgrade, and I took the opportunity of stretching my legs. Peter had come ashore for a smoke, and we wandered among the battered riverside streets, and looked at the broken arches of the great railway bridge which the Germans were working at like beavers. There was a big temporary pontoon affair to take the railway across, but I calculated that the main bridge would be ready inside a month. It was a clear, cold, blue day, and as one looked south one saw ridge after ridge of snowy hills. The upper streets of the city were still fairly whole, and there were shops open where food could be got. I remember hearing English spoken, and seeing some Red Cross nurses in the custody of Austrian soldiers coming from the railway station.

It would have done me a lot of good to have had a word with them. I thought of the gallant people whose capital this had been, how three times they had flung the Austrians back over the Danube, and then had only been beaten by the black treachery of their so-called allies. Somehow that morning in Belgrade gave both Peter and me a new purpose in our task. It was our business to put a spoke in the wheel of this monstrous bloody Juggernaut that was crushing the life out of the little heroic nations.

We were just getting ready to cast off when a distinguished party arrived at the quay. There were all kinds of uniforms—

German, Austrian, and Bulgarian, and amid them one stout gentleman in a fur coat and a black felt hat. They watched the barges up-anchor, and before we began to jerk into line I could hear the conversation. The fur coat was talking English.

"I reckon that's pretty good noos, General," it said; "if the English have run away from Gally-poly we can use these noo consignments for the bigger game. I guess it won't be long before we see the British lion moving out of Egypt with sore paws."

They all laughed. "The privilege of that spectacle may soon be ours," was the reply.

I did not pay much attention to the talk; indeed I did not realize till weeks later that that was the first tidings of the great evacuation of Cape Helles. What rejoiced me was the sight of Blenkiron, as bland as a barber among those swells. Here were two of the missionaries within reasonable distance of their goal.

CHAPTER 10

The Garden-House of Suliman the Red

WE REACHED Rustchuk on January 10, but by no means landed on that day. Something had gone wrong with the unloading arrangements, or more likely with the railway behind them, and we were kept swinging all day well out in the turbid river. On the top of this Captain Schenk got an ague, and by that evening was a blue and shivering wreck. He had done me well, and I reckoned I would stand by him. So I got his ship's papers, and the manifests of cargo, and undertook to see to the transhipment. It wasn't the first time I had tackled that kind of business, and I hadn't much to learn about steam cranes. I told him I was going on to Constantinople and would take Peter with me, and he was agreeable. He would have to wait at Rustchuk to get his return cargo, and could easily inspan a fresh engineer.

I worked about the hardest twenty-four hours of my life getting the stuff ashore. The landing officer was a Bulgarian, quite a competent man if he could have made the railways give him the trucks he needed. There was a collection of hungry German transport officers always putting in their oars, and being infernally insolent to everybody. I took the high and mighty line with them; and, as I had the Bulgarian commandant on my side, after about two hours' blasphemy got them quieted.

But the big trouble came the next morning when I had got nearly all the stuff aboard the trucks.

A young officer in what I took to be a Turkish uniform rode up with an aide-de-camp. I noticed the German guards saluting him, so I judged he was rather a swell. He came up to me and asked me very civilly in German for the way-bills. I gave him them and he looked carefully through them, marking certain items with a blue pencil. Then he coolly handed them to his aide-de-camp and spoke to him in Turkish.

"Look here, I want these back," I said. "I can't do without them, and we've no time to waste."

"Presently," he said, smiling, and went off.

I said nothing, reflecting that the stuff was for the Turks and they naturally had to have some say in its handling. The loading was practically finished when my gentleman returned. He handed me a neatly typed new set of way-bills. One glance at them showed that some of the big items had been left out.

"Here, this won't do," I cried. "Give me back the right set. This thing's no good to me."

For answer he winked gently, smiled like a dusky seraph, and held out his hand. In it I saw a roll of money.

"For yourself," he said. "It is the usual custom."

It was the first time anyone had ever tried to bribe me, and it made me boil up like a geyser. I saw his game clearly enough. Turkey would pay for the lot to Germany: probably had already paid the bill: but she would pay double for the things not on the way-bills, and pay to this fellow and his friends. This struck me as rather steep even for Oriental methods of doing business.

"Now look here, sir," I said, "I don't stir from this place till I get the correct way-bills. If you won't give me them, I will have every item out of the trucks and make a new list. But a correct list I have, or the stuff stays here till Doomsday."

He was a slim, foppish fellow, and he looked more puzzled than angry.

"I offer you enough," he said, again stretching out his hand.

At that I fairly roared. "If you try to bribe me, you infernal little haberdasher, I'll have you off that horse and chuck you in the river."

He no longer misunderstood me. He began to curse and threaten, but I cut him short.

"Come along to the commandant, my boy," I said, and I marched away, tearing up his typewritten sheets as I went and strewing them behind me like a paper chase.

We had a fine old racket in the commandant's office. I said it was my business, as representing the German Government, to see the stuff delivered to the consignee at Constantinople ship-shape and Bristol-fashion. I told him it wasn't my habit to proceed with cooked documents. He couldn't but agree with me, but there was that wrathful Oriental with his face as fixed as a Buddha.

"I am sorry, Rasta Bey," he said; "but this man is in the right."

"I have authority from the Committee to receive the stores," he said sullenly.

"Those are not my instructions," was the answer. "They are consigned to the Artillery commandant at Chataldja, General von Oesterzee."

The man shrugged his shoulders. "Very well. I will have a word to say to General von Oesterzee, and many to this fellow who flouts the Committee." And he strode away like an impudent boy.

The harassed commandant grinned. "You've offended his lordship, and he is a bad enemy. All those damned Comitadjis are. You would be well advised not to go on to Constantinople."

"And have that blighter in the red hat loot the trucks on the road. No, thank you. I am going to see them safe at Chataldja, or whatever they call the artillery depot."

I said a good deal more, but that is an abbreviated translation of my remarks. My word for "blighter" was *Trottel*, but I used some other expressions which would have ravished my Young Turk friend to hear. Looking back, it seems pretty ridiculous to have made all this fuss about guns which were going to be used against my own people. But I didn't see that at the time. My professional pride was up in arms, and I couldn't bear to have a hand in a crooked deal.

"Well, I advise you to go armed," said the commandant. "You will have a guard for the trucks, of course, and I will pick you good men. They may hold you up all the same. I can't help you once you are past the frontier, but I'll send a wire to Oesterzee and he'll make trouble if anything goes wrong. I still think you would have been wiser to humour Rasta Bey."

As I was leaving he gave me a telegram. "Here's a wire for your Captain Schenk." I slipped the envelope in my pocket and went out.

Schenk was pretty sick, so I left a note for him. At one o'clock I got the train started, with a couple of German Landwehr in each truck and Peter and I in a horse-box. Presently I remembered Schenk's telegram, which still reposed in my pocket. I took it out and opened it, meaning to wire it from the first station we stopped at. But I changed my mind when I read it. It was from some official at Regensburg, asking him to put under arrest and send back by the first boat a man called Brandt, who was believed to have come aboard at Absthafen on the 30th of December.

I whistled and showed it to Peter. The sooner we were at Constantinople the better, and I prayed we would get there before the fellow who sent this wire repeated it and got the commandant to send on the message and have us held up at Chataldja. For my back had fairly got stiffened about these munitions, and I was going to take any risk to see them safely delivered to their proper owner. Peter couldn't understand me at all. He still hankered after a grand destruction of the lot somewhere down the railway. But then, this wasn't the line of Peter's profession, and his pride was not at stake.

We had a mortally slow journey. It was bad enough in Bulgaria, but when we crossed the frontier at a place called Mustafa Pasha we struck the real supineness of the East. Happily I found a German officer there who had some notion of hustling, and, after all, it was his interest to get the stuff moved. It was the morning of the 16th, after Peter and I had been living like pigs on black bread and condemned tin stuff, that we came in sight of a blue sea on our right hand and knew we couldn't be very far from the end.

It was jolly near the end in another sense. We stopped at a station and were stretching our legs on the platform when I saw a familiar figure approaching. It was Rasta, with half a dozen Turkish gendarmes.

I called Peter, and we clambered into the truck next our horse-box. I had been half expecting some move like this and had made a plan.

The Turk swaggered up and addressed us. "You can get back to Rustchuk," he said. "I take over from you here. Hand me the papers."

"Is this Chataldja?" I asked innocently.

"It is the end of your affair," he said haughtily. "Quick, or it will be the worse for you."

"Now, look here, my son," I said; "you're a kid and know nothing. I hand over to General von Oesterzee and to no one else."

"You are in Turkey," he cried, "and will obey the Turkish Government."

"I'll obey the Government right enough," I said; "but if you're the Government I could make a better one with a bib and a rattle."

He said something to his men, who unslung their rifles.

"Please don't begin shooting," I said. "There are twelve armed guards in this train who will take their orders from me. Besides, I and my friend can shoot a bit."

"Fool!" he cried, getting very angry. "I can order up a regiment in five minutes."

"Maybe you can," I said; "but observe the situation. I am sitting on enough toluol to blow up this countryside. If you dare to come aboard I will shoot you. If you call in your regiment I will tell you what I'll do. I'll fire this stuff, and I reckon they'll be picking up the bits of you and your regiment off the Gallipoli peninsula."

He had put up a bluff—a poor one—and I had called it. He saw I meant what I said, and became silken.

"Good-bye, sir," he said. "You have had a fair chance and rejected it. We shall meet again soon, and you will be sorry for your insolence."

He strutted away and it was all I could do to keep from running after him. I wanted to lay him over my knee and spank him.

WE GOT safely to Chataldja, and were received by von Oesterzee like long-lost brothers. He was the regular gunner-officer, not thinking about anything except his guns and shells. I had to wait about three hours while he was checking the stuff with the invoices, and then he gave me a receipt which I still possess. I told him about Rasta, and he agreed that I had done right. It didn't make him as mad as I expected, because, you see, he got his stuff safe in any case. It was only that the wretched Turks had to pay twice for the lot of it.

He gave Peter and me luncheon, and was altogether very civil and inclined to talk about the war. I would have liked to hear what he had to say, for it would have been something to get the inside view of Germany's Eastern campaign, but I did not dare to wait. Any moment there might arrive an incriminating wire from Rustchuk. Finally he lent us a car to take us the few miles to the city.

So it came about that at five past three on the 16th day of January, with only the clothes we stood up in, Peter and I entered Constantinople.

I was in considerable spirits, for I had got the final lap successfully over, and I was looking forward madly to meeting my friends; but, all the same, the first sight was a mighty disappointment. I don't quite know what I had expected—a sort of fairyland Eastern city, all white marble and blue water, and stately Turks in surplices, and veiled houris, and roses and nightingales, and some sort of string band discoursing sweet music. I had forgotten that winter is pretty much the same everywhere. It was a drizzling day, with a south-east wind blowing, and the streets were long troughs of mud. The first part I struck looked like a dingy colonial suburb—wooden houses and corrugated iron roofs, and endless dirty, sallow children. There was a cemetery, I remember, with Turks' caps stuck at the head of each grave. Then we got into narrow steep streets which descended to a kind of big canal. I saw what I took to be mosques and minarets, and they were about as impressive as factory chimneys. By and by we crossed a bridge, and paid a penny for the privilege. If I had known it was the famous Golden Horn I would have looked at it with more interest, but I saw nothing save a lot of moth-eaten barges and some queer little boats like gondolas. Then we came into busier streets, where ramshackle cabs drawn by lean horses spluttered through the mud. I saw one old fellow who looked like my notion of a Turk, but most of the population had the appearance of London old-clothes men. All but the soldiers, Turk and German, who seemed well-set-up fellows.

Peter had paddled along at my side like a faithful dog, not saying a word, but clearly not approving of this wet and dirty metropolis.

"Do you know that we are being followed, Cornelis?" he said suddenly, "ever since we came into this evil-smelling dorp."

Peter was infallible in a thing like that. The news scared me badly, for I feared that the telegram had come to Chataldja. Then I thought it couldn't be that, for if von Oesterzee had wanted me he wouldn't have taken the trouble to stalk me. It was more likely my friend Rasta.

I found the ferry of Ratchik by asking a soldier and a German sailor there told me where the Kurdish Bazaar was. He pointed up a steep street which ran past a high block of warehouses with every window broken. Sandy had said the left-hand side coming down, so it must be the right-hand side going up. We plunged into it, and it was the filthiest place of all. The wind whistled up it and stirred the garbage. It seemed densely inhabited, for at all the doors there were groups of people squatting, with their heads covered, though scarcely a window showed in the blank walls.

The street corkscrewed endlessly. Sometimes it seemed to stop; then it found a hole in the opposing masonry and edged its way in. Often it was almost pitch dark; then would come a grey-ish twilight where it opened out to the width of a decent lane. To find a house in that murk was no easy job, and by the time we had gone a quarter of a mile I began to fear we had missed it. It was no good asking any of the crowd we met. They didn't look as if they understood any civilized tongue.

At last we stumbled on it—a tumble-down coffee-house, with A. Kuprasso above the door in queer amateur lettering. There was a lamp burning inside, and two or three men smoking at small wooden tables.

We ordered coffee, thick black stuff like treacle, which Peter anathematized. A negro brought it, and I told him in German I wanted to speak to Mr. Kuprasso. He paid no attention, so I shouted louder at him, and the noise brought a man out of the back parts.

He was a fat, oldish fellow with a long nose, very like the Greek traders you see on the Zanzibar coast. I beckoned to him and he waddled forward, smiling oilily. Then I asked him what he would take, and he replied, in very halting German, that he would have a sirop.

"You are Mr. Kuprasso," I said. "I wanted to show this place to my friend. He has heard of your garden-house and the fun there."

"The Signor is mistaken. I have no garden-house."

"Rot," I said; "I've been here before, my boy. I recall your shanty at the back and many merry nights there. What was it you called it? Oh, I remember—the Garden-House of Suliman the Red."

He put his finger to his lip and looked incredibly sly. "The Signor remembers that. But that was in the old happy days before war came. The place is long since shut. The people here are too poor to dance and sing."

"All the same I would like to have another look at it," I said, and I slipped an English sovereign into his hand.

He glanced at it in surprise and his manner changed. "The Signor is a Prince, and I will do his will." He clapped his hands and the negro appeared, and at his nod took his place behind a little side-counter.

"Follow me," he said, and led us through a long, noisome passage, which was pitch dark and very unevenly paved. Then he unlocked a door and with a swirl the wind caught it and blew it back on us.

We were looking into a mean little yard, with on one side a high curving wall, evidently of great age, with bushes growing in the cracks of it. Some scraggy myrtles stood in broken pots, and nettles flourished in a corner. At one end was a wooden building like a dissenting chapel, but painted a dingy scarlet. Its windows and skylights were black with dirt, and its door, tied with rope, flapped in the wind.

"Behold the Pavilion," Kuprasso said proudly.

"That is the old place," I observed with feeling. "What times I've seen there! Tell me, Mr. Kuprasso, do you ever open it?"

He put his thick lips to my ear.

"If the Signor will be silent I will tell him. It is sometimes open—not often. Men must amuse themselves even in war. Some of the German officers come here for their pleasure, and but last week we had the ballet of Mademoiselle Cici. The police approve—but not often, for this is no time for too much gaiety. I will tell you a secret. To-morrow afternoon there will be dancing—wonderful dancing! Only a few of my patrons know. Who, think you, will be there?"

He bent his head closer and said in a whisper—

"The Compagnie des Heures Roses."

"Oh, indeed," I said with a proper tone of respect, though I hadn't a notion what he meant.

"Will the Signor wish to come?"

"Sure," I said. "Both of us. We're all for the rose hours."

"Then the fourth hour after midday. Walk straight through the café and one will be there to unlock the door. You are newcomers here? Take the advice of Angelo Kuprasso and avoid the streets after nightfall. Stamboul is no safe place nowadays for quiet men."

I asked him to name an hotel, and he rattled off a list from which I chose one that sounded modest and in keeping with our get-up. It was not far off, only a hundred yards to the right at the top of the hill.

When we left his door the night had begun to drop. We hadn't gone twenty yards before Peter drew very near to me and kept turning his head like a hunted stag.

"We are being followed close, Cornelis," he said calmly.

Another ten yards and we were at a cross-road, where a little *place* faced a biggish mosque. I could see in the waning light a crowd of people who seemed to be moving towards us. I heard a high-pitched voice cry out a jabber of excited words, and it seemed to me that I had heard the voice before.

CHAPTER 11

The Companions of the Rosy Hours

WE BATTLED to a corner, where a jut of building stood out into the street. It was our only chance to protect our backs, to stand up with the rib of stone between us. It was only the work of seconds. One instant we were groping our solitary way in the darkness, the next we were pinned against a wall with a throaty mob surging round us.

It took me a moment or two to realize that we were attacked. Every man has one special funk in the back of his head, and mine was to be the quarry of an angry crowd. I hated the thought of it—the mess, the blind struggle, the sense of unleashed passions different from those of any single blackguard. It was a dark world to me, and I don't like darkness. But in my nightmares I had never imagined anything just like this. The narrow, fetid street, with the icy winds fanning the filth, the unknown tongue, the hoarse savage murmur, and my utter ignorance as to what it might all be about, made me cold in the pit of my stomach.

"We've got it in the neck this time, old man," I said to Peter, who had out the pistol the commandant at Rustchuk had given him. These pistols were our only weapons. The crowd saw them and hung back, but if they chose to rush us it wasn't much of a barrier two pistols would make.

Rasta's voice had stopped. He had done his work, and had

retired to the background. There were shouts from the crowd—
"*Alleman*" and a word "*Khafiyeh*" constantly repeated. I didn't
know what it meant at the time, but now I know that they were
after us because we were Boches and spies. There was no love
lost between the Constantinople scum and their new masters. It
seemed an ironical end for Peter and me to be done in because
we were Boches. And done in we should be. I had heard of the
East as a good place for people to disappear in; there were no inquisitive newspapers or incorruptible police.

I wished to Heaven I had a word of Turkish. But I made my
voice heard for a second in a pause of the din, and shouted that
we were German sailors who had brought down big guns for
Turkey, and were going home next day. I asked them what the
devil they thought we had done? I don't know if any fellow there
understood German; anyhow, it only brought a pandemonium of
cries in which that ominous word *Khafiyeh* was predominant.

Then Peter fired over their heads. He had to, for a chap was
pawing at his throat. The answer was a clatter of bullets on the
wall above us. It looked as if they meant to take us alive, and that
I was very clear should not happen. Better a bloody end in a
street scrap than the tender mercies of that bandbox bravo.

I don't quite know what happened next. A press drove down at
me and I fired. Someone squealed, and I looked the next moment
to be strangled. And then, suddenly, the scrimmage ceased, and
there was a wavering splash of light in that pit of darkness.

I never went through many worse minutes than these. When I
had been hunted in the past weeks there had been mystery
enough, but no immediate peril to face. When I had been up
against a real, urgent, physical risk, like Loos, the danger at any
rate had been clear. One knew what one was in for. But here was
a threat I couldn't put a name to, and it wasn't in the future, but
pressing hard at our throats.

And yet I couldn't feel it was quite real. The patter of the pistol bullets against the wall, like so many crackers, the faces felt
rather than seen in the dark, the clamour which to me was pure
gibberish, had all the madness of a nightmare. Only Peter,

cursing steadily in Dutch by my side, was real. And then the light came, and made the scene more eerie!

It came from one or two torches carried by wild fellows with long staves who drove their way into the heart of the mob. The flickering glare ran up the steep walls and made monstrous shadows. The wind swung the flame into long streamers, dying away in a fan of sparks.

And now a new word was heard in the crowd. It was *Chinganeh*, shouted not in anger but in fear.

At first I could not see the new-comers. They were hidden in the deep darkness under their canopy of light, for they were holding their torches high at the full stretch of their arms. They were shouting, too, wild shrill cries ending sometimes in a gush of rapid speech. Their words did not seem to be directed against us, but against the crowd. A sudden hope came to me that for some unknown reason they were on our side.

The press was no longer heavy against us. It was thinning rapidly and I could hear the scuffle as men made off down the side streets. My first notion was that these were the Turkish police. But I changed my mind when the leader came out into the patch of light. He carried no torch, but a long stave with which he belaboured the heads of those who were too tightly packed to flee.

It was the most eldritch apparition you can conceive. A tall man dressed in skins, with bare legs and sandal-shod feet. A wisp of scarlet cloth clung to his shoulders, and, drawn over his head down close to his eyes, was a skull-cap of some kind of pelt with the tail waving behind it. He capered like a wild animal, keeping up a strange high monotone that fairly gave me the creeps.

I was suddenly aware that the crowd had gone. Before us was only this figure and his half-dozen companions, some carrying torches and all wearing clothes of skin. But only the one who seemed to be their leader wore the skull-cap; the rest had bare heads and long tangled hair.

The fellow was shouting gibberish at me. His eyes were glassy, like a man who smokes hemp, and his legs were never still for a second. You would think such a figure no better than a mountebank, and yet there was nothing comic in it. Fearful and sinister and uncanny it was; and I wanted to do anything but laugh.

As he shouted he kept pointing with his stave up the street which climbed the hillside.

"He means us to move," said Peter. "For God's sake let us get away from this witch-doctor."

I couldn't make sense of it, but one thing was clear. These maniacs had delivered us for the moment from Rasta and his friends.

Then I did a dashed silly thing. I pulled out a sovereign and offered it to the leader. I had some kind notion of showing gratitude, and as I had no words I had to show it by deed.

He brought his stick down on my wrist and sent the coin spinning in the gutter. His eyes blazed, and he made his weapon sing round my head. He cursed me—oh, I could tell cursing well enough, though I didn't follow a word; and he cried to his followers and they cursed me too. I had offered him a mortal insult and stirred up a worse hornet's nest than Rasta's push.

Peter and I, with a common impulse, took to our heels. We were not looking for any trouble with demoniacs. Up the steep narrow lane we ran with that bedlamite crowd at our heels. The torches seemed to have gone out, for the place was black as pitch, and we tumbled over heaps of offal and splashed through running drains. The men were close behind us, and more than once I felt a stick on my shoulder. But fear lent us wings, and suddenly before us was a blaze of light and we saw the debouchment of our street in a main thoroughfare. The others saw it, too, for they slackened off. Just before we reached the light we stopped and looked round. There was no sound or sight behind us in the dark lane which dipped to the harbour.

"This is a queer country, Cornelis," said Peter, feeling his limbs for bruises. "Too many things happen in too short a time. I am breathless."

The big street we had struck seemed to run along the crest of the hill. There were lamps in it, and crawling cabs, and quite civilized-looking shops. We soon found the hotel to which Kuprasso had directed us, a big place in a courtyard with a very tumble-down-looking portico, and green sun shutters which rattled drearily in the winter's wind. It proved, as I had feared, to be packed to the door, mostly with German officers. With some trouble I got an interview with the proprietor, the usual Greek, and told him that we had been sent there by Mr. Kuprasso. That didn't affect him in the least, and we would have been shot into the street if I hadn't remembered about Stumm's pass.

So I explained that we had come from Germany with munitions and only wanted rooms for one night. I showed him the pass and blustered a good deal, till he became civil and said he would do the best he could for us.

That best was pretty poor. Peter and I were doubled up in a small room which contained two camp-beds and little else, and had broken windows through which the wind whistled. We had a wretched dinner of stringy mutton, boiled with vegetables, and a white cheese strong enough to raise the dead. But I got a bottle of whisky, for which I paid a sovereign, and we managed to light the stove in our room, fasten the shutters, and warm our hearts with a brew of toddy. After that we went to bed and slept like logs for twelve hours. On the road from Rustchuk we had had uneasy slumbers.

I woke next morning and, looking out from the broken window, saw that it was snowing. With a lot of trouble I got hold of a servant and made him bring us some of the treacly Turkish coffee. We were both in pretty low spirits. "Europe is a poor cold place," said Peter, "not worth fighting for. There is only one white man's land, and that is South Africa." At the time I heartily agreed with him.

I remember that, sitting on the edge of my bed, I took stock of our position. It was not very cheering. We seemed to have been amassing enemies at a furious pace. First of all, there was Rasta, whom I had insulted and who wouldn't forget it in a hurry. He had his crowd of Turkish riff-raff and was bound to get us sooner or later. Then there was the maniac in the skin hat. He didn't like Rasta, and I made a guess that he and his weird friends were of some party hostile to the Young Turks. But, on the other hand, he didn't like us, and there would be bad trouble the next time we met him. Finally, there was Stumm and the German Government. It could only be a matter of hours at the best before he got the Rustchuk authorities on our trail. It would be easy to trace us from Chataldja, and once they had us we were absolutely done. There was a big black dossier against us, which by no conceivable piece of luck could be upset.

It was very clear to me that, unless we could find sanctuary and shed all our various pursuers during this day, we should be done in for good and all. But where on earth were we to find sanctuary? We had neither of us a word of the language, and there was no way I could see of taking on new characters. For that we wanted friends and help, and I could think of none anywhere. Somewhere, to be sure, there was Blenkiron, but how could we get in touch with him? As for Sandy, I had pretty well given him up. I always thought his enterprise the craziest of the lot and bound to fail. He was probably somewhere in Asia Minor, and a month or two later would get to Constantinople and hear in some pot-house the yarn of the two wretched Dutchmen who had disappeared so soon from men's sight.

That rendezvous at Kuprasso's was no good. It would have been all right if we had got here unsuspected, and could have gone on quietly frequenting the place till Blenkiron picked us up. But to do that we wanted leisure and secrecy, and here we were with a pack of hounds at our heels. The place was horribly dangerous already. If we showed ourselves there we should be gathered in by Rasta, or by the German military police, or by the madman in the skin cap. It was a stark impossibility to hang about on the off-chance of meeting Blenkiron.

I reflected with some bitterness that this was the 17th day of January, the day of our assignation. I had had high hopes all the way down the Danube of meeting with Blenkiron—for I knew *he* would be in time—of giving him the information I had had the good fortune to collect, of piecing it together with what he had found out, and of getting the whole story which Sir Walter hungered for. After that, I thought it wouldn't be hard to get away by Rumania, and to get home through Russia. I had hoped to be back with my battalion in February, having done as good a bit of work as anybody in the war. As it was, it looked as if my information would die with me, unless I could find Blenkiron before the evening.

I talked the thing over with Peter, and he agreed that we were fairly up against it. We decided to go to Kuprasso's that afternoon, and to trust to luck for the rest. It wouldn't do to wander about the streets, so we sat tight in our room all morning, and swopped old hunting yarns to keep our minds from the beastly present. We got some food at midday—cold mutton and the same cheese, and finished our whisky. Then I paid the bill, for I didn't dare to stay there another night. About half past three we went into the street, without the foggiest notion where we would find our next quarters.

It was snowing heavily, which was a piece of luck for us. Poor old Peter had no greatcoat, so we went into a Jew's shop and bought a ready-made abomination, which looked as if it might have been meant for a dissenting parson. It was no good saving my money when the future was so black. The snow made the streets deserted, and we turned down the long lane which led to Ratchik ferry, and found it perfectly quiet. I do not think we met a soul till we got to Kuprasso's shop.

We walked straight through the café, which was empty, and down the dark passage, till we were stopped by the garden door. I knocked and it swung open. There was the bleak yard, now puddled with snow, and a blaze of light from the pavilion at the other end. There was a scraping of fiddles, too, and the sound of human talk. We paid the negro at the door, and passed from the bitter afternoon into a garish saloon.

There were forty or fifty people there, drinking coffee and sirops and filling the air with the fumes of latakia. Most of them were Turks in European clothes and the fez, but there were some German officers and what looked like German civilians—Army

Service Corps clerks, probably, and mechanics from the Arsenal. A woman in cheap finery was tinkling at the piano, and there were several shrill females with the officers. Peter and I sat down modestly in the nearest corner, where old Kuprasso saw us and sent us coffee. A girl who looked like a Jewess came over to us and talked French, but I shook my head and she went off again.

Presently a girl came on the stage and danced, a silly affair, all a clashing of tambourines and wriggling. I have seen native women do the same thing better in a Mozambique kraal. Another sang a German song, a simple, sentimental thing about golden hair and rainbows, and the Germans present applauded. The place was so tinselly and common that, coming to it from weeks of rough travelling, it made me impatient. I forgot that, while for the others it might be a vulgar little dancing-hall, for us it was as perilous as a brigands' den.

Peter did not share my mood. He was quite interested in it, as he was interested in everything new. He had a genius for living in the moment.

I remember there was a drop-scene on which was daubed a blue lake with very green hills in the distance. As the tobacco smoke grew thicker and the fiddles went on squealing, this tawdry picture began to mesmerize me. I seemed to be looking out of a window at a lovely summer landscape where there were no wars or danger. I seemed to feel the warm sun and to smell the fragrance of blossom from the islands. And then I became aware that a queer scent had stolen into the atmosphere.

There were braziers burning at both ends to warm the room, and the thin smoke from these smelt like incense. Somebody had been putting a powder in the flames, for suddenly the place became very quiet. The fiddles still sounded, but far away like an echo. The lights went down, all but a circle on the stage, and into that circle stepped my enemy of the skin cap.

He had three others with him. I heard a whisper behind me, and the words were those which Kuprasso had used the day before. These bedlamites were called the Companions of the Rosy Hours, and Kuprasso had promised great dancing.

I hoped to goodness they would not see us, for they had fairly given me the horrors. Peter felt the same, and we both made ourselves very small in that dark corner. But the new-comers had no eyes for us.

In a twinkling the pavilion changed from a common saloon, which might have been in Chicago or Paris, to a place of mystery—yes, and of beauty. It became the Garden-House of Suliman the Red, whoever that sportsman may have been. Sandy had said that the ends of the earth converged there, and he had been right. I lost all consciousness of my neighbours—stout German, frock-coated Turk, frowsy Jewess—and saw only strange figures leaping in a circle of light, figures that came out of the deepest darkness to make a big magic.

The leader flung some stuff into the brazier, and a great fan of blue light flared up. He was weaving circles, and he was singing something shrill and high, whilst his companions made a chorus with their deep monotone. I can't tell you what the dance was. I had seen the Russian ballet just before the war, and one of the men in it reminded me of this man. But the dancing was the least part of it. It was neither sound nor movement nor scent that wrought the spell, but something far more potent. In an instant I found myself reft away from the present with its dull dangers, and looking at a world all young and fresh and beautiful. The gaudy drop-scene had vanished. It was a window I was looking from, and I was gazing at the finest landscape on earth, lit by the pure clean light of morning.

It seemed to be part of the veld, but like no veld I had ever seen. It was wider and wilder and more gracious. Indeed, I was looking at my first youth. I was feeling the kind of immortal light-heartedness which only a boy knows in the dawning of his days. I had no longer any fear of these magic-makers. They were kindly wizards, who had brought me into fairyland.

Then slowly from the silence there distilled drops of music. They came like water falling a long way into a cup, each the essential quality of pure sound. We, with our elaborate harmonies, have forgotten the charm of single notes. The African natives know it, and I remember a learned man once telling me that the Greeks had the same art. Those silver bells broke out of infinite space, so exquisite and perfect that no mortal words could have been fitted to them. That was the music, I expect, that the morning stars made when they sang together.

Slowly, very slowly, it changed. The glow passed from blue to purple, and then to an angry red. Bit by bit the notes spun together till they had made a harmony—a fierce, restless harmony. And I was conscious again of the skin-clad dancers beckoning out of their circle.

There was no mistake about the meaning now. All the daintiness and youth had fled, and passion was beating the air— terrible, savage passion, which belonged neither to day nor night, life nor death, but to the half-world between them. I suddenly felt the dancers as monstrous, inhuman, devilish. The thick scents that floated from the brazier seemed to have a tang of new-shed blood. Cries broke from the hearers—cries of anger and lust and terror. I heard a woman sob, and Peter, who is as tough as any mortal, took tight hold of my arm.

I now realized that these Companions of the Rosy Hours were the only thing in the world to fear. Rasta and Stumm seemed feeble simpletons by contrast. The window I had been looking out of was changed to a prison wall—I could see the mortar between the massive blocks. In a second these devils would be smelling out their enemies like some foul witch-doctors. I felt the burning eyes of their leader looking for me in the gloom. Peter was praying audibly beside me, and I could have choked him. His infernal chatter would reveal us, for it seemed to me that there was no one in the place except us and the magic-workers.

THEN suddenly the spell was broken. The door was flung open and a great gust of icy wind swirled through the hall, driving clouds of ashes from the braziers. I heard loud voices without, and a hubbub began inside. For a moment it was quite dark, and then someone lit one of the flare lamps by the stage. It revealed nothing but the common squalor of a low saloon—white faces, sleepy eyes, and frowsy heads. The drop-piece was there in all its tawdriness.

The Companions of the Rosy Hours had gone. But at the door stood men in uniform. I heard a German a long way off murmur, "Enver's bodyguards," and I heard him distinctly; for, though I could not see clearly, my hearing was desperately acute. That is often the way when you suddenly come out of a swoon.

The place emptied like magic. Turk and German tumbled over each other, while Kuprasso wailed and wept. No one seemed to stop them, and then I saw the reason. Those guards had come for us. This must be Stumm at last. The authorities had tracked us down, and it was all up with Peter and me.

A sudden revulsion leaves a man with a low vitality. I didn't seem to care greatly. We were done, and there was an end of it. It was Kismet, the act of God, and there was nothing for it but to submit. I hadn't a flicker of a thought of escape or resistance. The game was utterly and absolutely over.

A man who seemed to be a sergeant pointed to us and said something to Kuprasso, who nodded. We got heavily to our feet and stumbled towards them. With one on each side of us we crossed the yard, walked through the dark passage and the empty shop, and out into the snowy street. There was a closed carriage waiting which they motioned to us to get into. It looked exactly like the Black Maria.

Both of us sat still, like truant schoolboys, with our hands on our knees. I didn't know where I was going and I didn't care. We seemed to be rumbling up the hill, and then I caught the glare of lighted streets.

"This is the end of it, Peter," I said.

"*Ja*, Cornelis," he replied, and that was all our talk.

By and by—hours later it seemed—we stopped. Someone opened the door and we got out, to find ourselves in a courtyard with a huge dark building around. The prison, I guessed, and I wondered if they would give us blankets, for it was perishing cold.

We entered a door, and found ourselves in a big stone hall. It was quite warm, which made me more hopeful about our cells. A man in some kind of uniform pointed to the staircase, up which we plodded wearily. My mind was too blank to take clear impressions, or in any way to forecast the future. Another warder met us and took us down a passage till we halted at a door. He stood aside and motioned us to enter.

I guessed that this was the governor's room, and we should be put through our first examination. My head was too stupid to think, and I made up my mind to keep perfectly mum. Yes, even if they tried thumbscrews. I had no kind of story, but I resolved not to give anything away. As I turned the handle I wondered idly what kind of sallow Turk or bulging-necked German we should find inside.

It was a pleasant room, with a polished wood floor and a big fire burning on the hearth. Beside the fire a man lay on a couch, with a little table drawn up beside him. On that table was a small glass of milk and a number of Patience cards spread in rows.

I stared blankly at the spectacle, till I saw a second figure. It was the man in the skin cap, the leader of the dancing maniacs. Both Peter and I backed sharply at the sight and then stood stock still.

For the dancer crossed the room in two strides and gripped both of my hands.

"Dick, old man," he cried, "I'm most awfully glad to see you again!"

CHAPTER 12

Four Missionaries See Light in Their Mission

A SPASM of incredulity, a vast relief, and that sharp joy which comes of reaction chased each other across my mind. I had come suddenly out of very black waters into an unbelievable calm. I dropped into the nearest chair and tried to grapple with something far beyond words.

"Sandy," I said, as soon as I got my breath, "you're an incarnate devil. You've given Peter and me the fright of our lives."

"It was the only way, Dick. If I hadn't come mewing like a tom-cat at your heels yesterday, Rasta would have had you long before you got to your hotel. You two have given me a pretty anxious time, and it took some doing to get you safe here. However, that is all over now. Make yourselves at home, my children."

"Over!" I cried incredulously, for my wits were still wool-gathering. "What place is this?"

"You may call it my humble home"—it was Blenkiron's sleek voice that spoke. "We've been preparing for you, Major, but it was only yesterday I heard of your friend."

I introduced Peter.

"Mr. Pienaar," said Blenkiron, "pleased to meet you. Well, as I was observing, you're safe enough here, but you've cut it mighty fine. Officially, a Dutchman called Brandt was to be arrested this afternoon and handed over to the German authorities. When

Germany begins to trouble about that Dutchman she will find difficulty in getting the body; but such are the languid ways of an Oriental despotism. Meantime the Dutchman will be no more. He will have ceased upon the midnight without pain, as your poet sings."

"But I don't understand," I stammered. "Who arrested us?"

"My men," said Sandy. "We have a bit of a graft here, and it wasn't difficult to manage it. Old Moellendorff will be nosing after the business to-morrow, but he will find the mystery too deep for him. That is the advantage of a Government run by a pack of adventurers. But, by Jove, Dick, we hadn't any time to spare. If Rasta had got you, or the Germans had had the job of lifting you, your goose would have been jolly well cooked. I had some unquiet hours this morning."

The thing was too deep for me. I looked at Blenkiron, shuffling his Patience cards with his old sleepy smile, and Sandy, dressed like some bandit in melodrama, his lean face as brown as a nut, his bare arms all tattooed with crimson rings, and the fox pelt drawn tight over brow and ears. It was still a nightmare world, but the dream was getting pleasanter. Peter said not a word, but I could see his eyes heavy with his own thoughts.

Blenkiron hove himself from the sofa and waddled to a cupboard.

"You boys must be hungry," he said. "My duodenum has been giving me hell as usual, and I don't eat no more than a squirrel. But I laid in some stores, for I guessed you would want to stoke up some after your travels."

He brought out a couple of Strassburg pies, a cheese, a cold chicken, a loaf, and three bottles of champagne.

"Fizz," said Sandy rapturously. "And a dry Heidsieck too! We're in luck, Dick, old man."

I never ate a more welcome meal, for we had starved in that dirty hotel. But I had still the old feeling of the hunted, and before I began I asked about the door.

"That's all right," said Sandy. "My fellows are on the stair and at the gate. If the *Metreb* are in possession, you may bet that other people will keep off. Your past is blotted out, clean vanished away, and you begin to-morrow morning with a new sheet. Blenkiron's the man you've got to thank for that. He was pretty certain you'd get here, but he was also certain that you'd arrive in a hurry with a good many inquiries behind you. So he arranged that you should leak away and start fresh."

"Your name is Richard Hanau," Blenkiron said, "born in Cleveland, Ohio, of German parentage on both sides. One of our brightest mining engineers, and the apple of Guggenheim's eye. You arrived this afternoon from Constanza, and I met you at the packet. The clothes for the part are in your bedroom next door. But I guess all that can wait, for I'm anxious to get to business. We're not here on a joy-ride, Major, so I reckon we'll leave out the dime-novel adventures. I'm just dying to hear them, but they'll keep. I want to know how our mutual inquiries have prospered."

He gave Peter and me cigars, and we sat ourselves in armchairs in front of the blaze. Sandy squatted cross-legged on the hearthrug and lit a foul old briar pipe, which he extricated from some pouch among his skins. And so began that conversation which had never been out of my thoughts for four hectic weeks.

"If I presume to begin," said Blenkiron, "it's because I reckon my story is the shortest. I have to confess to you, gentlemen, that I have failed."

He drew down the corners of his mouth till he looked a cross between a music-hall comedian and a sick child.

"If you were looking for something in the root of the hedge, you wouldn't want to scour the road in a high-speed automobile. And still less would you want to get a bird's-eye view in an aeroplane. That parable about fits my case. I have been in the clouds and I've been scorching on the pikes, but what I was wanting was in the ditch all the time, and I naturally missed it . . . I had the wrong stunt, Major. I was too high up and refined. I've been processing through Europe like Barnum's Circus, and living with generals and transparencies. Not that I haven't picked up a lot of noos, and got some very interesting sidelights on high politics.

But the thing I was after wasn't to be found on my beat, for those that knew it weren't going to tell. In that kind of society they don't get drunk and blab after their tenth cocktail. So I guess I've no contribution to make to quieting Sir Walter Bullivant's mind, except that he's dead right. Yes, sir, he has hit the spot and rung the bell. There is a mighty miracle-working proposition being floated in these parts, but the promoters are keeping it to themselves. They aren't taking in more than they can help on the ground floor."

Blenkiron stopped to light a fresh cigar. He was leaner than when he left London and there were pouches below his eyes. I fancy his journey had not been as fur-lined as he made out.

"I've found out one thing, and that is, that the last dream Germany will part with is the control of the Near East. That is what your statesmen don't figure enough on. She'll give up Belgium and Alsace-Lorraine and Poland, but by God! she'll never give up the road to Mesopotamia till you have her by the throat and make her drop it. Sir Walter is a pretty bright-eyed citizen, and he sees it right enough. If the worst happens, Kaiser will fling overboard a lot of ballast in Europe, and it will look like a big victory for the Allies, but he won't be beaten if he has the road to the East safe. Germany's like a scorpion: her sting's in her tail, and that tail stretches way down into Asia.

"I got that clear, and I also made out that it wasn't going to be dead easy for her to keep that tail healthy. Turkey's a bit of an anxiety, as you'll soon discover. But Germany thinks she can manage it, and I won't say she can't. It depends on the hand she holds, and she reckons it a good one. I tried to find out, but they gave me nothing but eyewash. I had to pretend to be satisfied, for the position of John S. wasn't so strong as to allow him to take liberties. If I asked one of the highbrows he looked wise and spoke of the might of German arms and German organization and German staff-work. I used to nod my head and get enthusiastic about these stunts, but it was all soft soap. She has a trick in hand—that much I know, but I'm darned if I can put a name to it. I pray to God you boys have been cleverer."

His tone was quite melancholy, and I was mean enough to feel rather glad. He had been the professional with the best chance. It would be a good joke if the amateur succeeded where the expert failed.

I looked at Sandy. He filled his pipe again, and pushed back his skin cap from his brows. What with his long dishevelled hair, his high-boned face, and stained eyebrows he had the appearance of some mad mullah.

"I went straight to Smyrna," he said. "It wasn't difficult, for you see I had laid down a good many lines in former travels. I reached the town as a Greek money-lender from the Fayum, but I had friends there I could count on, and the same evening I was a Turkish gipsy, a member of the most famous fraternity in Western Asia. I had long been a member, and I'm blood-brother of the chief boss, so I stepped into the part ready made. But I found out that the Company of the Rosy Hours was not what I had known it in 1910. Then it had been all for the Young Turks and reform; now it hankered after the old régime and was the last hope of the Orthodox. It had no use for Enver and his friends, and it did not regard with pleasure the *beaux yeux* of the Teuton. It stood for Islam and the old ways, and might be described as a Conservative Nationalist caucus. But it was uncommon powerful in the provinces, and Enver and Talaat daren't meddle with it. The dangerous thing about it was that it said nothing and apparently did nothing. It just bided its time and took notes.

"You can imagine that this was the very kind of crowd for my purpose. I knew of old its little ways, for with all its orthodoxy it dabbled a good deal in magic, and owed half its power to its atmosphere of the uncanny. The Companions could dance the heart out of the ordinary Turk. You saw a bit of one of our dances this afternoon, Dick—pretty good, wasn't it? They could go anywhere, and no questions asked. They knew what the ordinary man was thinking, for they were the best intelligence department in the Ottoman Empire—far better than Enver's *Khafiyeh*. And they were popular, too, for they had never bowed the knee to the *Nemesh*—the Germans who are squeezing out the life-blood of the Osmanli for their own ends. It would have been as much as the life of the Committee or its German masters was worth to lay a hand on us, for we clung together like leeches and we were not in the habit of sticking at trifles.

"Well, you may imagine it wasn't difficult for me to move where I wanted. My dress and the pass-word franked me any-where. I travelled from Smyrna by the new railway to Panderma on the Marmora, and got there just before Christmas. That was after Anzac and Suvla had been evacuated, but I could hear the guns going hard at Cape Helles. From Panderma I started to cross to Thrace in a coasting steamer. And there an uncommon funny thing happened—I got torpedoed.

"It must have been about the last effort of a British submarine in those waters. But she got us all right. She gave us ten minutes to take to the boats, and then sent the blighted old packet and a fine cargo of 6-inch shells to the bottom. There weren't many passengers, so it was easy enough to get ashore in the ship's boats. The submarine sat on the surface watching us, as we wailed and howled in the true Oriental way, and I saw the captain quite close in the conning-tower. Who do you think it was? Tommy Elliot, who lives on the other side of the hill from me at home.

"I gave Tommy the surprise of his life. As we bumped past him, I started the 'Flowers of the Forest'—the old version—on the antique stringed instrument I carried, and I sang the words very plain. Tommy's eyes bulged out of his head, and he shouted at me in English to know who the devil I was. I replied in the broadest Scots, which no man in the submarine or in our boat could have understood a word of. 'Maister Tammy,' I cried, 'what for wad ye skail a dacent tinkler lad intil a cauld sea? I'll gie ye your kail through the reek for this ploy the next time I forgaither wi' ye on the tap o'Caerdon.'

"Tommy spotted me in a second. He laughed till he cried, and as we moved off shouted to me in the same language to 'pit a stoot hert tae a stey brae.' I hope to Heaven he had the sense not to tell my father, or the old man will have had a fit. He never much approved of my wanderings, and thought I was safely anchored in the battalion.

"Well, to make a long story short, I got to Constantinople, and pretty soon found touch with Blenkiron. The rest you know . . . And now for business. I have been fairly lucky—but no more, for I haven't got to the bottom of the thing nor anything like it. But I've solved the first of Harry Bullivant's riddles. I know the meaning of *Kasredin*.

"Sir Walter was right, as Blenkiron has told us. There's a great stirring in Islam, something moving on the face of the waters. They make no secret of it. Those religious revivals come in cycles, and one was due about now. And they are quite clear about the details. A seer has arisen of the blood of the Prophet, who will restore the Khalifate to its old glories and Islam to its old purity. His sayings are everywhere in the Moslem world. All the orthodox believers have them by heart. That is why they are enduring grinding poverty and preposterous taxation, and that is why their young men are rolling up to the armies and dying without complaint in Gallipoli and Transcaucasia. They believe they are on the eve of a great deliverance.

"Now the first thing I found out was that the Young Turks had nothing to do with this. They are unpopular and unorthodox, and no true Turks. But Germany has. How, I don't know, but I could see quite plainly that in some subtle way Germany was regarded as a collaborator in the movement. It is that belief that is keeping the present régime going. The ordinary Turk loathes the Committee, but he has some queer perverted expectation from Germany. It is not a case of Enver and the rest carrying on their shoulders the unpopular Teuton; it is a case of the Teuton carrying the unpopular Committee. And Germany's graft is just this and nothing more—that she has some hand in the coming of the new deliverer.

"They talk about the thing quite openly. It is called the *Kaába-i-hurriyeh*, the Palladium of Liberty. The prophet himself is known as Zimrud—'the Emerald'—and his four Ministers are called also after jewels—Sapphire, Ruby, Pearl, and Topaz. You will hear their names as often in the talk of the towns and villages as you will hear the names of generals in England. But no one knew where Zimrud was or when he would reveal himself, though every week came his messages to the faithful. All that I could learn was that he and his followers were coming from the West.

"You will say, what about *Kasredin?* That puzzled me dreadfully, for no one used the phrase. The Home of the Spirit! It is an obvious cliché, just as in England some new sect might call itself the Church of Christ. Only no one seemed to use it.

"But by and by I discovered that there was an inner and an outer circle in this mystery. Every creed has an esoteric side which is kept from the common herd. I struck this side in Constantinople. Now there is a very famous Turkish *shaka* called *Kasredin*, one of those old half-comic miracle plays with an allegorical meaning which they call *orta oyun*, and which take a week to read. That tale tells of the coming of a prophet, and I found that the select of the faith spoke of the new revelation in terms of it. The curious thing is that in that tale the prophet is aided by one of the few women who play much part in the hagiology of Islam. That is the point of the tale, and it is partly a jest, but mainly a religious mystery. The prophet, too, is not called Emerald."

"I know," I said; "he is called Greenmantle."

Sandy scrambled to his feet, letting his pipe drop in the fireplace.

"Now how on earth did you find out that?" he cried.

Then I told them of Stumm and Gaudian and the whispered words I had not been meant to hear. Blenkiron was giving me the benefit of a steady stare, unusual from one who seemed always to have his eyes abstracted, and Sandy had taken to ranging up and down the room.

"Germany's in the heart of the plan. That is what I always thought. If we're to find the Kaábi-i-hurriyeh it is no good fossicking among the Committee or in the Turkish provinces. The secret's in Germany. Dick, you should not have crossed the Danube."

"That's what I half feared," I said. "But on the other hand it is obvious that the thing must come east, and sooner rather than later. I take it they can't afford to delay too long before they deliver the goods. If we can stick it out here we must hit the trail . . . I've got another bit of evidence. I have solved Harry Bullivant's third puzzle."

Sandy's eyes were very bright and I had an audience on wires.

"Did you say that in the tale of *Kasredin* a woman is the ally of the prophet?"

"Yes," said Sandy; "what of that?"

"Only that the same thing is true of Greenmantle. I can give you her name."

I fetched a piece of paper and a pencil from Blenkiron's desk and handed it to Sandy.

"Write down Harry Bullivant's third word."

He promptly wrote down "*v. I.*"

Then I told them of the other name Stumm and Gaudian had spoken. I told of my discovery as I lay in the woodman's cottage.

"The 'I' is not the letter of the alphabet, but the numeral. The name is von Einem—Hilda von Einem."

"Good old Harry," said Sandy softly. "He was a dashed clever chap. Hilda von Einem? Who and where is she? for if we find her we have done the trick."

Then Blenkiron spoke. "I reckon I can put you wise on that, gentlemen," he said. "I saw her no later than yesterday. She is a lovely lady. She happens also to be the owner of this house."

Both Sandy and I began to laugh. It was too comic to have stumbled across Europe and lighted on the very headquarters of the puzzle we had set out to unriddle.

But Blenkiron did not laugh. At the mention of Hilda von Einem he had suddenly become very solemn, and the sight of his face pulled me up short.

"I don't like it, gentlemen," he said. "I would rather you had mentioned any other name on God's earth. I haven't been long in this city, but I have been long enough to size up the various political bosses. They haven't much to them. I reckon they wouldn't stand up against what we could show them in the United States. But I have met the Frau von Einem, and that lady's a very different proposition. The man that will understand her has got to take a biggish size in hats."

"Who is she?" I asked.

"Why, that is just what I can't tell you. She was a great excavator of Babylonish and Hittite ruins, and she married a diplomat who went to glory three years back. It isn't what she has been, but what she is, and that's a mighty clever woman."

Blenkiron's respect did not depress me. I felt as if at last we had got our job narrowed to a decent compass, for I had hated casting about in the dark. I asked where she lived.

"That I don't know," said Blenkiron. "You won't find people unduly anxious to gratify your natural curiosity about Frau von Einem."

"I can find that out," said Sandy. "That's the advantage of having a push like mine. Meantime, I've got to clear, for my day's work isn't finished. Dick, you and Peter must go to bed at once."

"Why?" I asked in amazement. Sandy spoke like a medical adviser.

"Because I want your clothes—the things you've got on now. I'll take them off with me and you'll never see them again."

"You've a queer taste in souvenirs," I said.

"Say rather the Turkish police. The current in the Bosporus is pretty strong, and these sad relics of two misguided Dutchmen will be washed up to-morrow about Seraglio Point. In this game you must drop the curtain neat and pat at the end of each scene, if you don't want trouble later with the missing heir and the family lawyer."

CHAPTER 13

I Move in Good Society

I WALKED out of that house next morning with Blenkiron's arm in mine, a different being from the friendless creature who had looked vainly the day before for sanctuary. To begin with, I was splendidly dressed. I had a navy-blue suit with square padded shoulders, a neat black bow-tie, shoes with a hump at the toe, and a brown bowler. Over that I wore a greatcoat lined with wolf fur. I had a smart malacca cane, and one of Blenkiron's cigars in my mouth. Peter had been made to trim his beard, and, dressed in unassuming pepper-and-salt, looked with his docile eyes and quiet voice a very respectable servant. Old Blenkiron had done the job in style, for, if you'll believe it, he had brought the clothes all the way from London. I realized now why he and Sandy had been fossicking in my wardrobe. Peter's suit had been of Sandy's procuring, and it was not the fit of mine. I had no difficulty about the accent. Any man brought up in the colonies can get his tongue round American, and I flattered myself I made a very fair shape at the lingo of the Middle West.

The wind had gone to the south and the snow was melting fast. There was a blue sky above Asia, and away to the north masses of white cloud drifting over the Black Sea. What had seemed the day before the dingiest of cities now took on a strange beauty, the beauty of unexpected horizons and tongues of grey water winding below cypress-studded shores. A man's temper has a lot to do with his appreciation of scenery. I felt a free man once more, and could use my eyes.

That street was a jumble of every nationality on earth. There were Turkish regulars in their queer conical khaki helmets, and wild-looking levies who had no kin with Europe. There were squads of Germans in flat forage-caps, staring vacantly at novel sights, and quick to salute any officer on the side-walk. Turks in closed carriages passed, and Turks on good Arab horses, and Turks who looked as if they had come out of the Ark. But it was the rabble that caught the eye—very wild, pinched, miserable rabble. I never in my life saw such swarms of beggars, and you walked down that street to the accompaniment of entreaties for alms in all the tongues of the Tower of Babel. Blenkiron and I behaved as if we were interested tourists. We would stop and laugh at one fellow and give a penny to a second, passing comments in high-pitched Western voices.

We went into a café and had a cup of coffee. A beggar came in and asked alms. Hitherto Blenkiron's purse had been closed, but now he took out some small nickels and planked five down on the table. The man cried down blessings and picked up three. Blenkiron very swiftly swept the other two into his pocket.

That seemed to me queer, and I remarked that I had never before seen a beggar who gave change. Blenkiron said nothing, and presently we moved on and came to the harbour-side.

There were a number of small tugs moored alongside, and one or two bigger craft—fruit boats, I judged, which used to ply in the Aegean. They looked pretty well moth-eaten from disuse. We stopped at one of them and watched a fellow in a blue night-cap splicing ropes. He raised his eyes once and looked at us, and then kept on with his business.

Blenkiron asked him where he came from, but he shook his head, not understanding the tongue. A Turkish policeman came up and stared at us suspiciously, till Blenkiron opened his coat, as if by accident, and displayed a tiny square of ribbon, at which he saluted. Failing to make conversation with the sailor, Blenkiron flung him three of his black cigars. "I guess you can smoke, friend, if you can't talk," he said.

The man grinned and caught the three neatly in the air. Then to my amazement he tossed one of them back.

The donor regarded it quizzically as it lay on the pavement. "That boy's a connoisseur of tobacco," he said. As we moved away I saw the Turkish policeman pick it up and put it inside his cap.

We returned by the long street on the crest of the hill. There was a man selling oranges on a tray, and Blenkiron stopped to look at them. I noticed that the man shuffled fifteen into a cluster. Blenkiron felt the oranges, as if to see that they were sound, and pushed two aside. The man instantly restored them to the group, never raising his eyes.

"This ain't the time of year to buy fruit," said Blenkiron as we passed on. "Those oranges are rotten as medlars."

We were almost on our own doorstep before I guessed the meaning of the business.

"Is your morning's work finished?" I said.

"Our morning's walk?" he asked innocently.

"I said 'work.' "

He smiled blandly. "I reckoned you'd tumble to it. Why, yes, except that I've some figuring still to do. Give me half an hour and I'll be at your service, Major."

That afternoon, after Peter had cooked a wonderfully good luncheon, I had a heart-to-heart talk with Blenkiron.

"My business is to get noos," he said; "and before I start on a stunt I make considerable preparations. All the time in London when I was yelping at the British Government, I was busy with Sir Walter arranging things ahead. We used to meet in queer places and at all hours of the night. I fixed up a lot of connexions in this city before I arrived, and especially a noos service with your Foreign Office by way of Rumania and Russia. In a day or two I guess our friends will know all about our discoveries."

At that I opened my eyes very wide.

"Why, yes. You Britishers haven't any notion how wide-awake

your Intelligence Service is. I reckon it's easy the best of all the belligerents. You never talked about it in peace time, and you shunned the theatrical ways of the Teuton. But you had the wires laid good and sure. I calculate there isn't much that happens in any corner of the earth that you don't know within twenty-four hours. I don't say your highbrows use the noos well. I don't take much stock in your political push. They're a lot of silver-tongues, no doubt, but it ain't oratory that is wanted in this racket. The William Jennings Bryan stunt languishes in war time. Politics is like a chicken-coop, and those inside get to behave as if their little run were all the world. But if the politicians make mistakes it isn't from lack of good instruction to guide their steps. If I had a big proposition to handle and could have my pick of helpers I'd plump for the Intelligence Department of the British Admiralty. Yes, sir, I take off my hat to your Government sleuths."

"Did they provide you with ready-made spies here?" I asked in astonishment.

"Why, no," he said. "But they gave me the key, and I could make my own arrangements. In Germany I buried myself deep in the local atmosphere and never peeped out. That was my game, for I was looking for something in Germany itself, and didn't want any foreign cross-bearings. As you know, I failed where you succeeded. But so soon as I crossed the Danube I set about opening up my lines of communication, and I hadn't been two days in this metropolis before I had got my telephone exchange buzzing. Some time I'll explain the thing to you, for it's a pretty little business. I've got the cutest cypher . . . No, it ain't my invention. It's your Government's. Anyone, babe, imbecile, or dotard, can carry my messages—you saw some of them to-day—but it takes some mind to set the piece, and it takes a lot of figuring at my end to work out the results. Some day you shall hear it all, for I guess it would please you."

"How do you use it?" I asked.

"Well, I get early noos of what is going on in this cabbage-patch. Likewise I get authentic noos of the rest of Europe, and I can send a message to Mr. X. in Petrograd and Mr. Y. in London, or, if I wish, to Mr. Z. in Noo York. What's the matter with that for a post-office? I'm the best-informed man in Constantinople, for old General Liman only hears one side, and mostly lies at that, and Enver prefers not to listen at all. Also, I could give them points on what is happening at their very door, for our friend Sandy is a big boss in the best-run crowd of mountebanks that ever fiddled secrets out of men's hearts. Without their help I wouldn't have cut much ice in this city."

"I want you to tell me one thing, Blenkiron," I said. "I've been playing a part for the past month, and it wears my nerves to tatters. Is this job very tiring, for if it is, I doubt I may buckle up?"

He looked thoughtful. "I can't call our business an absolute rest-cure any time. You've got to keep your eyes skinned, and there's always the risk of the little packet of dynamite going off unexpected. But as these things go, I rate this stunt as easy. We've only got to be natural. We wear our natural clothes, and talk English, and sport a Teddy Roosevelt smile, and there isn't any call for theatrical talent. Where I've found the job tight was when I have got to be natural, and my naturalness was the same brand as that of everybody round about, and all the time I had to do unnatural things. It isn't easy to be going down town to business and taking cocktails with Mr. Carl Rosenheim, and next hour being engaged trying to blow Mr. Rosenheim's friends sky-high. And it isn't easy to keep up a part which is clean outside your ordinary life. I've never tried that. My line has always been to keep my normal personality. But you have, Major, and I guess you found it wearing."

"Wearing's a mild word," I said. "But I want to know another thing. It seems to me that the line you've picked is as good as could be. But it's a cast-iron line. It commits us pretty deep and it won't be a simple job to drop it."

"Why, that's just the point I was coming to," he said. "I was going to put you wise about that very thing. When I started out I figured on some situation like this. I argued that unless I had a very clear part with a big bluff in it I wouldn't get the confidences which I needed. We've got to be at the heart of the show, taking a real hand and not just looking on. So I settled I would be a big engineer—there was a time when there weren't many bigger in the United States than John S. Blenkiron. I talked large about what might be done in Mesopotamia in the way of washing the British down the river. Well, that talk caught on. They knew of my reputation as an hydraulic expert, and they were tickled to death to rope me in. I told them I wanted a helper, and I told them about my friend Richard Hanau, as good a German as ever supped sauerkraut, who was coming through Russia and Rumania as a benevolent neutral; but when he got to Constantinople would drop his neutrality and double his benevolence. They got reports on you by wire from the States—I arranged that before I left London. So you're going to be welcomed and taken to their bosoms just like John S. was. We've both got jobs we can hold down, and now you're in these pretty clothes you're the dead ringer of the brightest kind of American engineer . . . But we can't go back on our tracks. If we wanted to leave for Constanza next week they'd be very polite, but they'd never let us. We've got to go on with this adventure and nose our way down into Mesopotamia, hoping that our luck will hold . . . God knows how we will get out of it; but it's no good going out to meet trouble. As I observed before, I believe in an all-wise and beneficent Providence, but you've got to give Him a chance."

I am bound to confess the prospect staggered me. We might be let in for fighting—and worse than fighting—against our own side. I wondered if it wouldn't be better to make a bolt for it, and said so.

He shook his head. "I reckon not. In the first place we haven't finished our inquiries. We've got Greenmantle located right enough, thanks to you, but we still know mighty little about that holy man. In the second place it won't be as bad as you think. This show lacks cohesion, sir. It is not going to last for ever. I calculate that before you and I strike the site of the garden that Adam and Eve frequented there will be a queer turn of affairs. Anyhow, it's good enough to gamble on."

Then he got some sheets of paper and drew me a plan of the

disposition of the Turkish forces. I had no notion he was such a close student of war, for his exposition was as good as a staff lecture. He made out that the situation was none too bright anywhere. The troops released from Gallipoli wanted a lot of refitment, and would be slow in reaching the Transcaucasian frontier, where the Russians were threatening. The army of Syria was pretty nearly a rabble under the lunatic Djemal. There wasn't the foggiest chance of a serious invasion of Egypt being undertaken. Only in Mesopotamia did things look fairly cheerful, owing to the blunders of British strategy. "And you may take it from me," he said, "that if the old Turk mobilized a total of a million men, he has lost 40 per cent of them already. And if I'm anything of a prophet he's going pretty soon to lose more."

He tore up the papers and enlarged on politics. "I reckon I've got the measure of the Young Turks and their precious Committee. Those boys aren't any good. Enver's bright enough, and for sure he's got sand. He'll stick out a fight like a Vermont game-chicken, but he lacks the larger vision, sir. He doesn't understand the intricacies of the job no more than a sucking-child, so the Germans play with him, till his temper goes and he bucks like a mule. Talaat is a sulky dog who wants to batter mankind with a club. Both these boys would have made good cow-punchers in the old days, and they might have got a living out West as the gun-men of a Labour Union. They're about the class of Jesse James or Bill the Kid, excepting that they're college-reared and can patter languages. But they haven't the organizing power to manage the Irish vote in a ward election. Their one notion is to get busy with their firearms, and people are getting tired of the Black Hand stunt. Their hold on the country is just the hold that a man with a Browning has over a crowd with walking-sticks. The cooler heads in the Committee are growing shy of them, and an old fox like Djavid is lying low till his time comes. Now it doesn't want arguing that a gang of that kind has got to hang close together or they may hang separately. They've got no grip on the ordinary Turk, barring the fact that they are active and he is sleepy, and that they've got their guns loaded."

"What about the Germans here?" I asked.

Blenkiron laughed. "It is no sort of a happy family. But the Young Turks know that without the German boost they'll be strung up like Haman, and the Germans can't afford to neglect an ally. Consider what would happen if Turkey got sick of the game and made a separate peace. The road would be open for Russia to the Aegean. Ferdy of Bulgaria would take his depreciated goods to the other market, and not waste a day thinking about it. You'd have Rumania coming in on the Allies' side. Things would look pretty black for that control of the Near East on which Germany has banked her winnings. Kaiser says that's got to be prevented at all costs, but how is it going to be done?"

Blenkiron's face had become very solemn again. "It won't be done unless Germany's got a trump card to play. Her game's mighty near bust, but it's still got a chance. And that chance is a woman and an old man. I reckon our landlady has a bigger brain than Enver and Liman. She's the real boss of the show. When I came here, I reported to her, and presently you've got to do the same. I am curious as to how she'll strike you, for I'm free to admit that she impressed me considerable."

"It looks as if our job were a long way from the end," I said.

"It's scarcely begun," said Blenkiron.

THAT talk did a lot to cheer my spirits, for I realized that it was the biggest of big game we were hunting this time. I'm an economical soul, and if I'm going to be hanged I want a good stake for my neck.

Then began some varied experiences. I used to wake up in the morning, wondering where I should be at night, and yet quite pleased at the uncertainty. Greenmantle became a sort of myth with me. Somehow I couldn't fix any idea in my head of what he was like. The nearest I got was a picture of an old man in a turban coming out of a bottle in a cloud of smoke, which I remembered from a child's edition of the *Arabian Nights*. But if he was dim, the lady was dimmer. Sometimes I thought of her as a fat old German crone, sometimes as a harsh-featured woman like a schoolmistress with thin lips and eyeglasses. But I had to fit the East into the picture, so I made her young and gave her a touch of the languid houri in a veil. I was always wanting to pump Blenkiron on the subject, but he shut up like a rat-trap. He was looking for bad trouble in that direction, and was disinclined to speak about it beforehand.

We led a peaceful existence. Our servants were two of Sandy's lot, for Blenkiron had very rightly cleared out the Turkish care-takers, and they worked like beavers under Peter's eye, till I re-flected I had never been so well looked after in my life. I walked about the city with Blenkiron, keeping my eyes open, and speak-ing very civil. The third night we were bidden to dinner at Moellendorff's, so we put on our best clothes and set out in an ancient cab. Blenkiron had fetched a dress suit of mine, from which my own tailor's label had been cut and a New York one substituted.

General Liman and Metternich the Ambassador had gone up the line to Nish to meet the Kaiser, who was touring in those parts, so Moellendorff was the biggest German in the city. He was a thin, foxy-faced fellow, cleverish but monstrously vain, and he was not very popular either with the Germans or the Turks. He was polite to both of us, but I am bound to say that I got a bad fright when I entered the room, for the first man I saw was Gaudian.

I doubt if he would have recognized me even in the clothes I had worn in Stumm's company, for his eyesight was wretched. As it was, I ran no risk in dress clothes, with my hair brushed back and a fine American accent. I paid him high compliments as a fellow engineer, and translated part of a very technical conversa-tion between him and Blenkiron. Gaudian was in uniform, and I liked the look of his honest face better than ever.

But the great event was the sight of Enver. He was a slim fel-low of Rasta's build, very foppish and precise in his dress, with a smooth oval face like a girl's and rather fine straight black eye-brows. He spoke perfect German, and had the best kind of man-ners, neither pert nor overbearing. He had a pleasant trick, too, of appealing all round the table for confirmation, and so bringing everybody into the talk. Not that he spoke a great deal, but all he said was good sense, and he had a smiling way of saying it. Once or twice he ran counter to Moellendorff, and I could see there was no love lost between these two. I didn't think I wanted him as a friend—he was too cold-blooded and artificial; and I was pretty certain that I didn't want those steady black eyes as an enemy. But it was no good denying his quality. The little fellow was all cold courage, like the fine polished blue steel of a sword.

I fancy I was rather a success at that dinner. For one thing I could speak German, and so had a pull on Blenkiron. For another I was in a good temper, and really enjoyed putting my back into my part. They talked very high-flown stuff about what they had done and were going to do, and Enver was great on Gallipoli. I remember he said that he could have destroyed the whole British Army if it hadn't been for somebody's cold feet—at which Moellendorff looked daggers. They were so bitter about Britain and all her works that I gathered they were getting pretty panicky, and that made me as jolly as a sandboy. I'm afraid I was not free from bitterness myself on that subject. I said things about my own country that I sometimes wake in the night and sweat to think of.

Gaudian got on to the use of water power in war, and that gave me a chance.

"In my country," I said, "when we want to get rid of a mountain we wash it away. There's nothing on earth that will stand against water. Now, speaking with all respect, gentlemen, and as an absolute novice in the military art, I sometimes ask why this God-given weapon isn't more used in the present war. I haven't been to any of the fronts, but I've studied them some from maps and the newspapers. Take your German position in Flanders, where you've got the high ground. If I were a British general I reckon I would very soon make it no sort of position."

Moellendorff asked, "How?"

"Why, I'd wash it away. Wash away the fourteen feet of soil down to the stone. There's a heap of coal-pits behind the British front where they could generate power, and I judge there's ample water supply from the rivers and canals. I'd guarantee to wash you away in twenty-four hours—yes, in spite of all your big guns. It beats me why the British haven't got on to this notion. They used to have some bright engineers."

Enver was on the point like a knife, far quicker than Gaudian. He cross-examined me in a way that showed he knew how to approach a technical subject, though he mightn't have much technical knowledge. He was just giving me a sketch of the flooding in Mesopotamia when an aide-de-camp brought in a chit which fetched him to his feet.

"I have gossiped long enough," he said. "My kind host, I must leave you. Gentlemen all, my apologies and farewells."

Before he left he asked my name and wrote it down. "This is an unhealthy city for strangers, Mr. Hanau," he said in very good English. "I have some small power of protecting a friend, and what I have is at your disposal." This with the condescension of a king promising his favour to a subject.

The little fellow amused me tremendously, and rather impressed me too. I said so to Gaudian after he had left, but that decent soul didn't agree.

"I do not love him," he said. "We are allies—yes; but friends—no. He is no true son of Islam, which is a noble faith and despises liars and boasters and betrayers of their salt."

That was the verdict of one honest man on this ruler in Israel. The next night I got another from Blenkiron on a greater than Enver.

He had been out alone and had come back pretty late, with his face grey and drawn with pain. The food we ate—not at all bad of its kind—and the cold east wind played havoc with his dyspepsia. I can see him yet, boiling milk on a spirit-lamp, while Peter worked at a Primus stove to get him a hot-water bottle. He was using horrid language about his inside.

"My God, Major, if I were you with a sound stomach I'd fairly conquer the world. As it is, I've got to do my work with half my mind, while the other half is dwelling in my intestines. I'm like the child in the Bible that had a fox gnawing at its vitals."

He got his milk boiling and began to sip it.

"I've been to see our pretty landlady," he said. "She sent for me and I hobbled off with a grip full of plans, for she's mighty set on Mesopotamy."

"Anything about Greenmantle?" I asked eagerly.

"Why, no, but I have reached one conclusion. I opine that the hapless prophet has no sort of time with that lady. I opine that he will soon wish himself in Paradise. For if Almighty God ever created a female devil it's Madam von Einem."

He sipped a little more milk with a grave face.

"That isn't my duodenal dyspepsia, Major. It's the verdict of a ripe experience, for I have a cool and penetrating judgement, even if I've a deranged stomach. And I give it as my considered conclusion that that woman's mad and bad—but principally bad."

CHAPTER 14

The Lady of the Mantilla

SINCE that first night I had never clapped eyes on Sandy. He had gone clean out of the world, and Blenkiron and I waited anxiously for a word of news. Our own business was in good trim, for we were presently going east towards Mesopotamia, but unless we learned more about Greenmantle our journey would be a grotesque failure. And learn about Greenmantle we could not, for nobody by word or deed suggested his existence, and it was impossible of course for us to ask questions. Our only hope was Sandy, for what we wanted to know was the prophet's whereabouts and his plans. I suggested to Blenkiron that we might do more to cultivate Frau von Einem, but he shut his jaw like a rat-trap. "There's nothing doing for us in that quarter," he said. "That's the most dangerous woman on earth; and if she got any kind of notion that we were wise about her pet schemes I reckon you and I would very soon be in the Bosporus."

This was all very well; but what was going to happen if the two of us were bundled off to Bagdad with instructions to wash away the British? Our time was getting pretty short, and I doubted if we could spin out more than three days more in Constantinople. I felt just as I had felt with Stumm that last night when I was about to be packed off to Cairo and saw no way of avoiding it.

Even Blenkiron was getting anxious. He played Patience incessantly, and was disinclined to talk. I tried to find out something from the servants, but they either knew nothing or wouldn't speak—the former, I think. I kept my eyes lifting, too, as I walked about the streets, but there was no sign anywhere of the skin coats or the weird stringed instruments. The whole Company of the Rosy Hours seemed to have melted into the air, and I began to wonder if they had ever existed.

Anxiety made me restless, and restlessness made me want exercise. It was no good walking about the city. The weather had become foul again, and I was sick of the smells and the squalor and the flea-bitten crowds. So Blenkiron and I got horses, Turkish cavalry mounts with heads like trees, and went out through the suburbs into the open country.

It was a grey drizzling afternoon, with the beginnings of a sea fog which hid the Asiatic shores of the straits. It wasn't easy to find open ground for a gallop, for there were endless small patches of cultivation and the gardens of country houses. We kept on the high land above the sea, and when we reached a bit of downland came on squads of Turkish soldiers digging trenches. Whenever we let the horses go we had to pull up sharp for a digging party or a stretch of barbed wire. Coils of the beastly thing were lying loose everywhere, and Blenkiron nearly took a nasty toss over one. Then we were always being stopped by sentries and having to show our passes. Still the ride did us good and shook up our livers, and by the time we turned for home I was feeling more like a white man.

We jogged back in the short winter twilight, past the wooded grounds of white villas, held up every few minutes by transport-wagons and companies of soldiers. The rain had come on in real earnest, and it was two very bedraggled horsemen that crawled along the muddy lanes. As we passed one villa, shut in by a high white wall, a pleasant smell of wood smoke was wafted towards us, which made me sick for the burning veld. My ear, too, caught the twanging of a zither, which somehow reminded me of the afternoon in Kuprasso's garden-house.

I pulled up and proposed to investigate, but Blenkiron very testily declined.

"Zithers are as common here as fleas," he said. "You don't want to be fossicking around somebody's stables and find a horse-boy entertaining his friends. They don't like visitors in this country; and you'll be asking for trouble if you go inside those walls. I guess it's some old Buzzard's harem." Buzzard was his own private peculiar name for the Turk, for he said he had had as a boy a natural history book with a picture of a bird called the turkey-buzzard, and couldn't get out of the habit of applying it to the Ottoman people.

I wasn't convinced, so I tried to mark down the place. It seemed to be about three miles out from the city, at the end of a steep lane on the inland side of the hill coming from the Bosporus. I fancied somebody of distinction lived there, for a little farther on we met a big empty motor-car snorting its way up, and I had a notion that the car belonged to the walled villa.

Next day Blenkiron was in grievous trouble with his dyspepsia. About midday he was compelled to lie down, and having nothing better to do I had out the horses again and took Peter with me. It was funny to see Peter in a Turkish army-saddle, riding with the long Boer stirrup and the slouch of the backveld.

That afternoon was unfortunate from the start. It was not the mist and drizzle of the day before, but a stiff northern gale which blew sheets of rain in our faces and numbed our bridle hands. We took the same road, but pushed west of the trench-digging parties and got to a shallow valley with a white village among the cypresses. Beyond that there was a very respectable road which brought us to the top of a crest that in clear weather must have given a fine prospect. Then we turned our horses, and I shaped our course so as to strike the top of the long lane that abutted on the down. I wanted to investigate the white villa.

But we hadn't gone far on our road back before we got into trouble. It arose out of a sheep-dog, a yellow mongrel brute that came at us like a thunderbolt. It took a special fancy to Peter, and bit savagely at his horse's heels and sent it capering off the road. I should have warned him, but I did not realize what was happening, till too late. For Peter, being accustomed to mongrels in Kaffir kraals, took a summary way with the pest. Since it despised his whip, he out with his pistol and put a bullet through its head.

The echoes of the shot had scarcely died away when the row began. A big fellow appeared running towards us, shouting wildly. I guessed he was the dog's owner, and proposed to pay no attention. But his cries summoned two other fellows—soldiers by the look of them—who closed in on us, unslinging their rifles as they ran. My first idea was to show them our heels, but I had no desire to be shot in the back, and they looked like men who wouldn't stop short of shooting. So we slowed down and faced them.

They made as savage-looking a trio as you would want to avoid. The shepherd looked as if he had been dug up, a dirty ruffian with matted hair and a beard like a bird's nest. The two soldiers stood staring with sullen faces, fingering their guns, while the other chap raved and stormed and kept pointing at Peter, whose mild eyes stared unwinkingly at his assailant.

The mischief was that neither of us had a word of Turkish. I tried German, but it had no effect. We sat looking at them and they stood storming at us, and it was fast getting dark. Once I turned my horse round as if to proceed, and the two soldiers jumped in front of me.

They jabbered among themselves, and then one said very slowly: "He . . . want . . . pounds," and he held up five fingers. They evidently saw by the cut of our jib that we weren't Germans.

"I'll be hanged if he gets a penny," I said angrily, and the conversation languished.

The situation was getting serious, so I spoke a word to Peter. The soldiers had their rifles loose in their hands, and before they could lift them we had the pair covered with our pistols.

"If you move," I said, "you are dead." They understood that all right and stood stock still, while the shepherd stopped his raving and took to muttering like a gramophone when the record is finished.

"Drop your guns," I said sharply. "Quick, or we shoot."

The tone, if not the words, conveyed my meaning. Still staring at us, they let the rifles slide to the ground. The next second we had forced our horses on the top of them, and the three were off like rabbits. I sent a shot over their heads to encourage them. Peter dismounted and tossed the guns into a bit of scrub where they would take some finding.

This hold-up had wasted time. By now it was getting very dark, and we hadn't ridden a mile before it was black night. It was an annoying predicament, for I had completely lost my bearings and at the best I had only a foggy notion of the lie of the land. The best plan seemed to be to try and get to the top of a rise in the hope of seeing the lights of the city, but all the countryside was so pockety that it was hard to strike the right kind of rise.

We had to trust to Peter's instinct. I asked him where our line lay, and he sat very still for a minute sniffing the air. Then he pointed the direction. It wasn't what I would have taken myself, but on a point like that he was pretty near infallible.

Presently we came to a long slope which cheered me. But at the top there was no light visible anywhere—only a black void like the inside of a shell. As I stared into the gloom it seemed to me that there were patches of deeper darkness that might be woods.

"There is a house half-left in front of us," said Peter.

I peered till my eyes ached and saw nothing.

"Well, for Heaven's sake, guide me to it," I said, and with Peter in front we set off down the hill.

It was a wild journey, for darkness clung as close to us as a vest. Twice we stepped into patches of bog, and once my horse saved himself by a hair from going head forward into a gravel pit. We got tangled up in strands of wire, and often found ourselves rubbing our noses against tree-trunks. Several times I had to get down and make a gap in barricades of loose stones. But after a ridiculous amount of slipping and stumbling we finally struck what seemed the level of a road, and a piece of special darkness in front which turned out to be a high wall.

I argued that all mortal walls had doors, so we set to groping along it, and presently found a gap. There was an old iron gate on broken hinges, which we easily pushed open, and found ourselves on a back path to some house. It was clearly disused, for masses of rotting leaves covered it, and by the feel of it underfoot it was grass-grown.

We dismounted now, leading our horses, and after about fifty yards the path ceased and came out on a well-made carriage drive. So, at least, we guessed, for the place was as black as pitch. Evidently the house couldn't be far off, but in which direction I hadn't a notion.

Now, I didn't want to be paying calls on any Turk at that time of day. Our job was to find where the road opened into the lane, for after that our way to Constantinople was clear. One side the lane lay, and the other the house, and it didn't seem wise to take the risk of tramping up with horses to the front door. So I told Peter to wait for me at the end of the back-road, while I would prospect a bit. I turned to the right, my intention being if I saw the light of a house to return, and with Peter take the other direction.

I walked like a blind man in that nether-pit of darkness. The road seemed well kept, and the soft wet gravel muffled the sounds of my feet. Great trees overhung it, and several times I wandered into dripping bushes. And then I stopped short in my tracks, for I heard the sound of whistling.

It was quite close, about ten yards away. And the strange thing was that it was a tune I knew, about the last tune you would expect to hear in this part of the world. It was the Scots air: "Ca' the yowes to the knowes" which was a favourite of my father's.

The whistler must have felt my presence, for the air suddenly stopped in the middle of a bar. An unbounded curiosity seized me to know who the fellow could be. So I started in and finished it myself.

There was silence for a second, and then the unknown began again and stopped. Once more I chipped in and finished it.

Then it seemed to me that he was coming nearer. The air in that dank tunnel was very still, and I thought I heard a light foot. I think I took a step backward. Suddenly there was a flash of an electric torch from a yard off, so quick that I could see nothing of the man who held it.

Then a low voice spoke out of the darkness—a voice I knew well—and, following it, a hand was laid on my arm. "What the devil are you doing here, Dick?" it said, and there was something like consternation in the tone.

I told him in a hectic sentence, for I was beginning to feel badly rattled myself.

"You've never been in greater danger in your life," said the voice. "Great God, man, what brought you wandering here to-day of all days?"

You can imagine that I was pretty scared, for Sandy was the last man to put a case too high. And the next second I felt worse, for he clutched my arm and dragged me in a bound to the side of the road. I could see nothing, but I felt that his head was screwed round, and mine followed suit. And there, a dozen yards off, were the acetylene lights of a big motor-car.

It came along very slowly, purring like a great cat, while we pressed into the bushes. The headlights seemed to spread a fan far to either side, showing the full width of the drive and its borders, and about half the height of the over-arching trees. There was a figure in uniform sitting beside the chauffeur, whom I saw dimly in the reflex glow, but the body of the car was dark.

It crept towards us, passed, and my mind was just getting easy again when it stopped. A switch was snapped within, and the limousine was brightly lit up. Inside I saw a woman's figure.

The servant had got out and opened the door and a voice came from within—a clear soft voice speaking in some tongue I didn't understand. Sandy had started forward at the sound of it, and I followed him. It would never do for me to be caught skulking in the bushes.

I was so dazzled by the suddenness of the glare that at first I blinked and saw nothing. Then my eyes cleared and I found myself looking at the inside of a car upholstered in some soft dove-coloured fabric, and beautifully finished off in ivory and silver. The woman who sat in it had a mantilla of black lace over her head and shoulders, and with one slender jewelled hand she kept its fold over the greater part of her face. I saw only a pair of pale grey-blue eyes—these and the slim fingers.

I remember that Sandy was standing very upright with his hands on his hips, by no means like a servant in the presence of his mistress. He was a fine figure of a man at all times, but in those wild clothes, with his head thrown back and his dark brows drawn below his skull-cap, he looked like some savage king out of an older world. He was speaking Turkish, and glancing at me now and then as if angry and perplexed. I took the hint that he was not supposed to know any other tongue, and that he was asking who the devil I might be.

Then they both looked at me, Sandy with the slow unwinking stare of the gipsy, the lady with those curious, beautiful pale eyes. They ran over my clothes, my brand-new riding-breeches, my splashed boots, my wide-brimmed hat. I took off the last and made my best bow.

"Madam," I said, "I have to ask pardon for trespassing in your garden. The fact is, I and my servant—he's down the road with the horses and I guess you noticed him—the two of us went for a ride this afternoon, and got good and well lost. We came in by your back gate, and I was prospecting for your front door to find someone to direct us, when I bumped into this brigand-chief who didn't understand my talk. I'm American, and I'm here on a big Government proposition. I hate to trouble you, but if you'd send a man to show us how to strike the city I'd be very much in your debt."

Her eyes never left my face. "Will you come into the car?" she said in English. "At the house I will give you a servant to direct you."

She drew in the skirts of her fur cloak to make room for me, and in my muddy boots and sopping clothes I took the seat she pointed out. She said a word in Turkish to Sandy, switched off the light, and the car moved on.

Women had never come much my way, and I knew about as much of their ways as I knew about the Chinese language. All my life I had lived with men only, and rather a rough crowd at that. When I made my pile and came home I looked to see a little society, but I had first the business of the Black Stone on my hands, and then the war, so my education languished. I had never been in a motor-car with a lady before, and I felt like a fish on a dry sand-bank. The soft cushions and the subtle scents filled me with acute uneasiness. I wasn't thinking now about Sandy's grave words, or about Blenkiron's warning, or about my job and the part this woman must play in it. I was thinking only that I felt mortally shy. The darkness made it worse. I was sure that my companion was looking at me all the time and laughing at me for a clown.

The car stopped and a tall servant opened the door. The lady was over the threshold before I was at the step. I followed her heavily, the wet squelching from my field-boots. At that moment I noticed that she was very tall.

She led me through a long corridor to a room where two pillars held lamps in the shape of torches. The place was dark but for their glow, and it was as warm as a hothouse from invisible stoves. I felt soft carpets underfoot, and on the walls hung some tapestry or rug of an amazingly intricate geometrical pattern, but with every strand as rich as jewels. There, between the pillars, she turned and faced me. Her furs were thrown back, and the black mantilla had slipped down to her shoulders.

"I have heard of you," she said. "You are called Richard Hanau, the American. Why have you come to this land?"

"To have a share in the campaign," I said. "I'm an engineer, and I thought I could help out with some business like Mesopotamia."

"You are on Germany's side?" she asked.

"Why, yes," I replied. "We Americans are supposed to be noo-trals. That means we're free to choose any side we fancy. I'm for the Kaiser."

Her cool eyes searched me, but not in suspicion. I could see she wasn't troubled with the question whether I was speaking the truth. She was sizing me up as a man. I cannot describe that calm appraising look. There was no sex in it, nothing even of that implicit sympathy with which one human being explores the existence of another. I was a chattel, a thing infinitely removed from intimacy. Even so I have myself looked at a horse which I thought of buying, scanning his shoulders and hocks and paces. Even so must the old lords of Constantinople have looked at the slaves which the chances of war brought to their markets, assessing their usefulness for some task or other with no thought of a humanity common to purchased and purchaser. And yet—not quite. This woman's eyes were weighing me, not for any special duty, but for my essential qualities. I felt that I was under the scrutiny of one who was a connoisseur in human nature.

I see I have written that I knew nothing about women. But every man has in his bones a consciousness of sex. I was shy and perturbed, but horribly fascinated. This slim woman, poised exquisitely like some statue between the pillared lights, with her fair cloud of hair, her long delicate face, and her pale bright eyes, had the glamour of a wild dream. I hated her instinctively, hated her intensely, but I longed to arouse her interest. To be valued coldly by those eyes was an offence to my manhood, and I felt antagonism rising within me. I am a strong fellow, well set up, and rather above the average height, and my irritation stiffened me from heel to crown. I flung my head back and gave her cool glance for cool glance, pride against pride.

Once, I remember, a doctor on board ship who dabbled in hypnotism told me that I was the most unsympathetic person he had ever struck. He said I was about as good a mesmeric subject as Table Mountain. Suddenly I began to realize that this woman was trying to cast some spell over me. The eyes grew large and luminous, and I was conscious for just an instant of some will battling to subject mine. I was aware, too, in the same moment of a strange scent which recalled that wild hour in Kuprasso's garden-house. It passed quickly, and for a second her eyes drooped. I seemed to read in them failure, and yet a kind of satisfaction, too, as if they had found more in me than they expected.

"What life have you led?" the soft voice was saying.

I was able to answer quite naturally, rather to my surprise. "I have been a mining engineer up and down the world."

"You have faced danger many times?"

"I have faced danger."

"You have fought with men in battles?"

"I have fought in battles."

Her bosom rose and fell in a kind of sigh. A smile—a very beautiful thing—flitted over her face. She gave me her hand.

"The horses are at the door now," she said, "and your servant is with them. One of my people will guide you to the city."

She turned away and passed out of the circle of light into the darkness beyond . . .

Peter and I jogged home in the rain with one of Sandy's skin-clad Companions loping at our side. We did not speak a word, for my thoughts were running like hounds on the track of the past hours. I had seen the mysterious Hilda von Einem, I had spoken to her, I had held her hand. She had insulted me with the subtlest of insults and yet I was not angry. Suddenly the game I was playing became invested with a tremendous solemnity. My old antagonists, Stumm and Rasta and the whole German Empire, seemed to shrink into the background, leaving only the slim woman with her inscrutable smile and devouring eyes. "Mad and bad," Blenkiron had called her, "but principally bad." I did not think they were the proper terms, for they belonged to the narrow world of our common experience. This was something beyond and above it, as a cyclone or an earthquake is outside the decent routine of nature. Mad and bad she might be, but she was also great.

Before we arrived our guide had plucked my knee and spoken some words which he had obviously got by heart. "The Master says," ran the message, "expect him at midnight."

CHAPTER 15

An Embarrassed Toilet

I WAS soaked to the bone, and while Peter set off to look for dinner I went to my room to change. I had a rub down and then got into pyjamas for some dumb-bell exercises with two chairs, for that long wet ride had stiffened my arm and shoulder muscles. They were a vulgar suit of primitive blue, which Blenkiron had looted from my London wardrobe. As Cornelis Brandt I had sported a flannel nightgown.

My bedroom opened off the sitting-room, and while I was busy with my gymnastics I heard the door open. I thought at first it was Blenkiron, but the briskness of the tread was unlike his measured gait. I had left the light burning there, and the visitor, whoever he was, had made himself at home. I slipped on a green dressing-gown Blenkiron had lent me, and sallied forth to investigate.

My friend Rasta was standing by the table, on which he had laid an envelope. He looked round at my entrance and saluted.

"I come from the Minister of War, sir," he said, "and bring you your passports for to-morrow. You will travel by . . ." And then his voice tailed away and his black eyes narrowed to slits. He had seen something which switched him off the metals.

At that moment I saw it too. There was a mirror on the wall behind him, and as I faced him I could not help seeing my reflection. It was the exact image of the engineer on the Danube boat—blue jeans, *loden* cloak, and all. The accursed mischance of my costume had given him the clue to an identity which was otherwise buried deep in the Bosporus.

I am bound to say for Rasta that he was a man of quick action. In a trice he had whipped round to the other side of the table between me and the door, where he stood regarding me wickedly.

By this time I was at the table and stretched out a hand for the envelope. My one hope was nonchalance.

"Sit down, sir," I said, "and have a drink. It's a filthy night to move about in."

"Thank you, no, Herr Brandt," he said. "You may burn these passports for they will not be used."

"Whatever's the matter with you?" I cried. "You've mistaken the house, my lad. I'm called Hanau—Richard Hanau—and my partner's Mr. John S. Blenkiron. He'll be here presently. Never knew anyone of the name of Brandt, barring a tobacconist in Denver City."

"You have never been to Rustchuk?" he said with a sneer.

"Not that I know of. But, pardon me, sir, if I ask your name and your business here. I'm darned if I'm accustomed to be called by Dutch names or have my word doubted. In my country we consider that impolite as between gentlemen."

I could see that my bluff was having its effect. His stare began to waver, and when he next spoke it was in a more civil tone.

"I will ask pardon if I'm mistaken, sir, but you're the image of a man who a week ago was at Rustchuk, a man much wanted by the Imperial Government."

"A week ago I was tossing in a dirty little hooker coming from Constanza. Unless Rustchuk's in the middle of the Black Sea I've never visited the township. I guess you're barking up the wrong tree. Come to think of it, I was expecting passports. Say, do you come from Enver Damad?"

"I have that honour," he said.

"Well, Enver is a very good friend of mine. He's the brightest citizen I've struck this side of the Atlantic."

The man was calming down, and in another minute his suspicions would have gone. But at that moment, by the crookedest kind of luck, Peter entered with a tray of dishes. He did not notice Rasta, and walked straight to the table and plumped down his burden on it. The Turk had stepped aside at his entrance, and I saw by the look in his eyes that his suspicions had become a certainty. For Peter, stripped to shirt and breeches, was the identical shabby little companion of the Rustchuk meeting.

I had never doubted Rasta's pluck. He jumped for the door and had a pistol out in a trice pointing at my head.

"*Bonne fortune,*" he cried. "Both the birds at one shot." His hand was on the latch, and his mouth was open to cry. I guessed there was an orderly waiting on the stairs.

He had what you call the strategic advantage, for he was at the door while I was at the other end of the table and Peter at the side of it at least two yards from him. The road was clear before him, and neither of us was armed. I made a despairing step forward, not knowing what I meant to do, for I saw no light. But Peter was before me.

He had never let go of the tray, and now, as a boy skims a stone on a pond, he skimmed it with its contents at Rasta's head. The man was opening the door with one hand while he kept me covered with the other, and he got the contrivance fairly in the face. A pistol shot cracked out, and the bullet went through the tray, but the noise was drowned in the crash of glasses and crockery. The next second Peter had wrenched the pistol from Rasta's hand and had gripped his throat.

A dandified Young Turk, brought up in Paris and finished in Berlin, may be as brave as a lion, but he cannot stand in a rough-and-tumble against a backveld hunter, though more than double his age. There was no need for me to help him. Peter had his own way, learned in a wild school, of knocking the sense out of a foe. He gagged him scientifically, and trussed him up with his own belt and two straps from a trunk in my bedroom.

"This man is too dangerous to let go," he said, as if his

procedure were the most ordinary thing in the world. "He will be quiet now till we have time to make a plan."

At that moment there came a knocking at the door. That is the sort of thing that happens in melodrama, just when the villain has finished off his job neatly. The correct thing to do is to pale to the teeth, and with a rolling, conscience-stricken eye glare round the horizon. But that was not Peter's way.

"We'd better tidy up if we're to have visitors," he said calmly.

Now there was one of those big oak German cupboards against the wall which must have been brought in in sections, for complete it would never have got through the door. It was empty now, but for Blenkiron's hatbox. In it he deposited the unconscious Rasta, and turned the key. "There's enough ventilation through the top," he observed, "to keep the air good." Then he opened the door.

A magnificent *kavass* in blue and silver stood outside. He saluted and proffered a card on which was written in pencil, "Hilda von Einem."

I would have begged for time to change my clothes, but the lady was behind him. I saw the black mantilla and the rich sable furs. Peter vanished through my bedroom and I was left to receive my guest in a room littered with broken glass and a senseless man in the cupboard.

There are some situations so crazily extravagant that they key up the spirit to meet them. I was almost laughing when that stately lady stepped over my threshold.

"Madam," I said, with a bow that shamed my old dressing-gown and strident pyjamas. "You find me at a disadvantage. I came home soaking from my ride, and was in the act of changing. My servant has just upset a tray of crockery, and I fear this room's no fit place for a lady. Allow me three minutes to make myself presentable."

She inclined her head gravely and took a seat by the fire. I went into my bedroom, and as I expected found Peter lurking by the other door. In a hectic sentence I bade him get Rasta's orderly out of the place on any pretext, and tell him his master would return later. Then I hurried into decent garments, and came out to find my visitor in a brown study.

At the sound of my entrance she started from her dream and stood up on the hearthrug, slipping the long robe of fur from her slim body.

"We are alone?" she said. "We will not be disturbed?"

Then an inspiration came to me. I remembered that Frau von Einem, according to Blenkiron, did not see eye to eye with the Young Turks; and I had a queer instinct that Rasta could not be to her liking. So I spoke the truth.

"I must tell you that there's another guest here to-night. I reckon he's feeling pretty uncomfortable. At present he's trussed up on a shelf in that cupboard."

She did not trouble to look round.

"Is he dead?" she asked calmly.

"By no means," I said, "but he's fixed so he can't speak, and I guess he can't hear much."

"He was the man who brought you this?" she asked, pointing to the envelope on the table which bore the big blue stamp of the Ministry of War.

"The same," I said. "I'm not perfectly sure of his name, but I think they call him Rasta."

Not a flicker of a smile crossed her face, but I had a feeling that the news pleased her.

"Did he thwart you?" she asked.

"Why, yes. He thwarted me some. His head is a bit swelled, and an hour or two on the shelf will do him good."

"He is a powerful man," she said, "a jackal of Enver's. You have made a dangerous enemy."

"I don't value him at two cents," said I, though I thought grimly that as far as I could see the value of him was likely to be about the price of my neck.

"Perhaps you are right," she said with serious eyes. "In these days no enemy is dangerous to a bold man. I have come to-night, Mr. Hanau, to talk business with you, as they say in your country. I have heard well of you, and to-day I have seen you. I may have need of you, and you assuredly will have need of me . . ."

She broke off, and again her strange potent eyes fell on my face. They were like a burning searchlight which showed up every cranny and crack of the soul. I felt it was going to be horribly difficult to act a part under that compelling gaze. She could not mesmerize me, but she could strip me of my fancy dress and set me naked in the masquerade.

"What came you forth to seek?" she asked. "You are not like the stout American Blenkiron, a lover of shoddy power and a devotee of a feeble science. There is something more than that in your face. You are on our side, but you are not of the Germans with their hankerings for a rococo Empire. You come from America, the land of pious follies, where men worship gold and words. I ask, what came you forth to seek?"

As she spoke I seemed to get a vision of a figure, like one of the old gods looking down on human nature from a great height, a figure disdainful and passionless, but with its own magnificence. It kindled my imagination, and I answered with the stuff I had often cogitated when I had tried to explain to myself just how a case could be made out against the Allied cause.

"I will tell you, Madam," I said. "I am a man who has followed a science, but I have followed it in wild places, and I have gone through it and come out at the other side. The world, as I see it, had become too easy and cushioned. Men had forgotten their manhood in soft speech, and imagined that the rules of their smug civilization were the laws of the universe. But that is not the teaching of science, and it is not the teaching of life. We have forgotten the greater virtues, and we were becoming emasculated humbugs whose gods were our own weaknesses. Then came war, and the air was cleared. Germany, in spite of her blunders and her grossness, stood forth as the scourge of cant. She had the courage to cut through the bonds of humbug and to laugh at the fetishes of the herd. Therefore I am on Germany's side. But I came here for another reason. I know nothing of the East, but as I read history it is from the desert that the purification comes. When mankind is smothered with shams and phrases and painted idols a wind blows out of the wild to cleanse and simplify life. The world needs space and fresh air. The civilization we have boasted of is a toy-shop and a blind alley, and I hanker for the open country."

This confounded nonsense was well received. Her pale eyes had the cold light of the fanatic. With her bright hair and the long exquisite oval of her face she looked like some destroying fury of a Norse legend. At that moment I think I first really feared her; before I had half hated and half admired. Thank Heaven, in her absorption she did not notice that I had forgotten the speech of Cleveland, Ohio.

"You are of the Household of Faith," she said. "You will presently learn many things, for the Faith marches to victory. Meantime I have one word for you. You and your companion travel eastward."

"We go to Mesopotamia," I said. "I reckon these are our passports," and I pointed to the envelope.

She picked it up, opened it, and then tore it in pieces and tossed it in the fire.

"The orders are countermanded," she said. "I have need of you and you go with me. Not to the flats of the Tigris, but to the great hills. To-morrow you will receive new passports."

She gave me her hand and turned to go. At the threshold she paused, and looked towards the oak cupboard. "To-morrow I will relieve you of your prisoner. He will be safer in my hands."

SHE left me in a condition of pretty blank bewilderment. We were to be tied to the chariot-wheels of this fury, and started on an enterprise compared to which fighting against our friends at Kut seemed tame and reasonable. On the other hand, I had been spotted by Rasta, and had got the envoy of the most powerful man in Constantinople locked in a cupboard. At all costs we had to keep Rasta safe, but I was very determined that he should not be handed over to the lady. I was going to be no party to cold-blooded murder, which I judged to be her expedient. It was a pretty kettle of fish, but in the meantime I must have food, for I had eaten nothing for nine hours. So I went in search of Peter.

I had scarcely begun my long-deferred meal when Sandy entered. He was before his time, and he looked as solemn as a sick owl. I seized on him as a drowning man clutches a spar.

He heard my story of Rasta with a lengthening face.

"That's bad," he said. "You say he spotted you, and your subsequent doings of course would not disillusion him. It's an infernal nuisance, but there's only one way out of it. I must put him in charge of my own people. They will keep him safe and sound till he's wanted. Only he mustn't see me." And he went out in a hurry.

I fetched Rasta from his prison. He had come to his senses by this time, and lay regarding me with stony, malevolent eyes.

"I'm very sorry, sir," I said, "for what has happened. But you left me no alternative. I've got a big job on hand and I can't have it interfered with by you or anyone. You're paying the price of a suspicious nature. When you know a little more you'll want to apologize to me. I'm going to see that you are kept quiet and comfortable for a day or two. You've no cause to worry, for you'll suffer no harm. I give you my word of honour as an American citizen."

Two of Sandy's miscreants came in and bore him off, and presently Sandy himself returned. When I asked him where he was being taken, Sandy said he didn't know. "They've got their orders, and they'll carry them out to the letter. There's a big unknown area in Constantinople to hide a man, into which the *Khafiyeh* never enter."

Then he flung himself in a chair and lit his old pipe.

"Dick," he said, "this job is getting very difficult and very dark. But my knowledge has grown in the last few days. I've found out the meaning of the second word that Harry Bullivant scribbled."

"*Cancer?*" I asked.

"Yes. It means just what it reads and no more. Greenmantle is dying—has been dying for months. This afternoon they brought a German doctor to see him, and the man gave him a few hours of life. By now he may be dead."

The news was a staggerer. For a moment I thought it cleared up things. "Then that busts the show," I said. "You can't have a crusade without a prophet."

"I wish I thought it did. It's the end of one stage, but the start of a new and blacker one. Do you think that woman will be beaten by such a small thing as the death of her prophet? She'll find a substitute—one of the four Ministers, or someone else. She's a devil incarnate, but she has the soul of a Napoleon. The big danger is only beginning."

Then he told me the story of his recent doings. He had found out the house of Frau von Einem without much trouble, and had performed with his ragamuffins in the servants' quarters. The prophet had a large retinue, and the fame of his minstrels—for the Companions were known far and wide in the land of Islam— came speedily to the ears of the Holy Ones. Sandy, a leader in this most orthodox coterie, was taken into favour and brought to the notice of the four Ministers. He and his half-dozen retainers became inmates of the villa, and Sandy, from his knowledge of Islamic lore and his ostentatious piety, was admitted to the confidence of the household. Frau von Einem welcomed him as an ally, for the Companions had been the most devoted propagandists of the new revelation.

As he described it, it was a strange business. Greenmantle was dying and often in great pain, but he struggled to meet the demands of his protectress. The four Ministers, as Sandy saw them, were unworldly ascetics; the prophet himself was a saint, though a practical saint with some notions of policy; but the controlling brain and will were those of the lady. Sandy seemed to have won his favour, even his affection. He spoke of him with a kind of desperate pity.

"I never saw such a man. He is the greatest gentleman you can picture, with a dignity like a high mountain. He is a dreamer and a poet, too—a genius if I can judge these things. I think I can assess him rightly, for I know something of the soul of the East, but it would be too long a story to tell now. The West knows nothing of the true Oriental. It pictures him as lapped in colour and idleness and luxury and gorgeous dreams. But it is all wrong. The *Kâf* he yearns for is an austere thing. It is the austerity of the East that is its beauty and its terror . . . It always wants the same things at the back of its head. The Turk and the Arab came out of big spaces, and they have the desire of them in their bones. They settle down and stagnate, and by the by they degenerate into that appalling subtlety which is their ruling passion gone crooked. And then comes a new revelation and a great simplifying. They want to live face to face with God without a screen of ritual and images and priestcraft. They want to prune life of its foolish fringes and get back to the noble bareness of the desert. Remember, it is always the empty desert and the empty sky that cast their spell over them—these, and the hot, strong, antiseptic sunlight which burns up all rot and decay . . . It isn't inhuman. It's the humanity of one part of the human race. It isn't ours, it isn't as good as ours, but it's jolly good all the same. There are times when it grips me so hard that I'm inclined to forswear the gods of my fathers!

"Well, Greenmantle is the prophet of this great simplicity. He speaks straight to the heart of Islam, and it's an honourable message. But for our sins it's been twisted into part of that damned German propaganda. His unworldliness has been used for a cunning political move, and his creed of space and simplicity for the furtherance of the last word in human degeneracy. My God, Dick, it's like seeing St. Francis run by Messalina."

"The woman has been here to-night," I said. "She asked me what I stood for, and I invented some infernal nonsense which she approved of. But I can see one thing. She and her prophet may run for different stakes, but it's the same course."

Sandy started. "She has been here!" he cried. "Tell me, Dick, what do you think of her?"

"I thought she was about two parts mad, but the third part was uncommon like inspiration."

"That's about right," he said. "I was wrong in comparing her to Messalina. She's something a dashed sight more complicated. She runs the prophet just because she shares his belief. Only what in him is sane and fine, in her is mad and horrible. You see, Germany also wants to simplify life."

"I know," I said. "I told her that an hour ago, when I talked more rot to the second than any mortal man ever achieved. It will come between me and my sleep for the rest of my days."

"Germany's simplicity is that of the neurotic, not the primitive. It is megalomania and egotism and the pride of the man in the Bible that waxed fat and kicked. But the results are the same. She wants to destroy and simplify; but it isn't the simplicity of the ascetic, which is of the spirit, but the simplicity of the madman that grinds down all the contrivances of civilization to a featureless monotony. The prophet wants to save the souls of his people; Germany wants to rule the inanimate corpse of the world. But you can get the same language to cover both. And so you have the partnership of St. Francis and Messalina. Dick, did you ever hear of a thing called the Superman?"

"There was a time when the papers were full of nothing else," I answered. "I gather it was invented by a sportsman called Nietzsche."

"Maybe," said Sandy. "Old Nietzsche has been blamed for a great deal of rubbish he would have died rather than acknowledge. But it's a craze of the new, fatted Germany. It's a fancy type which could never really exist, any more than the Economic Man of the politicians. Mankind has a sense of humour which stops short of the final absurdity. There never has been, and there never could be a real Superman . . . But there might be a Superwoman."

"You'll get into trouble, my lad, if you talk like that," I said.

"It's true all the same. Women have got a perilous logic which we never have, and some of the best of them don't see the joke of life like the ordinary man. They can be far greater than men, for they can go straight to the heart of things. There never was a man so near the divine as Joan of Arc. But I think, too, they can be more entirely damnable than anything that ever was breeched, for they don't stop still now and then and laugh at themselves . . . There is no Superman. The poor old donkeys that fancy themselves in the part are either crack-brained professors who couldn't rule a Sunday-school class, or bristling soldiers with pint-pot heads who imagine that the shooting of a Duc d'Enghien made a Napoleon. But there is a Superwoman, and her name's Hilda von Einem."

"I thought our job was nearly over," I groaned, "and now it looks as if it hadn't well started. Bullivant said that all we had to do was to find out the truth."

"Bullivant didn't know. No man knows except you and me. I tell you, the woman has immense power. The Germans have trusted her with their trump card, and she's going to play it for all she is worth. There's no crime that will stand in her way. She has set the ball rolling, and if need be she'll cut all her prophets' throats and run the show herself . . . I don't know about your job, for honestly I can't quite see what you and Blenkiron are going to do. But I'm very clear about my own duty. She's let me into the business, and I'm going to stick to it in the hope that I'll find a chance of wrecking it . . . We're moving eastward to-morrow—with a new prophet if the old one is dead."

"Where are you going?" I asked.

"I don't know. But I gather it's a long journey, judging by the preparations. And it must be to a cold country, judging by the clothes provided."

"Well, wherever it is, we're going with you. You haven't heard the end of our yarn. Blenkiron and I have been moving in the best circles as skilled American engineers who are going to play Old Harry with the British on the Tigris. I'm a pal of Enver's now, and he has offered me his protection. The lamented Rasta brought our passports for the journey to Mesopotamia to-morrow, but an hour ago your lady tore them up and put them in the fire. We are going with her, and she vouchsafed the information that it was towards the great hills."

Sandy whistled long and low. "I wonder what the deuce she wants with you? This thing is getting dashed complicated, Dick . . . Where, more by token, is Blenkiron? He's the fellow to know about high politics."

The missing Blenkiron, as Sandy spoke, entered the room with his slow, quiet step. I could see by his carriage that for once he had no dyspepsia, and by his eyes that he was excited.

"Say, boys," he said, "I've got something pretty considerable in the way of noos. There's been big fighting on the Eastern border, and the Buzzards have taken a bad knock."

His hands were full of papers, from which he selected a map and spread it on the table.

"They keep mum about this thing in the capital, but I've been piecing the story together these last days and I think I've got it straight. A fortnight ago old man Nicholas descended from his mountains and scuppered his enemies there—at Kuprikeui, where the main road eastwards crosses the Araxes. That was only the beginning of the stunt, for he pressed on on a broad front, and the gentleman called Kiamil, who commands in those parts, was not up to the job of holding him. The Buzzards were shepherded in from north and east and south, and now the Muscovite is sitting down outside the forts of Erzerum. I can tell you they're pretty miserable about the situation in the highest quarters . . . Enver is sweating blood to get fresh divisions to Erzerum from Gally-poly, but it's a long road and it looks as if they would be too late for the fair . . . You and I, Major, start for Mesopotamy to-morrow, and that's about the meanest bit of bad luck that ever happened to John S. We're missing the chance of seeing the goriest fight of this campaign."

I picked up the map and pocketed it. Maps were my business, and I had been looking for one.

"We're not going to Mesopotamia," I said. "Our orders have been cancelled."

"But I've just seen Enver, and he said he had sent round our passports."

"They're in the fire," I said. "The right ones will come along to-morrow morning."

Sandy broke in, his eyes bright with excitement.

"The great hills! . . . We're going to Erzerum . . . Don't you see that the Germans are playing their big card? They're sending

Greenmantle to the point of danger in the hope that his coming will rally the Turkish defence. Things are beginning to move, Dick, old man. No more kicking the heels for us. We're going to be in it up to the neck, and Heaven help the best man . . . I must be off now, for I've a lot to do. *Au revoir.* We meet some time soon in the hills."

Blenkiron still looked puzzled, till I told him the story of that night's doings. As he listened, all the satisfaction went out of his face, and that funny, childish air of bewilderment crept in.

"It's not for me to complain, for it's in the straight line of our dooty, but I reckon there's going to be big trouble ahead of this caravan. It's Kismet, and we've got to bow. But I won't pretend that I'm not considerable scared at the prospect."

"Oh, so am I," I said. "The woman frightens me into fits. We're up against it this time all right. All the same I'm glad we're to be let into the real star metropolitan performance. I didn't relish the idea of touring the provinces."

"I guess that's correct. But I could wish that the good God would see fit to take that lovely lady to Himself. She's too much for a quiet man at my time of life. When she invites us to go in on the ground floor I feel like taking the elevator to the roof-garden."

CHAPTER 16

The Battered Caravanserai

Two days later, in the evening, we came to Angora, the first stage in our journey.

The passports had arrived next morning, as Frau von Einem had promised, and with them a plan of our journey. More, one of the Companions, who spoke a little English, was detailed to accompany us—a wise precaution, for no one of us had a word of Turkish. These were the sum of our instructions. I heard nothing more of Sandy or Greenmantle or the lady. We were meant to travel in our own party.

We had the railway to Angora, a very comfortable German *Schlafwagen*, tacked to the end of a troop-train. There wasn't much to be seen of the country, for after we left the Bosporus we ran into scuds of snow, and except that we seemed to be climbing on to a big plateau I had no notion of the landscape. It was a marvel that we made such good time, for that line was congested beyond anything I have ever seen. The place was crawling with the Gallipoli troops, and every siding was packed with supply trucks. When we stopped—which we did on an average about once an hour—you could see vast camps on both sides of the line, and often we struck regiments on the march along the railway track. They looked a fine, hardy lot of ruffians, but many were deplorably ragged, and I didn't think much of their boots. I wondered how they would do the five hundred miles of road to Erzerum.

Blenkiron played Patience, and Peter and I took a hand at picquet, but mostly we smoked and yarned. Getting away from that infernal city had cheered us up wonderfully. Now we were out on the open road, moving to the sound of the guns. At the worst, we should not perish like rats in a sewer. We would be all together, too, and that was a comfort. I think we felt the relief which a man who has been on a lonely out-post feels when he is brought back to his battalion. Besides, the thing had gone clean beyond our power to direct. It was no good planning and scheming, for none of us had a notion what the next step might be. We were fatalists now, believing in Kismet, and that is a comfortable faith.

All but Blenkiron. The coming of Hilda von Einem into the business had put a very ugly complexion on it for him. It was curious to see how she affected the different members of our gang. Peter did not care a rush; man, woman, and hippogriff were the same to him; he met it all as calmly as if he were making plans to round up an old lion in a patch of bush, taking the facts as they came and working at them as if they were a sum in arithmetic. Sandy and I were impressed—it's no good denying it: horribly impressed—but we were too interested to be scared, and we weren't a bit fascinated. We hated her too much for that. But she fairly struck Blenkiron dumb. He said himself it was just like a rattlesnake and a bird.

I made him talk about her, for if he sat and brooded he would get worse. It was a strange thing that this man, the most imperturbable and, I think, about the most courageous I have ever met, should be paralysed by a slim woman. There was no doubt about it. The thought of her made the future to him as black as a thunder-cloud. It took the power out of his joints, and if she was going to be much around, it looked as if Blenkiron might be counted out.

I suggested that he was in love with her, but this he vehemently denied.

"No; sir; I haven't got no sort of affection for the lady. My trouble is that she puts me out of countenance, and I can't fit her in as an antagonist. I guess we Americans haven't got the right poise for dealing with that kind of female. We've exalted our womenfolk into little tin gods, and at the same time left them out of the real business of life. Consequently, when we strike one playing the biggest kind of man's game we can't place her. We aren't used to regarding them as anything except angels and children. I wish I had had you boys' upbringing."

Angora was like my notion of some place such as Amiens in the retreat from Mons. It was one mass of troops and transport—the neck of the bottle, for more arrived every hour, and the only outlet was the single eastern road. The town was pandemonium into which distracted German officers were trying to introduce some order. They didn't worry much about us, for the heart of Anatolia wasn't a likely hunting-ground for suspicious characters. We took our passports to the commandant, who viséd them readily, and told us he'd do his best to get us transport. We spent the night in a sort of hotel, where all four crowded into one little bedroom, and next morning I had my work cut out getting a motorcar. It took four hours, and the use of every great name in the Turkish Empire, to raise a dingy sort of Studebaker, and another two to get the petrol and spare tyres. As for a chauffeur, love or money couldn't find him, and I was compelled to drive the thing myself.

We left just after midday and swung out into bare bleak downs patched with scrubby woodlands. There was no snow here, but a wind was blowing from the east which searched the marrow. Presently we climbed up into hills, and the road, though not badly engineered to begin with, grew as rough as the channel of a stream. No wonder, for the traffic was like what one saw on that awful stretch between Cassel and Ypres, and there were no gangs of Belgian roadmakers to mend it up. We found troops by the thousands striding along with their impassive Turkish faces, ox convoys, mule convoys, wagons drawn by sturdy little Anatolian horses, and, coming in the contrary direction, many shabby

Red Crescent cars and wagons of the wounded. We had to crawl for hours on end, till we got past a block. Just before the darkening we seemed to outstrip the first press, and had a clear run for about ten miles over a low pass in the hills. I began to get anxious about the car, for it was a poor one at the best, and the road was guaranteed sooner or later to knock even a Rolls-Royce into scrap iron.

All the same it was glorious to be out in the open again. Peter's face wore a new look, and he sniffed the bitter air like a stag. There floated up from little wayside camps the odour of wood smoke and dung-fires. That, and the curious acrid winter smell of great wind-blown spaces, will always come to my memory as I think of that day. Every hour brought me peace of mind and resolution. I felt as I had felt when the battalion first marched from Aire towards the firing-line, a kind of keying-up and wild expectation. I'm not used to cities, and lounging about Constantinople had slackened my fibre. Now, as the sharp wind buffeted us, I felt braced to any kind of risk. We were on the great road to the East and the border hills, and soon we should stand upon the farthest battle-front of the war. This was no commonplace intelligence job. That was all over, and we were going into the firing-line, going to take part in what might be the downfall of our enemies. I didn't reflect that we were among those enemies, and would probably share their downfall if we were not shot earlier. The truth is, I had got out of the way of regarding the thing as a struggle between armies and nations. I hardly bothered to think where my sympathies lay. First and foremost it was a contest between the four of us and a crazy woman, and this personal antagonism made the strife of armies only a dimly felt background.

We slept that night like logs on the floor of a dirty khan, and started next morning in a powder of snow. We were getting very high up now, and it was perishing cold. The Companion—his name sounded like Hussin—had travelled the road before and told me what the places were, but they conveyed nothing to me. All morning we wriggled through a big lot of troops, a brigade at least, who swung along at a great pace with a fine free stride that

I don't think I have ever seen bettered. I must say I took a fancy to the Turkish fighting man: I remembered the testimonial our fellows gave him as a clean fighter, and I felt very bitter that Germany should have lugged him into this dirty business. They halted for a meal, and we stopped, too, and lunched off some brown bread and dried figs and a flask of very sour wine. I had a few words with one of the officers who spoke a little German. He told me they were marching straight for Russia, since there had been a great Turkish victory in the Caucasus. "We have beaten the French and the British, and now it is Russia's turn," he said stolidly, as if repeating a lesson. But he added that he was mortally sick of war.

In the afternoon we cleared the column and had an open road for some hours. The land now had a tilt eastward, as if we were moving towards the valley of a great river. Soon we began to meet little parties of men coming from the East with a new look in their faces. The first lots of wounded had been the ordinary thing you see on every front, and there had been some pretence at organization. But these new lots were very weary and broken; they were often barefoot, and they seemed to have lost their transport and to be starving. You would find a group stretched by the roadside in the last stages of exhaustion. Then would come a party limping along, so tired that they never turned their heads to look at us. Almost all were wounded, some badly, and most were horribly thin. I wondered how my Turkish friend behind would explain the sight to his men, if he believed in a great victory. They had not the air of the backwash of a conquering army.

Even Blenkiron, who was no soldier, noticed it.

"These boys look mighty bad," he observed. "We've got to hustle, Major, if we're going to get seats for the last act."

That was my own feeling. The sight made me mad to get on faster, for I saw that big things were happening in the East. I had reckoned that four days would take us from Angora to Erzerum, but here was the second nearly over and we were not yet a third of the way. I pressed on recklessly, and that hurry was our undoing.

I have said that the Studebaker was a rotten old car. Its steering-gear was pretty dicky, and the bad surface and continual hairpin bends of the road didn't improve it. Soon we came into snow lying fairly deep, frozen hard and rutted by the big transport-wagons. We bumped and bounced horribly, and were shaken about like peas in a bladder. I began to be acutely anxious about the old boneshaker, the more as we seemed a long way short of the village I had proposed to spend the night in. Twilight was falling and we were still in an unfeatured waste, crossing the shallow glen of a stream. There was a bridge at the bottom of a slope—a bridge of logs and earth which had apparently been freshly strengthened for heavy traffic. As we approached it at a good pace the car ceased to answer to the wheel.

I struggled desperately to keep it straight, but it swerved to the left and we plunged over a bank into a marshy hollow. There was a sickening bump as we struck the lower ground, and the whole party were shot out into the frozen slush. I don't yet know how I escaped, for the car turned over and by rights I should have had my back broken. But no one was hurt. Peter was laughing, and Blenkiron, after shaking the snow out of his hair, joined him. For myself I was feverishly examining the machine. It was about as ugly as it could be, for the front axle was broken.

Here was a piece of hopeless bad luck. We were stuck in the middle of Asia Minor with no means of conveyance, for to get a new axle there was as likely as to find snowballs on the Congo. It was all but dark and there was no time to lose. I got out the petrol tins and spare tyres and cached them among some rocks on the hillside. Then we collected our scanty baggage from the derelict Studebaker. Our only hope was Hussin. He had got to find us some lodging for the night, and next day we would have a try for horses or a lift in some passing wagon. I had no hope of another car. Every automobile in Anatolia would now be at a premium.

It was so disgusting a mishap that we all took it quietly. It was too bad to be helped by hard swearing. Hussin and Peter set off on different sides of the road to prospect for a house, and

Blenkiron and I sheltered under the nearest rock and smoked savagely.

Hussin was the first to strike oil. He came back in twenty minutes with news of some kind of dwelling a couple of miles up the stream. He went off to collect Peter, and, humping our baggage, Blenkiron and I plodded up the waterside. Darkness had fallen thick by this time, and we took some bad tosses among the bogs. When Hussin and Peter overtook us they found a better road, and presently we saw a light twinkle in the hollow ahead.

It proved to be a wretched tumble-down farm in a grove of poplars—a foul-smelling, muddy yard, a two-roomed hovel of a house, and a barn which was tolerably dry and which we selected for our sleeping-place. The owner was a broken old fellow whose sons were all at the war, and he received us with the profound calm of one who expects nothing but unpleasantness from life.

By this time we had recovered our tempers, and I was trying hard to put my new Kismet philosophy into practice. I reckoned that if risks were foreordained, so were difficulties, and both must be taken as part of the day's work. With the remains of our provisions and some curdled milk we satisfied our hunger and curled ourselves up among the pease straw of the barn. Blenkiron announced with a happy sigh that he had now been for two days quit of his dyspepsia.

That night, I remember, I had a queer dream. I seemed to be in a wild place among mountains, and I was being hunted, though who was after me I couldn't tell. I remember sweating with fright, for I seemed to be quite alone and the terror that was pursuing me was more than human. The place was horribly quiet and still, and there was deep snow lying everywhere, so that each step I took was heavy as lead. A very ordinary sort of nightmare, you will say. Yes, but there was one strange feature in this one. The night was pitch-dark, but ahead of me in the throat of the pass there was one patch of light, and it showed a rum little hill with a rocky top: what we call in South Africa a *castrol* or saucepan. I had a notion that if I could get to that *castrol* I should be safe, and I panted through the drifts towards it with the avenger of blood at my heels. I woke, gasping, to find the winter morning struggling through the cracked rafters, and to hear Blenkiron say cheerily that his duodenum had behaved all night like a gentleman. I lay still for a bit trying to fix the dream, but it all dissolved into haze except the picture of the little hill, which was quite clear in every detail. I told myself it was a reminiscence of the veld, some spot down in the Wakkerstroom country, though for the life of me I couldn't place it.

I pass over the next three days, for they were one uninterrupted series of heart-breaks. Hussin and Peter scoured the country for horses, Blenkiron sat in the barn and played Patience, while I haunted the roadside near the bridge in the hope of picking up some kind of conveyance. My task was perfectly futile. The columns passed, casting wondering eyes on the wrecked car among the frozen rushes, but they could offer no help. My friend the Turkish officer promised to wire to Angora from some place or other for a fresh car, but, remembering the state of affairs at Angora, I had no hope from that quarter. Cars passed, plenty of them, packed with staff-officers, Turkish and German, but they were in far too big a hurry even to stop and speak. The only conclusion I reached from my roadside vigil was that things were getting very warm in the neighbourhood of Erzerum. Everybody on that road seemed to be in mad haste either to get there or to get away.

Hussin was the best chance, for, as I have said, the Companions had a very special and peculiar graft throughout the Turkish Empire. But the first day he came back empty-handed. All the horses had been commandeered for the war, he said; and though he was certain that some had been kept back and hidden away, he could not get on their track. The second day he returned with two—miserable screws and deplorably short in the wind from a diet of beans. There was no decent corn or hay left in that countryside. The third day he picked up a nice little Arab stallion: in poor condition, it is true, but perfectly sound. For these beasts we paid good money, for Blenkiron was well supplied and we had no time to spare for the interminable Oriental bargaining.

Hussin said he had cleaned up the countryside, and I believed him. I dared not delay another day, even though it meant leaving him behind. But he had no notion of doing anything of the kind. He was a good runner, he said, and could keep up with such horses as ours for ever. If this was the manner of our progress, I reckoned we would be weeks in getting to Erzerum.

We started at dawn on the morning of the fourth day, after the old farmer had blessed us and sold us some stale rye-bread. Blenkiron bestrode the Arab, being the heaviest, and Peter and I had the screws. My worst forebodings were soon realized, and Hussin, loping along at my side, had an easy job to keep up with us. We were about as slow as an ox-wagon. The brutes were unshod, and with the rough roads I saw that their feet would very soon go to pieces. We jogged along like a tinker's caravan, about five miles to the hour, as feckless a party as ever disgraced a highroad.

The weather was now a cold drizzle, which increased my depression. Cars passed us and disappeared in the mist, going at thirty miles an hour to mock our slowness. None of us spoke, for the futility of the business clogged our spirits. I bit hard on my lip to curb my restlessness, and I think I would have sold my soul there and then for anything that could move fast. I don't know any sorer trial than to be mad for speed and have to crawl at a snail's pace. I was getting ripe for any kind of desperate venture.

About midday we descended on a wide plain full of the marks of rich cultivation. Villages became frequent, and the land was studded with olive groves and scarred with water furrows. From what I remembered of the map I judged that we were coming to that champagne country near Siwas, which is the granary of Turkey, and the home of the true Osmanli stock.

Then at the turning of the road we came to the caravanserai.

It was a dingy, battered place, with the pink plaster falling in patches from its walls. There was a courtyard abutting on the road, and a flat-topped house with a big hole in its side. It was a long way from any battle-ground, and I guessed that some explosion had wrought the damage. Behind it, a few hundred yards off, a detachment of cavalry were encamped beside a stream, with their horses tied up in long lines of pickets.

And by the roadside, quite alone and deserted, stood a large new motor-car.

In all the road before and behind there was no man to be seen except the troops by the stream. The owners, whoever they were, must be inside the caravanserai.

I have said I was in the mood for some desperate deed, and lo and behold Providence had given me the chance! I coveted that car as I have never coveted anything on earth. At the moment all my plans had narrowed down to a feverish passion to get to the battlefield. We had to find Greenmantle at Erzerum, and once there we should have Hilda von Einem's protection. It was a time of war, and a front of brass was the surest safety. But, indeed, I could not figure out any plan worth speaking of. I saw only one thing—a fast car which might be ours.

I said a word to the others, and we dismounted and tethered our horses at the near end of the courtyard. I heard the low hum of voices from the cavalrymen by the stream, but they were three hundred yards off and could not see us. Peter was sent forward to scout in the courtyard. In the building itself there was but one window looking on the road, and that was in the upper floor. Meantime I crawled along beside the wall to where the car stood, and had a look at it. It was a splendid six-cylinder affair, brand new, with the tyres little worn. There were seven tins of petrol stacked behind as well as spare tyres, and, looking in, I saw map-cases and field-glasses strewn on the seats as if the owners had only got out for a minute to stretch their legs.

Peter came back and reported that the courtyard was empty. "There are men in the upper room," he said; "more than one, for I heard their voices. They are moving about restlessly, and may soon be coming out."

I reckoned that there was no time to be lost, so I told the others to slip down the road fifty yards beyond the caravanserai and be ready to climb in as I passed. I had to start the infernal thing, and there might be shooting.

I waited by the car till I saw them reach the right distance. I could hear voices from the second floor of the house and footsteps moving up and down. I was in a fever of anxiety, for any moment a man might come to the window. Then I flung myself on the starting handle and worked like a demon.

The cold made the job difficult, and my heart was in my mouth, for the noise in that quiet place must have woke the dead. Then, by the mercy of Heaven, the engine started, and I sprang to the driving seat, released the clutch, and opened the throttle. The great car shot forward, and I seemed to hear behind me shrill voices. A pistol bullet bored through my hat, and another buried itself in a cushion beside me.

In a second I was clear of the place and the rest of the party were embarking. Blenkiron got on the step and rolled himself like a sack of coals into the tonneau. Peter nipped up beside me, and Hussin scrambled in from the back over the folds of the hood. We had our baggage in our pockets and had nothing to carry.

Bullets dropped round us, but did no harm. Then I heard a report at my ear, and out of a corner of my eye saw Peter lower his pistol. Presently we were out of range, and, looking back, I saw three men gesticulating in the middle of the road.

"May the devil fly away with this pistol," said Peter ruefully. "I never could make good shooting with a little gun. Had I had my rifle . . ."

"What did you shoot for?" I asked in amazement. "We've got the fellows' car, and we don't want to do them any harm."

"It would have saved trouble had I had my rifle," said Peter, quietly. "The little man you call Rasta was there, and he knew you. I heard him cry your name. He is an angry little man, and I observe that on this road there is a telegraph."

CHAPTER 17

Trouble by the Waters of Babylon

From that moment I date the beginning of my madness. Suddenly I forgot all cares and difficulties of the present and future and became foolishly light-hearted. We were rushing towards the great battle where men were busy at my proper trade. I realized how much I had loathed the lonely days in Germany, and still more the dawdling week in Constantinople. Now I was clear of it all, and bound for the clash of armies. It didn't trouble me that we were on the wrong side of the battle-line. I had a sort of instinct that the darker and wilder things grew the better chance for us.

"Seems to me," said Blenkiron, bending over me, "that this joy-ride is going to come to an untimely end pretty soon. Peter's right. That young man will set the telegraph going, and we'll be held up at the next township."

"He's got to get to a telegraph office first," I answered. "That's where we have the pull on him. He's welcome to the screws we left behind, and if he finds an operator before the evening I'm the worst kind of a Dutchman. I'm going to break all the rules and bucket this car for what's she's worth. Don't you see that the nearer we get to Erzerum the safer we are?"

"I don't follow," he said slowly. "At Erzerum I reckon they'll be waiting for us with the handcuffs. Why in thunder couldn't those hairy ragamuffins keep the little cuss safe? Your record's a bit too precipitous, Major, for the most innocent-minded military boss."

"Do you remember what you said about the Germans being open to bluff? Well, I'm going to put up the steepest sort of bluff. Of course they'll stop us. Rasta will do his damnedest. But remember that he and his friends are not very popular with the Germans, and Madame von Einem is. We're her protégés, and the bigger the German swell I get before the safer I'll feel. We've got our passports and our orders, and he'll be a bold man that will stop us once we get into the German zone. Therefore I'm going to hurry as fast as God will let me."

It was a ride that deserved to have an epic written about it. The car was good, and I handled her well, though I say it who shouldn't. The road in that big central plain was fair, and often I knocked fifty miles an hour out of her. We passed troops by a circuit over the veld, where we took some awful risks, and once we skidded by some transport with our off wheels almost over the lip of a ravine. We went through the narrow streets of Siwas like a fire-engine, while I shouted out in German that we carried despatches for headquarters. We shot out of drizzling rain into brief spells of winter sunshine, and then into a snow blizzard which all but whipped the skin from our faces. And always before us the long road unrolled, with somewhere at the end of it two armies clinched in a death-grapple.

That night we looked for no lodging. We ate a sort of meal in the car with the hood up, and felt our way on in the darkness, for the headlights were in perfect order. Then we turned off the road for four hours' sleep, and I had a go at the map. Before dawn we started again, and came over a pass into the vale of a big river. The winter dawn showed its gleaming stretches, ice-bound among the sprinkled meadows. I called to Blenkiron:

"I believe that river is the Euphrates," I said.

"So," he said, acutely interested. "Then that's the waters of Babylon. Great snakes, that I should have lived to see the fields where King Nebuchadnezzar grazed! Do you know the name of that big hill, Major?"

"Ararat, as like as not," I cried, and he believed me.

We were among the hills now, great, rocky black slopes, and, seen through side-glens, a hinterland of snowy peaks. I remember I kept looking for the *castrol* I had seen in my dream. The thing had never left off haunting me, and I was pretty clear now that it did not belong to my South African memories. I am not a superstitious man, but the way that little *kranz* clung to my mind made me think it was a warning sent by Providence. I was pretty certain that when I clapped eyes on it I would be in for bad trouble.

All morning we travelled up that broad vale, and just before noon it spread out wider, the road dipped to the water's edge, and I saw before me the white roofs of a town. The snow was deep now, and lay down to the riverside, but the sky had cleared, and against a space of blue heaven some peaks to the south rose glittering like jewels. The arches of a bridge, spanning two forks of the stream, showed in front, and as I slowed down at the bend a sentry's challenge rang out from a block-house. We had reached the fortress of Erzingjan, the headquarters of a Turkish corps and the gate of Armenia.

I showed the man our passports, but he did not salute and let us move on. He called another fellow from the guard-house, who motioned us to keep pace with him as he stumped down a side lane. At the other end was a big barracks with sentries outside. The man spoke to us in Turkish, which Hussin interpreted. There was somebody in that barracks who wanted badly to see us.

"By the waters of Babylon we sat down and wept," quoted Blenkiron softly. "I fear, Major, we'll soon be remembering Zion."

I tried to persuade myself that this was merely the red tape of a frontier fortress, but I had an instinct that difficulties were in store for us. If Rasta had started wiring I was prepared to put up the brazenest bluff, for we were still eighty miles from Erzerum, and at all costs we were going to be landed there before night.

A fussy staff-officer met us at the door. At the sight of us he cried to a friend to come and look.

"Here are the birds safe. A fat man and two lean ones and a

savage who looks like a Kurd. Call the guard and march them off. There's no doubt about their identity."

"Pardon me, sir," I said, "but we have no time to spare and we'd like to be in Erzerum before the dark. I would beg you to get through any formalities as soon as possible. This man," and I pointed to the sentry, "has our passports."

"Compose yourself," he said impudently; "you're not going on just yet, and when you do it won't be in a stolen car." He took the passports and fingered them casually. Then something he saw there made him cock his eyebrows.

"Where did you steal these?" he asked, but with less assurance in his tone.

I spoke very gently. "You seem to be the victim of a mistake, sir. These are our papers. We are under orders to report ourselves at Erzerum without an hour's delay. Whoever hinders us will have to answer to General von Liman. We will be obliged if you will conduct us at once to the Governor."

"You can't see General Posselt," he said; "this is my business. I have a wire from Siwas that four men stole a car belonging to one of Enver Damad's staff. It describes you all, and says that two of you are notorious spies wanted by the Imperial Government. What have you to say to that?"

"Only that it is rubbish. My good sir, you have seen our passes. Our errand is not to be cried on the housetops, but five minutes with General Posselt will make things clear. You will be exceedingly sorry for it if you delay another minute."

He was impressed in spite of himself, and after pulling his moustache turned on his heel and left us. Presently he came back and said very gruffly that the Governor would see us. We followed him along a corridor into a big room looking out on the river, where an oldish fellow sat in an arm-chair by a stove, writing letters with a fountain pen.

This was Posselt, who had been Governor of Erzerum till he fell sick and Ahmed Fevzi took his place. He had a peevish mouth and big blue pouches below his eyes. He was supposed to be a good engineer and to have made Erzerum impregnable, but the look on his face gave me the impression that his reputation at the moment was a bit unstable.

The staff-officer spoke to him in an undertone.

"Yes, yes, I know," he said testily. "Are these the men? They look a pretty lot of scoundrels. What's that you say? They deny it. But they've got the car. They can't deny that. Here, you," and he fixed on Blenkiron, "who the devil are you?" Blenkiron smiled sleepily at him, not understanding one word, and I took up the parable.

"Our passports, sir, give our credentials," I said. He glanced through them, and his face lengthened.

"They're right enough. But what about this story of stealing a car?"

"It is quite true," I said, "but I would prefer to use a pleasanter word. You will see from our papers that every authority on the road is directed to give us the best transport. Our own car broke down, and after a long delay we got some wretched horses. It is vitally important that we should be in Erzerum without delay, so I took the liberty of appropriating an empty car we found outside an inn. I am sorry for the discomfort of the owners, but our business was too grave to wait."

"But the telegram says you are notorious spies!"

I smiled. "Who sent the telegram?"

"I see no reason why I shouldn't give you his name. It was Rasta Bey. You've picked an awkward fellow to make an enemy of."

I did not smile but laughed. "Rasta!" I cried. "He's one of Enver's satellites. That explains many things. I should like a word with you alone, sir."

He nodded to the staff-officer, and when he had gone I put on my most Bible face and looked as important as a provincial mayor at a royal visit.

"I can speak freely," I said, "for I am speaking to a soldier of Germany. There is no love lost between Enver and those I serve. I need not tell you that. This Rasta thought he had found a chance of delaying us, so he invents this trash about spies. Those

Comitadjis have spies on the brain . . . Especially he hates Frau von Einem."

He jumped at the name.

"You have orders from her?" he asked, in a respectful tone.

"Why, yes," I answered, "and those orders will not wait."

He got up and walked to a table, whence he turned a puzzled face on me. "I'm torn in two between the Turks and my own countrymen. If I please one I offend the other, and the result is a damnable confusion. You can go on to Erzerum, but I shall send a man with you to see that you report to headquarters there. I'm sorry, gentlemen, but I'm obliged to take no chances in this business. Rasta's got a grievance against you, but you can easily hide behind the lady's skirts. She passed through this town two days ago."

Ten minutes later we were coasting through the slush of the narrow streets with a stolid German lieutenant sitting beside me.

The afternoon was one of those rare days when in the pauses of snow you have a spell of weather as mild as May. I remembered several like it during our winter's training in Hampshire. The road was a fine one, well engineered, and well kept too, considering the amount of traffic. We were little delayed, for it was sufficiently broad to let us pass troops and transport without slackening pace. The fellow at my side was good-humoured enough, but his presence naturally put the lid on our conversation. I didn't want to talk, however. I was trying to piece together a plan, and making very little of it, for I had nothing to go upon. We must find Hilda von Einem and Sandy, and between us we must wreck the Greenmantle business. That done, it didn't matter so much what happened to us. As I reasoned it out, the Turks must be in a bad way, and, unless they got a fillip from Greenmantle, would crumple up before the Russians. In the rout I hoped we might get a chance to change our sides. But it was no good looking so far forward; the first thing was to get to Sandy.

Now I was still in the mood of reckless bravado which I had got from bagging the car. I did not realize how thin our story was, and how easily Rasta might have a big graft at headquarters.

If I had, I would have shot out the German lieutenant long before we got to Erzerum, and found some way of getting mixed up in the ruck of the population. Hussin could have helped me to that. I was getting so confident since our interview with Posselt that I thought I could bluff the whole outfit.

But my main business that afternoon was pure nonsense. I was trying to find my little hill. At every turn of the road I expected to see the *castrol* before us. You must know that ever since I could stand I have been crazy about high mountains. My father took me to Basutoland when I was a boy, and I reckon I have scrambled over almost every bit of upland south of the Zambesi, from the Hottentots Holland to the Zoutpansberg, and from the ugly yellow kopjes of Damaraland to the noble cliffs of Mont aux Sources. One of the things I had looked forward to in coming home was the chance of climbing the Alps. But now I was among peaks that I fancied were bigger than the Alps, and I could hardly keep my eyes on the road. I was pretty certain that my *castrol* was among them, for that dream had taken an almighty hold on my mind. Funnily enough, I was ceasing to think it a place of evil omen, for one soon forgets the atmosphere of nightmare. But I was convinced that it was a thing I was destined to see, and to see pretty soon.

Darkness fell when we were some miles short of the city, and the last part was difficult driving. On both sides of the road transport and engineers' stores were parked, and some of it strayed into the highway. I noticed lots of small details—machine-gun detachments, signalling parties, squads of stretcher-bearers—which mean the fringe of an army, and as soon as the night began the white fingers of searchlights began to grope in the skies.

And then, above the hum of the roadside, rose the voice of the great guns. The shells were bursting four or five miles away, and the guns must have been as many more distant. But in that upland pocket of plain in the frosty night they sounded most intimately near. They kept up their solemn litany, with a minute's interval between each—no *rafale* which rumbles like a drum, but the steady persistence of artillery exactly ranged on a target. I judged they must be bombarding the outer forts, and once there came a loud explosion and a red glare as if a magazine had suffered.

It was a sound I had not heard for five months, and it fairly crazed me. I remembered how I had first heard it on the ridge before Laventie. Then I had been half afraid, half solemnized, but every nerve had been quickened. Then it had been the new thing in my life that held me breathless with anticipation; now it was the old thing, the thing I had shared with so many good fellows, my proper work, and the only task for a man. At the sound of the guns I felt that I was moving in natural air once more. I felt that I was coming home.

We were stopped at a long line of ramparts, and a German sergeant stared at us till he saw the lieutenant beside me, when he saluted and we passed on. Almost at once we dipped into narrow twisting streets, choked with soldiers, where it was hard business to steer. There were few lights—only now and then the flare of a torch which showed the grey stone houses, with every window latticed and shuttered. I had put out my headlights and had only side lamps, so we had to pick our way gingerly through the labyrinth. I hoped we would strike Sandy's quarters soon, for we were all pretty empty, and a frost had set in which made our thick coats seem as thin as paper.

The lieutenant did the guiding. We had to present our passports, and I anticipated no more difficulty than in landing from the boat at Boulogne. But I wanted to get it over, for my hunger pinched me and it was fearsome cold. Still the guns went on, like hounds baying before a quarry. The city was out of range, but there were strange lights on the ridge to the east.

At last we reached our goal and marched through a fine old carved archway into a courtyard, and thence into a draughty hall.

"You must see the *Sektionschef*," said our guide. I looked round to see if we were all there, and noticed that Hussin had disappeared. It did not matter, for he was not on the passports.

We followed as we were directed through an open door. There was a man standing with his back towards us looking at a wall map, a very big man with a neck that bulged over his collar.

I would have known that neck among a million. At the sight of it I made a half-turn to bolt back. It was too late, for the door had closed behind us and there were two armed sentries beside it.

The man slewed round and looked into my eyes. I had a despairing hope that I might bluff it out, for I was in different clothes and had shaved my beard. But you cannot spend ten minutes in a death-grapple without your adversary getting to know you.

He went very pale, then recollected himself and twisted his features into the old grin.

"So," he said, "the little Dutchmen! We meet after many days."

It was no good lying or saying anything. I shut my teeth and waited.

"And you, Herr Blenkiron? I never liked the look of you. You babbled too much, like all your damned Americans."

"I guess your personal dislikes haven't got anything to do with the matter," said Blenkiron, calmly. "If you're the boss here, I'll thank you to cast your eye over these passports, for we can't stand waiting for ever."

This fairly angered him. "I'll teach you manners," he cried, and took a step forward to reach for Blenkiron's shoulder—the game he had twice played with me.

Blenkiron never took his hands from his coat pockets. "Keep your distance," he drawled in a new voice. "I've got you covered, and I'll make a hole in your bullet head if you lay a hand on me."

With an effort Stumm recovered himself. He rang a bell and fell to smiling. An orderly appeared to whom he spoke in Turkish, and presently a file of soldiers entered the room.

"I'm going to have you disarmed, gentlemen," he said. "We can conduct our conversation more pleasantly without pistols."

It was idle to resist. We surrendered our arms, Peter almost in tears with vexation. Stumm swung his legs over a chair, rested his chin on the back and looked at me.

"Your game is up, you know," he said. "These fools of Turkish police said the Dutchmen were dead, but I had the happier inspiration. I believed the good God had spared them for me. When I got Rasta's telegram I was certain, for your doings reminded me of a little trick you once played me on the Schwandorf road. But I didn't think to find this plump old partridge," and he smiled at Blenkiron. "Two eminent American engineers and their servant bound for Mesopotamia on business of high Government importance! It was a good lie; but if I had been in Constantinople it would have had a short life. Rasta and his friends are no concern of mine. You can trick them as you please. But you have attempted to win the confidence of a certain lady, and her interests are mine. Likewise you have offended me, and I do not forgive. By God," he cried, his voice growing shrill with passion, "by the time I have done with you your mothers in their graves will weep that they ever bore you!"

It was Blenkiron who spoke. His voice was as level as the chairman's of a bogus company, and it fell on that turbid atmosphere like acid on grease.

"I don't take no stock in high-falutin'. If you're trying to scare me by that dime-novel talk I guess you've hit the wrong man. You're like the sweep that stuck in the chimney, a bit too big for your job. I reckon you've a talent for romance that's just wasted in soldiering. But if you're going to play any ugly games on me I'd like you to know that I'm an American citizen, and pretty well considered in my own country and in yours, and you'll sweat blood for it later. That's a fair warning, Colonel Stumm."

I don't know what Stumm's plans were, but that speech of Blenkiron's put into his mind just the needed amount of uncertainty. You see, he had Peter and me right enough, but he hadn't properly connected Blenkiron with us, and was afraid either to hit out at all three, or to let Blenkiron go. It was lucky for us that the American had cut such a dash in the Fatherland.

"There is no hurry," he said blandly. "We shall have long happy hours together. I'm going to take you all home with me, for I am a hospitable soul. You will be safer with me than in the town gaol, for it's a trifle draughty. It lets things in, and it might let things out."

Again he gave an order, and we were marched out, each with a soldier at his elbow. The three of us were bundled into the back seat of the car, while two men sat before us with their rifles between their knees, one got up behind on the baggage rack, and one sat beside Stumm's chauffeur. Packed like sardines we moved into the bleak streets, above which the stars twinkled in ribbons of sky.

Hussin had disappeared from the face of the earth, and quite right too. He was a good fellow, but he had no call to mix himself up in our troubles.

CHAPTER 18

Sparrows on the Housetops

"I've often regretted," said Blenkiron, "that miracles have left off happening."

He got no answer, for I was feeling the walls for something in the nature of a window.

"For I reckon," he went on, "that it wants a good old-fashioned copper-bottomed miracle to get us out of this fix. It's plumb against all my principles. I've spent my life using the talents God gave me to keep things from getting to the point of rude violence, and so far I've succeeded. But now you come along, Major, and you hustle a respectable middle-aged citizen into an aboriginal mix-up. It's mighty indelicate. I reckon the next move is up to you, for I'm no good at the housebreaking stunt."

"No more am I," I answered; "but I'm hanged if I'll chuck up the sponge. Sandy's somewhere outside, and he's got a hefty crowd at his heels."

I simply could not feel the despair which by every law of common sense was due to the case. The guns had intoxicated me. I could still hear their deep voices, though yards of wood and stone separated us from the upper air.

What vexed us most was our hunger. Barring a few mouthfuls on the road we had eaten nothing since the morning, and as our diet for the past days had not been generous we had some leeway to make up. Stumm had never looked near since we were shoved into the car. We had been brought to some kind of house and bundled into a place like a wine-cellar. It was pitch dark, and after feeling round the walls, first on my feet and then on Peter's back, I decided that there were no windows. It must have been lit and ventilated by some lattice in the ceiling. There was not a stick of furniture in the place: nothing but a damp earth floor and bare stone sides. The door was a relic of the Iron Age, and I could hear the paces of a sentry outside it.

When things get to the pass that nothing you can do can better them, the only thing is to live for the moment. All three of us sought in sleep a refuge from our empty stomachs. The floor was the poorest kind of bed, but we rolled up our coats for pillows and made the best of it. Soon I knew by Peter's regular breathing that he was asleep, and I presently followed him . . .

I was awakened by a pressure below my left ear. I thought it was Peter, for it is the old hunter's trick of waking a man so that he makes no noise. But another voice spoke. It told me that there was no time to lose and to rise and follow, and the voice was the voice of Hussin.

Peter was awake, and we stirred Blenkiron out of heavy slumber. We were bidden take off our boots and hang them by their laces round our necks as country boys do when they want to go barefoot. Then we tiptoed to the door, which was ajar.

Outside was a passage with a flight of steps at one end which led to the open air. On these steps lay a faint shine of starlight, and by its help I saw a man huddled up at the foot of them. It was our sentry, neatly and scientifically gagged and tied up.

The steps brought us to a little courtyard about which the walls of the houses rose like cliffs. We halted while Hussin listened intently. Apparently the coast was clear and our guide led us to one side, which was clothed by a stout wooden trellis. Once it may have supported fig-trees, but now the plants were dead and only withered tendrils and rotten stumps remained.

It was child's play for Peter and me to go up that trellis, but it was the deuce and all for Blenkiron. He was in poor condition

and puffed like a grampus, and he seemed to have no sort of head
for heights. But he was as game as a buffalo, and started in gallantly till his arms gave out and he fairly stuck. So Peter and I
went up on each side of him, taking an arm apiece, as I had once
seen done to a man with vertigo in the Kloof Chimney on Table
Mountain. I was mighty thankful when I got him panting on the
top and Hussin had shinned up beside us.

We crawled along a broadish wall, with an inch or two of pow-
dery snow on it, and then up a sloping buttress on to the flat roof
of the house. It was a miserable business for Blenkiron, who
would certainly have fallen if he could have seen what was below
him, and Peter and I had to stand to attention all the time. Then
began a more difficult job. Hussin pointed out a ledge which took
us past a stack of chimneys to another building slightly lower,
this being the route he fancied. At that I sat down resolutely and
put on my boots, and the others followed. Frost-bitten feet would
be a poor asset in this kind of travelling.

It was a bad step for Blenkiron, and we only got him past it by
Peter and I spread-eagling ourselves against the wall and passing
him in front of us with his face towards us. We had no grip, and
if he had stumbled we should all three have been in the courtyard. But we got it over, and dropped as softly as possible on to
the roof of the next house. Hussin had his finger to his lips, and I
soon saw why. For there was a lighted window in the wall we had
descended.

Some imp prompted me to wait behind and explore. The
others followed Hussin and were soon at the far end of the roof,
where a kind of wooden pavilion broke the line, while I tried to
get a look inside. The window was curtained, and had two fold-
ing sashes which clasped in the middle. Through a gap in the
curtain I saw a little lamp-lit room and a big man sitting at a
table littered with papers.

I watched him, fascinated, as he turned to consult some document and made a marking on the map before him. Then he suddenly rose, stretched himself, cast a glance at the window, and
went out of the room, making a great clatter in descending the

wooden staircase. He left the door ajar and the lamp burning.

I guessed he had gone to have a look at his prisoners, in which case the show was up. But what filled my mind was an insane desire to get a sight of his map. It was one of those mad impulses which utterly cloud right reason, a thing independent of any plan, a crazy leap in the dark. But it was so strong that I would have pulled that window out by its frame, if need be, to get to that table.

There was no need, for the flimsy clasp gave at the first pull, and the sashes swung open. I scrambled in, after listening for steps on the stairs. I crumpled up the map and stuck it in my pocket, as well as the paper from which I had seen him copying. Very carefully I removed all marks of my entry, brushed away the snow from the boards, pulled back the curtain, got out and refastened the window. Still there was no sound of his return. Then I started off to catch up the others.

I found them shivering in the roof pavilion. "We've got to move pretty fast," I said, "for I've just been burgling old Stumm's private cabinet. Hussin, my lad, d'you hear that? They may be after us any moment, so I pray Heaven we soon strike better going."

Hussin understood. He led us at a smart pace from one roof to another, for here they were all the same height, and only low parapets and screens divided them. We never saw a soul, for a winter's night is not the time you choose to saunter on your housetop. I kept my ears open for trouble behind us, and in about five minutes I heard it. A riot of voices broke out, with one louder than the rest, and, looking back, I saw lanterns waving. Stumm had realized his loss and found the tracks of the thief.

Hussin gave one glance behind and then hurried us on at break-neck pace, with old Blenkiron gasping and stumbling. The shouts behind us grew louder, as if some eye quicker than the rest had caught our movement in the starlit darkness. It was very evident that if they kept up the chase we should be caught, for Blenkiron was about as useful on a roof as a hippo.

Presently we came to a big drop, with a kind of ladder down it, and at the foot a shallow ledge running to the left into a pit of darkness. Hussin gripped my arm and pointed down it. "Follow it," he whispered, "and you will reach a roof which spans a street. Cross it, and on the other side is a mosque. Turn to the right there and you will find easy going for fifty metres, well screened from the higher roofs. For Allah's sake keep in the shelter of the screen. Somewhere there I will join you."

He hurried us along the ledge for a bit and then went back, and with snow from the corners covered up our tracks. After that he went straight on himself, taking strange short steps like a bird. I saw his game. He wanted to lead our pursuers after him, and he had to multiply the tracks and trust to Stumm's fellows not spotting that they all were made by one man.

But I had quite enough to think of in getting Blenkiron along that ledge. He was pretty nearly foundered, he was in a sweat of terror, and as a matter of fact he was taking one of the biggest risks of his life, for we had no rope and his neck depended on himself. I could hear him invoking some unknown deity called Holy Mike. But he ventured gallantly, and we got to the roof which ran across the street. That was easier, though ticklish enough, but it was no joke skirting the cupola of that infernal mosque. At last we found the parapet and breathed more freely, for we were now under shelter from the direction of danger. I spared a moment to look round, and thirty yards off, across the street, I saw a weird spectacle.

The hunt was proceeding along the roofs parallel to the one we were lodged on. I saw the flicker of the lanterns, waved up and down as the bearers slipped in the snow, and I heard their cries like hounds on a trail. Stumm was not among them: he had not the shape for that sort of business. They passed us and continued to our left, now hid by a jutting chimney, now clear to view against the skyline. The roofs they were on were perhaps six feet higher than ours, so even from our shelter we could mark their course. If Hussin were going to be hunted across Erzerum it was a bad look-out for us, for I hadn't the foggiest notion where we were or where we were going to.

But as we watched we saw something more. The wavering

lanterns were now three or four hundred yards away, but on the roofs just opposite us across the street there appeared a man's figure. I thought it was one of the hunters, and we all crouched lower, and then I recognized the lean agility of Hussin. He must have doubled back, keeping in the dusk to the left of the pursuit, and taking big risks in the open places. But there he was now, exactly in front of us, and separated only by the width of the narrow street.

He took a step backward, gathered himself for a spring, and leaped clean over the gap. Like a cat he lighted on the parapet above us, and stumbled forward with the impetus right on our heads.

"We are safe for the moment," he whispered, "but when they miss me they will return. We must make good haste."

The next half-hour was a maze of twists and turns, slipping down icy roofs and climbing icier chimney-stacks. The stir of the city had gone, and from the black streets below came scarcely a sound. But always the great tattoo of guns beat in the east. Gradually we descended to a lower level, till we emerged on the top of a shed in a courtyard. Hussin gave an odd sort of cry, like a demented owl, and something began to stir below us.

It was a big covered wagon, full of bundles of forage, and drawn by four mules. As we descended from the shed into the frozen litter of the yard, a man came out of the shade and spoke low to Hussin. Peter and I lifted Blenkiron into the cart, and scrambled in beside him, and I never felt anything more blessed than the warmth and softness of that place after the frosty roofs. I had forgotten all about my hunger, and only yearned for sleep. Presently the wagon moved out of the courtyard into the dark streets.

Then Blenkiron began to laugh, a deep internal rumble which shook him violently and brought down a heap of forage on his head. I thought it was hysterics, the relief from the tension of the past hour. But it wasn't. His body might be out of training, but there was never anything the matter with his nerves. He was consumed with honest merriment.

"Say, Major," he gasped, "I don't usually cherish dislikes for my fellow men, but somehow I didn't cotton to Colonel Stumm. But now I almost love him. You hit his jaw very bad in Germany, and now you've annexed his private file, and I guess it's important or he wouldn't have been so mighty set on steeple-chasing over those roofs. I haven't done such a thing since I broke into neighbour Brown's woodshed to steal his tame 'possum, and that's forty years back. It's the first piece of genooine amusement I've struck in this game, and I haven't laughed so much since old Jim Hooker told the tale of 'Cousin Sally Dillard' when we were hunting ducks in Michigan and his wife's brother had an apoplexy in the night and died of it."

To the accompaniment of Blenkiron's chuckles I did what Peter had done in the first minute, and fell asleep.

When I woke it was still dark. The wagon had stopped in a courtyard which seemed to be shaded by great trees. The snow lay deeper here, and by the feel of the air we had left the city and climbed to higher ground. There were big buildings on one side, and on the other what looked like the lift of a hill. No lights were shown, the place was in profound gloom, but I felt the presence near me of others besides Hussin and the driver.

We were hurried, Blenkiron only half awake, into an outbuilding, and then down some steps to a roomy cellar. There Hussin lit a lantern, which showed what had once been a storehouse for fruit. Old husks still strewed the floor and the place smelt of apples. Straw had been piled in corners for beds, and there was a rude table and a divan of boards covered with sheepskins.

"Where are we?" I asked Hussin.

"In the house of the Master," he said. "You will be safe here, but you must keep still till the Master comes."

"Is the Frankish lady here?" I asked.

Hussin nodded, and from a wallet brought out some food—raisins and cold meat and a loaf of bread. We fell on it like vultures, and as we ate Hussin disappeared. I noticed that he locked the door behind him.

As soon as the meal was ended the others returned to their interrupted sleep. But I was wakeful now and my mind was sharp-set on many things. I got Blenkiron's electric torch and lay down on the divan to study Stumm's map.

The first glance showed me that I had lit on a treasure. It was the staff map of the Erzerum defences, showing the forts and the field-trenches, with little notes scribbled in Stumm's neat small handwriting. I got out the big map which I had taken from Blenkiron, and made out the general lie of the land. I saw the horseshoe of Deve Boyun to the east which the Russian guns were battering. Stumm's was just like the kind of squared artillery map we used in France, 1 in 10,000, with spidery red lines showing the trenches, but with the difference that it was the Turkish trenches that were shown in detail and the Russian only roughly indicated. The thing was really a confidential plan of the whole Erzerum *enceinte*, and would be worth untold gold to the enemy. No wonder Stumm had been in a wax at its loss.

The Deve Boyun lines seemed to me monstrously strong, and I remembered the merits of the Turk as a fighter behind strong defences. It looked as if Russia were up against a second Plevna or a new Gallipoli.

Then I took to studying the flanks. South lay the Palantuken range of mountains, with forts defending the passes, where ran the roads to Mush and Lake Van. That side, too, looked pretty strong. North in the valley of the Euphrates I made out two big forts, Tafta and Kara Gubek, defending the road from Olti. On this part of the map Stumm's notes were plentiful, and I gave them all my attention. I remembered Blenkiron's news about the Russians advancing on a broad front, for it was clear that Stumm was taking pains about the flank of the fortress.

Kara Gubek was the point of interest. It stood on a rib of land between two peaks, which from the contour lines rose very steep. So long as it was held it was clear that no invader could move down the Euphrates glen. Stumm had appended a note to the peaks—"*not fortified*"; and about two miles to the north-east there was a red cross and the name "*Prjevalsky*." I assumed that to be the farthest point yet reached by the right wing of the Russian attack.

Then I turned to the paper from which Stumm had copied the jottings on to his map. It was typewritten, and consisted of notes on different points. One was headed *Kara Gubek* and read: *No*

time to fortify adjacent peaks. Difficult for enemy to get batteries there,
but not impossible. This the real point of danger, for if Prjevalsky wins
the peaks Kara Gubek and Tafta must fall, and enemy will be on left
rear of Deve Boyun main position.

I was soldier enough to see the tremendous importance of this note. On Kara Gubek depended the defence of Erzerum, and it was a broken reed if one knew where the weakness lay. Yet, searching the map again, I could not believe that any mortal commander would see any chance in the adjacent peaks, even if he thought them unfortified. That was information confined to the Turkish and German staff. But if it could be conveyed to the Grand Duke he would have Erzerum in his power in a day. Otherwise he would go on battering at the Deve Boyun ridge for weeks, and long ere he won it the Gallipoli divisions would arrive, he would be outnumbered by two to one, and his chance would have vanished.

My discovery set me pacing up and down that cellar in a perfect fever of excitement. I longed for wireless, a carrier pigeon, an aeroplane—anything to bridge over that space of half a dozen miles between me and the Russian lines. It was maddening to have stumbled on vital news and to be wholly unable to use it. How could three fugitives in a cellar, with the whole hornet's nest of Turkey and Germany stirred up against them, hope to send this message of life and death?

I went back to the map and examined the nearest Russian positions. They were carefully marked. Prjevalsky in the north, the main force beyond Deve Boyun, and the southern columns up to the passes of the Palantuken but not yet across them. I could not know which was nearest to us till I discovered where we were. And as I thought of this I began to see the rudiments of a desperate plan. It depended on Peter, now slumbering like a tired dog on a couch of straw.

Hussin had locked the door and I must wait for information till he came back. But suddenly I noticed a trap in the roof, which had evidently been used for raising and lowering the cellar's stores. It looked ill-fitting and might be unbarred, so I pulled the table below it, and found that with a little effort I could raise the flap. I knew I was taking immense risks, but I was so keen on my plan that I disregarded them. After some trouble I got the thing prised open, and catching the edges of the hole with my fingers raised my body and got my knees on the edge.

It was the out-building of which our refuge was the cellar, and it was half filled with light. Not a soul was there, and I hunted about till I found what I wanted. This was a ladder leading to a sort of loft, which in turn gave access to the roof. Here I had to be very careful, for I might be overlooked from the high buildings. But by good luck there was a trellis for grape vines across the place, which gave a kind of shelter. Lying flat on my face I stared over a great expanse of country.

Looking north I saw the city in a haze of morning smoke, and, beyond, the plain of the Euphrates and the opening of the glen where the river left the hills. Up there, among the snowy heights, were Tafta and Kara Gubek. To the east was the ridge of Deve Boyun, where the mist was breaking before the winter's sun. On the roads up to it I saw transport moving, I saw the circle of the inner forts, but for a moment the guns were silent. South rose a great wall of white mountain, which I took to be the Palantuken. I could see the roads running to the passes, and the smoke of camps and horse-lines right under the cliffs.

I had learned what I needed. We were in the out-buildings of a big country house two or three miles south of the city. The nearest point of the Russian front was somewhere in the foothills of the Palantuken.

As I descended I heard, thin and faint and beautiful, like the cry of a wild bird, the muezzin from the minarets of Erzerum.

When I dropped through the trap the others were awake. Hussin was setting food on the table, and viewing my descent with anxious disapproval.

"It's all right," I said; "I won't do it again, for I've found out all I wanted. Peter, old man, the biggest job of your life is before you!"

CHAPTER 19

Greenmantle

PETER scarcely looked up from his breakfast.

"I'm willing, Dick," he said. "But you mustn't ask me to be friends with Stumm. He makes my stomach cold, that one."

For the first time he had stopped calling me "Cornelis." The day of make-believe was over for all of us.

"Not to be friends with him," I said, "but to bust him and all his kind."

"Then I'm ready," said Peter cheerfully. "What is it?"

I spread out the maps on the divan. There was no light in the place but Blenkiron's electric torch, for Hussin had put out the lantern. Peter got his nose into the things at once, for his intelligence work in the Boer War had made him handy with maps. It didn't want much telling from me to explain to him the importance of the one I had looted.

"That news is worth many a million pounds," said he, wrinkling his brows, and scratching delicately the tip of his left ear. It was a way he had when he was startled.

"How can we get it to our friends?"

Peter cogitated. "There is but one way. A man must take it. Once, I remember, when we fought the Matabele it was necessary to find out whether the chief Makapan was living. Some said he had died, others that he'd gone over the Portuguese border, but I believed he lived. No native could tell us, and since his kraal was well defended no runner could get through. So it was necessary to send a man."

Peter lifted up his head and laughed. "The man found the chief Makapan. He was very much alive, and made good shooting with a shot-gun. But the man brought the chief Makapan out of his kraal and handed him over to the Mounted Police. You remember Captain Arcoll, Dick—Jim Arcoll? Well, Jim laughed so much that he broke open a wound in his head, and had to have a doctor."

"You were that man, Peter," I said.

"*Ja.* I was the man. There are more ways of getting into kraals than there are ways of keeping people out."

"Will you take this chance?"

"For certain, Dick. I am getting stiff with doing nothing, and if I sit in houses much longer I shall grow old. A man bet me five pounds on the ship that I could not get through a trench-line, and if there had been a trench-line handy I would have taken him on. I will be very happy, Dick, but I do not say I will succeed. It is new country to me, and I will be hurried, and hurry makes bad stalking."

I showed him what I thought the likeliest place—in the spurs of the Palantuken mountains. Peter's way of doing things was all his own. He scraped earth and plaster out of a corner and sat down to make a little model of the landscape on the table, following the contours of the map. He did it extraordinarily neatly, for, like all great hunters, he was as deft as a weaver bird. He puzzled over it for a long time, and conned the map till he must have got it by heart. Then he took his field-glasses—a very good single Zeiss which was part of the spoils from Rasta's motor-car—and announced that he was going to follow my example and get on to the housetop. Presently his legs disappeared through the trap, and Blenkiron and I were left to our reflections.

Peter must have found something uncommon interesting, for he stayed on the roof the better part of the day. It was a dull job for us, since there was no light, and Blenkiron had not even the consolation of a game of Patience. But for all that he was in good spirits, for he had had no dyspepsia since we left Constantinople, and announced that he believed he was at last getting even with his darned duodenum. As for me I was pretty restless, for I could not imagine what was detaining Sandy. It was clear that our presence must have been kept secret from Hilda von Einem, for she was a pal of Stumm's, and he must by now have blown the gaff on Peter and me. How long could this secrecy last, I asked myself. We had now no sort of protection in the whole outfit. Rasta and the Turks wanted our blood: so did Stumm and the Germans; and once the lady found we were deceiving her she would want it most of all. Our only hope was Sandy, and he gave no sign of his existence. I began to fear that with him, too, things had miscarried.

And yet I wasn't really depressed, only impatient. I could never again get back to the beastly stagnation of that Constantinople week. The guns kept me cheerful. There was the devil of a bombardment all day, and the thought that our Allies were thundering there half a dozen miles off gave me a perfectly groundless hope. If they burst through the defence Hilda von Einem and her prophet and all our enemies would be overwhelmed in the deluge. And that blessed chance depended very much on old Peter, now brooding like a pigeon on the housetops.

It was not till the late afternoon that Hussin appeared again. He took no notice of Peter's absence, but lit a lantern and set it on the table. Then he went to the door and waited. Presently a light step fell on the stairs, and Hussin drew back to let someone enter. He promptly departed and I heard the key turn in the lock behind him.

Sandy stood there, but a new Sandy who made Blenkiron and me jump to our feet. The pelts and skin cap had gone, and he wore instead a long linen tunic clasped at the waist by a broad girdle. A strange green turban adorned his head, and as he pushed it back I saw that his hair had been shaved. He looked like some acolyte—a weary acolyte, for there was no spring in his walk or nerve in his carriage. He dropped numbly on the divan and laid his head in his hands. The lantern showed his haggard eyes with dark lines beneath them.

"Good God, old man, have you been sick?" I cried.

"Not sick," he said hoarsely. "My body is right enough, but the last few days I have been living in hell."

Blenkiron nodded sympathetically. That was how he himself would have described the company of the lady.

I marched across to him and gripped both his wrists.

"Look at me," I said, "straight in the eyes."

His eyes were like a sleep-walker's, unwinking, unseeing. "Great Heavens, man, you've been drugged!" I said.

"Drugged," he cried, with a weary laugh. "Yes, I have been drugged, but not by any physic. No one has been doctoring my food. But you can't go through hell without getting your eyes red-hot."

I kept my grip on his wrists. "Take your time, old chap, and tell us about it. Blenkiron and I are here, and old Peter's on the roof not far off. We'll look after you."

"It does me good to hear your voice, Dick," he said. "It reminds me of clean, honest things."

"They'll come back, never fear. We're at the last lap now. One more spurt and it's over. You've got to tell me what the new snag is. Is it that woman?"

He shivered like a frightened colt. "Woman!" he cried. "Does a woman drag a man through the nether-pit? She's a she-devil. Oh, it isn't madness that's wrong with her. She's as sane as you and as cool as Blenkiron. Her life is an infernal game of chess, and she plays with souls for pawns. She is evil—evil—evil . . ." And once more he buried his head in his hands.

It was Blenkiron who brought sense into this hectic atmosphere. His slow, beloved drawl was an antiseptic against nerves.

"Say, boy," he said, "I feel just like you about the lady. But our job is not to investigate her character. Her Maker will do that good and sure some day. We've got to figure how to circumvent her, and for that you've got to tell us what exactly's been occurring since we parted company."

Sandy pulled himself together with a great effort.

"Greenmantle died that night I saw you. We buried him secretly by her order in the garden of the villa. Then came the trouble about his successor . . . The four Ministers would be no party to a swindle. They were honest men, and vowed that their task now was to make a tomb for their master and pray for the rest of their days at his shrine. They were as immovable as a granite hill and she knew it . . . Then they, too, died."

"Murdered?" I gasped.

"Murdered . . . all four in one morning. I do not know how, but I helped to bury them. Oh, she had Germans and Kurds to do her foul work, but their hands were clean compared to hers. Pity me, Dick, for I have seen honesty and virtue put to the shambles and have abetted the deed when it was done. It will haunt me to my dying day."

I did not stop to console him, for my mind was on fire with his news.

"Then the prophet is gone, and the humbug is over," I cried.

"The prophet still lives. She has found a successor."

He stood up in his linen tunic.

"Why do I wear these clothes? Because I am Greenmantle. I am the Kaába-i-hurriyeh for all Islam. In three days' time I will reveal myself to my people and wear on my breast the green ephod of the prophet."

He broke off with an hysterical laugh.

"Only you see, I won't. I will cut my throat first."

"Cheer up!" said Blenkiron soothingly. "We'll find some prettier way than that."

"There is no way," he said, "no way but death. We're done for, all of us. Hussin got you out of Stumm's clutches, but you're in danger every moment. At the best you have three days, and then you, too, will be dead."

I had no words to reply. This change in the bold and unshakable Sandy took my breath away.

"She made me her accomplice," he went on. "I should have killed her on the graves of those innocent men. But instead I did all she asked and joined in her game . . . She was very candid, you know . . . She cares no more than Enver for the faith of Islam. She can laugh at it. But she has her own dreams, and they consume her as a saint is consumed by his devotion. She has told me them, and if the day in the garden was hell, the days since have been the innermost fires of Tophet. I think—it is horrible to say it—that she has got some kind of crazy liking for me. When we have reclaimed the East I am to be by her side when she rides on her milk-white horse into Jerusalem . . . And there have been moments—only moments, I swear to God—when I have been fired myself by her madness . . ."

Sandy's figure seemed to shrink and his voice grew shrill and wild. It was too much for Blenkiron. He indulged in a torrent of blasphemy such as I believe had never before passed his lips.

"I'm blessed if I'll listen to this God-darned stuff. It isn't delicate. You get busy, Major, and pump some sense into your afflicted friend."

I was beginning to see what had happened. Sandy was a man of genius—as much as anybody I ever struck—but he had the defects of such high-strung, fanciful souls. He would take more than mortal risks, and you couldn't scare him by any ordinary terror. But let his old conscience get cross-eyed, let him find himself in some situation which in his eyes involved his honour, and he might go stark crazy. The woman, who roused in me and Blenkiron only hatred, could catch his imagination and stir in him—for the moment only—an unwilling response. And then came bitter and morbid repentance, and the last desperation.

It was no time to mince matters. "Sandy, you old fool," I cried, "be thankful you have friends to keep you from playing the fool. You saved my life at Loos, and I'm jolly well going to get you through this show. I'm bossing the outfit now, and for all your confounded prophetic manners, you've got to take your orders from me. You aren't going to reveal yourself to your people, and still less are you going to cut your throat. Greenmantle will avenge the murder of his Ministers, and make that bedlamite woman sorry she was born. We're going to get clear away, and inside of a week we'll be having tea with the Grand Duke Nicholas."

I wasn't bluffing. Puzzled as I was about ways and means I had still the blind belief that we should win out. And as I spoke two legs dangled through the trap and a dusty and blinking Peter descended in our midst.

I took the maps from him and spread them on the table.

"First, you must know that we've had an almighty piece of luck. Last night Hussin took us for a walk over the roofs of Erzerum, and by the blessing of Providence I got into Stumm's room, and bagged his staff map . . . Look here . . . d'you see his notes? That's the danger-point of the whole defence. Once the Russians get that fort, Kara Gubek, they've turned the main position. And it can be got; Stumm knows it can; for these two adjacent hills are not held . . . It looks a mad enterprise on paper, but Stumm knows that it is possible enough. The question is: Will the Russians guess that? I say no, not unless someone tells them. Therefore, by hook or by crook, we've got to get that information through to them."

Sandy's interest in ordinary things was beginning to flicker up again. He studied the map and began to measure distances.

"Peter's going to have a try for it. He thinks there's a sporting chance of his getting through the lines. If he does—if he gets this map to the Grand Duke's staff—then Stumm's goose is cooked. In three days the Cossacks will be in the streets of Erzerum."

"What are the chances?" Sandy asked.

I glanced at Peter. "We're hard-bitten fellows and can face the truth. I think the chances against success are about five to one."

"Two to one," said Peter modestly. "Not worse than that. I don't think you're fair to me, Dick, my old friend."

I looked at that lean, tight figure and the gentle, resolute face, and I changed my mind. "I'm hanged if I think there are any odds," I said. "With anybody else it would want a miracle, but with Peter I believe the chances are level."

"Two to one," Peter persisted. "If it was evens I wouldn't be interested."

"Let me go," Sandy cried. "I talk the lingo, and can pass as a Turk, and I'm a million times likelier to get through. For God's sake, Dick, let me go."

"Not you. You're wanted here. If you disappear the whole show's busted too soon, and the three of us left behind will be strung up before morning . . . No, my son. You're going to escape, but it will be in company with Blenkiron and me. We've got to blow the whole Greenmantle business so high that the bits of it will never come to earth again . . . First, tell me how many of your fellows will stick by you? I mean the Companions."

"The whole half-dozen. They are very worried already about what has happened. She made me sound them in her presence, and they were quite ready to accept me as Greenmantle's successor. But they have their suspicions about what happened at the villa, and they've no love for the woman . . . They'd follow me through hell if I bade them, but they would rather it was my own show."

"That's all right," I cried. "It is the one thing I've been doubtful about. Now observe this map. Erzerum isn't invested by a long chalk. The Russians are round it in a broad half-moon. That means that all the west, south-west, and north-west is open and undefended by trench-lines. There are flanks far away to the north and south in the hills which can be turned, and once we get round a flank there's nothing between us and our friends . . . I've figured out our road," and I traced it on the map. "If we can make that big circuit to the west and get over that pass unobserved we're bound to strike a Russian column the next day. It'll be a rough road, but I fancy we've all ridden as bad in our time. But one thing we must have, and that's horses. Can we and your six ruffians slip off in the darkness on the best beasts in this township? If you can manage that, we'll do the trick."

Sandy sat down and pondered. Thank Heaven, he was thinking now of action and not of his own conscience.

"It must be done," he said at last, "but it won't be easy. Hussin's a great fellow, but as you know well, Dick, horses right up at the battle-front are not easy to come by. To-morrow I've got some kind of infernal fast to observe, and the next day that woman will be coaching me for my part. We'll have to give Hussin time . . . I wish to Heaven it could be to-night."

He was silent again for a bit, and then he said: "I believe the best time would be the third night, the eve of the revelation. She's bound to leave me alone that night."

"Right-o," I said. "It won't be much fun sitting waiting in this cold sepulchre; but we must keep our heads and risk nothing by being in a hurry. Besides, if Peter wins through, the Turk will be a busy man by the day after to-morrow."

The key turned in the door and Hussin stole in like a shade. It was the signal for Sandy to leave.

"You fellows have given me a new lease of life," he said. "I've got a plan now, and I can set my teeth and stick it out."

He went up to Peter and gripped his hand. "Good luck. You're the bravest man I've ever met, and I've seen a few." Then he turned abruptly and went out, followed by an exhortation from Blenkiron to "Get busy about the quadrupeds."

THEN we set about equipping Peter for his crusade. It was a simple job, for we were not rich in properties. His get-up, with his thick fur-collared greatcoat, was not unlike the ordinary Turkish officer seen in a dim light. But Peter had no intention of passing for a Turk, or indeed of giving anybody the chance of seeing him, and he was more concerned to fit in with the landscape. So he stripped off the greatcoat and pulled a grey sweater of mine over his jacket, and put on his head a woollen helmet of the same colour. He had no need of the map for he had long since got his route by heart, and what was once fixed in that mind stuck like wax; but I made him take Stumm's plan and paper, hidden below his shirt. The big difficulty, I saw, would be getting to the Russians without getting shot, assuming he passed the Turkish trenches. He could only hope that he would strike someone with a smattering of English or German. Twice he ascended to the roof and came back cheerful, for there was promise of wild weather.

Hussin brought in our supper, and Peter made up a parcel of food. Blenkiron and I had both small flasks of brandy and I gave him mine.

Then he held out his hand quite simply, like a good child who is going off to bed. It was too much for Blenkiron. With large tears rolling down his face he announced that, if we all came through, he was going to fit him into the softest berth that money could buy. I don't think he was understood, for old Peter's eyes had now the far-away absorption of the hunter who has found game. He was thinking only of his job.

Two legs and a pair of very shabby boots vanished through the trap, and suddenly I felt utterly lonely and desperately sad. The guns were beginning to roar again in the east, and in the intervals came the whistle of the rising storm.

CHAPTER 20

Peter Pienaar Goes to the Wars

This chapter is the tale that Peter told me—long after, sitting beside a stove in the hotel at Bergen, where we were waiting for our boat.

HE CLIMBED on the roof and shinned down the broken bricks of the outer wall. The out-building we were lodged in abutted on a road, and was outside the proper *enceinte* of the house. At ordinary times I have no doubt there were sentries, but Sandy and Hussin had probably managed to clear them off this end for a little. Anyhow he saw nobody as he crossed the road and dived into the snowy fields.

He knew very well that he must do the job in the twelve hours of darkness ahead of him. The immediate front of a battle is a bit too public for anyone to lie hidden in by day, especially when two or three feet of snow make everything kenspeckle. Now hurry in a job of this kind was abhorrent to Peter's soul, for, like all Boers, his tastes were for slowness and sureness, though he could hustle fast enough when haste was needed. As he pushed through the winter fields he reckoned up the things in his favour, and found the only one the dirty weather. There was a high, gusty wind, blowing scuds of snow but never coming to any great fall. The frost had gone, and the lying snow was as soft as butter.

That was all to the good, he thought, for a clear, hard night would have been the devil.

The first bit was through farmlands, which were seamed with little snow-filled water furrows. Now and then would come a house and a patch of fruit-trees, but there was nobody abroad. The roads were crowded enough, but Peter had no use for roads. I can picture him swinging along with his bent back, stopping every now and then to sniff and listen, alert for the foreknowledge of danger. When he chose he could cover country like an antelope.

Soon he struck a big road full of transport. It was the road from Erzerum to the Palantuken pass, and he waited his chance and crossed it. After that the ground grew rough with boulders and patches of thorn-trees, splendid cover where he could move fast without worrying. Then he was pulled up suddenly on the bank of a river. The map had warned him of it, but not that it would be so big.

It was a torrent swollen with melting snow and rains in the hills, and it was running fifty yards wide. Peter thought he could have swum it, but he was very averse to a drenching. "A wet man makes too much noise," he said, and besides, there was the off-chance that the current would be too much for him. So he moved up stream to look for a bridge.

In ten minutes he found one, a new-made thing of trestles, broad enough to take transport-wagons. It was guarded, for he heard the tramp of a sentry, and as he pulled himself up the bank he observed a couple of long wooden huts, obviously some kind of billets. These were on the near side of the stream, about a dozen yards from the bridge. A door stood open and a light showed in it, and from within came the sound of voices . . . Peter had a sense of hearing like a wild animal, and he could detect even from the confused gabble that the voices were German.

As he lay and listened someone came over the bridge. It was an officer, for the sentry saluted. The man disappeared in one of the huts. Peter had struck the billets and repairing shop of a squad of German sappers.

He was just going ruefully to retrace his steps and try to find a
good place to swim the stream when it struck him that the officer who had passed him wore clothes very like his own. He, too,
had had a grey sweater and a Balaclava helmet, for even a German officer ceases to be dressy on a mid-winter's night in Anatolia. The idea came to Peter to walk boldly across the bridge and
trust to the sentry not seeing the difference.

He slipped round a corner of the hut and marched down the
road. The sentry was now at the far end, which was lucky, for if
the worst came to the worst he could throttle him. Peter, mim-
icking the stiff German walk, swung past him, his head down as
if to protect him from the wind.

The man saluted. He did more, for he offered conversation.
The officer must have been a genial soul. "It's a rough night,
Captain," he said in German. "The wagons are late. Pray God,
Michael hasn't got a shell in his lot. They've begun putting over
some big ones."

Peter grunted good night in German and strode on. He was
just leaving the road when he heard a great halloo behind him.

The real officer must have appeared on his heels, and the sentry's doubts had been stirred. A whistle was blown, and, looking
back, Peter saw lanterns waving in the gale. They were coming
out to look for the duplicate.

He stood still for a second, and noticed the lights spreading
out south of the road. He was just about to dive off it on the
north side when he was aware of a difficulty. On that side a steep
bank fell to a ditch, and the bank beyond bounded a big flood.
He could see the dull ruffle of the water under the wind.

On the road itself he would soon be caught; south of it the
search was beginning; and the ditch itself was no place to hide,
for he saw a lantern moving up it. Peter dropped into it all the
same and made a plan. The side below the road was a little un-
dercut and very steep. He resolved to plaster himself against it,
for he would be hidden from the road, and a searcher in the ditch
would not be likely to explore the unbroken sides. It was always a
maxim of Peter's that the best hiding-place was the worst, the

least obvious to the minds of those who were looking for you.

He waited until the lights both in the road and the ditch came nearer, and then he gripped the edge with his left hand, where some stones gave him purchase, dug the toes of his boots into the wet soil and stuck like a limpet. It needed some strength to keep the position for long, but the muscles of his arms and legs were like whipcord.

The searcher in the ditch soon got tired, for the place was very wet, and joined his comrades on the road. They came along, running, flashing the lanterns into the trench, and exploring all the immediate countryside.

Then rose a noise of wheels and horses from the opposite direction. Michael and the delayed wagons were approaching. They dashed up at a great pace, driven wildly, and for one horrid second Peter thought they were going to spill into the ditch at the very spot where he was concealed. The wheels passed so close to the edge that they almost grazed his fingers. Somebody shouted an order and they pulled up a yard or two nearer the bridge. The others came up and there was a consultation.

Michael swore he had passed no one on the road.

"That fool Hannus has seen a ghost," said the officer testily. "It's too cold for this child's play."

Hannus, almost in tears, repeated his tale. "The man spoke to me in good German," he cried.

"Ghost or no ghost he is safe enough up the road," said the officer. "Kind God, that was a big one!" He stopped and stared at a shell-burst, for the bombardment from the east was growing fiercer.

They stood discussing the fire for a minute and presently moved off. Peter gave them two minutes' law and then clambered back to the highway and set off along it at a run. The noise of the shelling and the wind, together with the thick darkness, made it safe to hurry.

He left the road at the first chance and took to the broken country. The ground was now rising towards a spur of the Palan-tuken, on the far slope of which were the Turkish trenches. The night had begun by being pretty nearly as black as pitch; even the smoke from the shell explosions, which is often visible in darkness, could not be seen. But as the wind blew the snow-clouds athwart the sky patches of stars came out. Peter had a compass, but he didn't need to use it, for he had a kind of "feel" for landscape, a special sense which is born in savages and can only be acquired after long experience by the white man. I believe he could smell where the north lay. He had settled roughly which part of the line he would try, merely because of its nearness to the enemy. But he might see reason to vary this, and as he moved he began to think that the safest place was where the shelling was hottest. He didn't like the notion, but it sounded sense.

Suddenly he began to puzzle over queer things in the ground, and, as he had never seen big guns before, it took him a moment to fix them. Presently one went off at his elbow with a roar like the Last Day. These were Austrian howitzers—nothing over eight-inch, I fancy, but to Peter they looked like leviathans. Here, too, he saw for the first time a big and quite recent shell-hole, for the Russian guns were searching out the position. He was so interested in it all that he poked his nose where he shouldn't have been, and dropped plump into the pit behind a gun-emplacement.

Gunners all the world over are the same—shy people, who hide themselves in holes and hibernate and mortally dislike being detected.

A gruff voice cried "*Wer da?*" and a heavy hand seized his neck.

Peter was ready with his story. He belonged to Michael's wagon-team and had been left behind. He wanted to be told the way to the sappers' camp. He was very apologetic, not to say obsequious.

"It is one of those Prussian swine from the Marta bridge," said a gunner. "Land him a kick to teach him sense. Bear to your right, mannikin, and you will find a road. And have a care when you get there, for the Russkoes are registering on it."

Peter thanked them and bore off to the right. After that he

kept a wary eye on the howitzers, and was thankful when he got out of their area on to the slopes up the hill. Here was the type of country that was familiar to him, and he defied any Turk or Boche to spot him among the scrub and boulders. He was getting on very well, when once more, close to his ear, came a sound like the crack of doom.

It was the field-guns now, and the sound of a field-gun close at hand is bad for the nerves if you aren't expecting it. Peter thought he had been hit, and lay flat for a little to consider. Then he found the right explanation, and crawled forward very warily.

Presently he saw his first Russian shell. It dropped half a dozen yards to his right, making a great hole in the snow and sending up a mass of mixed earth, snow, and broken stones. Peter spat out the dirt and felt very solemn. You must remember that never in his life had he seen big shelling, and was now being landed in the thick of a first-class show without any preparation. He said he felt cold in his stomach, and very wishful to run away, if there had been anywhere to run to. But he kept on to the crest of the ridge, over which a big glow was broadening like sunrise. He tripped once over a wire, which he took for some kind of snare, and after that went very warily. By and by he got his face between two boulders and looked over into the true battlefield.

He told me it was exactly what the predikant used to say that Hell would be like. About fifty yards down the slope lay the Turkish trenches—they were dark against the snow, and now and then a black figure like a devil showed for an instant and disappeared. The Turks clearly expected an infantry attack, for they were sending up calcium rockets and Very flares. The Russians were battering their line and spraying all the hinterland, not with shrapnel, but with good, solid high-explosives. The place would be as bright as day for a moment, all smothered in a scurry of smoke and snow and debris, and then a black pall would fall on it, when only the thunder of the guns told of the battle.

Peter felt very sick. He had not believed there could be so much noise in the world, and the drums of his ears were splitting. Now, for a man to whom courage is habitual, the taste of fear—naked, utter fear—is a horrible thing. It seems to wash away all his manhood. Peter lay on the crest, watching the shells burst, and confident that any moment he might be a shattered remnant. He lay and reasoned with himself, calling himself every name he could think of, but conscious that nothing would get rid of that lump of ice below his heart.

Then he could stand it no longer. He got up and ran for his life.

But he ran forward.

It was the craziest performance. He went hell-for-leather over a piece of ground which was being watered with H.E., but by the mercy of Heaven nothing hit him. He took some fearsome tosses in shell-holes, but partly erect and partly on all fours he did the fifty yards and tumbled into a Turkish trench right on top of a dead man.

The contact with that body brought him to his senses. That men could die at all seemed a comforting, homely thing after that unnatural pandemonium. The next moment a crump took the parapet of the trench some yards to his left, and he was half buried in an avalanche.

He crawled out of that, pretty badly cut about the head. He was quite cool now and thinking hard about his next step. There were men all around him, sullen dark faces as he saw them when the flares went up. They were manning the parapets and waiting tensely for something else than the shelling. They paid no attention to him, for I fancy in that trench units were pretty well mixed up, and under a bad bombardment no one bothers about his neighbour. He found himself free to move as he pleased. The ground of the trench was littered with empty cartridge-cases, and there were many dead bodies.

The last shell, as I have said, had played havoc with the parapet. In the next spell of darkness Peter crawled through the gap and twisted among some snowy hillocks. He was no longer afraid of shells, any more than he was afraid of a veld thunderstorm. But he was wondering very hard how he should ever get to the

Russians. The Turks were behind him now, but there was the biggest danger in front.

Then the artillery ceased. It was so sudden that he thought he had gone deaf, and could hardly realize the blessed relief of it. The wind, too, seemed to have fallen, or perhaps he was sheltered by the lee of the hill. There were a lot of dead here also, and that he couldn't understand, for they were new dead. Had the Turks attacked and been driven back? When he had gone about thirty yards he stopped to take his bearings. On the right were the ruins of a large building set on fire by the guns. There was a blur of woods and the debris of walls round it. Away to the left another hill ran out farther to the east, and the place he was in seemed to be a kind of cup between the spurs. Just before him was a little ruined building, with the sky seen through its rafters, for the smouldering ruin on the right gave a certain light. He wondered if the Russian firing-line lay there.

Just then he heard voices—smothered voices—not a yard away and apparently below the ground. He instantly jumped to what this must mean. It was a Turkish trench—a communication trench. Peter didn't know much about modern warfare, but he had read in the papers, or heard from me, enough to make him draw the right moral. The fresh dead pointed to the same conclusion. What he had got through were the Turkish support trenches, not their firing-line. That was still before him.

He didn't despair, for the rebound from panic had made him extra courageous. He crawled forward, an inch at a time, taking no sort of risk, and presently found himself looking at the parados of a trench. Then he lay quiet to think out the next step.

The shelling had stopped, and there was that queer kind of peace which falls sometimes on two armies not a quarter of a mile distant. Peter said he could hear nothing but the far-off sighing of the wind. There seemed to be no movement of any kind in the trench before him, which ran through the ruined building. The light of the burning was dying, and he could just make out the mound of earth a yard in front. He began to feel hungry, and got out his packet of food and had a swig at the brandy flask. That comforted him, and he felt a master of his fate again. But the next step was not so easy. He must find out what lay behind that mound of earth.

Suddenly a curious sound fell on his ears. It was so faint that at first he doubted the evidence of his senses. Then as the wind fell it came louder. It was exactly like some hollow piece of metal being struck by a stick, musical and oddly resonant.

He concluded it was the wind blowing a branch of a tree against an old boiler in the ruin before him. The trouble was that there was scarcely enough wind now for that in this sheltered cup.

But as he listened he caught the note again. It was a bell, a fallen bell, and the place before him must have been a chapel. He remembered that an Armenian monastery had been marked on the big map, and he guessed it was the burned building on his right.

The thought of a chapel and a bell gave him the notion of some human agency. And then suddenly the notion was confirmed. The sound was regular and concerted—dot, dash, dot—dash, dot, dot. The branch of a tree and the wind may play strange pranks, but they do not produce the longs and shorts of the Morse Code.

This was where Peter's intelligence work in the Boer War helped him. He knew the Morse, he could read it, but he could make nothing of the signalling. It was either in some special code or in a strange language.

He lay still and did some calm thinking. There was a man in front of him, a Turkish soldier, who was in the enemy's pay. Therefore he could fraternize with him, for they were on the same side. But how was he to approach him without getting shot in the process? Again, how could a man send signals to the enemy from a firing-line without being detected? Peter found an answer in the strange configuration of the ground. He had not heard a sound until he was a few yards from the place, and they would be inaudible to men in the reserve trenches and even in the communication trenches. If somebody moving up the latter caught the noise, it would be easy to explain it naturally. But the wind blowing down the cup would carry it far in the enemy's direction.

There remained the risk of being heard by those parallel with the bell in the firing trenches. Peter concluded that that trench must be very thinly held, probably only by a few observers, and the nearest might be a dozen yards off. He had read about that being the French fashion under a big bombardment.

The next thing was to find out how to make himself known to this ally. He decided that the only way was to surprise him. He might get shot, but he trusted to his strength and agility against a man who was almost certainly wearied. When he had got him safe, explanations might follow.

Peter was now enjoying himself hugely. If only those infernal guns kept silent he would play out the game in the sober, decorous way he loved. So very delicately he began to wriggle forward to where the sound was.

The night was now as black as ink around him, and very quiet, too, except for soughings of the dying gale. The snow had drifted a little in the lee of the ruined walls, and Peter's progress was naturally very slow. He could not afford to dislodge one ounce of snow. Still the tinkling went on, now in greater volume. Peter was in terror lest it should cease before he got his man.

Presently his hand clutched at empty space. He was on the lip of the front trench. The sound was now a yard to his right, and with infinite care he shifted his position. Now the bell was just below him, and he felt the big rafter of the woodwork from which it had fallen. He felt something else—a stretch of wire fixed in the ground with the far end hanging in the void. That would be the spy's explanation if anyone heard the sound and came seeking the cause.

Somewhere in the darkness before him and below was the man, not a yard off. Peter remained very still, studying the situation. He could not see, but he could feel the presence, and he was trying to decide the relative position of the man and bell and their exact distance from him. The thing was not so easy as it looked, for if he jumped for where he believed the figure was, he might miss it and get a bullet in the stomach. A man who played so risky a game was probably handy with his firearms. Besides, if he should hit the bell, he would make a hideous row and alarm the whole front.

Fate suddenly gave him the right chance. The unseen figure stood up and moved a step, till his back was against the parados. He actually brushed against Peter's elbow, who held his breath.

There is a catch that the Kaffirs have which would need several diagrams to explain. It is partly a neck hold, and partly a paralysing backward twist of the right arm, but if it is practised on a man from behind, it locks him as sure as if he were handcuffed. Peter slowly got his body raised and his knees drawn under him, and reached for his prey.

He got him. A head was pulled backward over the edge of the trench, and he felt in the air the motion of the left arm pawing feebly but unable to reach behind.

"Be still," whispered Peter in German; "I mean you no harm. We are friends of the same purpose. Do you speak German?"

"*Nein*," said a muffled voice.

"English?"

"Yes," said the voice.

"Thank God," said Peter. "Then we can understand each other. I've watched your notion of signalling, and a very good one it is. I've got to get through to the Russian lines somehow before morning, and I want you to help me. I'm English—a kind of English, so we're on the same side. If I let go your neck will you be good and talk reasonably?"

The voice assented. Peter let go, and in the same instant slipped to the side. The man wheeled round and flung out an arm but gripped vacancy.

"Steady, friend," said Peter; "you mustn't play tricks with me or I'll be angry."

"Who are you? Who sent you?" asked the puzzled voice.

Peter had a happy thought. "The Companions of the Rosy Hours?" he said.

"Then are we friends indeed," said the voice. "Come out of the darkness, friend, and I will do you no harm. I am a good Turk, and I fought beside the English in Kordofan and learned their tongue. I live only to see the ruin of Enver, who has beggared my family and slain my twin brother. Therefore I serve the *Muscov ghiaours*."

"I don't know what the Musky Jaws are, but if you mean the Russians I'm with you. I've got news for them which will make Enver green. The question is, how I'm to get to them, and that is where you shall help me, my friend."

"How?"

"By playing that little tune of yours again. Tell them to expect within the next half-hour a deserter with an important message. Tell them, for God's sake, not to fire at anybody till they've made certain it isn't me."

The man took the blunt end of his bayonet and squatted beside the bell. The first stroke brought out a clear, searching note which floated down the valley. He struck three notes at slow intervals. For all the world, Peter said, he was like a telegraph operator calling up a station.

"Send the message in English," said Peter.

"They may not understand it," said the man.

"Then send it any way you like. I trust you, for we are brothers."

After ten minutes the man ceased and listened. From far away came the sound of a trench-gong, the kind of thing they used on the Western Front to give the gas-alarm.

"They say they will be ready," he said. "I cannot take down messages in the darkness, but they have given me the signal which means 'Consent.'"

"Come, that is pretty good," said Peter. "And now I must be moving. You take a hint from me. When you hear big firing up to the north get ready to beat a quick retreat, for it will be all up with that city of yours. And tell your folk, too, that they're making a bad mistake letting those fool Germans rule their land. Let them hang Enver and his little friends, and we'll be happy once more."

"May Satan receive his soul!" said the Turk. "There is wire before us, but I will show you a way through. The guns this evening made many rents in it. But haste, for a working party may be here presently to repair it. Remember there is much wire before the other lines."

Peter, with certain directions, found it pretty easy to make his way through the entanglement. There was one bit which scraped a hole in his back, but very soon he had come to the last posts and found himself in open country. The place, he said, was a graveyard of the unburied dead that smelt horribly as he crawled among them. He had no inducements to delay, for he thought he could hear behind him the movement of the Turkish working party, and was in terror that a flare might reveal him and a volley accompany his retreat.

From one shell-hole to another he wormed his way, till he struck an old ruinous communication trench which led in the right direction. The Turks must have been forced back in the past week, and the Russians were now in the evacuated trenches. The thing was half full of water, but it gave Peter a feeling of safety, for it enabled him to get his head below the level of the ground. Then it came to an end and he found before him a forest of wire.

The Turk in his signal had mentioned half an hour, but Peter thought it was nearer two hours before he got through that noxious entanglement. Shelling had made little difference to it. The uprights were all there, and the barbed strands seemed to touch the ground. Remember, he had no wire-cutter; nothing but his bare hands. Once again fear got hold of him. He felt caught in a net, with monstrous vultures waiting to pounce on him from above. At any moment a flare might go up and a dozen rifles find their mark. He had altogether forgotten about the message which had been sent, for no message could dissuade the ever-present death he felt around him. It was, he said, like following an old lion into bush when there was but one narrow way in, and no road out.

The guns began again—the Turkish guns from behind the

ridge—and a shell tore up the wire a short way before him. Under cover of the burst he made good a few yards, leaving large portions of his clothing in the strands. Then, quite suddenly, when hope had almost died in his heart, he felt the ground rise steeply. He lay very still, a star-rocket from the Turkish side lit up the place, and there in front was a rampart with the points of bayonets showing beyond it. It was the Russian hour for stand-to.

He raised his cramped limbs from the ground and shouted "Friend! English!"

A face looked down at him, and then the darkness again descended.

"Friend," he said hoarsely. "English."

He heard speech behind the parapet. An electric torch was flashed on him for a second. A voice spoke, a friendly voice, and the sound of it seemed to be telling him to come over.

He was now standing up, and as he got his hands on the parapet he seemed to feel bayonets very near him. But the voice that spoke was kindly, so with a heave he scrambled over and flopped into the trench. Once more the electric torch was flashed, and revealed to the eyes of the onlookers an indescribably dirty, lean, middle-aged man with a bloody head, and scarcely a rag of shirt on his back. The said man, seeing friendly faces around him, grinned cheerfully.

"That was a rough trek, friends," he said; "I want to see your general pretty quick, for I've got a present for him."

He was taken to an officer in a dug-out, who addressed him in French, which he did not understand. But the sight of Stumm's plan worked wonders. After that he was fairly bundled down communication trenches and then over swampy fields to a farm among trees. There he found staff-officers, who looked at him and looked at his map, and then put him on a horse and hurried him eastwards. At last he came to a big ruined house, and was taken into a room which seemed to be full of maps and generals.

The conclusion must be told in Peter's words.

"There was a big man sitting at a table drinking coffee, and when I saw him my heart jumped out of my skin. For it was the man I hunted with on the Pungwe in '98—him whom the Kaffirs called 'Buck's Horn,' because of his long curled moustaches. He was a prince even then, and now he is a very great general. When I saw him, I ran forward and gripped his hand and cried, '*Hoe gat het, Mynheer?*' and he knew me and shouted in Dutch, 'Damn, if it isn't old Peter Pienaar!' Then he gave me coffee and ham and good bread, and he looked at my map.

" 'What is this?' he cried, growing red in the face.

" 'It is the staff map of one Stumm, a German *skellum* who commands in yon city,' I said.

"He looked at it close and read the markings, and then he read the other paper which you gave me, Dick. And then he flung up his arms and laughed. He took a loaf and tossed it into the air so that it fell on the head of another general. He spoke to them in their own tongue, and they, too, laughed, and one or two ran out as if on some errand. I have never seen such merrymaking. They were clever men, and knew the worth of what you gave me.

"Then he got to his feet and hugged me, all dirty as I was, and kissed me on both cheeks.

" 'Before God, Peter,' he said, 'you're the mightiest hunter since Nimrod. You've often found me game, but never game so big as this!' "

The Little Hill

IT WAS a wise man who said that the biggest kind of courage was to be able to sit still. I used to feel that when we were getting shelled in the reserve trenches outside Vermelles. I felt it before we went over the parapets at Loos, but I never felt it so much as on the last two days in that cellar. I had simply to set my teeth and take a pull on myself. Peter had gone on a crazy errand which I scarcely believed could come off. There were no signs of Sandy; somewhere within a hundred yards he was fighting his own battles, and I was tormented by the thought that he might get jumpy again and wreck everything. A strange Companion brought us food, a man who spoke only Turkish and could tell us nothing; Hussin, I judged, was busy about the horses. If I could only have done something to help on matters I could have scotched my anxiety, but there was nothing to be done, nothing but wait and brood. I tell you I began to sympathize with the general behind the lines in a battle, the fellow who makes the plan which others execute. Leading a charge can be nothing like so nerve-shaking a business as sitting in an easy-chair and waiting on the news of it.

It was bitter cold, and we spent most of the day wrapped in our greatcoats and buried deep in the straw. Blenkiron was a marvel. There was no light for him to play Patience by, but he never complained. He slept a lot of the time, and when he was awake talked as cheerily as if he were starting out on a holiday. He had one great comfort, his dyspepsia was gone. He sang hymns constantly to the benign Providence that had squared his duodenum.

My only occupation was to listen for the guns. The first day after Peter left they were very quiet on the front nearest us, but in the late evening they started a terrific racket. The next day they never stopped from dawn to dusk, so that it reminded me of that tremendous forty-eight hours before Loos. I tried to read into this some proof that Peter had got through, but it would not work. It looked more like the opposite, for this desperate hammering must mean that the frontal assault was still the Russian game.

Two or three times I climbed on the housetop for fresh air. The day was foggy and damp, and I could see very little of the countryside. Transport was still bumping southward along the road to the Palantuken, and the slow wagon-loads of wounded returning. One thing I noticed, however. There was a perpetual coming and going between the house and the city. Motors and mounted messengers were constantly arriving and departing, and I concluded that Hilda von Einem was getting ready for her part in the defence of Erzerum.

These ascents were all on the first day after Peter's going. The second day, when I tried the trap, I found it closed and heavily weighted. This must have been done by our friends, and very right, too. If the house were becoming a place of public resort, it would never do for me to be journeying roofward.

Late on the second night Hussin reappeared. It was after supper, when Blenkiron had gone peacefully to sleep and I was beginning to count the hours till the morning. I could not close an eye during these days and not much at night.

Hussin did not light a lantern. I heard his key in the lock, and then his light step close to where we lay

"Are you asleep?" he said, and when I answered he sat down beside me.

"The horses are found," he said, "and the Master bids me tell you that we start in the morning three hours before dawn."

It was welcome news. "Tell me what is happening," I begged; "we have been lying in this tomb for three days and heard nothing."

"The guns are busy," he said. "The Allemans come to this place every hour, I know not for what. Also there has been a great search for you. The searchers have been here, but they were sent away empty . . . Sleep, my lord, for there is wild work before us."

I did not sleep much, for I was strung too high with expectation, and I envied Blenkiron his now eupeptic slumbers. But for an hour or so I dropped off, and my old nightmare came back. Once again I was in the throat of a pass, hotly pursued, straining for some sanctuary which I knew I must reach. But I was no longer alone. Others were with me: how many I could not tell, for when I tried to see their faces they dissolved in mist. Deep snow was underfoot, a grey sky was over us, black peaks were on all sides, but ahead in the mist of the pass was that curious *castrol* which I had first seen in my dream on the Erzerum road.

I saw it distinct in every detail. It rose to the left of the road through the pass, above a hollow where great boulders stood out in the snow. Its sides were steep, so that the snow had slipped off in patches, leaving stretches of glistening black shale. The *kranz* at the top did not rise sheer, but sloped at an angle of forty-five, and on the very summit there seemed a hollow, as if the earth within the rock-rim had been beaten by weather into a cup.

That is often the way with a South African *castrol*, and I knew it was so with this. We were straining for it, but the snow clogged us, and our enemies were very close behind.

Then I was awakened by a figure at my side. "Get ready, my lord," it said; "it is the hour to ride."

LIKE sleep-walkers we moved into the sharp air. Hussin led us out of an old postern and then through a place like an orchard to the shelter of some tall evergreen trees. There horses stood, champing quietly from their nosebags. "Good," I thought; "a feed of oats before a big effort."

There were nine beasts for nine riders. We mounted without a word and filed through a grove of trees to where a broken paling marked the beginning of cultivated land. There for the matter of twenty minutes Hussin chose to guide us through deep, clogging snow. He wanted to avoid any sound till we were well beyond earshot of the house. Then we struck a by-path which presently merged in a hard highway, running, as I judged, south-west by west. There we delayed no longer, but galloped furiously into the dark.

I had got back all my exhilaration. Indeed I was intoxicated with the movement, and could have laughed out loud and sung. Under the black canopy of the night perils are either forgotten or terribly alive. Mine were forgotten. The darkness I galloped into led me to freedom and friends. Yes, and success, which I had not dared to hope and scarcely even to dream of.

Hussin rode first, with me at his side. I turned my head and saw Blenkiron behind me, evidently mortally unhappy about the pace we set and the mount he sat. He used to say that horse-exercise was good for his liver, but it was a gentle amble and a short gallop that he liked, and not this mad helter-skelter. His thighs were too round to fit a saddle leather. We passed a fire in a hollow, the bivouac of some Turkish unit, and all the horses shied violently. I knew by Blenkiron's oaths that he had lost his stirrups and was sitting on his horse's neck.

Beside him rode a tall figure swathed to the eyes in wrappings, and wearing round his neck some kind of shawl whose ends floated behind him. Sandy, of course, had no European ulster, for it was months since he had worn proper clothes. I wanted to speak to him, but somehow I did not dare. His stillness forbade me. He was a wonderful fine horseman, with his firm English hunting seat, and it was as well, for he paid no attention to his beast. His head was still full of unquiet thoughts.

Then the air around me began to smell acrid and raw, and I saw that a fog was winding up from the hollows.

"Here's the devil's own luck," I cried to Hussin. "Can you guide us in a mist?"

"I do not know." He shook his head. "I had counted on seeing the shape of the hills."

"We've a map and compass, anyhow. But these make slow travelling. Pray God it lifts!"

Presently the black vapour changed to grey, and the day broke. It was little comfort. The fog rolled in waves to the horses' ears, and riding at the head of the party I could but dimly see the next rank.

"It is time to leave the road," said Hussin, "or we may meet inquisitive folk."

We struck to the left, over ground which was for all the world like a Scotch moor. There were pools of rain on it, and masses of tangled snow-laden junipers, and long reefs of wet slaty stone. It was bad going, and the fog made it hopeless to steer a good course. I had out the map and the compass, and tried to fix our route so as to round the flank of a spur of the mountains which separated us from the valley we were aiming at.

"There's a stream ahead of us," I said to Hussin. "Is it fordable?"

"It is only a trickle," he said, coughing. "This accursed mist is from Eblis." But I knew long before we reached it that it was no trickle. It was a hill stream coming down in spate, and, as I soon guessed, in a deep ravine. Presently we were at its edge, one long whirl of yeasty falls and brown rapids. We could as soon get horses over it as to the topmost cliffs of the Palantuken.

Hussin stared at it in consternation. "May Allah forgive my folly, for I should have known. We must return to the highway and find a bridge. My sorrow, that I should have led my lords so ill."

Back over that moor we went with my spirits badly damped. We had none too long a start, and Hilda von Einem would rouse heaven and earth to catch us up. Hussin was forcing the pace, for his anxiety was as great as mine.

Before we reached the road the mist blew back and revealed a wedge of country right across to the hills beyond the river. It was a clear view, every object standing out wet and sharp in the light of morning. It showed the bridge with horsemen drawn up across it, and it showed, too, cavalry pickets moving along the road.

They saw us at the same instant. A word was passed down the road, a shrill whistle blew, and the pickets put their horses at the bank and started across the moor.

"Did I not say this mist was from Eblis?" growled Hussin, as we swung round and galloped back on our tracks. "These cursed Zaptiehs have seen us, and our road is cut."

I was for trying the stream at all costs, but Hussin pointed out that it would do us no good. The cavalry beyond the bridge was moving up the other bank. "There is a path through the hills that I know, but it must be travelled on foot. If we can increase our lead and the mist cloaks us, there is yet a chance."

It was a weary business plodding up to the skirts of the hills. We had the pursuit behind us now, and that put an edge on every difficulty. There were long banks of broken screes, I remember, where the snow slipped in wreaths from under our feet. Great boulders had to be circumvented, and patches of bog, where the streams from the snows first made contact with the plains, mired us to our girths. Happily the mist was down again, but this, though it hindered the chase, lessened the chances of Hussin finding the path.

He found it nevertheless. There was the gully and the rough mule-track leading upwards. But there also had been a land-slip, quite recent from the marks. A large scar of raw earth had broken across the hillside, which with the snow above it looked like a slice cut out of an iced chocolate-cake.

We stared blankly for a second, till we recognized its hopelessness.

"I'm trying for the crags," I said. "Where there once was a way another can be found."

"And be picked off at their leisure by these marksmen," said Hussin grimly. "Look!"

The mist had opened again, and a glance behind showed me

the pursuit closing up on us. They were now less than three hundred yards off. We turned our horses and made off eastward along the skirts of the cliffs.

Then Sandy spoke for the first time. "I don't know how you fellows feel, but I'm not going to be taken. There's nothing much to do except to find a good place and put up a fight. We can sell our lives dearly."

"That's about all," said Blenkiron cheerfully. He had suffered such tortures on that gallop that he welcomed any kind of stationary fight.

"Serve out the arms," said Sandy.

The Companions all carried rifles slung across their shoulders. Hussin, from a deep saddle-bag, brought out rifles and bandoliers for the rest of us. As I laid mine across my saddle-bow I saw it was a German Mauser of the latest pattern.

"It's hell-for-leather till we find a place for a stand," said Sandy. "The game's against us this time."

Once more we entered the mist, and presently found better going on a long stretch of even slope. Then came a rise, and on the crest of it I saw the sun. Presently we dipped into bright daylight and looked down on a broad glen, with a road winding up it to a pass in the range. I had expected this. It was one way to the Palantuken pass, some miles south of the house where we had been lodged.

And then, as I looked southward, I saw what I had been watching for for days. A little hill split the valley, and on its top was a *kranz* of rocks. It was the *castrol* of my persistent dream.

On that I promptly took charge. "There's our fort," I cried. "If we once get there we can hold it for a week. Sit down and ride for it."

We bucketed down that hillside like men possessed, even Blenkiron sticking on manfully among the twists and turns and slithers. Presently we were on the road and were racing past marching infantry and gun teams and empty wagons. I noted that most seemed to be moving downward and few going up. Hussin screamed some words in Turkish that secured us a passage, but indeed our crazy speed left them staring. Out of a corner of my eye I saw that Sandy had flung off most of his wrappings and seemed to be all a dazzle of rich colour. But I had thought for nothing except the little hill, now almost fronting us across the shallow glen.

No horses could breast that steep. We urged them into the hollow, and then hastily dismounted, humped the packs, and began to struggle up the side of the *castrol*. It was strewn with great boulders, which gave a kind of cover that very soon was needed. For, snatching a glance back, I saw that our pursuers were on the road above us and were getting ready to shoot.

At normal times we would have been easy marks, but, fortunately, wisps and streamers of mist now clung about that hollow. The rest could fend for themselves, so I stuck to Blenkiron and dragged him, wholly breathless, by the least exposed route. Bullets spattered now and then against the rocks, and one sang unpleasantly near my head. In this way we covered three-fourths of the distance, and had only the bare dozen yards where the gradient eased off up to the edge of the *kranz*.

Blenkiron got hit in the leg, our only casualty. There was nothing for it but to carry him, so I swung him on my shoulders, and with a bursting heart did that last lap. It was hottish work, and the bullets were pretty thick about us, but we all got safely to the *kranz* and a short scramble took us over the edge. I laid Blenkiron inside the *castrol* and started to prepare our defence.

We had little time to do it. Out of the thin fog figures were coming, crouching in cover. The place we were in was a natural redoubt, except that there were no loopholes or sandbags. We had to show our heads over the rim to shoot, but the danger was lessened by the superb field of fire given by those last dozen yards of glacis. I posted the men and waited, and Blenkiron, with a white face, insisted on taking his share, announcing that he used to be handy with a gun.

I gave the order that no man was to shoot till the enemy had come out of the rocks on to the glacis. The thing ran right round the top, and we had to watch all sides to prevent them getting us in flank or rear. Hussin's rifle cracked out presently from the back, so my precautions had not been needless.

We were all three fair shots, though none of us up to Peter's miraculous standard, and the Companions, too, made good practice. The Mauser was the weapon I knew best, and I didn't miss much. The attackers never had a chance, for their only hope was to rush us by numbers, and, the whole party being not above two dozen, they were far too few. I think we killed three, for their bodies were left lying, and wounded at least six, while the rest fell back towards the road. In a quarter of an hour it was all over.

"They are dogs of Kurds," I heard Hussin say fiercely. "Only a Kurdish *ghiaour* would fire on the livery of the Kaába."

Then I had a good look at Sandy. He had discarded shawls and wrappings, and stood up in the strangest costume man ever wore in battle. Somehow he had procured field-boots and an old pair of riding-breeches. Above these, reaching well below his middle, he had a wonderful silken jibbah or ephod of a bright emerald. I call it silk, but it was like no silk I have ever known, so exquisite in the mesh, with such a sheen and depth in it. Some strange pattern was woven on the breast, which in the dim light I could not trace. I'll warrant no rarer or costlier garment was ever exposed to lead on a bleak winter hill.

Sandy seemed unconscious of his garb. His eye, listless no more, scanned the hollow. "That's only the overture," he cried. "The opera will soon begin. We must put a breastwork up in these gaps or they'll pick us off from a thousand yards."

I had meantime roughly dressed Blenkiron's wound with a linen rag which Hussin provided. It was from a ricochet bullet which had chipped into his left shin. Then I took a hand with the others in getting up earthworks to complete the circuit of the defence. It was no easy job, for we wrought only with our knives and had to dig deep down below the snowy gravel. As we worked I took stock of our refuge.

The *castrol* was a rough circle about ten yards in diameter, its interior filled with boulders and loose stones, and its parapet about four feet high. The mist had cleared for a considerable space, and I could see the immediate surroundings. West, beyond the hollow, was the road we had come, where now the remnants of the pursuit were clustered. North, the hill fell steeply to the valley bottom, but to the south, after a dip there was a ridge which shut the view. East lay another fork of the stream, the chief fork I guessed, and it was evidently followed by the main road to the pass, for I saw it crowded with transport. The two roads seemed to converge somewhere farther south of my sight.

I guessed we could not be very far from the front, for the noise of guns sounded very near, both the sharp crack of the field-pieces, and the deeper boom of the howitzers. More, I could hear the chatter of the machine-guns, a magpie note among the baying of hounds. I even saw the bursting of Russian shells, evidently trying to reach the main road. One big fellow—an eight-inch—landed not ten yards from a convoy to the east of us, and another in the hollow through which we had come. These were clearly ranging shots, and I wondered if the Russians had observation-posts on the heights to mark them. If so, they might soon try a curtain, and we should be very near its edge. It would be an odd irony if we were the target of friendly shells.

"By the Lord Harry," I heard Sandy say, "if we had a brace of machine-guns we could hold this place against a division."

"What price shells?" I asked. "If they get a gun up they can blow us to atoms in ten minutes."

"Please God the Russians keep them too busy for that," was his answer.

With anxious eyes I watched our enemies on the road. They seemed to have grown in numbers. They were signalling, too, for a white flag fluttered. Then the mist rolled down on us again, and our prospect was limited to ten yards of vapour.

"Steady," I cried; "they may try to rush us at any moment. Every man keep his eye on the edge of the fog, and shoot at the first sign."

For nearly half an hour by my watch we waited in that queer white world, our eyes smarting with the strain of peering. The sound of the guns seemed to be hushed, and everything grown deathly quiet. Blenkiron's squeal, as he knocked his wounded leg against a rock, made every man start.

THEN out of the mist there came a voice.

It was a woman's voice, high, penetrating, and sweet, but it spoke in no tongue I knew. Only Sandy understood. He made a sudden movement as if to defend himself against a blow.

The speaker came into clear sight on the glacis a yard or two away. Mine was the first face she saw.

"I come to offer terms," she said in English. "Will you permit me to enter?"

I could do nothing except take off my cap and say, "Yes, ma'am." Blenkiron, snuggled up against the parapet, was cursing furiously below his breath.

She climbed up the *kranz* and stepped over the edge as lightly as a deer. Her clothes were strange—spurred boots and breeches over which fell a short green kirtle. A little cap skewered with a jewelled pin was on her head, and a cape of some coarse country cloth hung from her shoulders. She had rough gauntlets on her hands, and she carried for weapon a riding-whip. The fog-crystals clung to her hair, I remember, and a silvery film of fog lay on her garments.

I had never before thought of her as beautiful. Strange, uncanny, wonderful, if you like, but the word beauty had too kindly and human a sound for such a face. But as she stood with heightened colour, her eyes like stars, her poise like a wild bird's, I had to confess that she had her own loveliness. She might be a devil, but she was also a queen. I considered that there might be merits in the prospect of riding by her side into Jerusalem.

Sandy stood rigid, his face very grave and set. She held out both hands to him, speaking softly in Turkish. I noticed that the six Companions had disappeared from the *castrol* and were somewhere out of sight on the farther side.

I do not know what she said, but from her tone, and above all from her eyes, I judged that she was pleading—pleading for his return, for his partnership in her great adventure; pleading, for all I knew, for his love.

His expression was like a death-mask, his brows drawn tight in a little frown and his jaw rigid.

"Madam," he said, "I ask you to tell your business quick and to tell it in English. My friends must hear it as well as me."

"Your friends!" she cried. "What has a prince to do with these hirelings? Your slaves, perhaps, but not your friends."

"My friends," Sandy repeated grimly. "You must know, Madam, that I am a British officer."

That was beyond doubt a clean staggering stroke. What she had thought of his origin God knows, but she had never dreamed of this. Her eyes grew larger and more lustrous, her lips parted as if to speak, but her voice failed her. Then by an effort she recovered herself, and out of that strange face went all the glow of youth and ardour. It was again the unholy mask I had first known.

"And these others?" she asked in a level voice.

"One is a brother officer of my regiment. The other is an American friend. But all three of us are on the same errand. We came east to destroy Greenmantle and your devilish ambitions. You have yourself destroyed your prophets, and now it is your turn to fail and disappear. Make no mistake, Madam; that folly is over. I will tear this sacred garment into a thousand pieces and scatter them on the wind. The people wait to-day for the revelation, but none will come. You may kill us if you can, but we have at least crushed a lie and done service to our country."

I would not have taken my eyes from her face for a king's ransom. I have written that she was a queen, and of that there is no manner of doubt. She had the soul of a conqueror, for not a flicker of weakness or disappointment marred her air. Only pride and the stateliest resolution looked out of her eyes.

"I said I came to offer terms. I will still offer them, though they are other than I thought. For the fat American, I will send him home safely to his own country. I do not make war on such as he. He is Germany's foe, not mine. You," she said, turning fiercely on me, "I will hang before dusk."

Never in my life had I been so pleased. I had got my revenge at last. This woman had singled me out above the others as the object of her wrath, and I almost loved her for it.

She turned to Sandy, and the fierceness went out of her face.

"You seek the truth," she said. "So also do I, and if we use a lie it is only to break down a greater. You are of my household in spirit, and you alone of all men I have seen are fit to ride with me on my mission. Germany may fail, but I shall not fail. I offer you the greatest career that mortal has known. I offer you a task which will need every atom of brain and sinew and courage. Will you refuse this destiny?"

I do not know what effect this vapouring might have had in hot scented rooms, or in the languor of some rich garden; but up on that cold hill-top it was as unsubstantial as the mist around us. It sounded not even impressive, only crazy.

"I stay with my friends," said Sandy.

"Then I will offer more. I will save your friends. They, too, shall share in my triumph."

This was too much for Blenkiron. He scrambled to his feet to speak the protest that had been wrung from his soul, forgot his game leg, and rolled back on the ground with a groan.

Then she seemed to make a last appeal. She spoke in Turkish now, and I do not know what she said, but I judged it was the plea of a woman to her lover. Once more she was the proud beauty, but there was a tremor in her pride—I had almost written tenderness. To listen to her was like horrid treachery, like eavesdropping on something pitiful. I know my cheeks grew scarlet and Blenkiron turned away his head.

Sandy's face did not move. He spoke in English.

"You can offer me nothing that I desire," he said. "I am the servant of my country, and her enemies are mine. I can have neither part nor lot with you. That is my answer, Madam von Einem."

Then her steely restraint broke. It was like a dam giving before a pent-up mass of icy water. She tore off one of her gauntlets and hurled it in his face. Implacable hate looked out of her eyes.

"I have done with you," she cried. "You have scorned me, but you have dug your own grave."

She leaped on the parapet and the next second was on the glacis. Once more the mist had fled, and across the hollow I saw a field-gun in place and men around it who were not Turkish. She waved her hand to them, and hastened down the hillside.

But at that moment I heard the whistle of a long-range Russian shell. Among the boulders there was the dull shock of an explosion and a mushroom of red earth. It all passed in an instant of time: I saw the gunners on the road point their hands and I heard them cry; I heard, too, a kind of sob from Blenkiron—all this before I realized myself what had happened. The next thing I saw was Sandy, already beyond the glacis, leaping with great bounds down the hill. They were shooting at him, but he heeded them not. For the space of a minute he was out of sight, and his whereabouts was shown only by the patter of bullets.

Then he came back—walking quite slowly up the last slope, and he was carrying something in his arms. The enemy fired no more; they realized what had happened.

He laid his burden down gently in a corner of the *castrol*. The cap had fallen off, and the hair was breaking loose. The face was very white but there was no wound or bruise on it.

"She was killed at once," I heard him saying. "Her back was broken by a shell-fragment. Dick, we must bury her here . . . You see, she . . . she liked me. I can make her no return but this."

We set the Companions to guard, and with infinite slowness, using our hands and our knives, we made a shallow grave below the eastern parapet. When it was done we covered her face with the linen cloak which Sandy had worn that morning. He lifted the body and laid it reverently in its place.

"I did not know that anything could be so light," he said.

It wasn't for me to look on at that kind of scene. I went to the parapet with Blenkiron's field-glasses and had a stare at our friends on the road. There was no Turk there, and I guessed why, for it would not be easy to use the men of Islam against the wearer of the green ephod. The enemy were German or Austrian, and they had a field-gun. They seemed to have got it laid on our fort; but they were waiting. As I looked I saw behind them a massive figure I seemed to recognize. Stumm had come to see the destruction of his enemies.

To the east I saw another gun in the fields just below the main road. They had got us on both sides, and there was no way of escape. Hilda von Einem was to have a noble pyre and goodly company for the dark journey.

Dusk was falling now, a clear bright dusk where the stars pricked through a sheen of amethyst. The artillery were busy all around the horizon, and towards the pass on the other road, where Fort Palantuken stood, there was the dust and smoke of a furious bombardment. It seemed to me, too, that the guns on the other fronts had come nearer. Deve Boyun was hidden by a spur of hill, but up in the north, white clouds, like the streamers of evening, were hanging over the Euphrates glen. The whole firmament hummed and twanged like a taut string that has been struck . . .

As I looked, the gun to the west fired—the gun where Stumm was. The shell dropped ten yards to our right. A second later another fell behind us.

Blenkiron had dragged himself to the parapet. I don't suppose he had ever been shelled before, but his face showed curiosity rather than fear.

"Pretty poor shooting, I reckon," he said.

"On the contrary," I said, "they know their business. They're bracketing . . ."

The words were not out of my mouth when one fell right among us. It struck the far rim of the *castrol*, shattering the rock, but bursting mainly outside. We all ducked, and barring some small scratches no one was a penny the worse. I remember that much of the debris fell on Hilda von Einem's grave.

I pulled Blenkiron over the far parapet, and called on the rest to follow, meaning to take cover on the rough side of the hill. But as we showed ourselves shots rang out from our front, shots fired from a range of a few hundred yards. It was easy to see what had happened. Riflemen had been sent to hold us in rear. They would not assault so long as we remained in the *castrol*, but they would block any attempt to find safety outside it. Stumm and his gun had us at their mercy.

We crouched below the parapet again. "We may as well toss for it," I said. "There's only two ways—to stay here and be shelled or try to break through those fellows behind. Either's pretty unhealthy."

But I knew there was no choice. With Blenkiron crippled we were pinned to the *castrol*. Our numbers were up all right.

CHAPTER 22

The Guns of the North

But no more shells fell.

The night grew dark and showed a field of glittering stars, for the air was sharpening again towards frost. We waited for an hour, crouching just behind the far parapets, but never came that ominous familiar whistle.

Then Sandy rose and stretched himself. "I'm hungry," he said. "Let's have out the food, Hussin. We've eaten nothing since before daybreak. I wonder what is the meaning of this respite?"

I fancied I knew.

"It's Stumm's way," I said. "He wants to torture us. He'll keep us hours on tenterhooks, while he sits over yonder exulting in what he thinks we're enduring. He has just enough imagination for that . . . He would rush us if he had the men. As it is, he's going to blow us to pieces, but do it slowly and smack his lips over it."

Sandy yawned. "We'll disappoint him, for we won't be worried, old man. We three are beyond that kind of fear."

"Meanwhile we're going to do the best we can," I said. "He's got the exact range for his whizz-bangs. We've got to find a hole somewhere just outside the *castrol*, and some sort of head-cover. We're bound to get damaged whatever happens, but we'll stick it out to the end. When they think they have finished with us and rush the place, there may be one of us alive to put a bullet through old Stumm. What do you say?"

They agreed, and after our meal Sandy and I crawled out to prospect, leaving the others on guard in case there should be an attack. We found a hollow in the glacis a little south of the *castrol*, and, working very quietly, managed to enlarge it and cut a kind of shallow cave in the hill. It would be no use against a direct hit, but it would give some cover from flying fragments. As I read the situation, Stumm could land as many shells as he pleased in the *castrol* and wouldn't bother to attend to the flanks. When the bad shelling began there would be shelter for one or two in the cave.

Our enemies were watchful. The riflemen on the east burnt Very flares at intervals, and Stumm's lot sent up a great star-rocket. I remember that just before midnight hell broke loose round Fort Palantuken. No more Russian shells came into our hollow, but all the road to the east was under fire, and at the Fort itself there was a shattering explosion and a queer scarlet glow which looked as if a magazine had been hit. For about two hours the firing was intense, and then it died down. But it was towards the north that I kept turning my head. There seemed to be something different in the sound there, something sharper in the report of the guns, as if shells were dropping in a narrow valley whose rock walls doubled the echo. Had the Russians by any blessed chance worked round that flank?

I got Sandy to listen, but he shook his head. "Those guns are a dozen miles off," he said. "They're no nearer than three days ago. But it looks as if the sportsmen on the south might have a chance. When they break through and stream down the valley, they'll be puzzled to account for what remains of us . . . We're no longer three adventurers in the enemy's country. We're the advance guard of the Allies. Our pals don't know about us, and we're going to be cut off, which has happened to advance guards before now. But all the same, we're in our own battle-line again. Doesn't that cheer you, Dick?"

It cheered me wonderfully, for I knew now what had been the

weight on my heart ever since I accepted Sir Walter's mission. It was the loneliness of it. I was fighting far away from my friends, far away from the true fronts of battle. It was a side-show which, whatever its importance, had none of the exhilaration of the main effort. But now we had come back to familiar ground. We were like the Highlanders cut off at Cité St. Auguste on the first day of Loos, or those Scots Guards at Festubert of whom I had heard. Only, the others did not know of it, would never hear of it. If Peter succeeded he might tell the tale, but most likely he was lying dead somewhere in the no-man's-land between the lines. We should never be heard of again any more, but our work remained. Sir Walter would know that, and he would tell our few belongings that we had gone out in our country's service.

We were in the *castrol* again, sitting under the parapets. The same thoughts must have been in Sandy's mind, for he suddenly laughed.

"It's a queer ending, Dick. We simply vanish into the infinite. If the Russians get through they will never recognize what is left of us among so much of the wreckage of battle. The snow will soon cover us, and when the spring comes there will only be a few bleached bones. Upon my soul it is the kind of death I always wanted." And he quoted softly to himself a verse of an old Scots ballad:

> *"Mony's the ane for him maks mane,*
> *But nane sall ken whar he is gane.*
> *Ower his white banes, when they are bare,*
> *The wind sall blaw for evermair."*

"But our work lives," I cried, with a sudden great gasp of happiness. "It's the job that matters, not the men that do it. And our job's done. We have won, old chap—won hands down—and there is no going back on that. We have won anyway; and if Peter has had a slice of luck, we've scooped the pool . . . After all, we never expected to come out of this thing with our lives."

Blenkiron, with his leg stuck out stiffly before him, was humming quietly to himself, as he often did when he felt cheerful. He had only one song, "John Brown's Body"; usually only a line at a time, but now he got as far as the whole verse:

> *"He captured Harper's Ferry, with his nineteen men so true,*
> *And he frightened old Virginny till she trembled through*
> *and through.*
> *They hung him for a traitor, themselves the traitor crew,*
> *But his soul goes marching along."*

"Feeling good?" I asked.

"Fine. I'm about the luckiest man on God's earth, Major. I've always wanted to get into a big show, but I didn't see how it would come the way of a homely citizen like me, living in a steam-warmed house and going down town to my office every morning. I used to envy my old dad that fought at Chattanooga, and never forgot to tell you about it. But I guess Chattanooga was like a scrap in a Bowery bar compared to this. When I meet the old man in Glory he'll have to listen some to me . . ."

It was just after Blenkiron spoke that we got a reminder of Stumm's presence. The gun was well laid, for a shell plumped on the near edge of the *castrol*. It made an end of one of the Companions who was on guard there, badly wounded another, and a fragment gashed my thigh. We took refuge in the shallow cave, but some wild shooting from the east side brought us back to the parapets, for we feared an attack. None came, nor any more shells, and once again the night was quiet.

I asked Blenkiron if he had any near relatives.

"Why, no, except a sister's son, a college-boy who has no need of his uncle. It's fortunate that we three have no wives. I haven't any regrets, neither, for I've had a mighty deal out of life. I was thinking this morning that it was a pity I was going out when I had just got my duodenum to listen to reason. But I reckon that's another of my mercies. The good God took away the pain in my stomach so that I might go to Him with a clear head and a thankful heart."

"We're lucky fellows," said Sandy; "we've all had our whack. When I remember the good times I've had I could sing a hymn of praise. We've lived long enough to know ourselves, and to shape ourselves into some kind of decency. But think of those boys who have given their lives freely when they scarcely knew what life meant. They were just at the beginning of the road, and they didn't know what dreary bits lay before them. It was all sunshiny and bright-coloured, and yet they gave it up without a moment's doubt. And think of the men with wives and children and homes that were the biggest things in life to them. For fellows like us to shirk would be black cowardice. It's small credit for us to stick it out. But when those others shut their teeth and went forward, they were blessed heroes . . ."

After that we fell silent. A man's thoughts at a time like that seem to be double-powered, and the memory becomes very sharp and clear. I don't know what was in the others' minds, but I know what filled my own . . .

I fancy it isn't the men who get most out of the world and are always buoyant and cheerful that most fear to die. Rather it is the weak-engined souls who go about with dull eyes, that cling most fiercely to life. They have not the joy of being alive which is a kind of earnest of immortality . . . I know that my thoughts were chiefly about the jolly things that I had seen and done; not regret, but gratitude. The panorama of blue moons on the veld unrolled itself before me, and hunter's nights in the bush, the taste of food and sleep, the bitter stimulus of dawn, the joy of wild adventure, the voices of old staunch friends. Hitherto the war had seemed to make a break with all that had gone before, but now the war was only part of the picture. I thought of my battalion, and the good fellows there, many of whom had fallen on the Loos parapets. I had never looked to come out of that myself. But I had been spared, and given the chance of a greater business, and I had succeeded. That was the tremendous fact, and my mood was humble gratitude to God and exultant pride. Death was a small price to pay for it. As Blenkiron would have said, I had got good value in the deal.

The night was getting bitter cold, as happens before dawn. It was frost again, and the sharpness of it woke our hunger. I got out the remnants of the food and wine and we had a last meal. I remember we pledged each other as we drank.

"We have eaten our Passover Feast," said Sandy. "When do you look for the end?"

"After dawn," I said. "Stumm wants daylight to get the full savour of his revenge."

SLOWLY the sky passed from ebony to grey, and black shapes of hill outlined themselves against it. A wind blew down the valley, bringing the acrid smell of burning, but something too of the freshness of morn. It stirred strange thoughts in me, and woke the old morning vigour of the blood which was never to be mine again. For the first time in that long vigil I was torn with a sudden regret.

"We must get into the cave before it is full light," I said. "We had better draw lots for the two to go."

The choice fell on one of the Companions and Blenkiron.

"You can count me out," said the latter. "If it's your wish to find a man to be alive when our friends come up to count their spoil, I guess I'm the worst of the lot. I'd prefer, if you don't mind, to stay here. I've made my peace with my Maker, and I'd like to wait quietly on His call. I'll play a game of Patience to pass the time."

He would take no denial, so we drew again, and the lot fell to Sandy.

"If I'm the last to go," he said, "I promise I don't miss. Stumm won't be long in following me."

He shook hands with his cheery smile, and he and the Companion slipped over the parapet in the final shadows before dawn.

BLENKIRON spread his Patience cards on a flat rock, and dealt out the Double Napoleon. He was perfectly calm, and hummed to himself his only tune. For myself I was drinking in my last draught of the hill air. My contentment was going. I suddenly felt bitterly loath to die.

Something of the same kind must have passed through Blenkiron's head. He suddenly looked up and asked, "Sister Anne, Sister Anne, do you see anybody coming?"

I stood close to the parapet, watching every detail of the landscape as shown by the revealing daybreak. Up on the shoulders of the Palantuken snowdrifts lipped over the edges of the cliffs. I wondered when they would come down as avalanches. There was a kind of croft on one hillside, and from a hut the smoke of breakfast was beginning to curl. Stumm's gunners were awake and apparently holding council. Far down on the main road a convoy was moving—I heard the creak of the wheels two miles away, for the air was deathly still.

Then, as if a spring had been loosed, the world suddenly leaped to a hideous life. With a growl the guns opened round all the horizon. They were especially fierce to the south, where a *rafale* beat as I had never heard it before. The one glance I cast behind me showed the gap in the hills choked with fumes and dust.

But my eyes were on the north. From Erzerum city tall tongues of flame leaped from a dozen quarters. Beyond, towards the opening of the Euphrates glen, there was the sharp crack of field-guns. I strained eyes and ears, mad with impatience, and I read the riddle.

"Sandy," I yelled, "Peter has got through. The Russians are round the flank. The town is burning. Glory to God, we've won, we've won!"

And as I spoke the earth seemed to split beside me, and I was flung forward on the gravel which covered Hilda von Einem's grave.

As I PICKED myself up, and to my amazement found myself uninjured, I saw Blenkiron rubbing the dust out of his eyes and arranging a disordered card. He was singing aloud:

> "He captured Harper's Ferry, with his nineteen men so true,
> And he frightened old Virginny . . ."

"Say, Major," he cried, "I believe this game of mine is coming out."

I was now pretty well mad. The thought that old Peter had won, that *we* had won beyond our wildest dreams, that if we died there were those coming who would exact the uttermost vengeance, rode my brain like a fever. I sprang on the parapet and waved my hand to Stumm, shouting defiance. Rifle shots cracked out from behind, and I leaped back just in time for the next shell.

The charge must have been short, for it was a bad miss, landing somewhere on the glacis. The next was better and crashed on the near parapet, carving a great hole in the rocky *kranz*. This time my arm hung limp, broken by a fragment of stone, but I felt no pain. Blenkiron seemed to bear a charmed life, for he was smothered in dust, but unhurt. He blew the dust away from his cards very gingerly and went on playing.

"Sister Anne," he asked, "do you see anybody coming?"

Then came a dud which dropped neatly inside on the soft ground. I was determined to break for the open and chance the rifle fire, for if Stumm went on shooting the *castrol* was certain death. I caught Blenkiron round the middle, scattering his cards to the winds, and jumped over the parapet.

"Don't apologize, Sister Anne," said he. "The game was as good as won. But for God's sake drop me, for if you wave me like the banner of freedom I'll get plugged sure and good."

My one thought was to get cover for the next minutes, for I had an instinct that our vigil was near its end. The defences of Erzerum were crumbling like sand-castles, and it was a proof of the tenseness of my nerves that I seemed to be deaf to the sound. Stumm had seen us cross the parapet, and he started to sprinkle all the surroundings of the *castrol*. Blenkiron and I lay like a working party between the lines caught by machine-guns, taking a pull on ourselves as best we could. Sandy had some kind of cover, but we were on the bare farther slope, and the riflemen on that side might have had us at their mercy.

But no shots came from them. As I looked east, the hillside, which a little before had been held by our enemies, was as empty as the desert. And then I saw on the main road a sight which for a second time made me yell like a maniac. Down that glen came a throng of men and galloping limbers—a crazy, jostling crowd, spreading away beyond the road to the steep slopes, and leaving behind it many black dots to darken the snows. The gates of the South had yielded, and our friends were through them.

At that sight I forgot all about our danger. I didn't give a cent for Stumm's shells. I didn't believe he could hit me. The fate which had mercifully preserved us for the first taste of victory would see us through to the end.

I remember bundling Blenkiron along the hill to find Sandy. But our news was anticipated. For down our own side-glen came the same broken tumult of men. More; for at their backs, far up at the throat of the pass, I saw horsemen—the horsemen of the pursuit. Old Nicholas had flung his cavalry in.

Sandy was on his feet, with his lips set and his eye abstracted. If his face hadn't been burned black by weather it would have been pale as a dish-clout. A man like him doesn't make up his mind for death and then be given his life again without being wrenched out of his bearings. I thought he didn't understand what had happened, so I beat him on the shoulders.

"Man, d'you see?" I cried. "The Cossacks! The Cossacks! God! how they're taking that slope! They're into them now. By Heaven, we'll ride with them! We'll get the gun horses!"

A little knoll prevented Stumm and his men from seeing what was happening farther up the glen, till the first wave of the rout was on them. He had gone on bombarding the *castrol* and its environs while the world was cracking over his head. The gun team was in the hollow below the road, and down the hill among the boulders we crawled, Blenkiron as lame as a duck, and me with a limp left arm.

The poor beasts were straining at their pickets and sniffing the morning wind, which brought down the thick fumes of the great bombardment and the indescribable babbling cries of a beaten army. Before we reached them that maddened horde had swept down on them, men panting and gasping in their flight, many of them bloody from wounds, many tottering in the first stages of collapse and death. I saw the horses seized by a dozen hands, and a desperate fight for their possession. But as we halted there our eyes were fixed on the battery on the road above us, for round it was now sweeping the van of the retreat.

I had never seen a rout before, when strong men come to the end of their tether and only their broken shadows stumble towards the refuge they never find. No more had Stumm, poor devil. I had no ill-will left for him, though coming down that hill I was rather hoping that the two of us might have a final scrap. He was a brute and a bully, but, by God! he was a man. I heard his great roar when he saw the tumult, and the next I saw was his monstrous figure working at the gun. He swung it south and turned it on the fugitives.

But he never fired it. The press was on him, and the gun was swept sideways. He stood up, a foot higher than any of them, and he seemed to be trying to check the rush with his pistol. There is power in numbers, even though every unit is broken and fleeing. For a second to that wild crowd Stumm was the enemy, and they had strength enough to crush him. The wave flowed round and then across him. I saw the butt-ends of rifles crash on his head and shoulders, and the next second the stream had passed over his body.

That was God's judgement on the man who had set himself above his kind.

Sandy gripped my shoulder and was shouting in my ear:

"They're coming, Dick. Look at the grey devils! . . . Oh, God be thanked, it's our friends!"

The next minute we were tumbling down the hillside, Blenkiron hopping on one leg between us. I heard dimly Sandy crying, "Oh, well done our side!" and Blenkiron declaiming about Harper's Ferry, but I had no voice at all and no wish to shout. I know the tears were in my eyes, and that if I had been left alone I would have sat down and cried with pure thankfulness. For sweeping down the glen came a cloud of grey cavalry on little wiry horses, a cloud which stayed not for the rear of the fugitives, but swept on like a flight of rainbows, with the steel of their lance-heads glittering in the winter sun. They were riding for Erzerum.

Remember that for three months we had been with the enemy and had never seen the face of an Ally in arms. We had been cut off from the fellowship of a great cause, like a fort surrounded by an army. And now we were delivered, and there fell around us the warm joy of comradeship as well as the exultation of victory.

We flung caution to the winds, and went stark mad. Sandy, still in his emerald coat and turban, was scrambling up the farther slope of the hollow, yelling greetings in every language known to man. The leader saw him, with a word checked his men for a moment—it was marvellous to see the horses reined in in such a break-neck ride—and from the squadron half a dozen troopers swung loose and wheeled towards us. Then a man in a grey overcoat and a sheepskin cap was on the ground beside us wringing our hands.

"You are safe, my old friends"—it was Peter's voice that spoke—"I will take you back to our army, and get you breakfast."

"No, by the Lord, you won't," cried Sandy. "We've had the rough end of the job and now we'll have the fun. Look after Blenkiron and these fellows of mine. I'm going to ride knee by knee with your sportsmen for the city."

Peter spoke a word, and two of the Cossacks dismounted. The next I knew I was mixed up in the cloud of greycoats, galloping down the road up which the morning before we had strained to the *castrol*.

That was the great hour of my life, and to live through it was worth a dozen years of slavery. With a broken left arm I had little hold on my beast, so I trusted my neck to him and let him have his will. Black with dirt and smoke, hatless, with no kind of uniform, I was a wilder figure than any Cossack. I soon was separated from Sandy, who had two hands and a better horse, and seemed resolute to press forward to the very van. That would have been suicide for me, and I had all I could do to keep my place in the bunch I rode with.

But, Great God! what an hour it was! There was loose shooting on our flank, but nothing to trouble us, though the gun team of some Austrian howitzer, struggling madly at a bridge, gave us a bit of a tussle. Everything flitted past me like smoke, or like the mad *finale* of a dream just before waking. I knew the living movement under me, and the companionship of men, but all dimly, for at heart I was alone, grappling with the realization of a new world. I felt the shadows of the Palantuken glen fading, and the great burst of light as we emerged on the wider valley. Somewhere before us was a pall of smoke seamed with red flames, and beyond the darkness of still higher hills. All that time I was dreaming, crooning daft catches of song to myself, so happy, so deliriously happy that I dared not try to think. I kept muttering a kind of prayer made up of Bible words to Him who had shown me His goodness in the land of the living.

But as we drew out from the skirts of the hills and began the long slope to the city, I woke to clear consciousness. I felt the smell of sheepskin and lathered horses, and above all the bitter smell of fire. Down in the trough lay Erzerum, now burning in many places, and from the east, past the silent forts, horsemen were closing in on it. I yelled to my comrades that we were nearest, that we would be first in the city, and they nodded happily and shouted their strange war-cries. As we topped the last ridge I saw below me the van of our charge—a dark mass on the snow—while the broken enemy on both sides were flinging away their arms and scattering in the fields.

In the very front, now nearing the city ramparts, was one man. He was like the point of the steel spear soon to be driven home. In the clear morning air I could see that he did not wear the uniform of the invaders. He was turbaned and rode like one possessed, and against the snow I caught the dark sheen of emerald. As he rode it seemed that the fleeing Turks were stricken still, and sank by the roadside with eyes strained after his unheeding figure . . .

Then I knew that the prophecy had been true, and that their prophet had not failed them. The long-looked-for revelation had come. Greenmantle had appeared at last to an awaiting people.

About the Author

JOHN Buchan was a man of many talents. Not only was he a well-known mystery writer, he was also a politician, lawyer, journalist, and diplomat. His accomplishments were many and lasting, and his crime novels in particular remain much admired even today.

Buchan was born in Perth, Scotland, on August 26, 1875, the oldest child of John Buchan, a Calvinist Presbyterian minister, and Helen Jane Buchan, a housewife. Along with his three brothers and one sister, Buchan was raised in a mining town in Fife. The family lived in a large gray manse on the coast. Buchan's father was a cheerful, music-loving soul who enjoyed singing traditional Scottish ballads and playing instruments. He also instilled a love of legends and storytelling in his children. In contrast, Buchan's mother was somewhat more reserved.

The family spent summers with Buchan's sheep-farming maternal grandparents in Broughton, in the Scottish border region. There, Buchan developed his passion for nature and the outdoors, spending endless hours exploring the woods, rivers, glens, and local wildlife. Much of his love for and knowledge of the Scottish landscape was apparent in his novels.

At age seventeen, Buchan won a scholarship to the University of Glasgow, where he studied classical literature and poetry. While there, Buchan wrote poetry and published essays in the Glasgow

University magazine to help meet expenses. In 1895, he attended Brasenose College at Oxford University, where he studied law.

After completing his education, Buchan moved to London in 1900 and worked as an apprentice in a law firm. However, he was lonely and unhappy, and after two years he decided to steer his career more toward diplomacy. He was appointed to a two-year post as private secretary to Lord Alfred Milner, the High Commissioner of South Africa. During this time, Buchan traveled extensively in southern Africa, and he would use much of what he saw and experienced in his crime fiction.

When Buchan returned to London around 1903, he became a director of Thomas Nelson & Sons publishers. A few years later, on July 15, 1907, he married Susan Charlotte Grosvenor. A year after that, their first child, Alice, was born. The couple eventually had three more children. Meanwhile, Buchan had not forgotten his knack for writing, and in 1910, he wrote his first adventure novel, *Prester John*, set in South Africa.

The era of World War I brought sadness to Buchan in the form of the deaths of several friends from Oxford, as well as the deaths of two of his brothers. In addition, Buchan became quite ill and was bedridden for several months. In the early part of 1914, Buchan wrote his most famous novel, *The Thirty-Nine Steps*, while recuperating. The novel was serialized in *Blackwood's Magazine* in July 1914 and published in book form the following year, to great acclaim.

After recovering sufficiently from his illness, in early 1915 Buchan became a war correspondent in France attached to the British Army. His primary job was to write articles for both *The Times* and *The Daily News* newspapers. Buchan covered such battles as Second Ypres and the Battle of Loos. Despite his other responsibilities, he continued to write fiction, and in 1916 he published *Greenmantle*, a sequel to *The Thirty-Nine Steps*. Buchan's books were well received, but he did not rest on his laurels. In 1917 he was put in charge of the British Army's newly formed Department of Information.

At the end of the war, Buchan began writing nonfiction books on historical topics along with his usual thrillers. His war